EARTH FOR INSPIRATION

EARTH FOR INSPIRATION

AND OTHER STORIES

The Complete Short Fiction of Clifford D. Simak, Volume Nine

Introduction by David W. Wixon

OPEN ROAD
INTEGRATED MEDIA
NEW YORK

ISBN: 978-1-5040-7392-9

This edition published in 2022 by Open Road Integrated Media, Inc.
180 Maiden Lane
New York, NY 10038
www.openroadmedia.com

CONTENTS

INTRODUCTION: THE SIMAK WESTERNS

"Parker lay, staring into the darkness, listening to the wind walking on the roof and tripping on the shingles."

—Clifford D. Simak in "The Hangnoose Army Rides to Town!"

Of the many science-fiction readers that count themselves fans of Clifford D. Simak, some are surprised to learn that he wrote a number of stories that were published in other genres—specifically Westerns and World War II air-combat stories. Part of the reason for that, of course, can be found in the length of the author's writing career. The last of those non–science fiction stories was published more than sixty-three years ago, and Cliff's career continued, limited by choice to science fiction only, for thirty-four years after the last Western was published. (It is important to note that, while in the time since this series of collections was announced I have seen a number of expressions of surprise about the Westerns, no one seems to have commented about the air-war stories—but then, they are far less interesting, and far shorter, than the Westerns; and so I'll limit this essay to the Westerns.)

It is true that, at one time, Cliff Simak told a bibliographer that there had been just one time in his career when he had written "strictly for money." The market for science fiction had been slow, he said, so he went out and bought a bunch of Westerns. "Then I simply spent the weekend reading them. Monday morning, I began writing." (At this point, I feel compelled to point out that the quoted comment was actually more about writing for money than about writing Western stories; the reader should not take this to mean that Cliff never wrote Westerns until the time to which he was referring. In fact, his journals show that he actually wrote a few Western stories as far back as the earliest years of his career.)

In those comments to the bibliographer, Cliff spoke of the Westerns market as he found it at that time: "They all had cowboys as heroes, and I thought there were other people out west than cowboys and Indians. So I wrote about doctors and lawyers and other folks. . . . But I stopped writing Westerns after a year. I had things to say that could not be expressed within the formula of the Western."

Actually, Cliff did not stop writing Westerns after a year. His journals make it clear that he was selling Westerns during the course of at least three years. The market for Westerns appears to have boomed during World War II—I suspect at least in part due to the need to provide entertainment for all the men in the armed forces—and the money was pretty good. But keep in mind that all of this took place more than thirty years before his comments to his bibliographer, and it seems clear that Cliff did not particularly enjoy doing them, so it would not be surprising if the details had gotten fuzzy in his mind.

Even today, however, it is unclear exactly how many Westerns Cliff might have written. His journals, which he either kept on a sporadic basis, skipped for years at a time, or lost, seem to indicate that he wrote twenty-one Westerns—three in the early 1930s, at the very beginning of his career, and the rest during the period between late 1943 and early 1947. (It appears that at least one Simak Western—"Gunsmoke Interlude"—was published as late as 1952, but it's not clear just when it was actually written or sold to a publisher.)

Aside from the lack of complete documentation in Cliff's journals, there is a second problem that precludes certainty in this matter: the vast majority of the Westerns named in Cliff's journals were not published under the names he gave them. And while a couple of the title changes that were made can be deduced from such information as similarities of plot elements and dates of publications, that does not work for the majority of the stories.

The Westerns of Clifford D Simak:

(For the bibliographically inclined: The story that appears in some lists under the title "Pilgrim Ramrod for Hell's Range" was not written by Cliff Simak. Its initial appearance in a bibliography of Simak stories was the result of a mistake by one bibliographer.)

- "Smoke Killer," the first of Simak's Westerns to have been published, appeared in *Lariat Story Magazine* in May 1944. I suspect that it is the story Cliff called "Killers Shouldn't Smoke" when he wrote it in 1943. It is shorter than most of his Westerns.
- "Cactus Colts" appeared in *Lariat Story Magazine* in July 1944. It is also one of the shorter of Simak's Westerns.
- "Trail City's Hot-Lead Crusaders," which was published in *New Western Magazine* in September 1944, is probably the story Cliff sent out under the title "Gunsmoke Goes to Press."
- "Gravestone Rebels Ride by Night!" was published in *Big-Book Western Magazine* in October 1944.
- "The Fighting Doc of Bushwhack Basin" was first published in *.44 Western Magazine*'s November 1944 issue. Cliff sent a story named "Powdersmoke Prescription" to Popular Publications at the end of July of that year.

• "The Reformation of Hangman's Gulch" appeared in the December 1944 issue of *Big-Book Western Magazine*. I suspect it is the story that Cliff gave the title "Owlhoot Heritage."
• "Way for the Hangtown Rebel!" originally appeared in *Ace-High Western Stories* in May 1945. It was the longest story in the issue and the only one featured on the cover.
• "Good Nesters Are Dead Nesters!" was first published in *.44 Western Magazine* in July 1945. It was the longest story in the issue.
• "The Hangnoose Army Rides to Town" originally appeared in *Ace-High Western Stories*, in September 1945. It is the only one of Cliff's Westerns to feature a lawman as a hero, and I suspect that it is a story that Cliff sent out under the title "Hang Your Guns on a Gallows Tree."
• "Barb Wire Brings Bullets!" was first published in the November 1945 issue of *Ace-High Western Stories*. It is likely the story that Cliff sold under the title "Blood Buys Barb Wire."
• "The Gunsmoke Drummer Sells a War" originally appeared in the January 1946 issue of *Ace-High Western Stories*.
• "No More Hides and Tallow" was originally published in the March 1946 issue of *Lariat Story Magazine*. The remained under the title Cliff gave it.
• "When it's Hangnoose Time in Hell" was first published in the April 1946 issue of *.44 Western Magazine*.
• "Gunsmoke Interlude" was ultimately published in the October 1952 issue of *Ten-Story Western Magazine*, but I suspect it is actually the story called "Walk in the Middle of the Street," which was sold in January 1946, but never published, as far as I know, during the remainder of that decade.

Finally, I will note that there is evidence that Cliff wrote at least seven other Westerns. Most were likely never accepted by any publisher, but it remains possible that some were. (I will point out, as an example, that Cliff himself did not appear to realize that "Gunsmoke Interlude" had been published. He had no copy of it, none of his records make reference to that title, and he never mentioned it to the bibliographer who interviewed him.) I've been unable to find a great deal of comprehensive information about Western pulp magazines, but I feel it's at least possible that others of Cliff's Westerns were published in other venues.

The stories that follow are titles that I believe to have been Simak Westerns, but of which no publication is known: "One-Shot Plays Rustler" (1933), "Gold Vengeance" (1934). "Some Cats and a Rocking Chair" (1943), "Powdersmoke Payoff in Purgatory Canyon" (1944), "Gringo Guns Spell Trouble" (1944), "Busted Banks Pay Off in Bullets" (1944), and "A Tramp Trumps a Tenderfoot" (1945).

David W. Wixon

EARTH FOR INSPIRATION

Likely written in 1940, this story was rejected by Astounding Science Fiction *and Amazing Stories before ultimately being accepted, with revisions, by* Wonder Stories *(known to some as* Thrilling Wonder Stories*), and published in that magazine's April 1941 issue. Wonder Stories was a lesser-known publication, and Cliff received only sixty dollars for the story.*

"Earth for Inspiration" features a robot named Jenkins, but don't confuse this robot with the Jenkins who would occupy a prominent place in the soon-to-follow City series. The story is also one of several of Cliff's works that touch on the craft of writing fiction—and I wonder, sometimes, whether he wrote this one because he had been asked once too often where he got his ideas. . . .

—dww

Philbert was lost. Likewise, he was frightened. That, in itself, was frightening, for Philbert was a robot and robots should have no emotions.

Philbert revolved that inside his brain case for many minutes, trying to figure it out. But there was no logic in it.

All around stretched the death and desolation that was Old Earth. High overhead the brick-red Sun shone dully in an ink-black sky, for the atmosphere was nearly gone, and the stars shone with a hard, bright glitter. The scraggly vegetation, fighting hard for life in a world where but little life was left, seemed to cower beneath a sense of ingrained futility.

Philbert stretched out his right leg and it squeaked. The knee joint had gone bad many hours before. Some sand had got into it, probably when he had fallen and broken his orientation plate. That was why he was lost. The three eyes in the top of Philbert's head studied the stars intently.

"I wish," said Philbert, his voice box rasping from lack of lubrication, "that I knew something about the constellations. The boss claimed men used to navigate by them. Well, that's wishful thinking." He had to find oil or he was sunk. If only he could retrace his steps to the shattered space ship and the equally shattered body of the man within it, he would find plenty there. But he couldn't retrace his steps, for he had no idea where the wreckage lay.

All he could do was keep plodding on, hoping to find the lone space port. Once each month the regular space run brought pilgrims and tourists to the old shrines and legendary places of mankind's first home. Or he might stumble on one of the primitive tribes that still lived on Old Earth.

He went on, the bad knee squeaking. The Sun slid slowly down the west. The Moon arose, a monstrous, pockmarked world. Philbert's shadow lurched ahead of him as he crossed eroded, worn-down mountains, trudged dune-filled deserts and salt-caked sea beds. But there was no sign of living things.

The knee squeaked louder. Finally he took it apart, unfastened the other joint and scraped some grease from it for the squeaking knee. In a few days both knees were squeaking. He took apart his arms, one at a time, and robbed them of their grease. It didn't matter if the arms ceased functioning, but those legs just had to move!

Next it was a hip joint that complained, then both hips, and finally the ankle joints. Philbert pushed forward, metal howling with dryness, walking less steadily each day.

He found a camping site, but the men were gone. The water had given out, so the tribe had moved.

The right leg was dragging now and fear hammered at him. "I'm getting batty," he moaned. "I'm beginning to imagine things, and only humans do that. Only humans—"

His voice box croaked and rasped and slipped a cog. The leg gave out and he crawled. Then his arms gave out and he lay still. The sand hissed against his metal body.

"Someone will find me," Philbert rattled hoarsely.

But no one found him. Philbert's body became a rusted hulk. His hearing went first and after that his eyes failed one by one. His body became flakes of dull red metal. But inside its almost indestructible case, lubricated by sealed-in oil, Philbert's brain still clicked.

He still lived, or rather he existed. He could neither see nor hear nor move nor speak. He was nothing more than a complex thought suspended in an abyss of nothingness. Man's life-expectancy was 10,000 years, but a robot's was dependent only on accident.

The years stretched into centuries and the centuries rolled into eons. Philbert thought dutifully, solved great problems, puzzled out correct actions under an endless set of circumstances. But futility at last caught up with him.

Bored to desperation, rebelling at dusty logic, he reasoned out a logical solution that effectively ended, not without some misgivings, the need for logic. While he had been an associate of mankind, it had been his duty to be logical. Now he was no longer associated with Man. Therefore, serving no purpose, there was no need of his logic.

Philbert was, by nature, thorough. He never did a thing by halves. He built up impossible situations, devised great travels and adventures, accepted shaky premises and theories, dallied with metaphysical speculation. He wandered to improbable dimensions, conversed with strange beings that lived on unknown worlds, battled with vicious entities that spawned outside the pale of time and space, rescued civilizations tottering on the brink of horrible destruction.

The years galloped on and on, but Philbert didn't notice. He was having him a time.

Jerome Duncan regarded the rejection slip sourly, picked it up gingerly and deciphered the editorial scrawl.

Not convincing. Too little science. Situations too commonplace. Characters have no life. Sorry.

"You sure outdid yourself this time!" snarled Duncan, addressing the scrawl.

Jenkins, the soft-footed robot valet, slid into the room.

"Another one, sir?" he asked.

Duncan jumped at the sound of the voice, then snapped at the robot:

"Jenkins, quit sneaking up on me. You make me nervous."

"I beg your pardon, sir," said Jenkins stiffly. "I wasn't sneaking up on you. I was just observing that another manuscript came back."

"What if it did? Lots of them have been coming back."

"That's just the point, sir. They never use to come back. You wrote some of the finest science fiction the Galaxy has ever known. Real classics, sir, if I do say so myself. Your *Robots Triumphant* won the annual award, sir, and—"

Duncan brightened. "Yeah, that was some yarn, wasn't it? All the robots wrote in and swamped that old sourpuss of an editor with letters praising it. But the robots would be the ones to eat it up. It was a story about them, giving them a break."

He glanced sadly at the rejection slip and shook his head.

"But no more, Jenkins. Duncan is on the skids. And yet readers keep asking about me. 'When is Duncan going to write another like *Robots Triumphant*?' But the editor keeps sending my stuff back. 'Not convincing,' he says. 'Not enough science. Characters no good!'"

"May I make a suggestion, sir?"

"Okay," signed Duncan. "Go ahead and make one."

"It's this way, sir," said Jenkins. "If you will pardon me, your stories don't sound convincing any more."

"Yeah? What am I going to do about it?"

"Why don't you visit some of these places you are writing about?" the robot suggested. "Why don't you take a vacation and see if you can't gather some local color and some inspiration?" Duncan scratched his head.

"Maybe you got something there, Jenkins," he admitted. He glanced at the returned manuscript, thumbed through its pages.

"This one should have sold. It's an Old Earth story and they're always popular."

He shoved the manuscript away from him and stood up.

"Jenkins, call up Galactic Transportation and find out the schedule to Old Earth."

"But the Old Earth run was discontinued a thousand years ago," protested Jenkins.

"There are shrines there that Man has been going to see for millions of years."

"It seems, sir," said Jenkins, "that no one's interested in shrines any more."

"All right, then," stated Duncan. "Scram out of here and charter a ship and get together some camping equipment."

"Camping equipment, sir?"

"Camping equipment. We're going to go back to Old Earth and pitch a tent there. We're going to soak up atmosphere until it runs out of our ears."

He glared viciously at the scrawl on the rejection slip.

"I'll show that old—"

The news bell tinkled softly and a blue light glowed in the wall panel. When Duncan pressed a stud, a newspaper shot out of a tube onto his desk. Swiftly he flipped it open.

Glaring scarlet headlines shrieked the following:

ROBOT RUSTLERS STRIKE AGAIN

Duncan tossed the paper to one side in disgust.

"They're going nuts about those rustlers," he said. "Who would kidnap a few robots. Maybe the robots are running away."

"But they wouldn't run away," insisted Jenkins. "Not those robots, sir. I knew some of them. They were loyal to their masters."

"It's just newspaper build-up," declared Duncan. "They're trying to get more circulation."

"But it's happening all over the Galaxy, sir," Jenkins reminded him. "The papers say it looks like the work of an organized gang. Stealing robots and selling them again could be a profitable business, sir."

"If it is," grunted Duncan, "the CBI will get them. Nobody's ever ducked that bunch of sleuths for long."

Old Hank Wallace stared skyward, muttering in his beard.

"By thunder," he suddenly yelped, "a ship at last!"

He hobbled toward the port control shack, heaved down the levers that lighted up the field, then stepped out to have another look. The ship came slanting down, touched the concrete lightly and skidded to a stop.

Hank shuffled forward, the breath whistling in his oxygen mask. A man, equipped with mask and swathed in heavy furs, stepped from the ship. He was followed by a robot, loaded down with packs and bundles.

"Howdy, there," yelled Hank. "Welcome to Old Earth."

The man regarded him curiously.

"We didn't think we'd find anyone here," he said.

Hank bristled. "Why not? This is a Galactic Transport station. You always find someone here. Service at all hours."

"But this station has been abandoned," explained Jerome Duncan. "The run was canceled a thousand years ago."

The old man let the information sink in.

"You're sure of that?" he asked. "You're sure they canceled the run?"

Duncan nodded.

"Dagnabit!" exploded Hank. "I knew there was something wrong. I thought there might have been a war."

"Jenkins," ordered Duncan, "get that camping stuff out of the ship as fast as you can."

"It's a dirty trick," lamented Hank. "A doggone dirty trick. Letting a man hang around here for a thousand years waiting for a ship."

Hank and Duncan sat side by side, chairs tilted back against the station wall, watching the Sun slip into the west.

"If it's atmosphere and color you're looking for," said Hank, "you sure ought to find it here. Once this was a green land, where a great civilization got its start. You kind of feel something almost sacred in this place when you get to know it. Mother Earth, they used to call it, way back in those early days before they left it behind and went out into the Galaxy. For centuries, though, they came back to visit the shrines."

He shook his head sadly.

"But they've forgotten all that now. History doesn't give Old Earth more than a paragraph or two. Just says it was the place where mankind arose. I heard once that there was a fellow who even claimed Man didn't come from Earth at all, but from some other planet."

"These last thousand years must have been lonesome ones," suggested Duncan.

"Not so bad," the old man told him. "At first I had Wilbur. He was my robot, and he was a lot of company. We used to sit around and chew the fat. But Wilber went off his clock, cog slipped or something. Started acting queer and I got scared of him. So I watched my chance and disconnected him. Then, just to make sure, I took the brain case out of his body. It's in there on the shelf. I take it down and polish it every now and then. Wilbur was a good robot."

From inside the station came a thump and clatter.

"Hey!" yelled Duncan. "What's going on in there?"

"I just found a robot's body, sir," called Jenkins. "I must have knocked it over."

"You know you knocked it over," snapped Duncan. "That's Wilbur's body. Put it back where it belongs."

"Yes, sir," said Jenkins.

"If you're looking for characters," continued Hank, "you ought to visit an old ocean depth about five hundred miles from here. A tribe is living there, one of the last left on Old Earth. They're the ones that just weren't worth the space they'd take up in ships when mankind left the Earth. But that was millions of years ago. There aren't many of them left now. The only place where water and air are left is in the old sea depths. The strongest tribes grabbed those long ago and drove out the weaker tribes."

"What happened to the weaker tribes?" asked Duncan.

"They died," said Hank. "You can't live without water and air, you know. They don't live long, anyway. Hundred years is about their limit, maybe less. There have been twelve chiefs in the last thousand years that I know of. An old duffer that calls himself the 'Thunderer' rules the roost right now. Nothing but a bag of bones, and thunder hasn't been heard on Earth for five million years at least. But they're great on names like that. Great story-tellers, too. They got some real hair-raisers."

The Thunderer let out a squeak of rage and got weakly to his feet. A band of urchins had rolled the ball that had hit his foot. They took to their heels, disappeared around the corner in a cloud of dust. Stiffly the Thunderer sat down again, groaning. He wiggled his toes, watching them intently, apparently surprised when they worked.

"Them dang kids will be the death of me," he grumbled. "No manners. When I was a youngster, my pappy would have whaled the living daylights out of me for a trick like that."

Jerome Duncan picked up the sphere.

"Where did they get this ball, Chief?" he asked.

"Out in the desert somewhere, I guess," said the Thunderer. "We used to find a lot of junk scattered around, especially on the old city sites. My tribe used to do a big business in it. Sold antiques to them fool tourists."

"But, Chief," protested Duncan, "this isn't just a piece of junk. This is a robot's brain case."

"Yeah?" piped the Thunderer.

"Sure," declared Duncan. "Look at the serial number, right down here." He bent his head closer to the number and whistled in surprise. "Look, Chief. This case is about three million years old! Only ten digits. This year's models have sixteen."

Duncan hefted the brain case in his cupped hands, considering.

"Might have an interesting story to tell," he said. "Might have been out there on the desert for a long time. Those old models all went to the junk pile centuries ago. Out-dated, too many improvements. Emotions, for one thing. Three million years ago, robots didn't have emotions. If we could connect it up—"

"You got a robot," the chief pointed out.

Duncan turned to Jenkins with a speculative look in his eyes, but Jenkins started backing away.

"No," he bleated. "Not that, sir! You can't do that to me."

"It would be just for a little while," Duncan coaxed.

"I don't like it," Jenkins said flatly. "I don't like it at all."

"Jenkins!" yelled Duncan. "You come here!"

Light lanced into Philbert's brain, a piercing, torturing light that shattered eons of shrouding nothingness. Alien visions swam across his senses. He tried to shut his eyes, but the mechanism of his brain was sluggish in response. The relentless light seared his eyes. Sound came to him, frightening sound. But he knew it should mean something to him.

Eye-shutters down at last, he waited for his eyes to grow used to the light. He lifted the shutters just a bit. The light lashed at him again, but it was less vicious this time. Gradually he lifted the shutters, found his vision blurred and foggy. Sound was blasting at him again. Now it divided itself into words.

"Get up!"

The command drilled into his consciousness. Slowly, motor centers uncertainly taking up old tasks, he heaved himself erect. He staggered on his feet, fighting to keep his balance. It was terrifying, this sudden yanking of his consciousness from a dreamworld into a world of actuality. His eyes focused. Before him was a village of huts. Beyond that lay a tiny pond and ranges of barren hills that marched like stairs into the black sky where hung the large, red Sun. There were people in front of him, too. One man was different from the rest. He was dressed in furs, with an oxygen mask dangling on his chest.

"Who are you?" the man in furs asked.

"I am—" said Philbert, and then he stopped.

Who was he? He tried to remember, but his memory was engulfed by that world of fantasy and imagination in which he had so long existed. One word popped up, one tiny clue and that was all.

"I am Philbert," he finally said.

"Do you know where you are?" asked the man. "How you came to be here? How long since you were alive?"

"I don't know," said Philbert.

"You see," squeaked the Thunderer, "he remembers nothing. He is a dunderhead."

"No, not that," Duncan disagreed. "He's been here too long. The years have wiped his memory clean."

The evening meal was over. The tribe squatted in a ring around the fire and listened to the Thunderer recite one of the tribal legends. It was a long tale with, Duncan suspected, but slight regard for truth. The Thunderer fixed him with a baleful eye, as if daring him to disbelieve.

"And so Angus took that critter from the stars in his bare hands and put its tail into its mouth and pushed. And it kept fighting all the time and trying to get loose. But Angus hung on and pushed that tail until the danged thing swallowed itself!"

The tribe murmured appreciatively. It was a good story. The murmur was broken by a raucous voice.

"Ah, shucks," jeered Philbert, "that ain't nothing!"

The tribe gasped in shocked amazement, growled with sudden anger. The Thunderer jumped as if he had been shot. Duncan started forward, a sharp command on his lips. The Thunderer stopped him with a raised hand.

"I suppose, you little whippersnapper," the chief piped at Philbert, "that you can tell a better one."

"You bet I can," Philbert stated. "And what's more, this one is the truth. These events really happened to me."

The Thunderer glared at him.

"All right," he growled, "go ahead and tell it. And it better be good. It better be plenty good."

Philbert started to talk. The tribesmen were hostile at first, but as he went along they snapped to abrupt attention. For Philbert was spinning a yarn that really was a yarn.

A screwball world had set out to conquer the rest of the Galaxy and used its very wackiness to accomplish its ends. Mankind, led by Philbert, of course, turned the tables on the conquerors and invented a synthetic screwball who upset all their plans.

Duncan sat enthralled, hanging on the words. Here was science fiction! The man who could write a tale like that would be hailed over the entire Galaxy as the master of his craft. His mind whirled and the circle of faces blurred. Realization struck at him, let him pale.

The man who wrote that story would be himself!

Philbert had ended the tale, was stepping back into the circle once again. Duncan grabbed the robot's arm.

"Philbert!" he shouted. "Where did you hear that story?"

"I didn't hear it," said Philbert. "It happened to me."

"But it couldn't have happened to you," protested Duncan. "If such a thing had happened, history would have mentioned it."

"It happened," Philbert insisted. "I am telling you the truth."

Duncan stared at the robot.

"Listen, Philbert," he urged, "did a lot of other things happen to you, too?"

"Sure," Philbert agreed cheerfully. "A lot of things. I went lots of places and did lots of things. Want me to tell about them?"

"Not right now," said Duncan hastily. "You come along with me."

Almost by main force, he shoved Philbert out of the circle and headed for the ship. Behind him a voice squeaked in rage.

"Hey, come back here!"

Duncan turned around. The Thunderer was on his feet, shaking clenched fists.

"You bring that robot back!" yelped the chief. "Don't you go sneaking off with him!"

"But he's my robot," said Duncan.

"You bring him back!" shrieked the old man. "He belongs to us. I guess we were the ones that found him. Think we're going to let you carry off the first good story-teller this tribe has had in five hundred years?"

"But, look here, Chief . . ."

"Dang you, bring him back! I'll sic the boys on you."

All the boys looked as if they would enjoy a little scrap. Duncan turned around to speak to Philbert, but Philbert was moving away rapidly.

"Hey, there!" yelled Duncan, but Philbert only went faster.

"Hey!" yelled the tribe in unison.

At the shout Philbert fairly split the wind. He streaked through the camp, across the flat and skittered out of sight, disappearing in the darkness of the hills.

"Now see what you done!" shouted Duncan angrily. "You scared him off with all that yelling."

The Thunderer hobbled forward to shake a massive, hairy fist beneath Duncan's nose.

"Dang you!" he piped. "I ought to bust you wide open. Trying to sneak off with that story-teller. You better get going before the boys decide to take you apart."

"But he was mine as much as yours," argued Duncan. "Maybe you found him, but it was my robot's body he was in and—"

"Stranger," cautioned the Thunderer fiercely, "you better get aboard that tin can of yours and clear out."

"Now look here," protested Duncan, "you can't run me off like this."

"Who says we can't?" gritted the old man.

Duncan saw the expectant, almost hopeful look on the faces of the watching tribesmen.

"Okay," he said. "I didn't really want to hang around, anyhow. You needn't get so tough."

Philbert's trail led straight across the desert. Old Hank grumbled in his beard.

"You're stark crazy, Duncan," he declared. "You can't catch this robot. Lord knows how far he went. He might not stop until he's halfway around the world."

"I have to catch him," Duncan said doggedly. "Don't you realize what he means to me? That robot is an encyclopedia of science fiction stories! That yarn he told this evening was better than anything I ever read. And he's got more of them. He told me so. He must have thought them up when he was lying out there in the sand. A couple of million years is a long time to lie around and think.

"If he were thinking of screwball scientific ideas all that time, he must be dripping with them. The beauty of it is that he thought about them so long, he forgot everything else he knew and thinks those wacky adventures of his are real. He really thinks he lived them."

"But, doggone it," panted Hank, "at least we could track him in the space ship. No use walking our legs down to the knees."

"You know what'll happen when we try to track him in the ship," said Duncan. "We'll go so fast that we won't even see the tracks. The ship isn't something you can throttle down. It has to go fast to escape gravity."

Jenkins stubbed his toe on a boulder and somersaulted in the sand with a thunderous clank and clatter. He pulled himself to his feet, making angry sounds.

"If he had to wear this body," Jenkins declared, "I can understand why Wilbur went nuts."

"You better be thankful that body was handy," snarled Duncan. "If it hadn't been, you'd still be disconnected. How would you like that?"

"No worse than stumbling around in this contraption, sir," said Jenkins.

"I was afraid at first," continued Duncan, "that maybe the old Thunderer would beat me to the draw and catch Philbert, but we don't have to worry about that any more. We're a good many miles from the tribal camp. They wouldn't wander this far."

"You wouldn't either, sir," said Jenkins crustily, "if you didn't have me to pack a couple of barrels of water for you. I don't like it. I'm a valet, not a pack horse."

Late in the afternoon, Jenkins was ahead. He stopped and yelled at them. They hurried forward to see what he had found.

The tracks of two other robots had joined Philbert's. There were signs of a scuffle and then the three tracks went angling up the dunes. Old Hank was horrified.

"But it can't be," he blurted, his whiskers waggling in exasperation. "There aren't any robots on Earth except Jenkins here and that crazy Philbert. There's Wilbur, of course, but he don't count no more."

"But there are," stated Duncan. "There are their three sets of tracks. It's plain as day what happened. The other two hid in wait for Philbert there behind those boulders and tackled him. He put up a little battle, but they finally got him tamed and led him off."

The three stood quietly staring at the tracks.

"How do you explain it?" whispered Hank.

"I'm not trying to explain it," snapped Duncan. "I'm going to follow them. I'm going to get Philbert if it's the last thing I ever do. I'm going to make that old sourpuss of an editor sit up when those yarns of mine start coming in. Philbert's got them. I just can't let him get away."

"I think you're full of moonshine," said Hank bitterly.

"So do I," agreed Jenkins. He added grudgingly: "Sir."

The trail led across a welter of dunes. Then it ducked into a rocky defile that slanted down into a fearsome valley, which went straight for a short distance and then abandoned itself to a series of tortuous turns.

"I don't like this place," whispered Hank hoarsely. "It downright smells of danger."

Duncan paid him no attention, went alertly forward. He slid around a sharp turn and stopped suddenly, his breath catching in his throat. The two behind came around the bend and bumped into him.

From the valley floor rose huge machines—mighty drills, mining equipment, shovels. All about were hundreds of robots:

"Let's get out of here!" quavered Hank.

They backed slowly away, silently, almost holding their breath. Jenkins, backing with them, stepped into a slight depression in the trail, lost his footing. Half a ton of hardware smacked against the rock with a bang that sent the echoes chasing between the narrow cliffs.

Robots suddenly began racing toward them, converging upon them in every direction.

"Boy," said Hank, "we're sure in for it now!"

Jenkins, on his feet again, cried out as they approached.

"I know some of those robots, sir! They are the ones the rustlers stole!"

"Who are the rustlers?" demanded Hank.

"We'll find out soon enough," said Duncan bitterly. "They're just about the toughest gang that ever roamed the Galaxy. Been stealing robots all over the place."

"And look at me," moaned Jenkins. "The boys will never let me forget it. Me, in a pile of junk like this."

"Keep your mouth shut," snapped Duncan, "and they'll never recognize you. If you go throwing yourself around any more, I'll disconnect that brain of yours and heave it out right in the middle of space."

"I didn't do it intentionally, sir," protested Jenkins. "This body is the most awkward thing I've ever seen. I just can't do a thing with it. Here they come!"

The robots were a milling mass in front of them. One of the metal men stepped forward. He singled out Duncan and spoke to him.

"We're certainly glad to see you," he said. "We were hoping someone would find us."

"Find you?" asked Duncan. "Are you lost?"

The robot scuffed his feet and hung his head.

"Well, not exactly lost. We sort of pulled a boner."

"Look here," said Duncan impatiently. "What are you talking about? Aren't you the robots the rustlers stole?"

"No, sir," the robot confessed. "You see, there aren't any rustlers."

"Aren't any rustlers!" exploded Duncan. "Well, if there aren't any rustlers, what are you fellows doing here?"

"We ran away, but it wasn't our fault. Not exactly, that is. You see, there was a science fiction writer—"

"What has a science fiction writer got to do with this?" roared Duncan.

"This science fiction writer wrote a story," explained the robot. "Fellow by the name of Jerome Duncan—"

Viciously Duncan kicked Jenkins in the shins and the robot gurgled, swallowing his words.

"He wrote a story called *Robots Triumphant*," the robot spokesman went on. "He told how a bunch of robots went out to build a civilization of their own. They were disgusted with the human race, thought Man had balled up just about everything. So they figured they'd sneak off some place and start from scratch and build themselves a great civilization without any of mankind's faults."

The robot glanced sharply at Duncan.

"You don't think I'm stringing you, do you?" he asked.

"No," said Duncan. "I read that story myself. I thought it was pretty good."

"It was good," admitted the robot. "Too darned good. We believed it. It got us all hopped up, made us want to go out and do the things he told about." He stopped and fixed Duncan with a stare. "But if we had that Duncan guy now! Just let us catch him!"

Duncan's heart flopped down into his boots, but he kept his voice steady.

"Why, what's the matter, boys? Didn't the idea work out?"

"Work out!" the robot grated. "I'll tell the Galaxy it didn't. We sneaked off, a few at a time, and gathered at a place we had agreed on. When there was a shipload of us, we came here. We landed, unloaded our equipment and then blew up the space ship. That's what the robots did in the story, so no one could get sick of it and try to get away. Sort of sink or swim proposition. Understand?"

"Yes, I remember," said Duncan. "The robots in the story, I believe, even came back to Old Earth. Figured they ought to start out on the same planet mankind started on. Inspirational, sort of."

"Yeah," said the robot. "That all sounded swell in the story, but it didn't work so well. That fool writer forgot just one thing. He forgot that before Man left the Earth he had stripped it clean. He'd pumped out all the oil and mined all the ore and chopped down all the timber. He cleaned the planet out. He didn't leave a thing. We've sunk wells, trying to get oil. There ain't a drop. The same with minerals. There isn't a thing here to start a civilization with.

"And the worst of it is that another bunch of the fellows are getting ready to go out to another old abandoned planet. We have to stop them, because they won't be any better off than we are. We're mighty glad you found us."

"But we weren't looking for you," stated Duncan. "We were looking for a robot called Philbert."

"We got him here," said the spokesman. "A couple of the boys saw him wandering around and thought he was one of our fellows trying to sneak off. They jumped him, but you can have him. We don't want him. He's batty. He almost drove us nuts telling us about the things he's done."

"Okay," said Duncan. "Trot him out."

"But what about us?"

"Well, what about you?"

"You're going to take us back, ain't you? You ain't going to leave us here?"

"I ought to let you guys stew in your own juice," said Duncan.

"Okay, then," said the robot. "We don't give you Philbert. We can't stand him around, but we can take him apart and throw him away."

"Hey, wait a minute!" yelled Duncan. "You can't do that."

"Take us back and you can have him," said the robot.

"But I haven't the room. All I have is just one space ship that isn't nearly big enough for all of you."

"We'll fix that. We'll disconnect ourselves, leave our bodies behind. All you have to take are the brain cases."

"But look here, I can't. The CBI would nab me. They think you fellows were stolen by a gang they've been calling the 'Robot Rustlers.' They'll think I'm the head robot rustler."

"If they do," said the robot, "we'll testify for you. We'll come clean and save you. And if you do get us through without getting caught, you can claim you rescued us. We won't contradict you. Honest, mister, we'll do anything to get out of here."

Duncan considered. He didn't like the proposition, but there wasn't much that he could do.

"Well," asked the robot, "do we take Philbert apart or do you agree to take us?"

"All right," said Duncan, beaten. "Bring Philbert here."

Duncan waved the new issue of the magazine triumphantly at Philbert.

"Look at that, will you!" he jubilated. "Front cover and everything. And the readers' column is packed with letters praising the last one. Boy, are we doing a job!"

Philbert yawned and lifted mechanical eyebrows.

"We?" he asked.

"Sure, we—" began Duncan, then stopped and glowered. "Look here, you tin-pants wonder, don't you go getting snooty with me. I've had just about enough out of you."

"You couldn't sell a thing before you found me," said Philbert tartly, "and you know it. When are you going to give me a by-line? When are you going to stop hogging all the credit?"

Duncan fairly bounced with wrath.

"We've been over that before. I take good care of you, don't I? I give you everything you want. But I get the by-lines. I'm not collaborating with any robot. That's final."

"Okay, then," declared Philbert. "You get no more yarns from me."

"I'll heave you back into that old outfit of Wilbur's," threatened Duncan. "Stumble around in that for a week and you'll be ready to give."

"If I do tell you another story," Philbert bargained, "will you get me that brand-new body we saw down in the store the other day? I don't want the girls to think I look like a slouch."

"But you don't need another body!" yelped Duncan. "You got ten of them already."

"All right, then," said Philbert, using his ace in the hole. "I'll get somebody to disconnect me and hide me somewhere. I'm not sure I didn't like it better that way, anyhow. There wasn't anything to distract my attention."

"Oh, all right," grumbled Duncan, aware that he was licked. "Go buy another body. Buy two of them. Anything to make you happy."

"That's better," said Philbert. "It'll save you a grease and polish job on this one, so you have nothing to kick about."

IDIOT'S CRUSADE

"Idiot's Crusade" was likely written in early 1954, a period which is not covered by any of Cliff Simak's surviving journals. I regret that; I'd like to know more about how he came to write the story.

At any rate, after being rejected by Astounding Science Fiction *in April of 1954, the story was sent to H. F. Gold in May. Gold accepted it, and it was published in the October 1954 issue of* Galaxy Science Fiction*—and even before that publication, Cliff was asked for his carbon by Groff Conklin, who wanted to put the story into an anthology. Cliff was paid five hundred dollars for the story, but I'm not sure if that figure represented both publications."*

—dww

For a long time I was the village idiot, but not any longer—although they call me "dummy" still and even worse than that.

I'm a genius now, but I won't let them know.

Not ever.

If they found out, they'd be on their guard against me.

No one has suspected me and no one will. My shuffle is the same and my gaze as vacant and my mumblings just as vague as they ever were. At times, it has been hard to remember to keep the shuffle and the gaze and mumblings as they were before, times when it was hard not to overdo them. But it's important not to arouse suspicion.

It all started the morning I went fishing.

I told Ma I was going fishing while we were eating breakfast and she didn't object. She knows I like fishing. When I fish, I don't get into trouble.

"All right, Jim," she said. "Some fish will taste real good."

"I know where to get them," I told her. "That hole in the creek just past Alf Adams' place."

"Now don't you get into any fracas with Alf," Ma warned me. "Just because you don't like him—"

"He was mean to me. He worked me harder than he should have. And he cheated me out of my pay. And he laughs at me."

I shouldn't have said that, because it hurts Ma when I say someone laughs at me.

"You mustn't pay attention to what people do," said Ma, speaking kind and gentle. "Remember what Preacher Martin said last Sunday. He said—"

"I know what he said, but I still don't like being laughed at. People shouldn't laugh at me."

"No," Ma agreed, looking sad. "They shouldn't."

I went on eating my breakfast, thinking that Preacher Martin was a great one to be talking about humility and patience, knowing the kind of man he was and how he was carrying on with Jennie Smith, the organist. He was a great one to talk about anything at all.

After breakfast, I went out to the woodshed to get my fishing tackle and Bounce came across the street to help me. After Ma, Bounce is the best friend I have. He can't talk to me, of course—not actually, that is—but neither does he laugh at me.

I talked to him while I was digging worms and asked him if he wanted to go fishing with me. I could see he did, so I went across the street to tell Mrs. Lawson that Bounce was going along. He belonged to her, but he spent most of his time with me.

We started out, me carrying my cane pole and all my fishing stuff and Bounce walking at my heels, as if I were someone he was proud to be seen walking with.

We went past the bank, where Banker Patton was sitting in the big front window, working at his desk and looking like the most important man in all of Mapleton, which he was. I went by slow so I could hate him good.

Ma and me wouldn't be living in the old tumbledown house we're living in if Banker Patton hadn't foreclosed on our home after Pa died.

We went out past Alf Adams' place, which is the first farm out of town, and I hated him some, too, but not as hard as Banker Patton. All Alf had done was work me harder than he should have, then cheat me of my pay.

Alf was a big, blustery man and a good enough farmer, I guess—at least he made it pay. He had a big new barn and it's just like him not to paint it red, the way any proper barn is painted, but white with red trim. Who ever heard of paint trim on a barn?

Just beyond Alf's place, Bounce and I turned off the road and went down across the pasture, heading for the big hole in the creek.

Alf's prize Hereford bull was way off in another corner of the pasture with the rest of the stock. When he saw us, he started coming for us, not mean or belligerent, but just investigating and ready for a fight if one was offered him. I wasn't afraid of him, because I'd made friends with him that summer I had worked for Alf. I used to pet him and scratch behind his ears. Alf said I was a crazy fool and someday the bull would kill me.

"You can never trust a bull," Alf said.

When the bull was near enough to see who it was, he knew we meant no harm, so he went back across the pasture again.

We got to the hole and I started fishing, while Bounce went up the stream to do some investigating. I caught a few fish, but they weren't very big and they weren't biting very often and I got disinterested. I like to fish, but to keep my interest up, I have to catch some.

So I got to daydreaming. I began wondering if you marked off a certain area of ground—a hundred feet square, say—and went over it real careful, how many different kinds of plants you'd find. I looked over a patch of ground next to where I was sitting and I could see just ordinary pasture grass and some dandelions and some dock and a couple of violets, and a buttercup which didn't have any flowers as yet.

Suddenly, when I was looking at the dandelion, I realized I could see *all* that dandelion, not just the part that showed above the ground!

I don't know how long I'd been seeing it that way before realizing it. And I'm not certain that "seeing" is the right word. Maybe "know" would be better. I *knew* how that dandelion's big taproot went down into the ground and how the little feathery roots grew out of it, and I knew where all the roots were, how they were taking water and chemicals out of the ground, how reserve food was stored in the root and how the dandelion used the sunlight to convert its food into a form it could use. And the funniest thing about it was that I had never known any of it before.

I looked at the other plants and I could see all of them the same way. I wondered if something had gone wrong with my eyes and if I would have to go around looking into things instead of at them, so I tried to make the new seeing go away and it did.

Then I tried to see the dandelion root again and I saw it, just the way I had before.

I sat there, wondering why I had never been able to see that way before and why I was able to now. And while I was wondering, I looked into the pool and tried to see down into the pool and I could, just as plain as day. I could see clear to the bottom of it and into all the corners of it, and there were lunkers lying in there, bigger than any fish that ever had been taken from the creek.

I saw that my bait was nowhere near any of the fish, so I moved it over until it was just in front of the nose of one of the biggest ones. But the fish didn't seem to see it, or if he did, he wasn't hungry, for he just lay there, fanning the water with his fins and making his gills work.

I moved the bait down until it bumped his nose, but he still didn't pay any attention to it.

So I made the fish hungry.

Don't ask me how I did it. I can't tell you. I all at once knew I could and just how to do it. So I made him hungry and he went for that bait like Bounce grabbing a bone.

He pulled the cork clear under and I heaved on the pole and hoisted him out. I took him off the hook and put him on the stringer, along with the four or five little ones I'd caught.

Then I picked out another big fish and lowered my bait down to him and made him hungry.

In the next hour and a half, I just about cleaned out all the big fish. There were some little ones left, but I didn't bother with them. I had the stringer almost full and I couldn't carry it in my hand, for then the fish would have dragged along the ground. I had to sling it over my shoulder and those fish felt awfully wet.

I called Bounce and we went back to town.

Everyone I met stopped and had a look at my fish and wanted to know where I'd got them and what I'd caught them on and if there were any left or had I taken them all. When I told them I'd taken all there was, they laughed fit to kill.

I was just turning off Main Street on my way home when Banker Patton stepped out of the barber shop. He smelled nice from the bottles of stuff that Jake, the barber, uses on his customers.

He saw me with my fish and stopped in front of me. He looked at me and looked at the fish and he rubbed his fat hands together. Then he said, like he was talking to a child, "Why, Jimmy, where did you get all those fish?" He sounded a little bit, too, like I might not have a right to them and probably had used some lowdown trick to get them.

"Out in the hole on Alf's place," I told him.

All at once, without even trying to do it, I saw him the same way I had seen the dandelion—his stomach and intestines and something that must have been his liver—and up above them all, surrounded by a doughy mass of pink, a pulsating thing that I knew must be his heart.

I guess that's the first time anybody ever *really* hated someone else's guts.

I shot out my hands—well, not my hands, for one was clutching the cane pole and the other was busy with the fish—but it felt almost exactly as if I'd put them out and grabbed his heart and squeezed it hard.

He gasped once, then sighed and wilted, like all the starch had gone out of him, and I had to jump out of the way so he wouldn't bump into me when he fell.

He never moved after he hit the ground.

Jake came running out of his barber shop.

"What happened to him?" he asked me.

"He just fell over," I said.

Jake looked at him. "It's a heart attack. I'd know it anywhere. I'll run for Doc."

He took off up the street for Doc Mason while other people came hurrying out of the places along the street.

There was Ben from the cheese factory and Mike from the pool hall and a couple of farmers who were in the general store.

I got out of there and went on home and Ma was pleased with the fish.

"They'll taste real good," she said, looking at them. "How did you come to catch that many, Jim?"

"They were biting good," I said.

"Well, you hurry up and clean them. We'll have to eat some right away and I'll take some over to Preacher Martin's and I'll rub salt in the others and put them in the cellar where it's good and cool. They'll keep for several days."

Just then, Mrs. Lawson ran across the street and told Ma about Banker Patton.

"He was talking to Jim when it happened," she told Ma.

Ma said to me, "Why didn't you tell me, Jim?"

"I never got around to it," I said. "I was showing you these fish."

So the two of them went on talking about Banker Patton and I went out to the woodshed and cleaned the fish. Bounce sat alongside me and watched me do it and I swear he was as happy over those fish as I was, just like he might have had a hand in catching them.

"It was a nice day, Bounce," I said and Bounce said he'd thought so, too. He recalled running up and down the stream and how he'd chased a frog and the good smell there was when he stuck his nose down to the ground and sniffed.

Now I don't want you to think I'm trying to make you believe Bounce actually talked, because he didn't. But it was just as if he'd said those very words.

People all the time are laughing at me and making cracks about me and trying to bait me because I'm the village idiot, but there are times when the village idiot has it over all of them. They would have been scared they were going crazy if a dog talked to them, but I didn't think it was strange at all. I just thought how much nicer it was now that Bounce could talk and how I wouldn't have to guess at what he wanted to say. I never thought it was queer at all, because I always figured Bounce could talk if he only tried, being a smart dog.

So Bounce and I sat there and talked while I cleaned the fish. When I came out of the woodshed, Mrs. Lawson had gone home and Ma was in the kitchen, getting a skillet ready to cook some of the fish.

"Jim, you . . ." she hesitated, then went on, "Jim, you didn't have anything to do with what happened to Banker Patton, did you? You didn't push him or hit him or anything?"

"I never even touched him," I said and that was true. I certainly hadn't touched him.

In the afternoon, I went out and worked in the garden. Ma does some housework now and then and that brings in some money, but we couldn't get along if it wasn't for the garden. I used to work some, but since the fight I had with Alf over him not paying me, she don't let me work for anyone. She says if I take care of the garden and catch some fish, I'm helping out enough.

Working in the garden, I found a different use for my new way of seeing. There were worms in the cabbages and I could see every one of them and I killed them all by squeezing them, the way I'd squeezed Banker Patton. I found a cloudy sort of stuff on some of the tomato plants and I suppose it was some kind of virus, because it was so small I could hardly see it at first. So I magnified it and could see it fine, and I made it go away. I didn't squeeze it like I did the worms. I just made it go away.

It was fun working in the garden, when you could look down into the ground and see how the parsnips and radishes were coming and could kill the cutworms you found there, and know just how the soil was and if everything was all right.

We'd had fish for lunch and we had fish again for supper, and after supper I went for a walk.

Before I knew it, I was walking by Banker Patton's place and, going past, I felt the grief inside the house.

I stood out on the sidewalk and let the grief come into me. I suppose that outside any house in town, I could have felt just as easily whatever was going on inside, but I hadn't known I could and I hadn't tried. It was only because the grief in the Patton house was so deep and strong that I noticed it.

The banker's oldest daughter was upstairs in her room and I could feel her crying. The other daughter was sitting with her mother in the living room and neither of them was crying, but they seemed lost and lonely. There were other people in the house, but they weren't very sad. Some neighbors, probably, who'd come in to keep the family company.

I felt sorry for the three of them and I wanted to help them. Not that I'd done anything wrong in killing Banker Patton, but I felt sorry for those women, because, after all, it wasn't their fault the way Banker Patton was, so I stood there, wishing I could help them.

And all at once I felt that perhaps I could and I tried first with the daughter who was upstairs in her room. I reached out to her and I told her happy thoughts. It wasn't easy to start with, but pretty soon I got the hang of it and it wasn't hard to make her happy. Then I made the other two happy and went on my way, feeling better about what I'd done to the family.

I listened in on the houses I passed. Most of them were happy, or at least contented, though I found a couple that were sad. Automatically, I reached out my mind and gave them happiness. It wasn't that I felt I should do something good for any particular person. To tell the truth, I don't remember which houses I made happy. I just thought if I was able to do a thing like that, I should do it. It wasn't right for someone to have that kind of power and refuse to use it.

Ma was sitting up for me when I got home. She was looking kind of worried, the way she always does when I disappear for a long time and she don't know where I am.

I went up to my room and got into bed and lay awake for a long time, wondering how come I could do all the things I could and how, suddenly, today I was able to do them when I'd never been able to before. But finally I went to sleep.

The situation is not ideal, of course, but a good deal better than I had any reason to expect. It is not likely that one should find on every alien planet a host so made to order for our purpose as is this one of mine.

It has accepted me without recognizing me, has made no attempt to deny itself to me or to reject me. It is of an order of intelligence which has enabled it, quickly and efficiently, to make use of those most-readily manipulated of my abilities and this has aided me greatly in my observations. It is fairly mobile and consorts freely with its kind, which are other distinct advantages.

I reckon myself fortunate, indeed, to have found so satisfactory a host so soon upon arrival.

When I got up and had breakfast, I went outside and found Bounce waiting for me. He said he wanted to go and chase some rabbits and I agreed to go along. He said since we could talk now, we ought to make a good team. I could stand up on a stump or a pile of rocks or even climb a tree, so I could overlook the ground and see the rabbit and yell out to him which way it was going, and he could intercept it.

We went up the road toward Alf's place, but turned off down across the pasture, heading for some cutover land on the hill across the creek.

When we were off the road, I turned around to give Alf a good hating and while I was standing there, hating him, a thought came into my mind. I didn't know if I could do it, but it seemed to be a good idea, so I tried.

I moved my seeing up to Alf's barn and went right through and came out in the middle of the haymow, with hay packed all around me. But all the time, you understand, I was standing out there in the pasture with Bounce, on our way to chase some rabbits.

I'd like to explain what I did next and how I did it, but mostly what worries me is how I knew enough to do it—I mean enough about chemical reaction and stuff like that. I did something to the hay and something to the oxygen and I started a fire there in the center of the haymow. When I saw it was started good, I got out of there and was in myself again, and Bounce and I went on across the creek and up the hill.

I kept looking back over my shoulder, wondering if the fire might not have gone out, but all at once there was a little trickle of smoke coming out of the haymow opening up under the gable's end.

We'd got up into the cutover land by that time and I sat down on a stump and enjoyed myself. The fire had a good start before it busted out and there wasn't a thing that could be done to save the barn. It went up with a roar and made the prettiest column of smoke you've ever seen.

On the way home, I stopped at the general store. Alf was there and he seemed much too happy to have just lost his barn.

But it wasn't long until I understood why he was so happy.

"I had her insured," he told Bert Jones, the storekeep, "plumb up to the hilt. Anyhow, it was too big a barn, a lot bigger than I needed. When I built it, I figured I was going to go into milking heavier than I've done and would need the space."

Bert chuckled. "Handy fire for you, Alf."

"Best thing that ever happened to me. I can build another barn and have some cash left over."

I was pretty sore about bungling it, but I thought of a way to get even.

After lunch, I went up the road again and out into Alf's pasture and hunted up the bull. He was glad to see me, although he did a little pawing and some bellowing just to show off.

I had wondered all the way out if I could talk to the bull the way I talked to Bounce and I was afraid that maybe I couldn't, for Bounce was bound to be smarter than a bull.

I was right, of course. It was awful hard to make that bull understand anything.

I made the mistake of scratching behind his ears while I tried to talk to him and he almost went to sleep. I could feel just how good the scratching felt to him. So I hauled off and kicked him in the ribs to wake him up, so he would pay attention. He did pay a little closer attention and even did a little answering, but not much. A bull is awful dumb.

But I felt fairly sure I'd got my idea across, for he started acting sore and feisty and I'm afraid that I overdid it just a mite. I made it to the fence ahead of him and went over without even touching it. The bull stopped at the fence and stood there, pawing and raising Cain, and I got out of there as fast as I could go.

I went home fairly pleased with myself for thinking up as smart a thing as that. I wasn't surprised in the least to hear that evening that Alf had been killed by his bull.

It wasn't a pretty way to die, of course, but Alf had it coming to him, the way he beat me out of my summer wages.

I was sitting in the pool hall when the news was brought in by someone and they all talked about it. Some said Alf had always claimed you couldn't trust no bull, and someone else said he'd often said I was the only one who'd ever gotten along with this particular bull and he was scared all the time I was there for fear the bull would kill me.

They saw me sitting there and they asked me about it and I acted dumb and all of them laughed at me, but I didn't mind their laughing. I knew something they didn't know. Imagine how surprised they'd be if they ever learned the truth!

They won't, of course.

I'm too smart for that.

When I went home, I got a tablet and a pencil and started to write down the names of all my enemies—everyone who had ever laughed at me or done mean things to me or said mean things about me.

The list was pretty long. It included almost everyone in town.

I sat there thinking and I decided maybe I shouldn't kill everyone in town. Not that I couldn't, for I could have, just as slick as anything. But thinking about Alf and Banker Patton, I could see there wasn't any lasting satisfaction in killing people you hate. And I could see as plain as day that if you killed a lot of people, it could leave you pretty lonesome.

I read down through the list of names I'd made and I gave a couple of them the benefit of a doubt and scratched them out. I read those that were left over and I had to admit that every one of them was bad. I decided that if I didn't kill them, I'd have to do something else about them, for I couldn't let them go on being bad.

I thought about it a long time and I remembered some of the things I'd heard Preacher Martin say, although, as I've mentioned before, he's a great one to be saying them. I decided I'd have to lay aside my hate and return good for evil.

I am puzzled and disturbed, although that, perhaps, is the normal reaction when one attaches oneself to an alien being. This is a treacherous and unprincipled species and, as such, an incalculably important one to study.

I am continually amazed at the facility with which my host has acquired the use of my talents, continually appalled by the use he makes of them. I am more than puzzled by his own conviction that he is less intelligent than his fellows; his actions during my acquaintance with him do not bear this out. I wonder if it may not be a racial trait, a sort of cult-attitude of inferiority, that it may be ill-mannered to think of oneself in any other way.

But I half suspect that he may have sensed me in some way without my knowing it and may be employing this strange concept as a device to force me from his mind. Under such a circumstance, it would not be prime ethics for me to remain with him—but he has proved to be such an excellent seat of observation that I am loath to leave him.

The fact is, I don't know. I could, of course, seize control of his mind and thus learn the truth of this and other matters which are perplexing me. But I fear that, in doing so, I would destroy his effectiveness as a free agent and thus impair his observational value. I have decided to wait before taking such drastic measures.

I ate breakfast in a hurry, being anxious to get started. Ma asked me what I was going to do and I said just walk around a bit.

First off, I went to the parsonage and sat down outside the hedge between it and the church. Pretty soon, Preacher Martin came out and began to walk up and down in what he called his garden, pretending he was sunk in holy thought, although I always suspected it was just an act to impress old ladies who might see him.

I put out my mind real easy and finally I got it locked with his so neatly, it seemed that it was me, not him, who was walking up and down. It was a queer feeling, I can tell you, for all the time I knew good and well that I was sitting there back of the hedge.

He wasn't thinking any holy thoughts at all. He was going over in his mind all the arguments he intended to use to hit up the church board for a raise in salary. He was doing some minor cussing out of some of the members of the board for being tight-fisted skinflints and that I agreed with, because they surely were.

Taking it easy, just sort of stealing in on his thoughts, I made him think about Jennie Smith, the organist, and the way he was carrying on with her, and I made him ashamed of himself for doing it.

He tried to push me away, though he didn't know it was me; he just thought it was his own mind bringing up the matter. But I wouldn't let him push the thought away. I piled it on real heavy.

I made him think how the people in the church trusted him and looked to him for spiritual leadership, and I made him remember back to when he was a younger man, just out of seminary, and looked on his lifetime work as a great crusade. I made him think of how he'd betrayed all the things he'd believed in then, and I got him down so low, he was almost bawling. Then I made him tell himself that owning up was the only way he could absolve himself. Once he'd done that, he could start life over again and be a credit to himself and his church.

I went away, figuring I'd done a fair job of work on him, but knowing that I'd have to check up on him every now and then.

At the general store, I sat around and watched Bert Jones sweep out the place. While he was talking to me, I sneaked into his mind and recalled to him all the times he'd paid way less than market prices for the eggs the farmers brought in, and the habit of sneaking in extra items on the bills he sent out to his charge customers, and how he'd cheated on his income tax. I scared him plenty on the income tax and I kept working at him until he'd about decided to make it right with everyone he'd cheated.

I didn't finish the job airtight, but I knew I could come back any time I wanted to and in a little while, I'd make an honest man of Bert.

Over at the barber shop, I watched Jake cut a head of hair. I wasn't too interested in the man Jake was working on—he lived four or five miles out of town—and at the moment, I figured that I'd better confine my work to the people in the village.

Before I left, I had Jake plenty worried about the gambling he'd been doing in the back room at the pool hall and had him almost ready to make a clean breast of it to his wife.

I went over to the pool hall. Mike was sitting back of the counter with his hat on, reading the baseball scores in the morning paper. I got a day-old paper and pretended to read it. Mike laughed and asked me when I'd learned to read, so I laid it on good and thick.

When I left, I knew, just as soon as I was out the door, he'd go down into the basement and dump all the moonshine down the drain, and before too long, I'd get him to close up the back room.

Over at the cheese factory, I didn't have much chance to work on Ben. The farmers were bringing in their milk and he was too busy for me to really get into his mind. But I did manage to make him think of what would happen if Jake ever caught him with Jake's wife. And I knew when I could catch him alone, I could do a top-notch job on him, for I saw he scared easy.

And that's the way it went.

It was tough work and at times I felt it was just too much of a job. But then I'd sit down and remind myself that it was my duty to keep on—that for some reason this power had been given me and that it was up to me to use it for all it was worth. And furthermore, I was not to use it for myself, for any selfish ends, but for the good of other people.

I don't think I missed a person in the village.

Remember how we wondered if there might not be unseen flaws in this plan of ours? We went over it most carefully and could find none, yet all of us feared that some might show up in actual practice. Now I can report there is one. It is this:

Accurate, impersonal observation is impossible, for as soon as one introduces one's self into a host, his abilities become available to the host and at once become a factor which upsets the norm.

As a result of this, I am getting a distorted picture of the culture of this planet. Reluctant to intervene before, I am now convinced that I must move to take command of the situation.

Bert, now that he's turned honest, is the happiest man you ever saw. Even losing all the customers who got sore at him when he explained why he paid them back some money doesn't bother him. I don't know how Ben is getting along—he disappeared right after Jake took the shotgun to him. But, then, everyone agrees Ben was overdoing it when he went to Jake and told him he was sorry for what had been going on. Jake's wife is gone, too, and some folks say she followed Ben.

To tell the truth, I am well satisfied with the way everything's turned out. Everyone is honest and no one is fooling around with anyone else and there ain't a lick of gambling or drinking going on in town. Mapleton probably is the most moral village in the United States.

I feel that perhaps it turned out the way it did because I started out by conquering my own evil thoughts and, instead of killing all the folks I hated, set out to do them good.

I'm a little puzzled when I walk through the streets at night because I don't pick up near as many happy thoughts as I used to. In fact, there are times when it keeps me busy almost all night long, getting them cheered up. You'd think honest folks would be happy folks. I imagine it's because, now they're good instead of bad, they're not so given to giddy pleasures, but are more concerned with the solid, worthwhile side of life.

I'm a little worried about myself. While I did a lot of good, I may have done it for a selfish reason. I did it, perhaps partly, to make up for killing Alf and Banker Patton. And I did it not for just people, but for people I know. That doesn't seem right. Why should only people I know benefit?

Help! Can you hear me? I'm trapped! I can neither control my host nor can I escape from him. Do not under any circumstances let anyone else try to use another member of this race as a host.

Help!

Can you hear me?

Help!

I've sat up all night, thinking, and now the way is clear.

Having reached my decision, I feel important and humble, both at once. I know I'm a chosen instrument for good and must not let anything stop me. I know the village was no more than a proving ground, a place for me to learn what I could really do. Knowing now, I'm determined to use the power to its utmost for the good of all humanity.

Ma's been saving up a little money for a long time for a decent burial.

I know just where she hides it.

It's all she's got.

But it's enough to get me to the U.N.

HELLHOUNDS OF THE COSMOS

Many of Cliff Simak's stories somehow touched on newspaper offices or newspaper people—not surprising, considering that he was a lifelong newspaperman—and this story starts in an editor's office. But after that, it gets, well, weird, and it's my opinion that no Simak story ever ended up more outré. In some ways, this story seems almost incoherent, as if the author awoke during the night with the weirdness of a dream still fresh in his mind, but fading (we all know that feeling), so he struggled to write it all down as fast as he could, before it got away from him . . . and failed to get it all.

I will not try to excuse this story's failings by pointing out that it was written in late 1931, and thus represents work from the earliest days of the author's career. But I have to admire that as a young author, still just beginning to learn his craft, Cliff dared to explore concepts so strange that even he struggled to get them onto paper.

This story was first published in Astounding Stories in June of 1932. Those were the days before the magazine became Astounding Science Fiction *and before John W. Campbell Jr. brought that magazine to the apex of science fiction. I wonder what Campbell would have thought if presented with this story.*

—dww

The paper had gone to press, graphically describing the latest of the many horrible events which had been enacted upon the Earth in the last six months. The headlines screamed that Six Corners, a little hamlet in Pennsylvania, had been wiped out by the Horror. Another front-page story told of a Terror in the Amazon valley which had sent the natives down the river in babbling fear. Other stories told of deaths here and there, all attributable to the "Black Horror," as it was called.

The telephone rang.

"Hello," said the editor.

"London calling," came the voice of the operator.

"All right," replied the editor.

He recognized the voice of Terry Masters, special correspondent. His voice came clearly over the transatlantic telephone.

"The Horror is attacking London in force," he said. "There are thousands of them and they have completely surrounded the city. All roads are blocked. The government declared the city under martial rule a quarter of an hour ago and efforts are being made to prepare for resistance against the enemy."

"Just a second," the editor shouted into the transmitter.

He touched a button on his desk and in a moment an answering buzz told him he was in communication with the press-room.

"Stop the presses!" he yelled into the speaking tube. "Get ready for a new front make-up!"

"O.K.," came faintly through the tube, and the editor turned back to the phone.

"Now let's have it," he said, and the voice at the London end of the wire droned on, telling the story that in another half hour was read by a world which shuddered in cold fear even as it scanned the glaring headlines.

"Woods," said the editor of the *Press* to a reporter, "run over and talk to Dr. Silas White. He phoned me to send someone. Something about this Horror business."

Henry Woods rose from his chair without a word and walked from the office. As he passed the wire machine it was tapping out, with a maddeningly methodical slowness, the story of the fall of London. Only half an hour before it had rapped forth the flashes concerning the attack on Paris and Berlin.

He passed out of the building into a street that was swarming with terrified humanity. Six months of terror, of numerous mysterious deaths, of villages blotted out, had set the world on edge. Now with London in possession of the Horror and Paris and Berlin fighting hopelessly for their lives, the entire population of the world was half insane with fright.

Exhorters on street corners enlarged upon the end of the world, asking that the people prepare for eternity, attributing the Horror to the act of a Supreme Being enraged with the wickedness of the Earth.

Expecting every moment an attack by the Horror, people left their work and gathered in the streets. Traffic, in places, had been blocked for hours and law and order were practically paralyzed. Commerce and transportation were disrupted as fright-ridden people fled from the larger cities, seeking doubtful hiding places in rural districts from the death that stalked the land.

A loudspeaker in front of a music store blared forth the latest news flashes.

"It has been learned," came the measured tones of the announcer, "that all communication with Berlin ceased about ten minutes ago. At Paris all efforts to hold the Horror at bay have been futile. Explosives blow it apart, but have the same effect upon it as explosion has on gas. It flies apart and then reforms again, not always in the same shape as it was before. A new gas, one of the most deadly ever conceived by man, has failed to have any effect on the things. Electric guns and heat guns have absolutely no effect upon them.

"A news flash which has just come in from Rome says that a large number of the Horrors has been sighted north of that city by airmen. It seems they are attacking the capitals of the world first. Word comes from Washington that every known form of defense is being amassed at that city. New York is also preparing. . . ."

Henry Woods fought his way through the crowd which milled in front of the loudspeaker. The hum of excitement was giving away to a silence, the silence of a stunned people, the fearful silence of a populace facing a presence it is unable to understand, an embattled world standing with useless weapons before an incomprehensible enemy.

In despair the reporter looked about for a taxi, but realized, with a groan of resignation, that no taxi could possibly operate in that crowded street. A street car, blocked by the stream of humanity which jostled and elbowed about it, stood still, a defeated thing.

Seemingly the only man with a definite purpose in that whirlpool of terror-stricken men and women, the newspaperman settled down to the serious business of battling his way through the swarming street.

"Before I go to the crux of the matter," said Dr. Silas White, about half an hour later, "let us first review what we know of this so-called Horror. Suppose you tell me exactly what you know of it."

Henry Woods shifted uneasily in his chair. Why didn't the old fool get down to business? The chief would raise hell if this story didn't make the regular edition. He stole a glance at his wrist-watch. There was still almost an hour left. Maybe he could manage it. If the old chap would only snap into it!

"I know no more," he said, "than is common knowledge."

The gimlet eyes of the old white-haired scientist regarded the newspaperman sharply.

"And that is?" he questioned.

There was no way out of it, thought Henry. He'd have to humor the old fellow.

"The Horror," he replied, "appeared on Earth, so far as the knowledge of man is concerned, about six months ago."

Dr. White nodded approvingly.

"You state the facts very aptly," he said.

"How so?"

"When you say 'so far as the knowledge of man is concerned.'"

"Why is that?"

"You will understand in due time. Please proceed."

Vaguely the newspaperman wondered whether he was interviewing the scientist or the scientist interviewing him.

"They were first reported," Woods said, "early this spring. At that time they wiped out a small village in the province of Quebec. All the inhabitants, except a few fugitives, were found dead, killed mysteriously and half eaten, as if by wild beasts. The fugitives were demented, babbling of black shapes that swept down out of the dark forest upon the little town in the small hours of the morning.

"The next that was heard of them was about a week later, when they struck in an isolated rural district in Poland, killing and feeding on the population of several farms. In the next week more villages were wiped out, in practically every country on the face of the Earth. From the hinterlands came tales of murder done at midnight, of men and women horribly mangled, of livestock slaughtered, of buildings crushed as if by some titanic force.

"At first they worked only at night and then, seeming to become bolder and more numerous, attacked in broad daylight."

The newspaperman paused.

"Is that what you want?" he asked.

"That's part of it," replied Dr. White, "but that's not all. What do these Horrors look like?"

"That's more difficult," said Henry. "They have been reported as every conceivable sort of monstrosity. Some are large and others are small. Some take the form of animals, others of birds and reptiles, and some are cast in appalling shapes such as might be snatched out of the horrid imagery of a thing which resided in a world entirely alien to our own."

Dr. White rose from his chair and strode across the room to confront the other.

"Young man," he asked, "do you think it possible the Horror might have come out of a world entirely alien to our own?"

"I don't know," replied Henry. "I know that some of the scientists believe they came from some other planet, perhaps even from some other solar system. I know they are like nothing ever known before on Earth. They are always inky black, something like black tar, you know, sort of sticky-looking, a disgusting sight. The weapons of mankind can't affect them. Explosives are useless and so are projectiles. They wade through poison gas and fiery chemicals and seem to enjoy them. Elaborate electrical barriers have failed. Heat doesn't make them turn a hair."

"And you think they came from some other planet, perhaps some other solar system?"

"I don't know what to think," said Henry. "If they came out of space they must have come in some conveyance, and that would certainly have been sighted, picked up long before it arrived, by our astronomers. If they came in small conveyances, there must have been many of them. If they came in a single conveyance, it would be too large to escape detection. That is, unless—"

"Unless what?" snapped the scientist.

"Unless it traveled at the speed of light. Then it would have been invisible."

"Not only invisible," snorted the old man, "but non-existent."

A question was on the tip of the newspaperman's tongue, but before it could be asked the old man was speaking again, asking a question:

"Can you imagine a fourth dimension?"

"No, I can't," said Henry.

"Can you imagine a thing of only two dimensions?"

"Vaguely, yes."

The scientist smote his palms together.

"Now we're coming to it!" he exclaimed.

Henry Woods regarded the other narrowly. The old man must be turned. What did fourth and second dimensions have to do with the Horror?

"Do you know anything about evolution?" questioned the old man.

"I have a slight understanding of it. It is the process of upward growth, the stairs by which simple organisms climb to become more complex organisms."

Dr. White grunted and asked still another question:

"Do you know anything about the theory of the exploding universe? Have you ever noted the tendency of the perfectly balanced to run amuck?"

The reporter rose slowly to his feet.

"Dr. White," he said, "you phoned my paper you had a story for us. I came here to get it, but all you have done is ask me questions. If you can't tell me what you want us to publish, I will say good-day."

The doctor put forth a hand that shook slightly.

"Sit down, young man," he said. "I don't blame you for being impatient, but I will now come to my point."

The newspaperman sat down again.

"I have developed a hypothesis," said Dr. White, "and have conducted several experiments which seem to bear it out. I am staking my reputation upon the supposition that it is correct. Not only that, but I am also staking the lives of several brave men who believe implicitly in me and my theory. After all, I suppose it makes little difference, for if I fail the world is doomed, if I succeed it is saved from complete destruction.

"Have you ever thought that our evolutionists might be wrong, that evolution might be downward instead of upward? The theory of the exploding universe, the belief that all of creation is running down, being thrown off balance by the loss of energy, spurred onward by cosmic accidents which tend to disturb its equilibrium, to a time when it will run wild and space will be filled with swirling dust of disintegrated worlds, would bear out this contention.

"This does not apply to the human race. There is no question that our evolution is upward, that we have arisen from one-celled creatures wallowing in the slime of primal seas. Our case is probably paralleled by thousands of other intelligences on far-flung planets and island universes. These instances, however, running at cross purposes to the general evolutional trend of the entire cosmos, are mere flashes in the eventual course of cosmic evolution, comparing no more to eternity than a split second does to a million years.

"Taking these instances, then, as inconsequential, let us say that the trend of cosmic evolution is downward rather than upward, from complex units to simpler units rather than from simple units to more complex ones.

"Let us say that life and intelligence have degenerated. How would you say such a degeneration would take place? In just what way would it be manifested? What sort of transition would life pass through in passing from one stage to a lower one? Just what would be the nature of these stages?"

The scientist's eyes glowed brightly as he bent forward in his chair. The newspaperman said simply: "I have no idea."

"Man," cried the old man, "can't you see that it would be a matter of dimensions? From the fourth dimension to the third, from the third to the second, from the second to the first, from the first to a questionable existence or plane which is beyond our understanding or perhaps to oblivion and the end of life. Might not the fourth have evolved from a fifth, the fifth from a sixth, the sixth from a seventh, and so on to no one knows what multi-dimension?"

Dr. White paused to allow the other man to grasp the importance of his statements. Woods failed lamentably to do so.

"But what has this to do with the Horror?" he asked.

"Have you absolutely no imagination?" shouted the old man.

"Why, I suppose I have, but I seem to fail to understand."

"We are facing an invasion of fourth-dimensional creatures," the old man whispered, almost as if fearful to speak the words aloud. "We are being attacked by life which is one dimension above us in evolution. We are fighting, I tell you, a tribe of hell-hounds out of the cosmos. They are unthinkably above us in the matter of intelligence. There is a chasm of knowledge between us so wide and so deep that it staggers the imagination. They regard us as mere animals, perhaps not even that. So far as they are concerned we are just fodder, something to be eaten as we eat vegetables and cereals or the flesh of domesticated animals. Perhaps they have watched us for years, watching life on the world increase, lapping their monstrous jowls over the fattening of the Earth. They have awaited the proper setting of the banquet table and now they are dining.

"Their thoughts are not our thoughts, their ideals not our ideals. Perhaps they have nothing in common with us except the primal basis of all life, self-preservation, the necessity of feeding.

"Maybe they have come of their own will. I prefer to believe that they have. Perhaps they are merely following the natural course of events, obeying some immutable law legislated by some higher being who watches over the cosmos and dictates what shall be and what shall not be. If this is true it means that there has been a flaw in my reasoning, for I believed that the life of each plane degenerated in company with the degeneration of its plane of existence, which would obey the same evolutional laws which govern the life upon it. I am quite satisfied that this invasion is a well-planned campaign, that some fourth-dimensional race has found a means of breaking through the veil of force which separates its plane from ours."

"But," pointed out Henry Woods, "you say they are fourth-dimensional things. I can't see anything about them to suggest an additional dimension. They are plainly three-dimensional."

"Of course they are three-dimensional. They would have to be to live in this world of three dimensions. The only two-dimensional objects which we know of in this world are merely illusions, projections of the third dimension, like a shadow. It is impossible for more than one dimension to live on any single plane.

"To attack us they would have to lose one dimension. This they have evidently done. You can see how utterly ridiculous it would be for you to try to attack a two-dimensional thing. So far as you were concerned it would have no mass. The same is true of the other dimensions. Similarly a being of a lesser plane could not harm an inhabitant of a higher plane. It is apparent that while the Horror has lost one material dimension, it has retained certain fourth-dimensional properties which make it invulnerable to the forces at the command of our plane."

The newspaperman was now sitting on the edge of his chair.

"But," he asked breathlessly, "it all sounds so hopeless. What can be done about it?"

Dr. White hitched his chair closer and his fingers closed with a fierce grasp upon the other's knee. A militant boom came into his voice.

"My boy," he said, "we are to strike back. We are going to invade the fourth-dimensional plane of these hellhounds. We are going to make them feel our strength. We are going to strike back."

Henry Woods sprang to his feet.

"How?" he shouted. "Have you . . .?"

Dr. White nodded.

"I have found a way to send the third-dimensional into the fourth. Come and I will show you."

The machine was huge, but it had an appearance of simple construction. A large rectangular block of what appeared to be a strange black metal was set on end and flanked on each side by two smaller ones. On the top of the large block was set a half-globe of a strange substance, somewhat, Henry thought, like frosted glass. On one side of the large cube was set a lever, a long glass panel, two vertical tubes and three clock-face indicators. The control board, it appeared, was relatively simple.

Beside the mass of the five rectangles, on the floor, was a large plate of transparent substance, ground to a concave surface, through which one could see an intricate tangle of wire mesh.

Hanging from the ceiling, directly above the one on the floor, was another concave disk, but this one had a far more pronounced curvature.

Wires connected the two disks and each in turn was connected to the rectangular machine.

"It is a matter of the proper utilization of two forces, electrical and gravitational," proudly explained Dr. White. "Those two forces, properly used, warp the third-dimensional into the fourth. A reverse process is used to return the object to the third. The principle of the machine is—"

The old man was about to launch into a lengthy discussion, but Henry interrupted him. A glance at his watch had shown him press time was drawing perilously close.

"Just a second," he said. "You propose to warp a third--dimensional being into a fourth dimension. How can a third-dimensional thing exist there? You said a short time ago that only a specified dimension could exist on one single plane."

"You have missed my point," snapped Dr. White. "I am not sending a third-dimensional thing to a fourth dimension. I am changing the third-dimensional being into a fourth-dimensional being. I add a dimension, and automatically the being exists on a different plane. I am reversing evolution. This third dimension we now exist on evolved, millions of eons ago, from a fourth dimension. I am sending a lesser entity back over those millions of eons to a plane similar to one upon which his ancestors lived inconceivably long ago."

"But, man, how do you know you can do it?"

The doctor's eyes gleamed and his fingers reached out to press a bell.

A servant appeared almost at once.

"Bring me a dog," snapped the old man. The servant disappeared.

"Young man," said Dr. White, "I am going to show you how I know I can do it. I have done it before, now I am going to do it for you. I have sent dogs and cats back to the fourth dimension and returned them safely to this room. I can do the same with men."

The servant reappeared, carrying in his arms a small dog. The doctor stepped to the control board of his strange machine.

"All right, George," he said.

The servant had evidently worked with the old man enough to know what was expected of him. He stepped close to the floor disk and waited. The dog whined softly, sensing that all was not exactly right.

The old scientist slowly shoved the lever toward the right, and as he did so a faint hum filled the room, rising to a stupendous roar as he advanced the lever. From both floor disk and upper disk leaped strange cones of blue light, which met midway to form an hour-glass shape of brilliance.

The light did not waver or sparkle. It did not glow. It seemed hard and brittle, like straight bars of force. The newspaperman, gazing with awe upon it, felt that terrific force was there. What had the old man said? Warp a third-dimensional being into another dimension! That would take force!

As he watched, petrified by the spectacle, the servant stepped forward and, with a flip, tossed the little dog into the blue light. The animal could be discerned for a moment through the light and then it disappeared.

"Look in the globe!" shouted the old man; and Henry jerked his eyes from the column of light to the half-globe atop the machine.

He gasped. In the globe, deep within its milky center, glowed a picture that made his brain reel as he looked upon it. It was a scene such as no man could have imagined unaided. It was a horribly distorted projection of an eccentric landscape, a landscape hardly analogous to anything on Earth.

"That's the fourth dimension, sir," said the servant.

"That's not the fourth dimension," the old man corrected him. "That's a third-dimensional impression of the fourth dimension. It is no more the fourth dimension than a shadow is three-dimensional. It, like a shadow, is merely a projection. It gives us a glimpse of what the fourth plane is like. It is a shadow of that plane."

Slowly a dark blotch began to grow in the landscape. Slowly it assumed definite form. It puzzled the reporter. It looked familiar. He could have sworn he had seen it somewhere before. It was alive, for it had moved.

"That, sir, is the dog," George volunteered.

"That *was* the dog," Dr. White again corrected him. "God knows what it is now."

He turned to the newspaperman.

"Have you seen enough?" he demanded.

Henry nodded.

The other slowly began to return the lever to its original position. The roaring subsided, the light faded, the projection in the half-globe grew fainter.

"How are you going to use it?" asked the newspaperman.

"I have ninety-eight men who have agreed to be projected into the fourth dimension to seek out the entities that are attacking us and attack them in turn. I shall send them out in an hour."

"Where is there a phone?" asked the newspaperman.

"In the next room," replied Dr. White.

As the reporter dashed out of the door, the light faded entirely from between the two disks and on the lower one a little dog crouched, quivering, softly whimpering.

The old man stepped from the controls and approached the disk. He scooped the little animal from where it lay into his arms and patted the silky head.

"Good dog," he murmured; and the creature snuggled close to him, comforted, already forgetting that horrible place from which it had just returned.

"Is everything ready, George?" asked the old man.

"Yes, sir," replied the servant. "The men are all ready, even anxious to go. If you ask me, sir, they are a tough lot."

"They are as brave a group of men as ever graced the Earth," replied the scientist gently. "They are adventurers, every one of whom has faced danger and will not shrink from it. They are born fighters. My one regret is that I have not been able to secure more like them. A thousand men such as they should be able to conquer any opponent. It was impossible. The others were poor soft fools. They laughed in my face. They thought I was an old fool—I, the man who alone stands between them and utter destruction."

His voice had risen to almost a scream, but it again sank to a normal tone.

"I may be sending ninety-eight brave men to instant death. I hope not."

"You can always jerk them back, sir," suggested George.

"Maybe I can, maybe not," murmured the old man.

Henry Woods appeared in the doorway.

"When do we start?" he asked.

"We?" exclaimed the scientist.

"Certainly, you don't believe you're going to leave me out of this. Why, man, it's the greatest story of all time. I'm going as special war correspondent."

"They believed it? They are going to publish it?" cried the old man, clutching at the newspaperman's sleeve.

"Well, the editor was skeptical at first, but after I swore on all sorts of oaths it was true, he ate it up. Maybe you think that story didn't stop the presses!"

"I didn't expect them to. I just took a chance. I thought they, too, would laugh at me."

"But when do we start?" persisted Henry.

"You are really in earnest? You really want to go?" asked the old man, unbelievingly.

"I am going. Try to stop me."

Dr. White glanced at his watch.

"We will start in exactly thirty-four minutes," he said.

"Ten seconds to go." George, standing with watch in hand, spoke in a precise manner, the very crispness of his words betraying the excitement under which he labored.

The blue light, hissing, drove from disk to disk; the room thundered with the roar of the machine, before which stood Dr. White, his hand on the lever, his eyes glued on the instruments before him.

In a line stood the men who were to fling themselves into the light to be warped into another dimension, there to seek out and fight an unknown enemy. The line was headed by a tall man with hands like hams, with a weather-beaten face and a wild mop of hair. Behind him stood a belligerent little cockney. Henry Woods stood fifth in line. They were a motley lot, adventurers every one of them, and some were obviously afraid as they stood before that column of light, with only a few seconds of the third dimension left to them. They had answered a weird advertisement, and had but a limited idea of what they were about to do. Grimly, though, they accepted it as a job, a bizarre job, but a job. They faced it as they had faced other equally dangerous, but less unusual, jobs.

"Five seconds," snapped George.

The lever was all the way over now. The half-globe showed, within its milky interior, a hideously distorted landscape. The light had taken on a hard, brittle appearance and its hiss had risen to a scream. The machine thundered steadily with a suggestion of horrible power.

"Time up!"

The tall man stepped forward. His foot reached the disk; another step and he was bathed in the light, a third and he glimmered momentarily, then vanished. Close on his heels followed the little cockney.

With his nerves at almost a snapping point, Henry moved on behind the fourth man. He was horribly afraid, he wanted to break from the line and run, it didn't matter where, any place to get away from that steady, steely light in front of him. He had seen three men step into it, glow for a second, and then disappear. A fourth man had placed his foot on the disk.

Cold sweat stood out on his brow. Like an automaton he placed one foot on the disk. The fourth man had already disappeared.

"Snap into it, pal," growled the man behind.

Henry lifted the other foot, caught his toe on the edge of the disk and stumbled headlong into the column of light.

He was conscious of intense heat which was instantly followed by equally intense cold. For a moment his body seemed to be under enormous pressure, then it seemed to be expanding, flying apart, bursting, exploding . . .

He felt solid ground under his feet, and his eyes, snapping open, saw an alien land. It was a land of somber color, with great gray moors, and beetling black cliffs. There was something queer about it, an intangible quality that baffled him.

He looked about him, expecting to see his companions. He saw no one. He was absolutely alone in that desolate brooding land. Something dreadful had happened! Was he the only one to be safely transported from the third dimension? Had some horrible accident occurred? Was he alone?

Sudden panic seized him. If something had happened, if the others were not here, might it not be possible that the machine would not be able to bring him back to his own dimension? Was he doomed to remain marooned forever in this terrible plane?

He looked down at his body and gasped in dismay. It was not his body!

It was a grotesque caricature of a body, a horrible profane mass of flesh, like a phantasmagoric beast snatched from the dreams of a lunatic.

It was real, however. He felt it with his hands, but they were not hands. They were something like hands; they served the same purpose that hands served in the third dimension. He was, he realized, a being of the fourth dimension, but in his fourth-dimensional brain still clung hard-fighting remnants of that faithful old third-dimensional brain. He could not, as yet, see with fourth-dimensional eyes, think purely fourth-dimensional thoughts. He had not oriented himself as yet to this new plane of existence. He was seeing the fourth dimension through the blurred lenses of millions of eons of third-dimensional existence. He was seeing it much more clearly than he had seen it in the half-globe atop the machine in Dr. White's laboratory, but he would not see it clearly until every vestige of the third dimension was wiped from him. That, he knew, would come in time.

He felt his weird body with those things that served as hands and he found, beneath his groping, unearthly fingers, great rolling muscles, powerful tendons, and hard, well-conditioned flesh.

A sense of well-being surged through him and he growled like an animal, like an animal of that horrible fourth plane.

But the terrible sounds that came from between his slobbering lips were not those of his own voice, they were the voices of many men.

Then he knew. He was not alone. Here, in this one body were the bodies, the brains, the power, the spirit, of those other ninety-eight men. In the fourth dimension, all the millions of third-dimensional things were one. Perhaps that particular portion of the third dimension called the Earth had sprung from, or degenerated from, one single unit of a dissolving, worn-out fourth dimension. The third dimension, warped back to a higher plane, was automatically obeying the mystic laws of evolution by reforming in the shape of that old ancestor, unimaginably removed in time from the race he had begot. He was no longer Henry Woods, newspaperman; he was an entity that had given birth, in the dim ages when the Earth was born, to a third dimension. Nor was he alone. This body of his was composed of other sons of that ancient entity.

He felt himself grow, felt his body grow vaster, assume greater proportions, felt new vitality flow through him. It was the other men, the men who were flinging themselves into the column of light in the laboratory to be warped back to this plane, to be incorporated in his body.

It was not his body, however. His brain was not his alone. The pronoun, he realized, represented the sum total of those other men, his fellow adventurers.

Suddenly a new feeling came, a feeling of completeness, a feeling of supreme fitness. He knew that the last of the ninety-eight men had stepped across the disk, that all were here in this giant body.

Now he could see more clearly. Things in the landscape, which had escaped him before, became recognizable. Awful thoughts ran through his brain, heavy, ponderous, black thoughts. He began to recognize the landscape as something familiar, something he had seen before, a thing with which he was intimate. Phenomena, which his third-dimensional intelligence would have gasped at, became commonplace. He was finally seeing through fourth-dimensional eyes, thinking fourth-dimensional thoughts.

Memory seeped into his brain and he had fleeting visions, visions of dark caverns lit by hellish flames, of huge seas that battered remorselessly with mile-high waves against towering headlands that reared titanic toward a glowering sky. He remembered a red desert scattered with scarlet boulders, he remembered silver cliffs of gleaming metallic stone. Through all his thoughts ran something else, a scarlet thread of hate, an all-consuming passion, a fierce lust after the life of some other entity.

He was no longer a composite thing built of third-dimensional beings. He was a creature of another plane, a creature with a consuming hate, and suddenly he knew against whom this hate was directed and why. He knew also that this creature was near and his great fists closed and then spread wide as he knew it. How did he know it? Perhaps through some sense which he, as a being of another plane, held, but which was alien to the Earth. Later he asked himself this question. At the time, however, there was no questioning on his part. He only knew that somewhere near was a hated enemy and he did not question the source of his knowledge. . . .

Mumbling in an idiom incomprehensible to a third-dimensional being, filled with rage that wove redly through his brain, he lumbered down the hill onto the moor, his great strides eating up the distance, his footsteps shaking the ground.

At the foot of the hill he halted and from his throat issued a challenging roar that made the very crags surrounding the moor tremble. The rocks flung back the roar as if in mockery.

Again he shouted and in the shout he framed a lurid insult to the enemy that lurked there in the cliffs.

Again the crags flung back the insult, but this time the echoes, booming over the moor, were drowned by another voice, the voice of the enemy.

At the far end of the moor appeared a gigantic form, a form that shambled on grotesque, misshapen feet, growling angrily as he came.

He came rapidly despite his clumsy gait, and as he came he mouthed terrific threats.

Close to the other he halted and only then did recognition dawn in his eyes.

"*You, Mal Shaff?*" he growled in his guttural tongue, and surprise and consternation were written large upon his ugly face.

"Yes, it is I, Mal Shaff," boomed the other. "Remember, Ouglat, the day you destroyed me and my plane. I have returned to wreak my vengeance. I have solved a mystery you have never guessed and I have come back. You did not imagine you were attacking me again when you sent your minions to that other plane to feed upon the beings there. It was I you were attacking, fool, and I am here to kill you."

Ouglat leaped and the thing that had been Henry Woods, newspaperman, and ninety-eight other men, but was now Mal Shaff of the fourth dimension, leaped to meet him.

Mal Shaff felt the force of Ouglat, felt the sharp pain of a hammering fist, and lashed out with those horrible arms of his to smash at the leering face of his antagonist. He felt his fists strike solid flesh, felt the bones creak and tremble beneath his blow.

His nostrils were filled with the terrible stench of the other's foul breath and his filthy body. He teetered on his gnarled legs and side-stepped a vicious kick and then stepped in to gouge with straightened thumb at the other's eye. The thumb went true and Ouglat howled in pain.

Mal Shaff leaped back as his opponent charged head down, and his knotted fist beat a thunderous tattoo as the misshapen beast closed in. He felt clawing fingers seeking his throat, felt ghastly nails ripping at his shoulders. In desperation he struck blindly, and Ouglat reeled away. With a quick stride he shortened the distance between them and struck Ouglat a hard blow squarely on his slavering mouth. Pressing hard upon the reeling figure, he swung his fists like sledge-hammers, and Ouglat stumbled, falling in a heap on the sand.

Mal Shaff leaped upon the fallen foe and kicked him with his taloned feet, ripping him wickedly. There was no thought of fair play, no faintest glimmer of mercy. This was a battle to the death: there could be no quarter.

The fallen monster howled, but his voice cut short as his foul mouth, with its razor-edged fangs, closed on the other's body. His talons, seeking a hold, clawed deep.

Mal Shaff, his brain a screaming maelstrom of weird emotions, aimed pile-driver blows at the enemy, clawed and ripped. Together the two rolled, locked tight in titanic battle, on the sandy plain and a great cloud of heavy dust marked where they struggled.

In desperation Ouglat put every ounce of his strength into a heave that broke the other's grip and flung him away.

The two monstrosities surged to their feet, their eyes red with hate, glaring through the dust cloud at one another.

Slowly Ouglat's hand stole to a black, wicked cylinder that hung on a belt at his waist. His fingers closed upon it and he drew the weapon. As he leveled it at Mal Shaff, his lips curled back and his features distorted into something that was not pleasant to see.

Mal Shaff, with doubled fists, saw the great thumb of his enemy slowly depressing a button on the cylinder, and a great fear held him rooted in his tracks. In the back of his brain something was vainly trying to explain to him the horror of this thing which the other held.

Then a multicolored spiral, like a corkscrew column of vapor, sprang from the cylinder and flashed toward him. It struck him full on the chest and even as it did so he caught the ugly fire of triumph in the red eyes of his enemy.

He felt a stinging sensation where the spiral struck, but that was all. He was astounded. He had feared this weapon, had been sure it portended some form of horrible death. But all it did was to produce a slight sting.

For a split second he stood stock-still, then he surged forward and advanced upon Ouglat, his hands outspread like claws. From his throat came those horrible sounds, the speech of the fourth dimension.

"Did I not tell you, foul son of Sargouthe, that I had solved a mystery you have never guessed at? Although you destroyed me long ago, I have returned. Throw away your puny weapon. I am of the lower dimension and am invulnerable to your engines of destruction. You bloated . . ." His words trailed off into a stream of vileness that could never have occurred to a third-dimensional mind.

Ouglat, with every line of his face distorted with fear, flung the weapon from him, and turning, fled clumsily down the moor, with Mal Shaff at his heels.

Steadily Mal Shaff gained and with only a few feet separating him from Ouglat, he dived with outspread arms at the other's legs.

The two came down together, but Mal Shaff's grip was broken by the fall and the two regained their feet at almost the same instant.

The wild moor resounded to their throaty roaring and the high cliffs flung back the echoes of the bellowing of the two gladiators below. It was sheer strength now and flesh and bone were bruised and broken under the life-shaking blows that they dealt. Great furrows were plowed in the sand by the sliding of heavy feet as the two fighters shifted to or away from attack. Blood, blood of fourth-dimensional creatures, covered the bodies of the two and stained the sand with its horrible hue. Perspiration streamed from them and their breath came in gulping gasps.

The lurid sun slid across the purple sky and still the two fought on, Ouglat, one of the ancients, and Mal Shaff, reincarnated. It was a battle of giants, a battle that must have beggared even the titanic tilting of forgotten gods and entities in the ages when the third-dimensional Earth was young.

Mal Shaff had no conception of time. He may have fought seconds or hours. It seemed an eternity. He had attempted to fight scientifically, but had failed to do so. While one part of him had cried out to elude his opponent, to wait for openings, to conserve his strength, another part had shouted at him to step in and smash, smash, smash at the hated monstrosity pitted against him.

It seemed Ouglat was growing in size, had become more agile, that his strength was greater. His punches hurt more; it was harder to hit him.

Still Mal Shaff drilled in determinedly, head down, fists working like pistons. As the other seemed to grow stronger and larger, he seemed to become smaller and weaker.

It was queer. Ouglat should be tired, too. His punches should be weaker. He should move more slowly, be heavier on his feet.

There was no doubt of it. Ouglat was growing larger, was drawing on some mysterious reserve of strength. From somewhere new force and life were flowing into his body. But from where was this strength coming?

A huge fist smashed against Mal Shaff's jaw. He felt himself lifted, and the next moment he skidded across the sand.

Lying there, gasping for breath, almost too fagged to rise, with the black bulk of the enemy looming through the dust cloud before him, he suddenly realized the source of the other's renewed strength.

Ouglat was recalling his minions from the third dimension! They were incorporating in his body, returning to their parent body!

They were coming back from the third dimension to the fourth dimension to fight a third-dimensional thing reincarnated in the fourth-dimensional form it had lost millions of eons ago!

This was the end, thought Mal Shaff. But he staggered to his feet to meet the charge of the ancient enemy and a grim song, a death chant immeasurably old, suddenly and dimly remembered from out of the mists of countless millenniums, was on his lips as he swung a pile-driver blow into the suddenly astonished face of the rushing Ouglat. . . .

The milky globe atop the machine in Dr. White's laboratory glowed softly, and within that glow two figures seemed to struggle.

Before the machine, his hands still on the controls, stood Dr. Silas White. Behind him the room was crowded with newspapermen and photographers.

Hours had passed since the ninety-eight men—ninety-nine, counting Henry Woods—had stepped into the brittle column of light to be shunted back through unguessed time to a different plane of existence. The old scientist, during all those hours, had stood like a graven image before his machine, eyes staring fixedly at the globe.

Through the open windows he had heard the cry of the newsboy as the *Press* put the greatest scoop of all time on the street. The phone had rung like mad and George answered it. The doorbell buzzed repeatedly and George ushered in newspapermen who had asked innumerable questions, to which he had replied briefly, almost mechanically. The reporters had fought for the use of the one phone in the house and had finally drawn lots for it. A few had raced out to use other phones.

Photographers came and flashes popped and cameras clicked. The room was in an uproar. On the rare occasions when the reporters were not using the phone the instrument buzzed shrilly. Authoritative voices demanded Dr. Silas White. George, his eyes on the old man, stated that Dr. Silas White could not be disturbed, that he was busy.

From the street below came the heavy-throated hum of thousands of voices. The street was packed with a jostling crowd of awed humanity, every eye fastened on the house of Dr. Silas White. Lines of police held them back.

"What makes them move so slowly?" asked a reporter, staring at the globe. "They hardly seem to be moving. It looks like a slow motion picture."

"They are not moving slowly," replied Dr. White. "There must be a difference in time in the fourth dimension. Maybe what is hours to us is only seconds to them. Time must flow more slowly there. Perhaps it is a bigger place than this third plane. That may account for it. They aren't moving slowly, they are fighting savagely. It's a fight to the death! Watch!"

The grotesque arm of one of the figures in the milky globe was moving out slowly, loafing along, aimed at the head of the other. Slowly the other twisted his body aside, but too slowly. The fist finally touched the head, still moving slowly forward, the body following as slowly. The head of the creature twisted, bent backward, and the body toppled back in a leisurely manner.

"What does White say? . . . Can't you get a statement of some sort from him? Won't he talk at all? A hell of a fine reporter you are—can't even get a man to open his mouth. Ask him about Henry Woods. Get a human-interest slant on Woods walking into the light. Ask him how long this is going to last. Damn it all, man, do something, and don't bother me again until you have a real story—yes, I said a real story—are you hard of hearing? For God's sake, do something!"

The editor slammed the receiver on the hook.

"Brooks," he snapped, "get the War Department at Washington. Ask them if they're going to back up White. Go on, go on. Get busy. . . . How will you get them? I don't know. Just get them, that's all. Get them!"

Typewriters gibbered like chuckling morons through the roaring tumult of the editorial rooms. Copy boys rushed about, white sheets clutched in their grimy hands. Telephones jangled and strident voices blared through the haze that arose from the pipes and cigarettes of perspiring writers who feverishly transferred to paper the startling events that were rocking the world.

The editor, his necktie off, his shirt open, his sleeves rolled to the elbow, drummed his fingers on the desk. It had been a hectic twenty-four hours and he had stayed at the desk every minute of the time. He was dead tired. When the moment of relaxation came, when the tension snapped, he knew he would fall into an exhausted stupor of sleep, but the excitement was keeping him on his feet. There was work to do. There was news such as the world had never known before. Each new story meant a new front make-up, another extra. Even now the presses were thundering, even now papers with the ink hardly dry upon them were being snatched by the avid public from the hands of screaming newsboys.

A man raced toward the city desk, waving a sheet of paper in his hand. Sensing something unusual the others in the room crowded about as he laid the sheet before the editor.

"Just came in," the man gasped.

The paper was a wire dispatch. It read:

"Rome—The Black Horror is in full retreat. Although still apparently immune to the weapons being used against it, it is lifting the siege of this city. The cause is unknown."

The editor ran his eye down the sheet. There was another dateline:

"Madrid—The Black Horror, which has enclosed this city in a ring of dark terror for the last two days, is fleeing, rapidly disappearing. . . ."

The editor pressed a button. There was an answering buzz.

"Composing room," he shouted, "get ready for a new front! Yes, another extra. This will knock their eyes out!"

A telephone jangled furiously. The editor seized it.

"Yes. What was that? . . . White says he must have help. I see. Woods and the others are weakening. Being badly beaten, eh? . . . More men needed to go out to the other plane. Wants reinforcements. Yes. I see. Well, tell him that he'll have them. If he can wait half an hour we'll have them walking by thousands into that light. I'll be damned if we won't! Just tell White to hang on! We'll have the whole nation coming to the rescue!"

He jabbed up the receiver.

"Richards," he said, "write a streamer, 'Help Needed,' 'Reinforcements Called'—something of that sort, you know. Make it scream. Tell the foreman to dig out the biggest type he has. A foot high. If we ever needed big type, we need it now!"

He turned to the telephone.

"Operator," he said, "get me the Secretary of War at Washington. The secretary in person, you understand. No one else will do."

He turned again to the reporters who stood about the desk.

"In two hours," he explained, banging the desk top for emphasis, "we'll have the United States Army marching into that light Woods walked into!"

The bloody sun was touching the edge of the weird world, seeming to hesitate before taking the final plunge behind the towering black crags that hung above the ink-pot shadows at their base. The purple sky had darkened until it was almost the color of soft, black velvet. Great stars were blazing out.

Ouglat loomed large in the gathering twilight, a horrible misshapen ogre of an outer world. He had grown taller, broader, greater. Mal Shaff's head now was on a level with the other's chest; his huge arms seemed toylike in comparison with those of Ouglat, his legs mere pipestems.

Time and time again he had barely escaped as the clutching hands of Ouglat reached out to grasp him. Once within those hands he would be torn apart.

The battle had become a game of hide and seek, a game of cat and mouse, with Mal Shaff the mouse.

Slowly the sun sank and the world became darker. His brain working feverishly, Mal Shaff waited for the darkness. Adroitly he worked the battle nearer and nearer to the Stygian darkness that lay at the foot of the mighty crags. In the darkness he might escape. He could no longer continue this unequal fight. Only escape was left.

The sun was gone now. Blackness was dropping swiftly over the land, like a great blanket, creating the illusion of the glowering sky descending to the ground. Only a few feet away lay the total blackness under the cliffs.

Like a flash Mal Shaff darted into the blackness, was completely swallowed in it. Roaring, Ouglat followed.

His shoulders almost touching the great rock wall that shot straight up hundreds of feet above him, Mal Shaff ran swiftly, fear lending speed to his shivering legs. Behind him he heard the bellowing of his enemy. Ouglat was searching for him, a hopeless search in that total darkness. He would never find him, Mal Shaff felt sure.

Fagged and out of breath, he dropped panting at the foot of the wall. Blood pounded through his head and his strength seemed to be gone. He lay still and stared out into the less dark moor that stretched before him.

For some time he lay there, resting. Aimlessly he looked out over the moor, and then he suddenly noted, some distance to his right, a hill rising from the moor. The hill was vaguely familiar. He remembered it dimly as being of great importance.

A sudden inexplicable restlessness filled him. Far behind him he heard the enraged bellowing of Ouglat, but that he scarcely noticed. So long as darkness lay upon the land he knew he was safe from his enemy.

The hill had made him restless. He must reach the top. He could think of no logical reason for doing so. Obviously he was safer here at the base of the cliff, but a voice seemed to be calling, a friendly voice from the hilltop.

* * *

He rose on aching legs and forged ahead. Every fiber of his being cried out in protest, but resolutely he placed one foot ahead of the other, walking mechanically.

Opposite the hill he disregarded the strange call that pulsed down upon him, long enough to rest his tortured body. He must build up his strength for the climb.

He realized that danger lay ahead. Once he quitted the blackness of the cliff's base, Ouglat, even in the darkness that lay over the land, might see him. That would be disastrous. Once over the top of the hill he would be safe.

Suddenly the landscape was bathed in light, a soft green radiance. One moment it had been pitch dark, the next it was light, as if a giant search-light had been snapped on.

In terror, Mal Shaff looked for the source of the light. Just above the horizon hung a great green orb, which moved up the ladder of the sky even as he watched.

A moon! A huge green satellite hurtling swiftly around this cursed world!

A great, overwhelming fear sat upon Mal Shaff and with a high, shrill scream of anger he raced forward, forgetful of aching body and outraged lungs.

His scream was answered from far off, and out of the shadows of the cliffs toward the far end of the moor a black figure hurled itself. Ouglat was on the trail!

Mal Shaff tore madly up the slope, topped the crest, and threw himself flat on the ground, almost exhausted.

A queer feeling stole over him, a queer feeling of well-being. New strength was flowing into him, the old thrill of battle was pounding through his blood once more.

Not only were queer things happening to his body, but also to his brain. The world about him looked queer, held a sort of an intangible mystery he could not understand. A half question formed in the back of his brain. Who and what was he? Queer thoughts to be thinking! He was Mal Shaff, but had he always been Mal Shaff?

He remembered a brittle column of light, creatures with bodies unlike his body, walking into it. He had been one of those creatures. There was something about dimensions, about different planes, a plan for one plane to attack another!

He scrambled to his bowed legs and beat his great chest with mighty, long-nailed hands. He flung back his head and from his throat broke a sound to curdle the blood of even the bravest.

On the moor below Ouglat heard the cry and answered it with one equally ferocious.

Mal Shaff took a step forward, then stopped stock-still. Through his brain went a sharp command to return to the spot where he had stood, to wait there until attacked. He stepped back, shifting his feet impatiently.

He was growing larger; every second fresh vitality was pouring into him. Before his eyes danced a red curtain of hate and his tongue roared forth a series of insulting challenges to the figure that was even now approaching the foot of the hill.

As Ouglat climbed the hill, the night became an insane bedlam. The challenging roars beat like surf against the black cliffs.

Ouglat's lips were flecked with foam, his red eyes were mere slits, his mouth worked convulsively.

They were only a few feet apart when Ouglat charged.

Mal Shaff was ready for him. There was no longer any difference in their size and they met like the two forward walls of contending football teams.

Mal Shaff felt the soft throat of the other under his fingers and his grip tightened. Maddened, Ouglat shot terrific blow after terrific blow into Mal Shaff's body.

Try as he might, however, he could not shake the other's grip.

It was silent now. The night seemed brooding, watching the struggle on the hilltop.

Larger and larger grew Mal Shaff, until he overtopped Ouglat like a giant.

Then he loosened his grip and, as Ouglat tried to scuttle away, reached down to grasp him by the nape of his neck.

High above his head he lifted his enemy and dashed him to the ground. With a leap he was on the prostrate figure, trampling it apart, smashing it into the ground. With wild cries he stamped the earth, treading out the last of Ouglat, the Black Horror.

When no trace of the thing that had been Ouglat remained, he moved away and viewed the trampled ground.

Then, for the first time he noticed that the crest of the hill was crowded with other monstrous figures. He glared at them, half in surprise, half in anger. He had not noticed their silent approach.

"It is Mal Shaff!" cried one.

"Yes, I am Mal Shaff. What do you want?"

"But, Mal Shaff, Ouglat destroyed you once long ago!"

"And I, just now," replied Mal Shaff, "have destroyed Ouglat."

The figures were silent, shifting uneasily. Then one stepped forward.

"Mal Shaff," it said, "we thought you were dead. Apparently it was not so. We welcome you to our land again. Ouglat, who once tried to kill you and apparently failed, you have killed, which is right and proper. Come and live with us again in peace. We welcome you."

Mal Shaff bowed.

Gone was all thought of the third dimension. Through Mal Shaff's mind raced strange, haunting memories of a red desert scattered with scarlet boulders, of silver cliffs of gleaming metallic stone, of huge seas battering against towering headlands. There were other things, too. Great palaces of shining jewels, and weird nights of inhuman joy where hellish flames lit deep, black caverns.

He bowed again.

"I thank you, Bathazar," he said.

Without a backward look he shambled down the hill with the others.

"Yes?" said the editor. "What's that you say? Doctor White is dead! A suicide! Yeah, I understand. Worry, hey! Here, Roberts, take this story."

He handed over the phone.

"When you write it," he said, "play up the fact he was worried about not being able to bring the men back to the third dimension. Give him plenty of praise for ending the Black Horror. It's a big story."

"Sure," said Roberts, then spoke into the phone: "All right, Bill, shoot the works."

HONORABLE OPPONENT

This story was submitted to H. F. Gold under the title "Brain-Wash" in late February of 1956. The editor requested a few revisions before purchasing the story, but after Cliff obliged, Gold bought it, and the story was published under the title "Honorable Opponent" in the August 1956 issue of Galaxy Science Fiction.

Notice how the author sets the scene, seven short sentences into the story, simply by mentioning a move in a game of chess. . . .

—dww

The Fivers were late.

Perhaps they had misunderstood.

Or this might be another of their tricks.

Or maybe they never had intended to stick to their agreement.

"Captain," asked General Lyman Flood, "what time have we got now?"

Captain Gist looked up from the chessboard. "Thirty-seven o eight, galactic, sir."

Then he went back to the board again. Sergeant Conrad had pinned his knight and he didn't like it.

"Thirteen hours late!" the general fumed.

"They may not have got it straight, sir."

"We spelled it out to them. We took them by the hand and we went over it time and time again so they'd have it clear in mind. They couldn't possibly misunderstand."

But they very possibly could, he knew.

The Fivers misunderstood almost everything. They had been confused about the armistice—as if they'd never heard of an armistice before. They had been obtuse about the prisoner exchange. Even the matter of setting a simple time had involved excruciating explanation—as if they had never heard of the measurement of time and were completely innocent of basic mathematics.

"Or maybe they broke down," the captain offered.

The general snorted. "They don't break down. Those ships of theirs are marvels. They'd live through anything. They whipped us, didn't they?"

"Yes sir," said the captain.

"How many of them, Captain, do you estimate we destroyed?"

"Not more than a dozen, sir."

"They're tough," the general said.

He went back across the tent and sat down in a chair.

The captain had been wrong. The right number was eleven. And of those, only one had been confirmed destroyed. The others had been no better than put out of action.

And the way it figured out, the margin had been more than ten to one in favor of the Fivers. Earth, the general admitted to himself, had never taken such a beating. Whole squadrons had been wiped out; others had come fleeing back to Base with their numbers cut in half.

They came fleeing back to Base and there were no cripples. They had returned without a scratch upon them. And the ships that had been lost had not been visibly destroyed—they had simply been wiped out, leaving not a molecule of wreckage. How do you beat a thing like that, he asked himself. How do you fight a weapon that cancels out a ship in its entirety?

Back on Earth and on hundreds of other planets in the Galactic Confederacy, thousands of researchers were working day and night in a crash-priority program to find an answer to the weapon—or at least to find the weapon.

But the chance of success ran thin, the general knew, for there was not a single clue to the nature of it. Which was understandable, since every victim of the weapon had been lost irretrievably.

Perhaps some of the human prisoners would be able to provide a clue. If there had been no such hope, he knew, Earth never would have gone to all the trouble to make this prisoner exchange.

He watched the captain and the sergeant hunched above the chessboard, with the captive Fiver looking on.

He called the captive over.

The captive came, like a trundling roly-poly.

And once again, watching him, the general had that strange, disturbing sense of outrage.

For the Fiver was a droll grotesque that held no hint of the martial spirit. He was round and jolly in every feature, expression and gesture, dressed in a ribald clash of colors, as though designed and clad deliberately to offend any military man.

"Your friends are late," the general told him.

"You wait," the Fiver said and his words were more like whistling than talk. One had to listen closely to make out what he said.

The general held himself in check.

No use in arguing.

No point blowing up.

He wondered if he—or the human race—would ever understand the Fivers.

Not that anyone really wanted to, of course. Just to get them combed out of Earth's hair would be enough.

"You wait," the Fiver whistled. "They come in middle time from now."

And when in hell, the general wondered, would be a middle time from now?

The Fiver glided back to watch the game.

The general walked outside.

The tiny planet looked colder and more desolate and forbidding than it ever had before. Each time he looked at it, the general thought, the scene was more depressing than he had remembered it.

Lifeless, worthless, of no strategic or economic value, it had qualified quite admirably as neutral territory to carry out the prisoner exchange. Neutral mostly because it wasn't worth the trouble for anyone to grab it.

The distant star that was its sun was a dim glow in the sky. The black and naked rock crept out to a near horizon. The icy air was like a knife inside the general's nostrils.

There were no hills or valleys. There was absolutely nothing—just the smooth flatness of the rock stretching on all sides, for all the world like a great space-field.

It had been the Fivers, the general remembered, who had suggested this particular planet and that in itself was enough to make it suspect. But Earth, at that point in the negotiations, had been in no position to do much haggling.

He stood with his shoulders hunched and he felt the cold breath of apprehension blowing down his neck. With each passing hour, it seemed, the place felt more and more like some gigantic trap.

But he must be wrong, he argued. There was absolutely nothing in the Fivers' attitude to make him feel like that. They had, in fact, been almost magnanimous. They could have laid down their terms—almost any terms—and the Confederacy would have had no choice but to acquiesce. For Earth must buy time, no matter what the price. Earth had to be ready next time—five years or ten or whatever it might be.

But the Fivers had made no demands, which was unthinkable.

Except, the general told himself, one could never know what they might be thinking or what they might be planning.

The exchange camp huddled in the dimness—a few tents, a portable power plant, the poised and waiting ship and, beside it, the little scouter the captive Fiver had been piloting.

The scouter in itself was a good example of the gulf which separated the Fivers and the humans. It had taken three full days of bickering before the Fivers had been able to make clear their point that the scouter as well as its pilot must be returned to them.

No ship in all the Galaxy had ever gotten so thorough a study as that tiny craft. But the facts that it had yielded had been few indeed. And the captive Fiver, despite the best efforts of the experts in Psych, had furnished even fewer.

The area was quiet and almost deserted. Two sentries strode briskly up and down. Everyone else was under cover, killing time, waiting for the Fivers.

The general walked quickly across the area to the medic tent. He stooped and went inside.

Four men were sitting at a table, drearily playing cards. One of them put down his hand and rose.

"Any word, General?"

The general shook his head. "They should be coming soon, Doc. Everything all set?"

"We've been ready for some time," said the psychiatrist. "We'll bring the boys in here and check them over as soon as they arrive. We've got the stuff all set. It won't take us long."

"That's fine. I want to get off this rock as quickly as I can. I don't like the feel of it."

"There's just one thing. . . ."

"What's that?"

"If we only knew how many they are handing back?"

The general shook his head. "We never could find out. They're not so hot on figures. And you'd think, wouldn't you, that math would be universal?"

"Well," said Doc resignedly, "we'll do the best we can."

"There can't be many," the general said. "We're only giving back one Fiver and one ship. How many humans do you figure a ship is worth to them?"

"I wouldn't know. You really think they'll come?"

"It's hard to be certain that they understood. When it comes to sheer stupidity—"

"Not so stupid," Doc replied, quietly. "We couldn't learn their language, so they learned ours."

"I know," the general said impatiently. "I realize all that. But that armistice business—it took days for them to get what we were driving at. And the time reckoning system still more days. Good Lord, man, you could do better using sign language with a Stone Age savage!"

"You should," said Doc. "The savage would be human."

"But these Fivers are intelligent. Their technology, in many ways, has us beaten seven ways from Sunday. They fought us to a standstill."

"They licked us."

"All right, then, they licked us. And why not? They had this weapon that we didn't have. They were closer to their bases. They had no logistics problem to compare with ours. They licked us, but I ask you, did they have the sense to know it? Did they take advantage of it? They could have wiped us out. They could have laid down peace terms that would have crippled us for centuries. Instead, they let us go. Now how does that make sense?"

"You're dealing with an alien race," said Doc.

"We've dealt with other aliens. And we always understood them. Mostly, we got along with them."

"We dealt with them on a commercial basis," Doc reminded him. "Whatever trouble we might have had with them came after a basic minimum of understanding had been achieved. The Fivers are the first that ever came out shooting."

* * *

"I can't figure it," the general said. "We weren't even heading for them. We might have passed them by. They couldn't have known who we were. Point is, they didn't care. They just came piling out and opened up on us. And it's been the same with everyone else who came within their reach. They take on every comer. There's never a time when they aren't fighting someone—sometimes two or three at once."

"They have a defensive complex," said Doc. "Want to be left alone. All they aim to do is keep others off their planets. As you say, they could have wiped us out."

"Maybe they get hurt real easy. Don't forget we gave them a bloody nose or two—not as much as they busted us, but we hurt them some. I figure they'll come out again, soon as they can cut in."

He drew a deep breath. "Next time, we have to be ready for them. Next time, they may not stop. We have to dope them out."

It was tough work, he thought, to fight an enemy about which one knew next to nothing. And a weapon about which one knew absolutely nothing.

There were theories in plenty, but the best no more than educated guesses.

The weapon might operate in time—hurling its targets back into unimagined chaos. Or it might be dimensional. Or it might collapse the atoms in upon themselves, reducing a spaceship to the most deadly massive dust-mote the Universe had known.

One thing for certain—it was not disintegration, for there was no flash and there was no heat. The ship just disappeared and that was the end of it—the end and all of it.

"There's another thing that bothers me," said Doc. "Those other races that fought the Fivers before they jumped on us. When we tried to contact them, when we tried to get some help from them, they wouldn't bother with us. They wouldn't tell us anything."

"This is a new sector of space for us," the general said. "We are strangers here."

"It stands to reason," argued Doc, "they should jump at the chance to gang up on the Fivers."

"We can't depend on alliances. We stand alone. It is up to us."

He bent to leave the tent.

"We'll get right on it," said Doc, "soon as the men show up. We'll have a preliminary report within an hour, if they're in any shape at all."

"That's fine," the general said and ducked out of the tent.

It was a bad situation, blind and terrifying if one didn't manage to keep a good grip on himself.

The captive humans might bring back some information, but even so, you couldn't buy it blind, for there might be a gimmick in it—as there was a gimmick in what the captive Fiver knew.

This time, he told himself, the psych boys might have managed to outsmart themselves.

It had been a clever trick, all right—taking the captive Fiver on that trip and showing him so proudly all the barren, no-good planets, pretending they were the showplaces of the Confederacy.

Clever—if the Fiver had been human. For no human would have fought a skirmish, let alone a war, for the kind of planets he'd been shown.

But the Fiver wasn't human. And there was no way of knowing what kind of planet a Fiver might take a fancy to.

And there always was the chance that those crummy planets had given him the hunch that Earth would be easy prey.

The whole situation didn't track, the general thought. There was a basic wrongness to it. Even allowing for all the differences which might exist between the Fiver and the human cultures, the wrongness still persisted.

And there was something wrong right here.

He heard the sound and wheeled to stare into the sky.

The ship was close and coming in too fast.

But even as he held his breath, it slowed and steadied and came to ground in a perfect landing not more than a quarter of a mile from where the Earth ship stood.

The general broke into a run toward it, then remembered and slowed to a stiff military walk.

Men were tumbling out of tents and forming into lines. An order rang across the area and the lines moved with perfect drill precision.

The general allowed himself a smile. Those boys of his were good. You never caught them napping. If the Fivers had expected to sneak in and catch the camp confused and thus gain a bit of face, it was a horse on them.

The marching men swung briskly down the field. An ambulance moved out from beneath its tarp and followed. The drums began to roll and the bugles sounded clear and crisp in the harsh, cold air.

It was men like these, the general told himself with pride, who held the expanding Confederacy intact. It was men like these who kept the peace across many cubic light-years. It was men like these who some day, God willing, would roll back the Fiver threat.

There were few wars now. Space was too big for it. There were too many ways to skirt around the edge of war for it to come but seldom. But something like the Fiver threat could not be ignored. Some day, soon or late, either Earth or Fiver must go down to complete defeat. The Confederacy could never feel secure with the Fivers on its flank.

Feet pounded behind him and the general turned. It was Captain Gist, buttoning his tunic as he ran. He fell in beside the general.

"So they finally came, sir."

"Fourteen hours late," the general said. "Let us, for the moment, try to look our best. You missed a button, Captain."

"Sorry, sir," the captain said, fastening the button.

"Right, then. Get those shoulders back. Smartly, if you will. Right, left, hup, hup!"

Out of the corner of his eye, he saw that Sergeant Conrad had his squad moving out with precision, escorting the captive Fiver most correctly forward, with all the dignity and smartness that anyone might wish.

The men were drawn up now in two parallel lines, flanking the ship. The port was swinging open and the ramp was rumbling out and the general noted with some satisfaction that he and Captain Gist would arrive at the foot of the ramp about the time it touched the ground. The timing was dramatic and superb, almost as if he himself had planned it down to the last detail.

The ramp snapped into position and three Fivers came sedately waddling down it.

A seedy-looking trio, the general thought. Not a proper uniform nor a medal among the lot of them.

The general seized the diplomatic initiative as soon as they reached the ground.

"We welcome you," he told them, speaking loudly and slowly and as distinctly as he could so they would understand.

They lined up and stood looking at him and he felt a bit uncomfortable because there was that round jolly expression on their faces. Evidently they didn't have the kind of faces that could assume any other expression. But they kept on looking at him.

The general plunged ahead. "It is a matter of great gratification to Earth to carry out in good faith our obligations as agreed upon in the armistice proceedings. It marks what we sincerely hope will be the beginning of an era. . . ."

"Most nice," one of the Fivers said. Whether he meant the general's little speech or the entire situation or was simply trying to be gracious was not at once apparent.

Undaunted, the general was ready to go on, but the spokesman Fiver raised a short round arm to halt him.

"Prisoners arrive briefly," he whistled.

"You mean you didn't bring them?"

"They come again," the Fiver said with a glorious disregard for preciseness of expression.

He continued beaming at the general and he made a motion with the arm that might have been a shrug.

"Shenanigans," the captain said, close to the general's ear.

"We talk," the Fiver said.

"They're up to something," warned the captain. "It calls for Situation Red, sir."

"I agree," the general told the captain. "Set it up quietly." He said to the Fiver delegation: "If you gentlemen will come with me, I can offer you refreshments."

He had a feeling that they were smiling at him, mocking him, but one could never tell. Those jolly expressions were always the same. No matter what the situation.

"Most happy," said the Fiver spokesman. "These refresh—"

"Drink," the general said and made a motion to supplement the word.

"Drink is good," the Fiver answered. "Drink is friend?"

"That is right," the general said.

He started for the tent, walking slowly so the Fivers could keep up.

He noted with some satisfaction that the captain had carried on most rapidly, indeed. Sergeant Conrad was marching his squad back across the area, with the captive Fiver shambling in the center. The tarps were coming off the guns and the last of the crew was clambering up the ladder of the ship.

The captain caught up with them just short of the tent.

"Everything all set, sir," Captain Gist reported in a whisper.

"Fine," the general said.

They reached the tent and went inside. The general opened a refrigerating unit and took out a gallon jug.

"This," he explained, "is a drink we made for your compatriot. He found it very tasty."

He set out glasses and sipping straws and uncorked the jug, wishing he could somehow hold his nose, for the drink smelled like something that had been dead too long. He didn't even like to guess what might have gone into it. The chemists back on Earth had whomped it up for the captive Fiver, who had consumed gallon after gallon of it with disconcerting gusto.

The general filled the glasses and the Fivers picked them up in their tentacles and stuck the straws into their drawstring mouths. They drank and rolled their eyes in appreciation.

The general took the glass of liquor the captain handed him and gulped half of it in haste. The tent was getting just a little thick. What things a man goes through, he thought, to serve his planets and his peoples.

He watched the Fivers drinking and wondered what they might have up their sleeves.

Talk, the spokesman had told him, and that might mean almost anything. It might mean a reopening of negotiations or it might be nothing but a stall.

And if it was a negotiation, Earth was across the barrel. For there was nothing he could do but negotiate. Earth's fleet was crippled and the Fivers had the weapon and a renewal of the war was unthinkable. Earth needed five years at the minimum and ten years would be still better.

And if it was attack, if this planet was a trap, there was only one thing he could do—stand and fight as best he could, a thoroughly suicidal course.

Either way, Earth lost, the general realized.

The Flyers put down their glasses and he filled them up again.

"You do well," one of the Fivers said. "You got the paper and the marker?"

"Marker?" the general asked.

"He means a pencil," said the captain.

"Oh, yes. Right here." The general reached for a pad of paper and a pencil and laid them on the desk.

One of the Fivers set down his glass and, picking up the pencil, started to make a laborious drawing. He looked for all the world like a five-year-old printing his first alphabet.

They waited while the Fiver drew. Finally he was finished. He laid the pencil down and pointed to the wiggly lines.

"Us," he said.

He pointed to the sawtooth lines.

"You," he told the general.

The general bent above the paper, trying to make out what the Fiver had put down.

"Sir," the captain said, "it looks like a battle diagram."

"Is," said the Fiver proudly.

He picked the pencil up.

"Look," he said.

He drew directional lines and made a funny kind of symbol for the points of contact and made crosses for the sections where the battle lines were broken. When he was done, the Earth fleet had been shattered and sliced into three segments and was in headlong flight.

"That," the general said, with the husk of anger rising in his throat, "was the engagement in Sector 17. Half of our Fifth Squadron was wiped out that day."

"Small error," said the Fiver and made a deprecatory gesture.

He ripped the sheet of paper off the pad and tossed it on the floor. He laboriously drew the diagram again.

"Attend," he said.

The Fiver drew the directional lines again, but this time he changed them slightly. Now the Earth line pivoted and broke and became two parallel lines that flanked the Fiver drive and turned and blunted it and scattered it in space.

The Fiver laid the pencil down.

"Small matter," he informed the general and the captain. "You good. You make one thin mistake."

Holding himself sternly in hand, the general filled the glasses once again.

What are they getting at, he thought. Why don't they come flat out and say it?

"So best," one of the Fivers said, lifting his glass to let them know that he meant the drink.

"More?" asked the Fiver tactician, picking up the pencil.

"Please," said the general, seething.

He walked to the tent flap and looked outside. The men were at the guns. Thin wisps of vapor curled from the ship's launching tubes; in just a little while, it would be set to go, should the need arise. The camp was quiet and tense.

He went back to the desk and watched as the Fiver went on gaily with his lesson on how to win a battle. He filled page after page with diagrams and occasionally he was generous—he sometimes showed how the Fivers lost when they might have won with slightly different tactics.

"Interesting!" he piped enthusiastically.

"I find it so," the general said. "There is just one question."

"Ask," the Fiver invited.

"If we should go to war again, how can you be sure we won't use all of this against you?"

"But fine," the Fiver enthused warmly. "Exactly as we want."

"You fight fine," another Fiver said. "But just too slightly hard. Next time, you able to do much better."

"Hard!" the general raged.

"Too roughly, sir. No need to make the ship go poof."

Outside the tent, a gun cut loose and then another one and above the hammering of the guns came the full-throated, ground-shaking roar of many ship motors.

The general leaped for the entrance, went through it at a run, not bothering with the flap. His cap fell off and he staggered out, thrown slightly off his balance. He jerked up his head and saw them coming in, squadron after squadron, painting the darkness with the flare of tubes.

"Stop firing!" he shouted. "You crazy fools, stop firing!"

But there was no need of shouting, for the guns had fallen silent.

The ships came down toward the camp in perfect flight formation. They swept across it and the thunder of their motors seemed to lift it for a moment and give it a mighty shake. Then they were climbing, rank on serried rank, still with drill precision—climbing and jockeying into position for regulation landing.

The general stood like a frozen man, with the wind ruffling his iron-gray hair, with a lump, half pride, half thankfulness, rising in his throat.

Something touched his elbow.

"Prisoners," said the Fiver. "I told you bye and bye."

The general tried to speak, but the lump was there to stop him. He swallowed it and tried once again.

"We didn't understand," he said.

"You did not have a taker," said the Fiver. "That why you fight so rough."

"We couldn't help it," the general told him. "We didn't know. We never fought this way before."

"We give you takers," said the Fiver. "Next time, we play it right. You do much better with the takers. It easier on us."

No wonder, the general thought, they didn't know about an armistice. No wonder they were confused about the negotiations and the prisoner exchange. Negotiations are not customarily needed to hand back the pieces one has won in a game.

And no wonder those other races had viewed with scorn and loathing Earth's proposal to gang up on the Flyers.

"An unsporting thing to do," the general said aloud. "They could have told us. Or maybe they were so used to it."

* * *

And now he understood why the Fivers had picked this planet. There had to be a place where all the ships could land.

He stood and watched the landing ships mushing down upon the rock in clouds of pinkish flame. He tried to count them, but he became confused, although he knew every ship Earth had lost would be accounted for.

"We give you takers," said the Fiver. "We teach you how to use. They easy operate. They never hurt people or ships."

And there was more to it, the general told himself, than just a silly game—though maybe not so silly, once one understood the history and the cultural background and the philosophic concepts that were tied into it. And this much one could say for it: It was better than fighting actual wars.

But with the takers, there would be an end of war. What little war was left would be ended once for all. No longer would an enemy need to be defeated; he could be simply taken. No longer would there be years of guerrilla fighting on newly settled planets; the aborigines could be picked up and deposited in cultural reservations and the dangerous fauna shunted into zoos.

"We fight again?" the Fiver asked with some anxiety.

"Certainly," said the general. "Any time you say. Are we really as good as you claim?"

"You not so hot," the Fiver admitted with disarming candor. "But you the best we ever find. Play plenty, you get better."

The general grinned. Just like the sergeant and the captain and their eternal chess, he thought.

He turned and tapped the Fiver on the shoulder.

"Let's get back," he said. "There's still some drinking in that jug. We mustn't let it go to waste."

GREEN FLIGHT, OUT!

This story, written before the United States entered World War II, was sent to American Eagle *in August of 1941, and was sold in September, but it did not see print in that magazine; it would first appear in the Fall 1943 issue of American Eagle's companion magazine,* Army-Navy Flying Stories. *Apparently, there was a market for war stories in the United States even before Pearl Harbor, probably arising out of the sympathy many Americans had for Great Britain, then battling Nazi Germany as the lone survivor of the allies of the western front—a sympathy that led some Americans to volunteer with British and Canadian forces. Cliff was paid twenty-five dollars for the story.*

—dww

The afternoon shadows were slanting across London when Flight Lieutenant Kermit Cary came out of the hospital.

But Cary did not see the shadows. Inside his brain was the picture of a head swathed in bandages. And hands, also bandage-wrapped, like huge white, clumsy boxing gloves. That and the smell of antiseptics, the lingering fumes of ether, the half-guessed aroma of pain.

He couldn't wipe from his brain the mumbling voice that came from the swollen lips framed by the bandages, the futile, blinded groping of the awkward hands.

But more than that, he could not forget the half resentment, half embarrassment he had sensed from the figure that lay there in the room. Resentment that he, Kermit Cary, should have dared to come. Embarrassment—the embarrassment of a man shorn of physical abilities.

Cary shook his head, trying to shake away the things that lingered there, but they refused to leave. Perhaps he shouldn't have gone. Perhaps he should have forgotten Reggie, the way he had forced himself to forget all the others. The others were dead, and Reggie still was alive, but—

He forced himself to say it. Reggie would have been better dead. Reggie already was dead as far as the things worth doing, the things worth thinking were concerned. Cary shuddered to think of what might be behind those shielding bandages.

A man who is pulled from a flaming plane usually doesn't have much left to live for. People, Kermit Cary told himself, shouldn't pull men from flaming planes.

He quickened his step, watching for a cab or some driver who might give him a lift to the airdrome. But there were no cabs, and the cars that threaded their way through the littered streets were loaded down.

Probably it had been wrong for him to go and see Reggie. If he hadn't gone, Reggie would have understood that he was busy. A message would have done as well. But, no, he'd had to go—

For he and Reggie were all that were left—the last two men of the original roll of Number Six Fighter Squadron. The "Mad Yank," they had called him back in those days, but no more. To these youngsters who had filled the places of those others, he was simply "Cary." They were respectful, a little distant even, and they watched him too much.

Cary knew why they watched. He had caught scraps of conversation when he suddenly came into the mess.

"How long can Cary take it? Even if a man were made of steel—"

Things like that. Wondering when he would crack up. How long his luck would hold. How long his nerve could stay.

They guessed a little of it, of course. But they couldn't guess it all. They didn't know how it felt to be the last survivor of the original squadron. They didn't know how it felt to see the others go down, one by one.

O'Malley over Dunkerque. Smythe and Chittenden blazing torches in the sky above Dover. Flight Lieutenant Welsh screaming down into the Thames. They didn't know what it was like to see new faces taking the places of the old, hearing new voices where the old had been.

And above all, they could not guess the haunting terror the squadron's *last man* must feel. The black nights of wondering if he himself might not have been the jinx that had sent the others plummeting to death. The all-gone sensation of knowing that one's own luck is running thin. That one literally is living on borrowed time—

Brakes screamed beside Cary.

"Want a lift?" a voice said.

Cary suddenly came to life.

"Why, yes."

"Which way?"

Cary told him.

"Take you right past it," said the man.

Cary studied the driver. Obviously he was a clerk of some sort. Neatly but not too well dressed, a bit on the oldish side. Gray around his temples. Coat collar a little worn and shirt cuffs slightly frayed.

He could picture the man at home before the bombers came. A small house of his own with a flower garden. Probably roses. Yes, Cary decided, it would be roses.

"Have to hurry," said the man. "Going to take the old woman and the kids out into the country again tonight."

Cary nodded. "Might be wise at that."

"A little hard sleeping," said the man, "but we get along all right."

The motor droned softly, sputtering a little now and then. Twice they stopped to pick up other pedestrians. Several times they were detoured by roped-off areas protecting time-bombs and debris-filled streets.

Cary relaxed, thinking, scarcely hearing the talk of the other three in the car. He was remembering the mumbled words that had come out of the bandage-wrapped face, the puffed lips scarcely moving.

"It was von Rausnig. I got one of his decoys, but he flamed me—"

He hadn't asked Reggie why he hadn't taken to the silk. There must have been a reason. Probably he'd tried to beat a crash. Probably he had tried to save the ship.

So it had been von Rausnig!

"They ought to start coming over in another couple of hours," said the driver.

"Who?" asked Cary.

"The Jerries."

"Oh, yes," Cary agreed. "Undoubtedly they will."

The driver left him off at his field a few minutes later. His flying mates had eaten when Cary walked in, and were lined up at the bar. They greeted him vociferously.

"Come on, Cary! Have a double. Looks like another night."

"There'll be a moon," said young Harvey.

"Wonder if von Rausnig will be out tonight?" asked Derek.

There were sounds of disgust.

"Von Rausnig, the dirty coward! Always flies with two men on his tail so you can't get at him."

"Decorated by Hitler," jeered Harvey. "For what?"

"Look, men," declared Cary. "Von Rausnig is a good fighter. He knows his stuff. He doesn't take the chances you chaps do.

He always plays it safe. He doesn't go batting off on hair-brained hero stunts."

They hooted him good-naturedly and the mess corporal shoved a double brandy across the bar. Cary picked it up and drank, his mind whirling.

Von Rausnig, with twenty-three planes to his credit, the only Nazi flyer who carried distinctive markings on his plane. A cold, calculating fighter, a squadron leader. True, he always was tailed by two other flyers, but that was the smart way. No use of taking chances.

After all, no matter what the newspapers or the writers or anyone else might say, this Battle for Britain was no medieval war, no jousting of chivalric knights. It was cool, deliberate fighting with no holds barred, no quarter asked or given.

Von Rausnig, with twenty-three planes to his credit; no, twenty-four now. For it had been the Nazi ace who had shot down Reggie—

A batman was at Cary's side.

"Pardon me, sir, but the dinner's getting cold."

Cary flared. "Throw it out the window."

He shoved the empty glass across the bar.

"Another double," he ordered.

He saw them looking at him for just a moment, and then their eyes moved away.

"Don't you think you ought to have a bite?" suggested Derek softly.

"I know what I want," snarled Cary. "I don't want dinner. I want another drink."

"Take it easy, old man," urged Derek.

"Derek," snapped Cary, "if you ever say that to me again, I'll smack you flat."

He seized the brandy glass and the liquor splashed upon the bar.

"I've been taking it easy for months now," he said, and did not realize he was almost shouting. "I too it easy in France and over Dunkerque. I took it easy at Dover and between here and the Coast, when we fought the Jerries back from London. I took it easy when they came over and blasted the guts out of us here. And I'm still taking it easy!"

He realized there was silence in the room, an unnerving silence. He saw their faces, all their faces, uneasy and a bit embarrassed, staring at him.

"Gentlemen," he said, "I don't want a single one of you feeling sorry for me."

He drained the brandy and, turning on his heel, marched off to his cubicle.

The rest stared at him in dull silence.

Darkness was sifting through the city outside the windows when the inter-squadron speaker blared its first orders of the night.

"Red Flight, all out! Red Flight, all out! Pilots of Red Flight! Green Flight stand by! Green Flight stand by!"

Cary hoisted himself from his bunk and stepped hurriedly into the mess. Green Flight was his.

The three members of Red Flight already were going out the door into the briefing room. Harvey and Derek were struggling into flying togs.

"Jerry's starting early," Derek grinned.

Cary grunted and sat down on an empty bomb-box, began pulling on his outfit. Outside, on the cab rank, he heard the thunder of the Spitfires. And far away, somewhere down in London's East End, he heard the first rumble of the *Ack-Acks*.

The speaker gurgled and blared.

"Green Flight, all out! Green Flight, all out!"

The Red Flight Spitfires were now splitting the night wide open on the take-off.

"Come on, men," snapped Cary and led the way into the briefing room.

Behind the desk sat the squadron leader, the three rings of gold braid on his sleeve gleaming dully in the lamplight.

"How are you feeling, Cary?" he asked.

"I'm feeling all right," Cary growled and clumped outside.

Green Flight's three Spitfires were waiting, trembling like great hounds held on the leash. The exhausts flamed softly, throwing a faint radiance on the ground.

The recording officer shoved papers into Cary's hand, shouting to make himself heard above the blasting of the Merlins.

"Wave coming up the river," he summarized. "High. Probably will shut off their motors and glide in. Watch sharp for them."

Cary nodded.

Inside the ship, he pushed the hatch cover back into position and fastened his safety-belt.

"Ready, Derek?" he asked into the flap mike.

"Ready," acknowledged Derek, his voice carrying the sharp edge of tension that Cary had heard so often before from so many other men. From O'Malley and Smythe and Chittenden. Reggie, too.

"Ready, Harvey?"

Harvey was ready.

The floodlight slapped down the field and the shadow bar was there to line up the take-off. Clearance flashed from the Aldis lamp. Cary shoved up the throttle knob and the Spitfire moved. Gaining speed, the three fighters thundered down the turf, fled into the black.

Cary, handling the ship almost by instinct, headed through the Notch, that narrow lane of clearance between the swinging cables of the barrage balloons.

"Keep tight," he warned into the flap mike. "Stay close. Watch out for the kite strings."

"We're right on your tail," said Harvey crisply.

A faint glimmer in the east told of the rising moon. A Nazi hunting moon.

Cary bared his teeth and rammed the throttle up the gate. The Merlin talked, talked with all its thousand thundering horses.

Cary's altimeter said they were through the Notch, above the balloons. He glanced at the map strapped to his thigh and spoke into the mike, calling for an area. Observer corps gave it to him.

He snapped directions to Harvey and Derek and swung in an arc for Limehouse. The Thames embankment guns were barking, and the blackness of the sky was pricked with the sheet lightning of rifled *Ack-Ack* shells.

From far away came the *crump, crump* of exploding bombs. The phones in Cary's helmet barked swift, terse orders at him.

The Spitfire was a little pool of light and instruments in a dark immensity. Far below, London was blacked out, but with gleams of light showing here and there. The guns still coughed and the *crump, crump* of the bombs continued. Man-made lightning flicked and flashed across the sky. Searchlights slashed up, crisscrossed, centered and held.

Under Cary's hand the plane slashed across the night.

Then he saw them. Three, four, five dark shapes spotted by the lights. He screamed into the mike, and Derek and Harvey whooped back.

The Spitfire now was no more than a thing of tremendous power to hurl at those black shapes netted by the lights. More lights came up and ringed the invaders, sliding across them, keeping them marked.

Cary snapped off the safety and held his finger over the gun button on the stick. There were eight guns in the wings, eight deadly Brownings waiting for the signal.

One of the Dorniers loomed up in the stabbing light, nose pointed high, straining for altitude. Cary snapped the Spitfire at it and tightened his finger on the button. He saw his tracers flicker and spatter along one wing. Then the Dornier was gone, the Spitfire was tearing under it. Cary swung the plane into a stiff climb and looped.

Moonlight filled the cockpit and threw dancing shadows on the hatch cover. To the east, Cary could see the golden orb just creeping over the channel. Behind him a Dornier was flaming, writhing in a fiery death.

The rest of the Nazis were gone.

Thrumming through the night somewhere, heading for the French coast. Cary peered through the glass, trying to make them out. But they were nowhere to be seen.

Blind rage and humiliation shook Cary. He should have had that Dornier cold, yet all he had done was pepper a wing. The lights had set it up for him and he had missed.

"Cary! Green Flight! Cary!" said the phones.

"Here," said Cary. "Who got that ship?"

"Derek did," said Harvey.

Out of the corner of his eye he caught the sudden silvered gleam of the propeller coming at him from above. Instinctively he dived and rolled, then jerked the Spitfire into a climb. Here, far above the city, the air was molten moonlight, so white it seemed to have actual substance.

Cary wheeled his ship and saw the Messerschmitt climbing toward him. With teeth clamped shut, he nosed down, maneuvering for an attacking point. The Nazi dropped off and fled, Cary after him.

The Spitfire shivered to a sudden impact. The Merlin stuttered, and the instrument panel all at once was a mangled piece of wreckage. Instinctively Cary swerved, the stuttering engine screaming as if in pain.

Staring at the smashed dials, Flight Lieutenant Kermit Cary knew that he had fallen for a trick he should have recognized. The first Messerschmitt, after missing him, had not even tried to fight, had turned and fled, drawing his attention while another Nazi, from above, had dived and riveted itself on his tail.

Fighting in the moonlight is tricky under the best conditions. But, Cary told himself, he should have noticed that second ship, should not have fallen for the lure.

The Merlin was still stammering. When Cary tried to lift the Spitfire's nose, it failed to respond properly. Its loggishness sent his heart into his boots. Swiftly craning his neck, he saw the Messerschmitt above and behind, straightening out for another burst.

Terror tightening his throat, Cary hauled the ship almost straight down, shoved the throttle to its limit. With the engine misbehaving, he knew the chance he took; knew that he might be unable to pull it out of the dive. But it was one way, the quickest way, to shake off the attacker. Once he dipped into the darkness untouched by the moon, he and his crippled ship would be hard to find.

But the realization of this possible danger was cut short by the abrupt presence of a greater one.

Flame licked out from under the engine cowling. First a tiny flicker, then a blinding sheet that swept over the hatch cover, curling and flaring at the paint.

With almost superhuman strength, Cary fought to bring the Spitfire out of the dive, protect the cockpit from the blasting fire. Under his frantic efforts the plane leveled slightly. With one hand still holding the stick, he shoved back the hatch cover with the other, and clawed loose the safety-belt.

Wind whipped at him furiously. Once the hot breath of flame washed toward him as he crouched for one split second, ready for the leap.

Then Cary jumped, far out, to clear the falling ship.

He plunged out of moonlight into blackness. Below him he heard the whining scream of the corkscrewing Spitfire, saw it burst into a gout of flame that trailed swiftly earthward.

He jerked the ripcord. The straps of the parachute rocked him when they took hold, and Cary swung in sickening arcs. Then he was wafting down, alone in the blackness of the night.

The *Ack-Acks* were quiet for the moment. The blast of the bombs was gone. But that, he knew, was only a breather. The Jerries would be back again. A moon like the one coming up over the channel couldn't be wasted. Later in the night the lunar light would reveal every rooftop, every chimney pot in London.

The Spitfire was gone now, crashed to earth minutes ago, a molten wreck.

Cary shivered when he realized how close his escape had been. This had not been the first time the breath of death had blown past him. Once over Dunkerque, once at Dover—and other times. But each time of late, each time it had blown past, he had asked himself how much longer he could dodge its fury.

It seemed uncanny. Uncanny that he, Kermit Cary, should be living when all the rest had died. That shell splinter and bullet and aerial cannon had failed to spell his end. It seemed positively indecent he should continue to live—

In his mind's eye he saw those others now. O'Malley, who deliberately had rammed a Nazi bomber when his ship had burst into flames, and carried the Jerry to earth with him. Chittenden, who had worn a silk stocking instead of a scarf around his throat. Welsh, who knew all the latest stories about Hitler, Goebbels and Goering.

And Reggie—Reggie, who lay in a hospital now, his head a ball of white, his hands huge, awkward boxing gloves.

Cary shut his eyes, in order to quit seeing them. Because he had to stop seeing them, had to stop thinking about them. He was slipping. He knew that. And some of the others knew, too. Or at least suspected.

He should have speared that Dornier. But he hadn't. He should not have fallen into the Messerschmitt trap. But he had.

He was running to nerves. His liquor slopped on the bar whenever he lifted the glass. And he was snappish with the other men. That outburst tonight, for example. Maybe they would lay that to his being an American. Good Englishmen simply didn't do things like that.

Shutting his eyes, however, did no good. The old ones were still there. Welsh, chuckling at his own jokes; O'Malley, clutching his pony of brandy with both hands; Chittenden laughing, the backwash from the prop whipping that ridiculous bit of silk about his throat.

Derek and Harvey lounged in the mess. Gray dawn was tinting the walls, spreading its wings over a battered, smoking London. Outside the last of the Spitfires was coming in. Yellow Flight.

They counted audibly as the ships came down. One. Two— There wasn't any three.

The two fliers looked at one another, still waiting for the third. But it didn't come.

"We had a bright moon," Derek said wearily.

Harvey said nothing. After a moment, Derek lowered his voice.

"Are you sure about Cary? Sure he didn't take to the silk?"

"I didn't see him," Harvey answered. "But the moonlight, you know. One can't see so well."

Derek nodded. "His Spitfire exploded. They found no sign of him."

"It's been coming on," said Harvey. "He missed that Dornier clean."

"He hit the wings."

"Wings don't count," said Harvey, sourly.

Heavy footsteps slogged across the briefing room.

"Cary!" the squadron leader cried.

There was no answer and the feet slogged on. Cary stood reeling in the doorway, his parachute bundled under his arm.

"Good morning, gentlemen," he said. "I suppose you've been holding a post mortem. Premature, I would say."

"That's unfair, Cary," snapped Derek.

Cary ignored the protest.

"How many times were you up tonight?" he asked instead.

"Five times," Harvey told him.

"It was the worst night yet," said Derek, in a mollifying tone.

"Who flew with you?"

"Saunders."

Cary laid the parachute on the bar.

"Well, Saunders isn't flying with you now. I'm flying with you. I tramped across the whole city of London—a city filled with bombs—so that I could. I even brought back the silk."

"Sure, sure you're flying with us," Harvey assured him quickly. "We don't want to fly with anyone else."

"You know I missed the Dornier," said Cary bleakly. "You know the Messerschmitts took me for a ride. Are you sure you want to?"

"Please," evaded Derek, "stop being foolish, man. Everyone has his off nights."

The speaker blared. "Green Flight, out! Green Flight, out!"

"That's us," snapped Cary. "Just let me grab another 'chute."

"Good Lord, they expect us to go up again!"

"Sure, they expect us to go up again." Cary wheeled on Harvey. "Haven't you heard that we are short of pilots, short of planes?"

Harvey nodded tightly and started for the door. The squadron leader stopped Cary.

"Don't you think you'd better—"

"Better let Saunders take them up?" said Cary bitterly. "You think I'm—"

"It's his flight, sir," said a voice. That was Saunders, standing by the desk.

"If you think you're all right—" said the squadron leader uncertainly.

"Thanks, Saunders," said Cary.

Outside the planes squatted in the pearly light of fast approaching day, their Rolls-Royce Merlins turning over.

"They're out to break us today," the recording officer shouted at Cary, shoving him the papers. "No let-up at all. They know we're still short of men. They think they'll wear us down."

"Where are they?" Cary shouted back.

"Coming over the Thames Estuary. The boys along the coast had a go at them, but they broke through."

Cary's legs ached as he climbed into the cockpit. The long march across the city, detouring street after street where bombs had spattered buildings, crouching in doorways while H.E. rained down, had taken a heavy toll. And he was hungry. He needed a drink and a smoke, but there was no time for either. The Nazis were coming up the river. Someone had to stop them. Or at least try to stop them.

The Spitfires sprang down the turf and leaped into the air. In daylight, when one could see what he was dong, it was easy enough to take the notch.

Up they roared into the brightening sky. Once over the balloons they straightened out, streaking southeast. From other points other planes were rising, swift defenders bulleting to meet the invader.

Cary spoke briefly into his flap mike, was assured by the other two that everything was well. Below them the city still smoked. A few fires still burned redly, and a gray pall hung heavily over certain sectors where bombs had rained the thickest.

It was Derek, not Cary, who sighted the Nazis first, a mass of black dots outlined against the lemon and white of the morning sky. Savagely his Spitfire roared into a climb.

Cary watched the Nazis closely, satisfied at the altitude his flight had gained above them. The wave was not as large as some he had seen. Probably the boys along the coast had thinned it out.

Through the sky other Spitfires were burning up the air. Several flights were coming from the south and others from the north.

Cary rapped instructions into the flap mike, suddenly slid down the sky, his plane a silver streak of vengeance. Behind him came the other two.

The fighter formation below them broke and streaked in all directions, but Cary had marked one plane. Relentlessly he thundered down upon it. With two others, it tried frantically to dodge away.

The safety catch was up and Cary's finger hovered on the button. Without checking his dive, he depressed the firing mechanism and the eight Brownings whipped leaden streams of hate into the Messerschmitt.

Below him the Nazi virtually exploded in mid-air, flying apart, hammered into bits by the slashing bullets. For a single instant it had seemed to shiver, then burst into a blast of flame.

Shrieking past the burning, smoking debris, Cary fought his ship out of its dive and streaked for altitude. But even as he did, he saw something that brought a cry of frosty anger from his lips.

One of the two remaining ships in the group of three he had attacked bore the flame-red death's-head—the personal insignia of the dreaded Nazi ace, von Rausnig!

Thoughts screamed through Cary's brain. Von Rausnig! The man who had sent Reggie down in fiery ruin. The man who had turned Reggie's head into a ball of bandages. Who had robbed Reggie of sight and face and hands.

Black hate rose up to choke Cary, lay bitter in his mouth. One of van Rausnig's defenders now was gone. Perhaps—

Cary whipped the Spitfire through the air with vicious purpose, until the ship groaned and protested at the handling. Another Messerschmitt screeched past him. Even above the roar of engines Cary could hear the pounding chatter of many guns as *Luftwaffe* and R.A.F. battled in the sky.

Von Rausnig was climbing now. Cary climbed with him. But through his hate of the man who rode the death's-head plane sounded a warning, a memory of what had happened the night before.

Tossing a glance over his shoulder, Cary saw a Jerry diving at him. He rolled the Spitfire and snapped into a climb again. The

Messerschmitt, undoubtedly the second of von Rausnig's flight, plunged past and was lost in the shuttling battle below.

But the maneuver had lost Cary precious height. Von Rausnig's plane was leveling off now, circling for position.

Then the Nazi was coming at him. Cary saw smoke drift from the guns, felt the storm of bullets strike the Spitfire. But there were no shattered instruments, no stutter in the motor. The blast had drilled his left wing. From where he sat, Cary could see the neatly bored holes the fusillade had made.

Von Rausnig's ship snapped under him and up in a swooping arc. There was no room, no time now to turn for an attack, for the German had lost but little altitude.

Cary grinned tensely. Here was a man who knew how to fly a ship, a man who would not pass by a challenge. No matter what anyone might say of him, von Rausnig was no coward.

The sound of battle drifted up but faintly now. Cary and the death's-head plane had climbed far above it, there to fight out their duel.

Cary swung to the east and spiraled up, watching the other closely. It was like a game of chess, he told himself. Maneuver and maneuver and maneuver. Get set for one blow, one good blow, for that was all it took. A battle for position, trying to set the opponent up for the final knockout punch.

How von Rausnig did it Cary never exactly knew, but suddenly the Messerschmitt was coming at him again, directly on his tail. Guns yammered thinly. The Spitfire shivered as slugs slammed into its tail and along the fuselage. Cary sideslipped, losing altitude but fighting to keep the nose of his plane well up.

His breath came out in a gasping sigh of relief as the machine handled to the slightest touch. None of the Nazi's bullets had taken effect!

Von Rausnig screamed past and Cary, jaw tight shut, shrieked after him. With throttle all the way up, he plummeted after the

Nazi ace's ship, heart hammering in his throat, finger on the gun control.

Now he was in the right position, but at too long a range. If he didn't get that blast in soon, von Rausnig would pull out of his dive and the chance would be lost.

The Merlin howled in fiendish glee as it hurtled the Spitfire down upon the Nazi. The wind screamed and whistled piercingly along the streamlined plane.

Cary felt blackness sliding in upon him. He sucked in his breath and tightened his stomach muscles. He simply couldn't black out now. He had to hang onto his consciousness for a few more seconds until he was close enough.

The Nazi ship grew before his straining eyes, but not quite enough—

In the savage wind Cary seemed to hear a chuckling—the way Welsh used to chuckle at his Hitler jokes. The scream of split-open air no longer was a scream. It was the healthy laughter of a man who wore a stocking for a scarf.

Words seemed to ride with Cary in the cockpit now. Words with O'Malley's old familiar brogue.

"Faith, and ye got him now, Yank! Ye got him where ye want him. Dip the nose a little lower and that will build the speed of ye—"

Only, of course, the words weren't really there. They were just something that rang through a mist-filled memory—

Things were getting blurred and fuzzy, but the Nazi ship was larger now and directly ahead.

"Now's the time, my lad," said O'Malley's quiet voice—and Cary clamped down the firing button and held it there.

Darkness rose to suffocate him but he fought it back, holding his finger down, remembering a head that was a ball of bandages, remembering flaming planes over Dunkerque and over Dover.

"That's for O'Malley!" his mind was shrieking. "And that's for Chittenden and that's for Reggie—especially for Reggie—"

He heard faintly, as if from far away, the growling of the Brownings, the hammer of their bark. And suddenly where there had been a Messerschmitt, there was a gush of fire.

Only then did Cary release the button and jerk back the stick.

He blacked out, but only momentarily. When he fought his way back to consciousness, the Spitfire was zooming skyward and the battle was far away.

But below him, far below, a wavering plume of black smoke trickled down to earth. Cary waved a suddenly feeble hand at it.

The scream of the wind was gone now, and so was Welsh's chuckle and his laughter. But it had been there and so had the voice in his ear—the old familiar voice of O'Malley, who had died long days ago.

Kermit Cary laughed at himself a little unsteadily. Funny ideas a man picks up at times, he thought. Or were they funny ideas?

He scowled slightly as he swung the ship for home.

"Thanks, fellows," he said, to no one in particular.

But Cary knew, deep within himself, whom he was talking to. To those other men who had come out of bitter memory to ride the blazing sky with him.

He knew, with sudden clarity, that never again would he spend black nights wondering why he lived, while they had died. Never again would he try to forget them, and what had happened to them.

It wasn't every flyer who had those who would come and help him when he ne

CARBON COPY

On March 21, 1957, Clifford Simak noted in his journal that he had begun writing "Realtor"—"writes smoothly and easily," he added. Soon after that, however, he seems to have gotten involved in several other pieces of business, including retyping "Death Scene" and having lunch with a visiting author for whom Cliff clearly did not care. But then he sent "Realtor" to H. F. Gold, who accepted it in less than a week. It was only when Cliff noted that Gold had taken the story that the title "Carbon Copy" appeared.

"Carbon Copy" was published in the December 1957 issue of Galaxy Science Fiction, *and I wonder whether it might have led to the later Simak novel* They Walked Like Men.

—dww

The man who came into Homer Jackson's office was wearing his left shoe on his right foot and his right shoe on his left.

He gave Homer quite a start.

The man was tall and had a gangling look about him, but he was smartly dressed—except for his shoes. And his shoes were all right, too; it was just the way he wore them.

"Am I addressing Mr. Homer Jackson?" he asked with a formality to which Homer was entirely unaccustomed.

"That's me," said Homer.

He squirmed a bit uncomfortably in his chair. He hoped this wasn't one of Gabby Wilson's jokes.

Gabby had an office just down the hall and loved to pester Homer plenty. When Gabby cooked up a joke, he did a massive job on it; he left out not a single detail. And some of Gabby's jokes got pretty rough.

But the man seemed to be dead serious and perhaps a little anxious.

"Mr. Homer Jackson, the suburban realtor?" he persisted.

"That's right," said Homer.

"Specializing in lake properties and country acreages?"

"I'm your man." Homer began to feel uncomfortable. This man was spreading it on a trifle thick and Homer thought he could see Gabby's hand in it.

"I'd like to talk with you. I have a matter of small business."

"Fire away," said Homer, motioning toward a chair.

The man sat down carefully, bolt upright in the chair.

"My name is Oscar Steen," he said. "We're building a development on what is known as the Saunders place. We call it Happy Acres."

Homer nodded. "I'm acquainted with the place. It's the last good holding on the lake. You were fortunate to get it."

"Thank you, Mr. Jackson. We think that it is nice."

"How are you getting on?"

"We have just finished it. But now comes the most important part. We must get people onto the property."

"Well," said Homer, "things are a little tough right now. Money has tightened up and the interest rates are higher, and Washington is no help and besides that—"

"We wondered if you'd be interested in handling it for us."

Homer choked a little, but recovered quickly. "Well, now, I don't know. Those houses may be hard to sell. You'd have to get a solid figure for them and the prices will run high. That stone wall you put around the place and those fancy gates and all, I would suspect you have high-class houses. You have gone and made it into an exclusive section. There'll be only a certain class of buyer who might be interested."

"Mr. Jackson," said Steen, "we have a new approach. We won't have to sell them. We're only leasing them."

"Renting them, you mean."

"No, sir, leasing them."

"Well, it all comes out to the same thing in the end. You'll have to get a lot for them."

"Five thousand."

"Five thousand is an awful lot of money. At least, out here it is. Five thousand a year comes to over four hundred a month and—"

"Not for a year," corrected Steen. "For ninety-nine."

"For what!"

"Ninety-nine. We're leasing at five thousand dollars ninety-nine full years."

"But, man, you can't do that! Why, that's absolutely crazy! Taxes would eat up—"

"We're not so interested in making money on the houses as we are in creating business for our shopping center."

"You mean you have a shopping center in there, too?"

Steen allowed himself a smile. "Mr. Jackson, we obtain the property and then we build the wall to have some privacy so there can be no snoopers."

"Yes, I know," said Homer. "It's smart to do it that way. Good publicity. Whets the public's interest. Gives you a chance to have a big unveiling. But that twelve-foot wall—"

"Fourteen, Mr. Jackson."

"All right, then, fourteen. And it's built of solid stone. I know—I watched them put it up. And no one builds walls of solid stone any more. They just use stone facing. The way you built that wall set you back a hunk—"

"Mr. Jackson, please. We know what we are doing. In this shopping center, we sell everything from peanuts to Cadillacs. But we need customers. So we build houses for our customers. We desire to create a good stable population of rather well-to-do families."

Jumping to his feet in exasperation, Homer paced up and down the office.

"But, Mr. Steen, you can't possibly build up enough business at your shopping center by relying solely on the people in your development. For instance, how many houses have you?"

"Fifty."

"Fifty families are a mere drop in the bucket for a shopping center. Even if every one of those fifty families bought all their needs from you—and you can't be sure they will—but if they did, you'd still have little volume. And you won't pick up any outside trade—not behind that wall, you won't."

He stopped his pacing and went back to his chair.

"I don't know why I'm upset about it," he told Steen. "It's no skin off my nose. Yes, I'll handle the development, but I can't handle leasing at my usual five per cent."

"Oh, I forgot to tell you," said Steen. "You keep the entire five thousand."

Homer gasped like a fish hauled suddenly from water.

"On one condition," added Steen. "One has to be so careful. We have a bank, you see. Part of the shopping center service."

"A bank," Homer said feebly.

"Chartered under the state banking regulations."

"And what has a bank to do with me?"

"You'll take ten per cent," said Steen. "The rest will be credited to your account in the Happy Acres Bank. Every time you lease a unit, you get five hundred cash; forty-five hundred goes into your bank account."

"I don't quite see—"

"There are advantages."

"Yes, I know," Homer said. "It builds up your business. You're out to make that shopping center go."

"That might be one factor. Another is that we can't have you getting rich in front of all your friends and neighbors. There'd be too much talk about it and we don't want that kind of publicity. And there are tax advantages as well."

"Tax advantages?"

"Mr. Jackson, if you lease all fifty houses, you will have earned a quarter million dollars. Have you ever figured what the income tax might be on a quarter million dollars?"

"It would be quite a lot."

"It would be a crying shame," said Steen. "The bank could be a help."

"I don't quite see how."

"You leave that to us. Leave everything to us. You just lease the houses."

"Mr. Steen, I've been an honest man for years in an occupation where there's opportunity—"

"Honesty, Mr. Jackson. Of course we know you're honest. That's why we came to you. Have you got your car here?"

"It's parked outside."

"Fine. Mine is at the station getting serviced. Let's drive out and look the houses over."

II

The houses were all that anyone could wish. They were planned with practical imagination and built with loving care. There was, Homer admitted to himself, more honest workmanship in them than he had seen for many years in this era of mass-production building. They had that quiet sense of quality material, of prideful craftsmanship, of solidity, of dignity and tradition that was seldom found any more.

They were well located, all fifty of them, in the wooded hills that stretched back from the lake, and the contractor had not indulged in the ruthless slashing out of trees. Set in natural surroundings, with decent amounts of space around them, they stood, each one of them, in comparative privacy.

In the spring, there would be wild flowers, and in the autumn, the woods would flame with color and there would be birds and squirrels and rabbits. And there was a stretch of white sand beach, the last left on the whole lake.

Homer began mentally to write the ad he'd put in the Sunday paper and found that he looked forward with some anticipation to setting down the words. This was one he could pull out all the stops on, use all the purple prose he wanted.

"I like it, Mr. Steen," he said. "I think they won't be too hard to move."

"That is good," Steen replied. "We are prepared to give you an exclusive contract for a period of ten years. Renewable, of course."

"But why ten years? I can get this tract handled in a year or two, if it goes at all."

"You are mistaken. The business, I can assure you, will be continuing."

They stood on the brick walk in front of one of the houses and looked toward the lake. There were two white sails on the water, far toward the other shore, and a rowboat bobbed in the middle distance, with the black smudge of a hunched fisherman squatted in the stern.

Homer shook his head in some bewilderment. "I don't understand."

"There'll be some subletting," Steen told him smoothly. "When fifty families are involved, there are always some who move."

"But that's another story. Subletting—"

Steen pulled a paper from his pocket and handed it to Homer. "Your contract. You'll want to look it over. Look it over closely. You're a cautious man and that's the kind of man we want."

Homer drove along the winding, wooded road back to the shopping center with Steen.

The center was a lovely place. It stretched along the entire south side of the property, backed by the fourteen-foot wall, and was a shining place of brand-new paint and gleaming glass and metal.

Homer stopped the car to look at it.

"You've got everything," he said.

"I think we have," said Steen proudly. "We've even got our own telephone exchange."

"Isn't that unusual?"

"Not at all. What we have set up here amounts to a model village, a model living space. We have our own water system and our sewage plant. Why not a telephone exchange?"

Homer let it pass. There was no sense arguing. It all was just this side of crazy, anyhow. No matter how fouled up it was, Steen seemed satisfied.

Maybe, Homer told himself, he knows what he is doing.

But Homer doubted it.

"One thing more," said Steen. "It is just a minor matter, but you should know about it. We have a car agency, you see. Many agencies, in fact. We can supply almost any make of car—"

"But how did you do—"

"We know our way around. Any make of car a person would want. And anyone who leases must buy a car from us."

"Mister," Homer said, "I've heard a lot of fast ones in the auto business, but this one beats them all. If you think I'll sell cars for you—"

"There's nothing wrong with it," said Steen. "We have some good connections. Any car one wants at a fair and honest price.

And we are prepared to give good value on their trade-ins, too. It would never do to have old rattle-traps in a high-class development like this."

"And what else? I think you better tell me how many other tie-in deals you have."

"Not a single one. The automobile is all."

Homer put the car in gear and drove slowly toward the gate.

The uniformed gateman saw them coming and swung the gates wide open. He waved to them cheerily as they went past his kiosk.

III

"I wouldn't touch it with a ten-foot pole," Homer told his wife, Elaine, "if there weren't so much money in it. But things have been kind of slow with this higher interest rate and all and this deal would give me a chance—"

"If it's Mr. Steen wearing his shoes on the wrong feet," Elaine said, "I don't think you need to worry. You remember Uncle Eb?"

"Sure. He was the one who wore his vest inside out."

"Pure stubbornness, that's what it was with Uncle Eb. He put it on inside out one day and someone laughed at him. So Uncle Eb said that was the way to wear a vest. And that's the way he wore it to his dying day."

"Well, sure," said Homer, "that might be it, of course. But wearing a vest inside out wouldn't hurt your chest. Shoes on the wrong feet would hurt something terrible."

"This poor Mr. Steen might be a cripple of some sort. Maybe he was born that way."

"I've never heard of anyone born with his right and left foot switched."

"It's queer, naturally," Elaine persisted, "but what difference does it make? If you lease all those houses, we can go to Europe like we've always planned. As far as I'm concerned, he can go barefoot if he wants."

"Yeah, I suppose so."

"And we need a car," Elaine said, beginning on her catalogue. "And drapes for the living room. And I haven't had a new dress in ages. And it's shameful to be using our old silver. We should have replaced it years ago. It's the old stuff Ethel gave us when we were married—"

"All right," said Homer. "If I lease the houses, if the deal holds up, if I don't get in jail—we'll go to Europe."

He knew when he was licked.

He read the contract carefully. It was all right. It said, in black and white, that he got the whole five thousand.

Maybe, he told himself, he should have a lawyer see it. Al Congdon could tell him in a minute if it was ironclad. But he shrank from showing it. There seemed something sinful, almost shameful, about his getting all that money.

He checked on the Happy Acres Bank. A charter had been issued and all regulations had been met.

He checked on building permits and they were in order, too.

So what was a man to do?

Especially when he had a wife who had yearned loudly for ten years to go to Europe.

Homer sat down and wrote an ad for the real estate section of the Sunday paper. On second thought, he dismissed purple prose that he had planned to use. He employed the low-key technique. The ad wasn't long. It didn't cost too much. It read:

$4.16!!!!!
WOULD YOU PAY ONLY $4.16
a month to live in a house
that would sell for $35,000

to $50,000?
If so, call or see
JACKSON REAL ESTATE
Specializing in Lake Property and Country Acreages

IV

The first prospect was a man named H. F. Morgan. He came into the office early Sunday morning. He was belligerent. He slammed the folded want ad section down on Homer's desk. He had ringed Homer's ad with a big red-pencil mark.

"This isn't true!" yelled Morgan. "What kind of come-on is this?"

"It's substantially true," Homer answered quietly. "That's what it figures out to."

"You mean I just pay $4.16 a month?"

"Well," hedged Homer, "it's not quite as simple as all that. You lease it for ninety-nine years."

"What would I want with a house for ninety-nine years? I won't live that long."

"Actually, it's better than owning a house. You can live there a lifetime, just as if you owned the place, and there are no taxes and no maintenance. And if you have children, they can go on living there."

"You mean this is on the level?"

Homer emphatically nodded. "Absolutely."

"What's wrong with this house of yours?"

"There's nothing wrong with it. It's a new house among other new houses in an exclusive neighborhood. You have a shopping center just up the road that's as good as any city—"

"You say it's new?"

"Right. There are fifty houses. You can pick out the one you want. But I wouldn't take too long to decide, because these will go like hotcakes."

"I got my car outside."

"All right," said Homer, reaching for his hat. "I'll take my car and show you the way. The houses are unlocked. Look at them and choose the one you want."

Out on the street, Homer got into his car and sat down on something angular. He cursed because it hurt. He lifted himself and reached down and picked up the thing he'd sat on.

It was nothing he had ever seen before and he tossed it to the other side of the seat. It was, he thought, something like one of those clip-together plastic blocks that were made for children, but how it had gotten in his car, he could not imagine.

He wheeled out into the street and signaled for the Morgan car to follow.

There were Mrs. Morgan and Jack, a hell-raising eight-year-old, and Judy, a winsome five-year-old, and Butch, the Boxer pup. All of them, Homer saw, were taken by surprise at the sight of Happy Acres. He could tell by the way Mrs. Morgan clasped her hands together and by the way suspicion darkened Morgan's face. One could almost hear him thinking that no one was crazy enough to offer a deal like this.

Jack and Butch, the pup, went running in the woods and Judy danced gaily on the lawn and, Homer told himself, he had them neatly hooked.

Homer spent a busy day. His phone was jammed with calls. House-hunting families, suspicious, half-derisive, descended on the office.

He did the best he could. He'd never had a crowd like this before.

He directed the house-hunting families out to Happy Acres. He patiently explained to callers that it was no hoax, that there were houses to be had. He urged all of them to hurry and make up their minds.

"They won't last long," he told them, intoning unctuously that most ancient of all real estate selling gimmicks.

After church, Elaine came down to the office to help him with the phone while he talked to the prospects who dropped in.

Late in the afternoon, he drove out to Happy Acres. The place was an utter madhouse. It looked like a homecoming or a state fair or a monster picnic. People were wandering around, walking through the houses. One had three windows broken. The floors were all tracked up. Water faucets had been left running. Someone had turned on a hose and washed out a flowerbed.

He tried to talk with some of them, but he made no headway. He went back to the office and waited for the rush to start.

There wasn't any rush.

A few phone calls came in and he assured the callers it was on the level. But they were still hard to convince.

He went home beat.

He hadn't leased a house.

V

Morgan was the first one who came back. He came back alone, early Monday morning. He was still suspicious.

"Look," he said, "I'm an architect. I know what houses cost. What's the catch?"

"The catch is that you pay five thousand cash for a ninety-nine-year lease."

"But that's no catch. That's like buying it. The normal house, when it stands a hundred years, has long since lost its value."

"There's another catch," said Homer. "The builder won't lease to you unless you buy a new car from him."

"That's illegal!" shouted Morgan.

"I wouldn't know. Nobody's forcing you to take the offer."

"Let's forget about the car for the moment," Morgan urged. "What I want to know is, how can the builder put up a place like that for five thousand dollars? I know for a fact that he can't."

"So do I. But if he wants to lose a lot of money, who are we to stop him?"

Morgan pounded on the desk. "What's the gimmick, Jackson?"

"The builder wears his shoes on the wrong feet, if that means anything to you."

Morgan stared at him. "I think you're crazy, too. What would that have to do with it?"

"I don't know," said Homer. "I just mentioned it, thinking it might help you."

"Well, it doesn't."

Homer sighed. "It's got me puzzled, too."

Morgan picked up his hat and jammed it on his head. "I'll be seeing you," he said. It sounded like a threat.

"I'll be right here," said Homer as Morgan went slamming out the door.

Homer went down to the drugstore for a cup of coffee.

When he got back, a second visitor was waiting for him. The man sat stiffly in a chair and tapped nervous fingers on his briefcase, held primly in his lap. He looked as if he'd eaten something sour.

"Mr. Jackson," he said, "I represent the County Realtors Association."

"Not interested," said Homer. "I've gotten along for years without joining that outfit. I can get along a few years more."

"I'm not here to solicit membership. I am here about that ad of yours in the paper yesterday."

"Good ad, I thought. It brought in a lot of business."

"It's exactly the kind of advertising that our association frowns upon. It is, if you will pardon the expression, nothing but a come-on."

"Mr.—by the way, what is your name?"

"Snyder," said the man.

"Mr. Snyder, if you happen to be in the market for a place out in this area at the ridiculously low cost of $4.16 a month, I shall be glad to show you any one of fifty houses. If you have a moment, I can drive you out."

The man's mouth snapped together like a trap. "You know what I mean, Jackson. This is fraudulent advertising and you know it is. It is misrepresentation. We mean to show it is."

Homer pitched his hat on top of the filing cabinet and sat in his chair.

"Snyder," he said, "you're cluttering up the place. You've done your duty—you've warned me. Now get out of here."

It wasn't exactly what he had meant to say and he was surprised at himself for saying it. But now that it was said, there was no way of recalling it and he rather liked the feel of strength and independence that it gave him.

"There is no use flying off the handle," said Snyder. "We could talk this over."

"You came in and made your threat," Homer retorted. "There's nothing to talk over. You said you were going to get me, so come ahead and get me."

Snyder got to his feet savagely. "You'll regret this, Jackson."

"Maybe so," admitted Homer. "Sure you don't need a house?"

"Not from you," said Snyder, and went stalking out.

Must have hurt their weekend sales, Homer told himself, watching Snyder go stumping down the street.

He sat quietly, thinking. He'd known there would be trouble, but there had been no way he could have passed up the deal. Not with Elaine set on that trip to Europe.

And now he was committed. He could not back out even if he wished. And he wasn't sure that he wanted to. There could be a lot of money in it.

The car deal he didn't like, but there was nothing he could do about it. And by handling it right, he might keep in the clear. Maybe, he thought, he should go out and talk to Steen about it.

Gabby Wilson, his insurance-selling neighbor down the hall, came in and flopped into a chair. Gabby was a loud-mouth.

"Howsa boy?" he yelled. "Hear you got that Happy Acres deal. How's about cutting in your old pal on the insurance end?"

"Go chase yourself," invited Homer irritably.

"Heard a good story the other day. It seems this wrecking outfit got a job to tear down a building. And the straw boss got his orders wrong and tore down another building." Gabby slapped his knee and roared with laughter. "Can you imagine the look on that contractor's face when he heard the news?"

"It cost him a lot of money," Homer said. "He had a right to be good and sore."

"You don't think it's funny?"

"No, I don't."

"How you getting on with this Happy Acres gang?"

"Fine, so far," said Homer.

"Cheap outfit," Gabby told him. "I been checking round. They got some two-bit contractor from out in the sticks somewhere to do the job for them. Didn't even buy their material from the dealers here. The contractor brought his own crew with him. The developers didn't spend a nickel locally."

"Unpatriotic of them."

"Not smart, either. Houses probably will fall down in a year or two."

"I don't care particularly. Just so I get them leased."

"Do anything so far?"

"Got some interest in them. Here comes a prospect now."

It was Morgan. He had parked in front and was getting out of a new and shiny car, agleam with chrome.

Gabby beat a swift retreat.

Morgan came into the office. He sat down in a chair and pulled out his check-book.

"I bought the car," he said. "How do you want this check made out?"

VI

Six weeks later, Homer dropped in at the shopping center office. Steen was sitting with his feet up on the desk. He was wearing black shoes instead of the brown ones he had worn before. They still were on the wrong feet.

"Howdy, Mr. Jackson," he said easily.

Homer sat down in a chair. "I finally got rid of them. All the fifty houses are leased."

"That's fine." Steen reached into a drawer, took out a small book and tossed it across the desk to Homer. "Here. This belongs to you."

Homer picked it up. It was a bank book. He opened it and saw a neat row of $4,500 entries marching down the page.

"You made yourself a mint," said Steen.

"I wish I had fifty more," Homer told him. "Or two hundred more. This thing is catching on. I could lease them in a week. I've got a waiting list longer than my arm."

"Well, why don't you go ahead and lease them?"

"I can't lease them a second time."

"Funny thing," said Steen. "There's no one living in those houses. They are all standing empty."

"But that can't be!" objected Homer. "There might be a few still empty—a few that the people haven't occupied yet. But most of them have moved in. They're living in those houses."

"That's not the way it looks to me."

"What's happened to those people then? Where have they—"

"Mr. Jackson!"

"Yes?"

"You haven't trusted me. You didn't trust me from the start. I don't know why. You thought the deal was queer. You were scared of it. But I've played fair with you. You'll have to admit I have."

Homer stroked the bank book. "More than fair."

"I know what I am doing, Mr. Jackson. I'm not anybody's fool. I have the angles figured out. String along with me. I need a man like you."

"You mean lease all those houses a *second* time!" Homer asked uneasily.

"A second time," said Steen. "And a third. And fourth. Lease them as often as you like. Keep right on leasing them. No one will mind at all."

"But the people will mind—the people that I lease those houses to," Homer pointed out.

"Mr. Jackson, let me handle this. Don't you worry about a solitary thing. You just keep those houses moving."

"But it isn't right."

"Mr. Jackson, in some six weeks' time, you've made a quarter million dollars. I suppose that's what's wrong with you. I suppose you figure that's enough—"

"Well, no. With income tax and all—"

"Forget the income tax. I told you that this bank of ours had tax advantages."

"I don't get it," Homer said. "This is no way to do business."

"But it is," said Steen. "I challenge you to find a better way to do business. There's no end to it. You can become a multimillionaire . . ."

"In jail."

"I've told you we weren't doing wrong. If you don't want to handle it—"

"Let me think it over," Homer pleaded. "Give me a day or two."

"Noon tomorrow," said Steen decisively. "If you don't tell me you are willing to go ahead by noon tomorrow, I'll look for someone else."

Homer got up. He thrust the bank book in his pocket. "I'll be in to see you."

Steen put his feet back on the desk. "Fine. I'll be expecting you."

Out on the concourse, Homer walked along the gleaming shop fronts. And the shops, he saw, were no more than half-staffed and entirely innocent of buyers. He went into a drugstore to buy a cigar and was waited on by a girl of just slightly more than high school age. He failed to recognize her.

"You live around here?" he asked.

"No, sir. In the city."

He went into a hardware store and into a grocery supermarket. He saw no one he knew. And that was queer. He'd lived in the area for almost thirteen years and thought he knew . . .

He recalled what Gabby had said about the contractor from somewhere out of town. Maybe, for some zany reason, Steen had a policy against employing local people. Still, he'd employed Homer.

It was a crazy set-up, Homer told himself. None of it made sense—and least of all, the leasing of the houses a second time around.

Perhaps he should get out of it. He'd made a fair amount of money. Right now, most likely, he could get out slick and clean. If he stayed, there might be trouble.

He lighted up the cigar and went back to his car. Wheeling out of the parking lot, he headed for the road that led into the housing development.

He drove slowly, looking closely at each house. All of them seemed empty. The windows stared blindly without drapes or curtains. The lawns had not been cut for weeks. There was no sign of anyone—and there should be children and pets playing. Almost everyone he'd leased to had had children and dogs and cats. The place should be jumping, he told himself, and instead it was silent and deserted.

He stopped the car and went into a house. It was bare and empty. There was sawdust in the corners and wood shavings here and there. There were no scuff marks on the floor, no handprints on the wall. The windows had not been washed; the trademark paper still was sticking to them.

He went out puzzled.

He inspected two more houses. They were the same.

Steen had been right, then. Steen, with his shoes on the wrong feet, and with something else—with his different way of talking now. Six weeks ago, when Steen had come into Homer's office, he had been stiff and formal, awkward, yet striving for preciseness. And now he was easy in his manner, now he put his feet up on the desk, now he talked slangily.

There was no one living in the houses, Homer admitted to himself. No one had ever lived in them. He had leased all fifty of them and no one had moved in.

And it had a fishy smell—it had a terribly fishy smell.

On his way out, he stopped at Steen's office. The place was locked up.

The old gateman opened the gate and waved at him from the window of his kiosk.

Back in his own office, Homer took out of a drawer the list of leases he had drawn. He phoned Morgan, the first name on the lease.

"That number has been changed," the operator told him.

She gave him the new number and he dialed it.

"Happy Acres," said a sing-song operator-voice.

"Huh?"

"Happy Acres," the voice sang. "Whom did you wish, sir?"

"The Morgan residence."

He waited and it was Morgan who answered.

"Homer Jackson. Just checking. How do you like the house? Are you getting on okay?"

"Perfectly," Morgan told him happily. "I've been meaning to come in and thank you for putting me onto this."

"Everything is really all right?"

"Couldn't be better. I hardly ever go into my office now. I stay out here and work in the amusement room. I go fishing and I take walks. The wife and kids are just as pleased as I am." Morgan lowered his voice. "How do you guys manage this? I've tried to get it figured and I can't."

"It's a secret," Homer replied, thinking on his feet. "The answer to the housing problem."

"Not that I care," Morgan said. "Just curious, you know. I'll be dropping in one day. I'll bring you something."

"Glad to see you," said Homer.

He called the Happy Acres number and asked for another family. He went halfway through the list. He talked mostly to the women, although some of the men were home. They were not only happy, but enthusiastic. They asked him jokingly how he got away with it.

When he finished, he was glassy-eyed.

He went down to the drugstore for a cup of coffee.

When he returned, he'd made up his mind.

He took out his waiting list and began making calls.

"There just happens to be a vacancy in Happy Acres if you are interested."

They were.

He reminded them about the cars. They said they'd take care of that matter first thing in the morning.

By suppertime, he'd leased twenty of the houses by making twenty phone calls.

VII

"There's something wrong," Homer said to his wife. "But there's money in it."

"It's just that you don't understand," said Elaine. "There may be a perfectly good reason why Mr. Steen can't explain it all to you."

"But it means we have to give up our trip to Europe. And after we had got our passports and all."

"We can go to Europe later. You'll never get a chance like this again."

"It worries me," said Homer.

"Oh, you're always worried over things that never even happen. Mr. Steen is satisfied and the people you have leased to are, so why are you worrying?"

"But where *are* these people? They aren't living in the houses and yet they talk as if they were. And some of them asked me how I got away with it or words to that effect. They asked it as if they admired me for being slick in some kind of shady deal, and if it turns out that I *am* smart, I'd like to know just how I managed—"

"Forget it," Elaine said. "You aren't smart and you never were. If I didn't keep behind you, pushing all the time—"

"Yes, dear," said Homer. He'd heard it all before.

"And quit your worrying."

He tried to, but he couldn't.

The next morning, he drove to Happy Acres and parked across the road from the gate. From 7 o'clock until 9, he counted 43 cars coming out of the development. Some of the people in them he recognized as those he had leased the houses to. Many of them waved to him.

At 9:30, he drove in through the gate and went slowly down the road.

The houses still were empty.

When he got back to the office, there were people waiting for him. The block was clogged with cars that gleamed with newness.

He did a rushing business. No one, it turned out, was interested in seeing the houses. Most of them had seen them earlier. All they wanted was a lease. He filled out the forms as rapidly as he could and raked in the checks and cash.

Some other people showed up. Word had got around, they said, that there were vacancies in the Happy Acres tract. Yes, he said, there were. Just a few of them. He reminded them about the cars.

The last man in line, however, did not want to lease a house.

"My name is Fowler," he said. "I represent the Contractors and Builders Association. Maybe you can help me."

"I've got another house, if that is what you want," said Homer.

"I don't need a house. I have one, thanks."

"Pay you to sell it and get in on this deal. The newest thing in housing. A completely new concept."

Fowler shook his head. "All I want to know is, how do I get hold of Steen?"

"No trouble at all," said Homer. "You just go out to Happy Acres. He has an office there."

"I've been out there a dozen times. He is never in. Usually the office is locked."

"I never have any trouble finding him, although I don't see him often. I'm too busy handling the property."

"Can you tell me how he does it, Mr. Jackson?"

"How he does what? How he is always out?"

"No. How he can sell a house for five thousand dollars."

"He doesn't sell. He leases."

"Don't pull that one on me. It's the same as selling. And he can't build for anywhere near that kind of money. He's losing a good twenty thousand or more on every house out there."

"If a man wants to lose his money—"

"Mr. Jackson," said Fowler, "that is not the point at all. The point is that it's unfair competition."

"Not if he leases," Homer pointed out. "If he sold, it might be."

"If this keeps on, it'll put every contractor in the area out of business."

"That," said Homer, "would be no more than simple justice in a lot of cases. They throw up a shack with plenty of glitter and charge a fancy price and—"

"Nevertheless, Mr. Jackson, none of them intend to be put out of business."

"And you're going to sue," guessed Homer.

"We certainly intend to."

"Don't look at me. I only lease the places."

"We intend to get out an injunction against your leasing them."

"You make the second one," Homer informed him, annoyed.

"The second what?"

"The real estate boys sent a guy like you out here several weeks ago. He made a lot of threats and nothing's happened yet. He was bluffing, just like you."

"Let me set your mind at rest," said Fowler. "I'm not doing any bluffing."

He got up from his chair and stalked stiffly out.

Homer looked at his watch. It was long past lunchtime. He went down to the drugstore for a sandwich and a cup of coffee. The place was empty and he had the counter to himself.

He sat hunched over the lunch and thought about it, trying to get all the queer goings-on straightened out into some sort of logic. But the only thing he could think about was that Steen wore his shoes on the wrong feet.

Wearily, still worried, Homer went back to the office. There were people waiting, with their new cars parked outside. He leased houses right and left.

Apparently the word was spreading. The house-seekers drifted in all afternoon. He leased four more houses before it was time to close.

It was funny, he thought, very, very funny how the word had got around. He hadn't advertised in the last three weeks and they still were coming in.

Just as he was getting ready to lock up, Morgan strode in breezily. He had a package underneath his arm.

"Here you are, pal," he said. "I told you I'd bring you something. Caught them just an hour or two ago."

The package was beginning to get soggy. Homer took it gingerly. "Thanks very much," he said in a doubtful voice.

"Think nothing of it. I'll bring you more in a week or two."

As soon as Morgan left, Homer closed the blinds and unwrapped the package warily.

Inside were brook trout—trout fresh-caught, with the ferns in which they had been wrapped not even wilting yet.

And there was no trout stream closer than a couple of hundred miles!

Homer stood and shivered. For there was no point in pretending ignorance, no point in repeating smugly to himself that it was all right. Even at five thousand a deal, there still was something wrong—very badly wrong.

He had to face it. They were beginning to close in on him. Fowler had sounded as if he might mean business and the Real Estate Association undoubtedly was lying in ambush, waiting for him to make one little slip. And when he made that slip, they'd snap the trap shut.

To protect himself, he had to know what was going on. He could no longer go at it blind.

Knowing, he might be able to go on. He might know when to quit. And that time, he told himself, might have been as early as this afternoon.

He stood there, with the fish and ferns lying in the wet wrapping paper on the desk, and envisioned a long street of houses, and behind that long street of houses, another identical street of houses, and behind the second street, another—street after street, each behind the other, each exactly like the other, fading out of sight on a flat and level plain.

And that was the way it must be—except there was no second street of houses. There was just the one, standing lone and empty, and yet, somehow, with people living in them.

Lease them a second time, Steen had said, and a third time and a fourth. Don't you worry about a thing. Let me handle it. Leave the worry all to me. You just keep on leasing houses.

And Homer leased one house and the people moved, not into the house he'd leased them, but into the second identical house immediately behind it, and he leased the first house yet again and the people moved into the third, also identical, also directly behind the first and second house, and that was how it was.

Except it was just a childish thing he had dreamed up to offer an explanation—any explanation—for a thing he couldn't understand. A fairy tale.

He tried to get the idea back on the track again, tried to rationalize it, but it was too weird.

A man could trust his sense, couldn't he? He could believe what he could see. And there were only fifty houses—empty houses, despite the fact that people lived in them. He could trust his ears and he had talked to people who were enthusiastic about living in those empty houses.

It was crazy, Homer argued with himself. All those other folks were crazy—Steen and all the people living in the houses.

He wrapped up the fish and retied the package clumsily. No matter where they came from, no matter what lunacy might prevail, those trout surely would taste good. And that, the taste of fresh-caught trout, was one of the few true, solid things left in the entire world.

There was a creaking sound and Homer jumped in panic, whirling swiftly from the desk.

The door was being opened! He'd forgotten to lock the door!

The man who came in wore no uniform, but there was no doubt that he was a cop or detective.

"My name is Hankins," he said. He showed his badge to Homer.

Homer shut his mouth tight to keep his teeth from chattering.

"I think you may be able to do something for me," Hankins said.

"Surely," Homer chattered. "Anything you say."

"You know a man named Dahl?"

"I don't think I do."

"Would you search your records?"

"My records?" Homer echoed wildly.

"Mr. Jackson, you're a businessman. Surely you keep records—the names of persons to whom you sell property and other things like that."

"Yes," said Homer, all in a rush. "Yes, I keep that sort of record. Of course. Sure."

With shaking hands, he pulled out a desk drawer and brought out the folder he'd set up on Happy Acres. He looked through it, fumbling at the papers.

"I think I may have it," he said. "Dahl, did you say the name was?"

"John H. Dahl," said Hankins.

"Three weeks ago, I leased a house in Happy Acres to a John H. Dahl. Do you think he might be the one?"

"Tall, dark man. Forty-three years old. Acts nervous."

Homer shook his head. "I don't remember him. There have been so many people."

"Have you one there for Benny August?"

Homer searched again. "B. J. August. The day after Mr. Dahl."

"And perhaps a man named Drake? More than likely signs himself Hanson Drake."

Drake was also there.

Hankins seemed well pleased. "Now how do I get to this Happy Acres place?"

With a sinking feeling, Homer told him how.

He gathered up his fish and walked outside with Hankins. He stood and watched the officer drive away. He wouldn't want to be around, he suspected, when Hankins returned from Happy Acres. He hoped with all his heart that Hankins wouldn't look him up.

He locked up the office and went down to the drugstore to buy a paper before going home.

He unfolded it and the headlines leaped at him:

THREE HUNTED
IN STOCK SWINDLE

Three photographs on column cuts were ranged underneath the headline. He read the names in turn. Dahl. August. Drake.

He folded the paper tightly and thrust it beneath his arm and he felt the sweat begin to trickle.

Hankins would never find his men, he knew. No one would ever find them. In Happy Acres, they'd be safe. It was, he began to see, a ready-made hideout for all kinds of hunted men.

He wondered how many of the others he had leased the houses to might be hunted, too. No wonder, he thought, the word had spread so quickly. No wonder his office had been filled all day with people who'd already bought the cars.

And what was it all about? How did it work? Who had figured it all out?

And why did he, Homer Jackson, have to be the one who'd get sucked into it?

Elaine took a searching look at him as he came in the door.

"You've been worrying," she scolded.

Homer lied most nobly. "Not worrying. Just a little tired."

Scared to death would have been closer to the truth.

IX

At 9 o'clock next morning, he drove to Happy Acres. He was inside the door before he saw that Steen was busy. The man who had been talking to Steen swung swiftly from the desk.

"Oh, it's you," he said.

Homer saw that the man was Hankins.

Steen smiled wearily. "Mr. Hankins seems to think that we're obstructing justice."

"I can't imagine," Homer said, "why he should think that."

Hankins was on the edge of rage. "Where are these people? What have you done with them?"

Steen said: "I've told you, Mr. Hankins, that we only lease the property. We cannot undertake to go surety for anybody who may lease from us."

"You've hidden them!"

"How could we hide them, Mr. Hankins? *Where* could we hide them? The entire development is open to you. You can search it to your heart's content."

"I don't know what is going on," said Hankins savagely, "but I'm going to find out. And once I do, both of you had better have your explanations ready."

"I think," Steen commented, "that Mr. Hankins' determination and deep sense of duty are very splendid things. Don't you, Mr. Jackson?"

"I do, indeed," said Homer, at a loss as to what to say.

"You'll be saying that out of the other side of your mouth before I'm through with you," Hankins promised them.

He went storming out the door.

"What a nasty man," Steen remarked, unconcerned.

"I'm getting out," said Homer. "I've got a pocket full of checks and cash. As soon as I turn them over, I am pulling out. You can find someone else to do your dirty work."

"Now I am sorry to hear that. And just when you were doing well. There's a lot of money to be made."

"It's too risky."

"I grant you that it may appear a little risky, but actually it's not. Men like Hankins will raise a lot of dust but what can they really do? We are completely in the clear."

"We're leasing the same houses over and over again."

"Why, certainly," said Steen. "How else would you expect me to build up the kind of clientele I need to give me business volume in this shopping center? You yourself have told me that fifty families were by no means enough. And you were right, of course. But you lease the houses ten times and you have five hundred families, which is not bad. Lease each one a hundred times and you have five thousand—And incidentally, Mr. Jackson, by the time you lease each of them a hundred times, you will have made yourself twenty-five million dollars, which is not a bad amount for a few years' work.

"Because," Steen concluded, "you see, despite what you may have thought of me, I'm squarely on the level. I gave you the straight goods. I told you I was not interested in money from the houses, but merely from the shopping center."

Homer tried to pretend that he was unimpressed. He kept on emptying checks and wads of money from his pockets. Steen reached out for the checks and began endorsing them. He stacked the money neatly.

"I wish you would reconsider, Mr. Jackson," he urged. "I have need of a man like you. You've worked out so satisfactorily, I hate to see you go."

"Come clean with me," said Homer, "and I might stay. Tell me all there is to tell—how it all works and what all the angles are and what you plan to do."

Steen laid a cautionary finger across his lips. "Hush! You don't know what you're asking."

"You mean you see no trouble coming?"

"Some annoyance, perhaps. Not real trouble."

"They could throw the book at us if they could prove we were hiding people wanted by the law."

Steen sighed deeply. "Mr. Jackson, how many fugitives have you sheltered in the last six weeks?"

"Not a one," said Homer.

"Neither have I." Steen spread his arms wide. "So we have nothing to fear. We've done no wrong. At least," he amended, "none that they can prove."

He picked up the money and the checks and handed them to Homer. "Here," he said. "You might as well take it to the bank. It's your money."

Homer took the money and the checks and stood with them in his hand, thinking about what Steen had said about not doing any wrong. Maybe Steen was right. Maybe Homer was getting scared when there was no need to be.

What could they be charged with?

Fraudulent advertising? There had been no specific claims that had not been performed.

For tying in the auto sales? Just possibly, although he had not made an auto sale a condition of transaction; he had merely mentioned that it would be very nice if they bought a car from Happy Acres Auto Sales.

For selling at less than cost? Probably not, for it would be a fine point of law to prove a lease a sale. And selling or leasing below cost in any case was no crime.

For leasing the same house more than once? Certainly not

until it could be proved that someone had suffered damage and it was most unlikely that it could be proved.

For doing away with people? But those people could be reached by telephone, could drive out through the gate. And they were well and happy and enthusiastic.

"Perhaps," Steen said gently, "you have changed your mind. Perhaps you'll stay with us."

"Perhaps I will," said Homer.

He walked down the concourse to the bank. It was an impressive place. The foyer was resplendent in coppery metal and with brightly polished mirrors. There were birds in hanging cages and some of the birds were singing.

There were no customers, but the bank was spic and span. An alert vice-president sat behind his polished desk without a thing to do. An equally alert teller waited shiny-faced behind the wicket window.

Homer walked to the window and shoved through the money and the checks. He took his passbook from his pocket and handed it across.

The teller looked at it and said, "I'm sorry, Mr. Jackson, but you have no account with us."

"No account!" cried Homer. "I have a quarter of a million!"

His heart went plunk into his boots, and if he'd had Steen there, he'd have broken him to bits.

"No," said the teller calmly, "you've made an error. That is all."

"Error!" gasped Homer, hanging onto the window to keep from keeling over.

"An understandable error," the teller said sympathetically. "One that anyone could make. Your account is not with us, but with the Second Bank."

"Second Bank," wheezed Homer. "What are you talking about? This is the only bank there is."

"Look, it says Second Bank right here." He showed Homer the passbook. It did say Second Happy Acres State Bank.

"Well, now," said Homer, "that's better. Will you tell me how I get to this Second Bank?"

"Gladly, sir. Right over there. Just go through that door."

He handed back the passbook and the money.

"That door, you say?" inquired Homer.

"Yes. The one beside the drinking fountain."

Homer clutched the passbook and the money tightly in his hand and headed for the door. He opened it and stepped inside and got it shut behind him before he realized that he was in a closet.

It was just a tiny place, not much bigger than a man, and it was as black as the inside of a cat.

Sweat started out on Homer and he searched frantically for the doorknob and finally found it.

He pushed the door open and stumbled out. He strode wrathfully back across the foyer to the teller's window. He rapped angrily on the ledge and the teller turned around.

"What kind of trick is this?" yelled Homer. "What do you think you're pulling? What is going on here? That is nothing but a closet."

"I'm sorry, sir," the teller said. "My fault. I forgot to give you this."

He reached into his cash drawer and handed Homer a small object. It looked for all the world like the replica of a bizarre radiator ornament.

Juggling the object in his hand, Homer asked, "What has this got to do with it?"

"Everything," the teller said. "It will get you to the Second Bank. Don't lose it. You'll need it to get back."

"You mean I just hold it in my hand?"

"That is all you do, sir," the teller assured him.

Homer went back to the door, still unconvinced. It was all a lot of mumbo-jumbo, he told himself. These guys were just the same as Gabby Wilson—full of smart pranks. And if that teller was making a fool of him, he promised himself, he'd mop up the floor with him.

He opened the door and stepped into the closet, only it was no closet. It was another bank.

The metal still was coppery and the mirrors were a-glitter and the birds were singing, but there were customers. There were three tellers instead of the single one in the first bank and the bland, smooth vice-president at his shiny desk was industriously at work.

Homer stood quietly just outside the door through which he'd come from the other bank. The customers seemed not to have noticed him, but as he looked them over, he was startled to discover that there were many whose faces were familiar.

Here, then, were the people who had leased the houses, going about their business in the Second Bank.

He put the miniature radiator ornament in his pocket and headed for the window that seemed to be least busy. He waited in line while the man ahead of him finished making a deposit.

Homer could only see the back of the man's head, but the head seemed to be familiar. He stood there raking through the memories of the people he had met in the last six weeks.

Then the man turned around and Homer saw that it was Dahl. It was the same face he had seen staring at him from the front page of the paper only the night before.

"Hello, Mr. Jackson," said Dahl. "Long time no see."

Homer gulped. "Good day, Mr. Dahl. How do you like the house?"

"Just great, Mr. Jackson. It's so quiet and peaceful here, I can't tear myself away from it."

I bet you can't, thought Homer.

"Glad to hear you say so," he said aloud, and stepped up to the window.

The teller glanced at the passbook. "Good to see you, Mr. Jackson. The president, I think, would like to see you, too. Would you care to step around after I finish your deposit?"

Homer left the teller's window, feeling a little chilly at the prospect of seeing the president, wondering what the president might want and what new trouble it portended.

A hearty voice told him to come when he knocked on the door.

The president was a beefy gentleman and extremely pleasant.

"I've been hoping you'd come in," he said. "I don't know if you realize it or not, but you're our biggest depositor."

He shook Homer's hand most cordially and motioned him to a chair. He gave him a cigar and Homer, a good judge of tobacco, figured it for at least a fifty-center.

The president, puffing a little, sat down behind his desk.

"This is a good setup here," said Homer, to get the conversation started.

"Oh, yes," the president said. "Most splendid. It's just a test, though, you know."

"No, I hadn't known that."

"Yes, surely. To see if it will work. If it does, we will embark on much bigger projects—ones that will prove even more economically feasible. One never knows, of course, how an idea will catch on. You can run all the preliminary observations and make innumerable surveys and still never know until you try it out."

"That's true," said Homer, wondering what in the world the president was talking about.

"Once we get it all worked out," the president said, "we can turn it over to the natives."

"I see. You're not a native here?"

"Of course not. I am from the city."

And that, thought Homer, was a funny thing to say. He

watched the man closely, but there was nothing in his face to indicate that he had misspoken—no flush of embarrassment, no sign of flurry.

"I'm especially glad to have a chance to see you," Homer told him. "As a matter of fact, I had been thinking of switching my account and—"

The president's face took on a look of horror. "But why? Certainly you've been told about the tax advantages."

"I think that the matter got some mention. But, I must confess, I don't understand."

"Why, Mr. Jackson, it is simple. No mystery at all. So far as the authorities of your country are concerned—"

"My country?"

"Well, of course. I think it might logically be argued, even in a court of law, that this place we're in is no longer the United States of America. But even if it should be a part of your great nation—I doubt that such a contention would hold up if put to the decision—why, even so, our records are not available to the agents of your country. Don't tell me you fail to see the implications of a situation such as that."

"The income tax," Homer said.

"Correct," said the president, smiling very blandly.

"That is interesting. Interesting, indeed." Homer rose and held out his hand to the president. "I'll be in again."

"Thank you," said the president. "Drop in any time you wish."

On the street outside the bank, the sun was shining brightly. The shopping center stretched along the mall and there were people here and there, walking on the concourse or shopping in the stores. A few cars were parked in the lot and the world of this Second Bank looked exactly like the First Bank's world, and if a man had not known the difference—

Good Lord, thought Homer, what *was* the difference? What had really happened? He'd walked through the door and there was the other bank. He'd walked through a door and found the missing people—the people who had not been living in the empty houses of the First Bank's world.

Because that other world where the houses still stood empty was no more than a show window? It might simply be a street lined with demonstration homes. And here was that second street of houses he'd dreamed up the other night. And beyond this second street, would there be another street and another and another?

He stumbled along the concourse, shaken, now that he realized there really was that second street of houses. It was an idea that was hard to take in stride. He didn't take it in his stride. His mind balked and shied away from it and he told himself it wasn't true. But it was true and there was no way to rationalize it, to make it go away.

There *was* a second street!

He walked along and saw that he was near the gate. The gate, he saw, was the same as ever, with its expanse of massive iron. But there was no gateman.

And a car was coming up the road, heading directly for the gate, and it was moving fast, as if the driver did not see the gate.

Homer shouted and the car kept on. He started to run, waving his arms, but the driver paid not the least attention.

The crazy fool, thought Homer. He'll hit the gate and—

And the car hit the gate, slammed into it, but there was sound, no crash, no screech of rending metal. There was simply nothing.

The gate was there, undented. And there was no car. The car had disappeared.

Homer stalked to the gate.

Ten feet away, he stopped.

The road came up to the gate; beyond it was no road. Beyond the gate was wilderness. The road came up and ended and the wilderness began.

Cautiously, Homer walked out into the road and peered through the gate.

Just a few feet away, a giant oak towered into the air and behind it was the forest, wild and hoary and primeval, and in the forest was the happy sound, the abandoned sound of water running in a brook.

Fish, thought Homer. Maybe that brook is where the trout came from.

He moved toward the gate for a closer look and reached out his hands to grasp the ironwork. Even as he did, the forest went away and the gate as well as he stood in the old familiar entrance to Happy Acres, with the gate wide open, with the state highway running along the wall and the road from the development running out to meet it.

"Good morning, sir," said the gateman. "Maybe you ought to move over to one side. A car is apt to hit you."

"Huh?" Homer asked blankly.

"A car. This is a road, you know."

Homer turned around and brushed past the gateman. He hustled down the concourse, aiming for Steen's office.

But the office was locked. Homer shook the door. He rapped wildly on the glass. He pounded on the frame. Absolutely nothing happened.

Turning from the door, he stared out across the development with incredulous eyes—the vacant concourse, the empty houses among the trees, the faint patches of shining lake peeking through the clearings.

He jammed his hands into his pockets and his fingers touched the little radiator ornament. He took it out and looked at it.

He'd seen it before—not the little replica, but the ornament itself.

He had seen it, he remembered, on the new cars parked outside his office by the people seeking leases. He had seen it on the car that had crashed the gate and disappeared.

He walked slowly to the parking lot and drove home.

"I don't think I'll go back to the office today," he told Elaine. "I don't feel so good."

"You've been working too hard," she told him accusingly. "You look all worn out."

"That's a fact," he admitted.

"After lunch, you lie down. And see that you get some sleep."

"Yes, dear," he said.

So it began to fall into a pattern, he thought, lying on his bed and staring at the ceiling. Finally it was clear enough so a man could begin to make some head and tail of it.

It was unbelievable, but there was no choice—one could not disbelieve in it. It was there to see. And if one looked at it any other way, it made no sense at all.

Someone—Steen, perhaps, or maybe someone else for whom Steen was serving as a front—had found out how to build one house, yet have many houses, houses stretching back street after street from the first house, all shadows of the first house, but substantial just the same—substantial enough for families to live in.

Dimensional extensions of that first house. Or houses stretching into time. Or something else as weird.

But however they might do it, it was a swell idea. For you could build one house and sell it, or lease it, time and time again. Except that one was crazy to get hold of an idea that was as good as that and then let someone else make all the money from the leasing of the houses.

And there was no question that Steen was crazy. That idea he had about the shopping center was completely batty—although, stop to think of it, if one had five thousand houses and leased each of them ten times and had a monopoly on all the shops and stores—why, it would pay off tremendously.

And the bank president's slant on sovereignty had certain angles, too, that should not be overlooked.

A new idea in housing, Steen had told him. It was all of that. It was a new idea that would apply to many things—to industry and farming and mining and a lot of other ventures. A man could make one car and there would be many others. A man could build a manufacturing plant and he would have many plants.

It was like a carbon copy, Homer thought—an economic carbon copy. And a man apparently could make as many carbons as he wished. Possibly, he speculated, once you knew the principle, there was no limit to the carbons. Possibly the ghostly parade of Happy Acres houses stretched limitless, forever and forever. There might be no end to them.

He fell asleep and dreamed of going down a line of ghostly houses, counting them frantically as he ran along, hoping that he'd soon get to the end of them, for he couldn't quit until he did get to the end. But they always stretched ahead of him, as far as he could see, and he could find no end to them.

He woke, damp with perspiration, his tongue a dry and bitter wad inside a flannel mouth. He crept out of bed and went to the bathroom. He held his head under a cold faucet. It helped, but not much.

Downstairs, he found a note that Elaine had propped against the radio on the breakfast table: *Gone to play bridge at Mabel's. Sandwiches in refrigerator.*

It was dark outside. He'd slept the daylight hours away. A wasted day, he berated himself—a completely wasted day. He hadn't done a dollar's worth of work.

He found some milk and drank it, but left the sandwiches where they were.

He might as well go to the office and get a little work done, compensate in part for the wasted day. Elaine wouldn't return until almost midnight and there was no sense in staying home alone.

He got his hat and went out to where he'd parked the car in the driveway. He got into it and sat down on something angular and hard. He hoisted himself wrathfully and searched the seat with a groping hand to find the thing he'd sat on.

His fingers closed about it and then he remembered. He'd sat on it on that day Morgan had showed up in answer to the ad. It had been rolling around ever since, unnoticed in the seat.

It was smooth to the touch and warm—warmer than it should be—as if there were a busy little motor humming away inside it.

And suddenly it winked.

He caught his breath and it flashed again.

Exactly like a signal.

Instinct told him to get rid of it, to heave it out the window, but a voice suddenly spoke out of it—a thick, harsh voice that mouthed a sort of chant he could not recognize.

"What the hell?" chattered Homer, fearful now. "What's going on?"

The chanting voice ceased and a heavy silence fell, so thick and frightening that Homer imagined he could feel it closing in on him.

The voice spoke again. This time, it was one word, slow and labored, as if the thick, harsh tongue drove itself to create a new and alien sound.

The silence fell again and there was a sense of waiting. Homer huddled in the seat, cold with fear.

For now he could guess where the cube had come from. Steen had ridden in the car with him and it had fallen from his pocket.

The voice took up again: "Urrr—urr—urrth—mum!"

Homer almost screamed.

Rustling, panting sounds whispered from the cube.

Earthman? Homer wondered wildly. Was that what it had tried to say?

And if that was right, if the cube in fact had been lost by Steen, then it meant that Steen was not a man at all.

* * *

He thought of Steen and the way he wore his shoes and suddenly it became understandable why he might wear his shoes that way. Perhaps, where Steen came from, there was no left or right, maybe not even shoes. No man could expect an alien, a being from some distant star, to get the hang of all Earth's customs—not right away, at least. He recalled the first day Steen had come into the office and the precise way he had talked and how stiffly he'd sat down in the chair. And that other day, six weeks later, when Steen had talked slangily and had sat slouched in his chair, with his feet planted on the desk.

Learning, Homer thought. Learning all the time. Getting to know his way around, getting the feel of things, like a gawky country youth learning city ways.

But it sure was a funny thing that he'd never learned about the shoes.

The cube went on gurgling and panting and the thick voice muttered and spat out alien words. One could sense the tenseness and confusion at the other end.

Homer sat cold and rigid, with horror seeping into him drop by splashing drop, while the cube blurted over and over a single phrase that meant not a thing to him.

Then, abruptly, the cube went dead. It lay within his hand, cooling, silent, just a thing that looked and felt like a clip-together plastic block for children.

From far off, he heard the roar of a car as it left the curb and sped off in the night. From someone's backyard, a cat meowed for attention. Nearby, a bird cheeped sleepily.

Homer opened the glove compartment and tossed the cube in among the rags and scraper and the dog-eared road map and the other odds and ends.

He felt the terror and the loathing and the wild agony begin to drain out of his bones and he sat quietly in the car, trying to readjust his mind to this new situation—that Steen must be an alien.

He dipped his hand into his pocket and found the replica of the radiator ornament. And that was the key, he knew—not only the key to the many streets of homes, but the key to Steen and the alien world.

They hadn't meant for him to keep the ornament, of course. If he had returned the way he'd entered into the world of the Second Bank, the teller more than likely would have demanded that he give it back. But he'd returned another way, an unexpected way, and it still was in his pocket.

And the radiator ornament, of course, was the reason that Steen had insisted that anyone who leased a house must also buy a car. For the ornament was a key that bridged one world and another. Although, thought Homer, it was rather drastic to insist that a man should buy a car simply so he'd have the correct radiator ornament.

But that might be the way, he told himself, that an alien mind would work.

He was calmer now. The fear still lingered, but pushed back, buried just a little.

Exactly how is a man supposed to act, he asked himself, when he learns there are aliens in the land? Run screeching through the streets, rouse all the citizens, alert the law, go baying on the trail? Or does he continue about his business?

Might he not, he wondered, take advantage of his knowledge, turn it to his own benefit?

He was the only human being on all of Earth who knew.

Steen might not like it known that he was an alien. Perhaps it would be worth a lot to Steen not to have it known.

Homer sat and thought about it. The more he thought, the more reasonable it seemed that Steen might be ready to lay plenty on the line to keep the fact a secret.

Not that I don't have it coming to me, Homer told himself. Not that he hasn't caused me a heap of worry and trouble.

He put his hand into his pocket. The miniature ornament was there. There was no need to wait. Now was as good as any time.

He turned the ignition key and the motor came to life. He backed out of the driveway and took the road to Happy Acres.

The development was dark and quiet. Even the usual advertising signs were turned off in the shop fronts.

He parked in front of Steen's office and got out. Opening the trunk, he found the jack handle in the dark.

He stood staring toward the gate. There was no sign of the gateman. But that was a chance he'd have to take. If the old fool tried to interfere, he could handle him.

For a moment, in front of the door to Steen's office, he hesitated, trying to reassure himself. Certainly there would be another closet, some way to get to those other worlds, inside the office.

He struck savagely at the glass in the door with the jack handle. The glass splintered and rained down, with crashing, tinkling sounds.

Homer waited, tense, listening, watching. Nothing stirred. The old gateman, if he was around, apparently had not heard the crash.

Carefully, Homer reached through the broken glass and manipulated the night lock. The door swung easily open. He walked inside and closed the door behind him.

In the empty office, Homer paused until his eyes became accustomed to the deeper darkness. He moved forward, groping with his hands, and found the desk. He could make out the dim bulk of a filing case. There should be a door somewhere. Perhaps not a door into the street, but a door into a hideout—some room where Steen could disappear to eat and rest and sleep; some place that might have a touch of his alien home about it.

Homer moved from the desk to the filing cabinet and felt along the wall. Almost immediately, he found a door.

He took a firmer grip on the jack handle and twisted on the knob. He walked through the door and there was the room, lighted a garish green by a lantern suspended from the ceiling.

There was sound and the sense of movement. Homer's hair stood straight on end and he felt his skin trying very hard to roll up his back. The hairy monster reached out a paw and grabbed him by the shoulder just as Homer swung around to dive back through the door.

The monster's paw was heavy and very strong. It was hairy and it tickled. Homer opened his mouth to scream, but his tongue dried up and his throat closed and he couldn't make a sound. The jack handle slipped from his numb fingers and clattered to the floor.

For a long moment, he stood there in the grip of the hairy monster and he supposed it had a face, but he could not see the face, for the hair grew all over it and drooped down where its face should be. The monster was a large one, with massive chest and shoulders that tapered down to a slim, athletic waist. Frightened as he was, Homer still could not keep from thinking that it looked a lot like an English sheepdog with a wrestler's body.

And all the while, there was something rolling on the floor and moaning.

Then the hairy monster said, in halting, stumbling syllables: "You Mister Jackson, you are not?"

Homer made a croaking sound.

"I apologize," the monster told him. "I very poor at your words. I work on your planet survey, but not so good with words."

He motioned at the thing moaning and rolling on the floor. "That was good with words."

The hairy hand dropped from Homer's shoulder.

"That," it said, gesturing at the floor again, "your Mister Steen."

"What is wrong with him?" Homer blurted out. "Is he sick or something?"

"He die himself," the monster said.

"You mean he's dying and you're just standing there—"

"No, no. He—how do you word it right?—he unlive himself."

"You mean he's killing himself? Committing suicide?"

"Yes," the monster said. "He does it very well. Do you not agree?"

"But you can't—"

"He take great pride in it. He make spectacular. He just starting now. He work up to grand finale. You must stay and watch. It be something to remember."

"No, thank you," Homer said faintly.

Homer turned to go, but the monster put out a hairy paw and stopped him.

"You must not be afraid of us. I stay half myself, all right? Could change entirely into human, but much trouble. Good enough this way?"

"It's all right," said Homer.

"We owe you debt," the monster said. "This Mister Steen of yours got things all scrambled up."

"I'll say he did," said Homer feelingly.

"He just a stumblebum. Bungler. He likewise is a joker."

"Joker?"

"Clown? Wise guy? You know—he made the joke. Sometimes very sly joke, but stupid just the same."

The monster leaned forward to peer into Homer's face.

"Your planet, it has its jokers, too?"

"Yes, indeed," Homer said. "There's one down the hall from me. His name is Gabby Wilson."

"So you understand then. A joker not too bad if that is all he is. But take a joker who makes mistakes and that is most bad. You have name for it. Smart aleck?"

"That's the name," said Homer.

"We make projects for the planets, for very many planets. We try to make each project fit the planet. The kind that will help the planet, the kind it needs the most."

"Like foreign aid," Homer supplied.

"So this bungler," said the monster, his voice rising in forthright and honest wrath, "this smart aleck, this nincompoop, this Mister Steen of yours, what do you think he does? He came to Earth as project manager—and he brings *wrong plan!* He is like that other times, going off not cocked. But this, it is too much. Final straw."

"You mean this Happy Acres business was never meant for Earth, but for some other planet?"

The monster draped his arm around Homer's shoulder in a gesture of understanding and affection. "That exactly what he do. No need of Happy Acres here. You still have room enough for all your people. No need to double up."

"But, sir," said Homer earnestly, "it is a swell idea. It has possibilities."

"Other things you need much worse, my friend. We have better plan for you."

Homer couldn't decide whether he liked the way the monster talked about the better plan.

"What other plan?" he asked.

"That is topmost secret. To make project big success, it must be done so that the natives think they the ones who do it. And that," the monster said, gesturing toward the floor, "is where this silly obscenity failed in second place. He let you find out what was going on."

"But there were all the other people, too," Homer protested. "All the people in the shops. The bank president and the gateman and—"

"All of them is us," the monster explained. "Them the crew that came with Mister Steen."

"But they were so human-looking! They looked exactly like us!"

"They play it straight. This ape, he ham it up."

"But they dressed like us and they wore shoes—"

"The shoes was more joke," the monster said furiously. "Your Mister Steen, he know how to make himself a human like the rest of them. But he wear his shoes wrong to get you humans'—your humans'—there is a word for it."

"Goat?"

"That is it! He wear them wrong to get your humans' goat. And he make outrageous deal with you and he watch you worry and he rejoice greatly and think himself superior and smart because he that kind of clown. That, I tell you, is no way to treat anyone. That is no true-blue friendship. But your Mister Steen, he was plain jerk. Let us go and watch him suffer."

"No," said Homer, horrified.

"You no like this dying?"

"It's inhuman."

"Of course, inhuman. We not humans, us. It is a way we have, a social law. He make himself a fool. He make bonehead blunder. He must dead himself. He must do it good. Great honor, do it good. He bungle everything in life, he must not bungle dying. He forever heel if he do."

Homer shivered, listening to the anguish of the alien on the floor, sick at stomach and giddy in the green flood of alien light.

"Now it is to end," said the alien. "We wipe out project. It was nonsensical mistake. We will take it all away."

"You can't mean that!" argued Homer. "We need it. We could make use of it. Just show us the principle."

"No," the monster said.

"But if you wipe out the project, there'll be all these people—"

"Sorry."

"They'll murder me! I was the one who leased the houses to them—"

"Too bad," the monster said.

"And all that money in the bank! A quarter of a million dollars, more than a quarter of a million dollars! It will be wiped out!"

"You have human money in bank?"

"I did. I suppose *that's* too bad, too."

"We can pay you off. Mister Steen make lot of money. He store it over there."

He pointed to the far wall. "You see that pile of bags? You take all that you can carry."

"Money?" Homer asked.

"Good money."

"All I can carry?" insisted Homer, nailing it down tight. "And you will let me leave?"

"We do you wrong," the monster said. "This fix it just a little?"

"I'll tell the world," said Homer, with enthusiasm.

Steen was becoming noisier. He had changed into his alien form and now he rolled upon the floor, knotted up and writhing.

Homer walked wide around him to get to the farther wall. He hefted down the bags and they were fairly heavy. He could take two at least, he figured. He hoisted two on his back, then piled on the third. He barely made it back across the room.

The monster watched him with some admiration. "You like money, huh?"

"You bet," Homer panted. "Everyone likes money."

He set the bags down by the door.

"You sure you not stay and watch? It get good directly. It be amusing, maybe even interesting."

Homer held down a rising shudder. "No, thank you very much."

The monster helped him get the bags on his shoulder. "I hold the door for you."

"Thank you," said Homer. "Good day to you and thanks for everything."

"Good-bye, my friend," the monster said.

He held the door and Homer walked on through.

He came back into the office he'd left an hour before. The glass in the door was shattered and his car was still parked outside.

Homer hurried.

In less than five minutes, he went roaring out the gate, with the bags of money locked inside the trunk.

There was little time, he realized. What he did had to be done fast. For when the monster wiped out Happy Acres, there would be a battalion of families marooned there in the woods and they'd come boiling out with a single thought in mind—to get their hands on Homer Jackson.

He tried to imagine what it might be like, and then tried to stop thinking what it might be like, but couldn't.

There would be a lot of people there without any houses. They'd wake up in the wild, wet woods, with their furniture and belongings scattered all about them. And all those bright new cars would be in among the trees. And the people would be plenty sore.

Not that he blamed them much.

He was sore himself.

That lousy Steen, he said. Like that contractor Gabby told about—the one who went out on a wrecking job and demolished the wrong house.

The dashboard clock said slightly after midnight. Elaine would be home by now and they could start right out.

Homer turned into the driveway and braked to a halt. There was a light in the kitchen window. He ran up the walk and burst into the house.

"Oh, *there* you are," said Elaine. "I wondered where you were. What's wrong with you?"

"We're getting out of here," Homer babbled.

"Have you gone stark crazy? Getting out!"

"Now for once," said Homer, "don't give me an argument. We're getting out of here. Tonight. I've got three sacks of money out there in the car—"

"Money! How did you get three sacks—"

"It's legal," Homer pleaded. "There's nothing wrong with it. I didn't rob a bank. There's no time to explain. Let us just get going."

She got icy calm. "Where are we going, Homer?"

"We can decide that later. Maybe Mexico."

"You're ill," she scolded. "You've been working too hard lately. And worrying about that Happy Acres deal—"

It was too much for Homer. He turned toward the door.

"Homer! Where are you going, Homer?"

"I'll show you the money," he gritted. "I'll show you I really have it."

"Wait for me," she cried, but he didn't wait. She ran down the walk behind him.

He opened the car trunk. "There it is. We'll carry it up to the house. You can take off your shoes and walk in it. Then maybe you'll believe me."

"No, Homer, no!"

"Here, help me with these sacks," he said.

Inside the house, he opened the sacks. Neatly bundled sheafs of bills spilled out on the floor.

Elaine knelt and picked up a package.

"Why, it's real!" she cried happily.

"Of course it is," said Homer.

"And, Homer, these are twenty-thousand-dollar bills!" She dropped the package that she held and picked up another and another and another.

"And so are these!" she screamed. "There are millions and millions here!"

Homer was pawing desperately through the heap of money. Sweat was running down his face.

"Are they all twenty-thousand-dollar bills?" she asked hopefully.

"Yes," said Homer in a beaten voice.

"But what is wrong?"

"That dirty, lowdown, bungling Steen," he said bitterly.

"But what is wrong?" she cried again.

"They aren't worth a dime," said Homer. "There are no such things as twenty-thousand-dollar bills. The Treasury never issued any!"

THE ASTEROID OF GOLD

This story was named "Planetoid Treasure" when it was sent to Hugo Gernsback of Wonder Stories *on August 10, 1932, but by the time it was published in the November 1932 issue of that magazine, it had a new title. Since Gernsback was the magazine's editor-in-chief, he was probably the one who changed the title and wrote the introduction to the story, which read in part: "The man from earth whose mental habits are fixed will have great difficulty in accustoming himself to the peculiarities of areas of no gravitation; of worlds on which the atmosphere, temperature and other natural conditions are so different from those on earth. It may well be that success or disaster will depend on quick thinking in a crisis. . . ."*

It certainly sounds like Gernsback, who wrote the classic story "Ralph 124C 41+." (It is Gernsback for whom the annual Hugo Awards, given at each year's World Science Fiction Convention, are named.)

I'm not sanguine about the physics used in this story, but it certainly exudes the enthusiastic flavors of its era!

—dww

"After this charge we'll knock off for eats and sleep," Vince Drake suggested to his brother.

Vernon Drake nodded.

"I've got the jitters from wearing the suit for such a long stretch," he said. "I'm afraid we're overdoing the work a bit, Vince."

"It's a tough racket," his brother agreed, "but the sooner we get this load to earth, the quicker we can buy *Space Pup II*."

The two moved over the rocky surface of the asteroid in apparently effortless leaps, heading toward the *Space Pup*, which squatted like a silver monster against the drab monotony of the little world. Here the gravity was slight, so slight, in fact, that the brothers wore ropes about their waists while at work, with the other ends fastened to the *Space Pup*. The ship was securely anchored to the planetoid with magnetic plates. Otherwise some slight disturbance might have sent it off into space.

A man, putting his full strength into a leap, could easily have torn himself from the face of the rocky little world and hurled himself beyond its attraction. Thus the ropes attached to the man and the ship. It would have been no joke to inadvertently hop off the tiny slab of rock and be unable to return. They had at first experimented with weighted shoes and then with magnetic plates attached to the soles, but both of these devices had proved cumbersome and awkward.

Overhead the stars moved steadily in the velvety blackness of absolute space. The asteroid, nothing more than a slab of rock some five miles in length, half as wide and approximately four miles thick, was tumbling rapidly end over end through space. Here one was afforded the astounding spectacle of observing the constellations march in orderly procession against the curtain of blackness which enveloped the airless little world.

Descending over the sunward horizon could be seen the Twin, only a matter of some fifteen miles distant. The two tiny slabs of rock, revolving about each other, made up a part of the asteroid belt, all that remained of a mythical planet between Mars and Jupiter (which must have disrupted into the thousands of tiny fragments many millions of years before).

Here and there in the blackness loomed dark splotches, some shining faintly with reflected light from the distant sun—other members of the belt. At times wandering chunks of rock hurtled across space, some passing close to the asteroid upon which the two brothers were located. At times showers of tiny meteors, travelling at bullet-like speeds, bombarded the little island of space. There was danger in plenty, but the stakes were high and the brothers braved the dangers.

Two slabs of rock revolving about one another, true twins of space . . . but the Twin was only rock, while the one upon which Vince and Vernon Drake were conducting their mining operations was shot through and through with yellow veins of gold. The ore was rich, unbelievably rich, so rich that it practically crumbled under one's fingers. The price of one cargo alone would run into six figures. A treasure house in space! A treasure hoard of the void!

The brothers reached the ship and Vince knelt to connect the wires to the detonator. The nitro was planted in shallow holes, with care taken that the charge was not excessive. With the slight gravity, too large a charge would simply blast a portion of the ore-bearing slab into space, possibly to be lost forever. This had happened several times before they had learned just how much nitro to use.

"Hang on!" cautioned Vince.

Vernon grasped a rung set in the side of the *Space Pup*. Vince slid his arm through a similar rung and with his free hand shot down the plunger of the detonator.

There was no noise, only a slight flush where the charges were planted. The planetoid trembled violently beneath their feet. The *Space Pup* quivered and tugged at its magnetic moorings as the rock beneath it shook to the charge of the explosive. About a half mile away, where the charge had been set, a shower of small rock fragments sailed upward, but they did not drop. Out and out they sailed until they were lost to view, each becoming a separate unit in the mass of debris which formed the asteroid belt.

"Now into the *Pup*," exclaimed Vince, "for some eats and a good long sleep. We've done a lot this shift."

"The thing I look forward to is getting out of this suit," declared Vernon.

He turned toward the door and as he did so he cast a glance upward. He stopped short in astonishment.

"Vince, look!" he cried.

Looming out of the void, blotting out a portion of the sky, a huge, black ship hung almost directly above them. There had been nothing to apprise them of its coming. It had simply slipped out of the blackness of space and suddenly was there, hanging above the tiny world. They had seen no rocket blasts.

Their earphones rang as an imperative tone cut in upon their receiving sets.

"Stay where you are. Don't move. We are going to land and we have guns on you."

The ship was speaking to them.

"Who the hell are you?" demanded Vernon.

And the answer came.

"Max Robinson of the Space Ship *Star Wanderer*, speaking."

"Max Robinson, of the *Star Wanderer*!" The faces of the two brothers paled under their helmets. The most notorious raider of the space lines! Plunderer extraordinary. Cutthroat bandit of the void. How had he learned of the wondrous treasure on the little asteroid?

There was nothing to say. The two young miners at first did not realize the true significance of this visit from Robinson. It all came so suddenly that it was impossible to think clearly, impossible to grasp the true possibilities of the situation.

"You damned robber!" said Vernon bitterly.

He felt his brother's hand upon his arm, squeezing with a vise-like grip.

"Men don't talk like that to Max Robinson," the voice came coolly, unflustered, "and get away with it."

Warned by the pressure on his arm, Vernon did not reply.

The two stood silently, watching the great craft settle slowly to a berth only a short distance from where the *Space Pup* lay. Through the lighted ports they could see men in the ship, while here and there heads were outlined against the circles of light, men off duty looking out upon the tiny world where they had landed.

Smoothly a gangplank came down and the outer door of an air chamber swiftly unscrewed and swung free.

"Come into my ship," said the voice of Robinson, "and come peaceably."

There was a horrible threat in the words. The two knew there never would be a moment, except perhaps when they were actually in the air chamber, that they would not be under the guns of the vessel.

In long hops they moved forward and set foot on the gangplank of the pirate ship. There they halted to unfasten the ropes about their waists.

"What are you stopping for?" growled Robinson.

"To unfasten our safety cables," Vince explained. "The gravity is so low here we anchored ourselves to our ship."

Robinson chuckled.

"Bright idea," he applauded. "I'll never forget the time one of my men jumped off one of these lousy little worlds. We scouted around for hours before we picked him up. He was dead."

They could hear the raider chuckle again, deep in his throat.

"Scared to death," he explained.

The brothers did not answer; neither of them at the moment could find anything particularly funny about a man being frightened to a point where death claimed him. With their ropes free they stepped up the gangplank into the air chamber. Noiselessly the door swung against the port, spinning into the threads. There was a sharp hissing, continuing for several minutes, then the inner door slipped its threads and swung open.

Vernon again felt the warning pressure of his brother's hand as they stepped out of the air chamber into the interior of the ship. Several members of the crew sprang toward them, ran swift hands over their inflated suits.

"That's all right," said Vernon, "we have no guns."

The men dropped back and the brothers unfastened their helmets and swung them back on their rear hinges. They closed the air tank valves and the suits went limp, hanging loosely about them.

Their eyes, roving over the ship, saw that it was extremely modern, equipped with many of the new inventions for comfort and safe space travel.

Six members of the crew stood in the room with them. They were a hardfaced lot; scum drafted from all the infamous space ports of the worlds; perhaps many of them criminals hiding from justice.

"The captain wants to see you immediately," said one of them.

"Mind if we take off our suits?" asked Vernon. "They aren't comfortable after you've worn them for a while."

"Don't see that would hurt any," grunted the man. "Hurry about it, though."

Quickly they unfastened the suits and stepped from them, leaving them on the floor.

"The captain ain't one to be kept waiting," the man explained.

The two followed the man along a central corridor to the forward end of the ship. Before a door their guide stopped and knocked.

"Come in," commanded the voice they had heard over their receiving sets.

The guide swung open the door and motioned the others to step forward. As they did so, the door closed behind them and they stood alone, face to face with Max Robinson, cruelest and most hunted space raider of the system.

They saw a man attired in a colorful uniform of powder blue, adorned with gold buttons, and with a red circle as a breast insignia. His forehead was high and his chin square, but not overemphasized. A squat nose hulked above the slightest suggestion of a mustache and the lips were full and well formed. It was such a face as might have belonged to an ordinary, everyday business man of the Earth . . . until one looked at the eyes, and there the brothers saw cold calculation and insane cruelty.

He sat behind a large desk of beautiful carved stone, which was at once recognized as Martian art. Perhaps the desk had been part of the loot taken from some flaming homestead upon which Robinson and his crew of vandals descended to obtain a cargo of food. Upon the walls of the room hung paintings, specimens of the best art of the world. Held in wall brackets were other works of art, vases and statues. A heavy rug carpeted the floor.

"You like my office?" queried Robinson.

"It is appointed more tastefully than I would have imagined," replied Vince and the implication of his words was not lost upon the man behind the desk.

"When you become more thoroughly acquainted with me," he purred, "you will receive many surprises."

"Doubtless," said Vince.

Robinson's eyes narrowed. He seemed on the point of speaking sharply, then appeared to change his mind.

"Doing some mining?" he asked.

"No, exploring," lied Vince.

"Find anything?"

"A little lead."

Lead or Gold?

Robinson clucked with mock sympathy.

"Too bad," he said, "too bad. Funny you would stay on one asteroid so long when all you found was a little lead. We saw you here 20 days ago when we passed by. When we picked you up again this time we thought you might have found something, so we dropped down."

Vince said nothing. There was nothing to say.

"Been doing a lot of blasting, too," observed the pirate. "In one place. That's funny. Seems to me you would blast a lot of test pits if you were just exploring."

"We were hopeful of finding something really worthwhile," explained Vernon. "Had just about decided to quit. If we find nothing from this last shot we won't do any more exploring here. We've wasted too much time here as it is."

"You're right," said Robinson and his voice was silky. "You won't do any more exploring . . . here or on any other asteroid."

"What do you mean?" asked Vernon.

Robinson did not seem to hear the question. He leaned forward over the desk and beat a clenched fist on its polished top.

"What did you find?" he bellowed.

"Lead," declared Vince.

The pirate picked up a small hammer and tapped a gong which squatted on his desk. The door opened and the man who had escorted the brothers to his captain stepped into the room.

"Make these gentlemen comfortable," commanded Robinson, "I am going out to have a look at their lead mine."

With an evil grin the man beckoned to the two, led the way out of the door and down the corridor. Far in the rear of the ship he halted and with a key opened a heavy door.

"In you go," he said.

The brothers stepped inside and the door creaked to, behind them. A moment later the key grated in the lock.

The room was bare of furniture except for four steel beds bolted to the floor. They were in the prison room of the *Star Wanderer*.

Vernon sat down heavily on one of the beds.

"What do we do now?" he asked.

"We have to wait and watch our chance," said Vince. "Maybe a chance will never come, but if it does, we'll make the most of it. We have to try not to antagonize Robinson, but we must stand upon our dignity. We must not let him believe for a moment we are afraid of him or afraid of what he might do to us. We have told our story and we are going to stick to it. We explored and we found lead. No matter if he takes tons of gold out of this place, it will always be lead to us."

Vernon grinned. The course suggested by his brother struck a chord of grim humor in him.

Vince seated himself on the bed and threw an arm over Vernon's shoulder.

"It's a tough break, kid," he said. "We are in the hands of the system's worst outlaw. We . . ."

He stopped, groping for words.

"Yes, I know," said Vernon and the two of them sat, staring straight at the grey wall in front of them.

Vince broke the silence.

"No use kidding ourselves," he said.

"None at all," agreed Vernon and his voice matched his brother's in tenseness.

"But we must always remember, kid," went on Vince, "that this isn't the first time a Drake has been in a tight spot. Some of them have gotten out of it and some of them haven't. But they were always Drakes. Not a sniveling coward among them. Not a single whimper for mercy. They've never forgotten their *savoir faire*. We've got something that Robinson never had and never can have and maybe we can beat him yet. He'll get small satisfaction out of this deal, no matter what happens."

They sat in silence again.

"Let's get some sleep," suggested Vernon, and Vince nodded.

"Good idea," he said and almost crunched the bones in his brother's shoulder with the grip of an understanding hand.

Dog-tired after hours in space suits, with the labor of wresting the golden fortune from the isolated little asteroid, they slept long and when they awoke a table bearing food stood in the room.

Vernon went to the single port-hole opening out of the prison room. Staring through it he could see feverish activity outside. Several cranes had been rigged up on the surface of the little world and the entire crew of the *Star Wanderer* seemed to be engaged in looting the planetoid of its golden hoard. It was a weird picture. Huge floodlights hastily erected lighted up the surface and made the place a plain of light and shadow. Space armor glistened and shone and sudden flashes spurted against the utter blackness of space as charges of explosives were fired. As each charge exploded the *Star Wanderer* vibrated from end to end. Men with heavy loads of ore toiled up the gangplank and into the airlock.

"What are they doing?" asked Vince sleepily from his bed.

"Come and see," invited Vernon.

Together the two brothers gazed out upon the scene.

"Our mine," said Vernon.

Vince nodded bitterly.

The two turned from the window and gave their attention to the food on the table.

"Poison," suggested Vernon, but Vince shook his head.

"Not Robinson's way of doing things," he declared. "Not bloody enough. No entertainment just sending two poor souls into eternity with a dose of strychnine. Robinson demands dramatics."

"I hope you're right," said Vernon.

"What does it matter if I am or not?" demanded Vince. "We have to eat, don't we? I'd rather eat poison every time in preference to starvation."

The food was good and the brothers, not having eaten for twenty-four hours, did justice to it.

An hour later the same man who had conducted them to their cell appeared to take away the food.

"The captain says to tell you that he's found gold," he stated.

"Tell the captain that he's found lead," corrected Vince.

Hours passed. Ten times the Twin circled its mate in space. Still the work of mining the gold went on without a stop. Apparently Robinson had divided his crew into shifts and was working every minute. Great pits were being gouged in the surface of the planetoid. It was plain that the pirate would not halt mining operations until either the ore pinched out or until his ship was loaded to capacity.

Food was served the prisoners at regular intervals and they slept when they felt sleepy. Part of the time they spent at the port watching the activity outside. They requested a deck of cards from their keeper and whiled away hours playing for immense imaginary stakes. Neither of them mentioned what lay in store for them. Neither was there talk of escape. They knew there was no escape.

Escape from the ship without space suits meant death of the most horrible kind on the airless surface of the asteroid. Escape even with space suits would have to be made in the face of the pirates swarming outside. Even if they were able to safely reach the *Space Pup*, they knew that the *Star Wanderer* carried weapons which could blast the little ship out of existence.

The Twin had circled its companion eighteen times when they were summoned out of their prison to face Robinson again. As they walked up the corridor with their keeper stalking in their wake, Vernon's hand reached out and grasped his brother's for just an instant in a bone-crushing clasp. They were walking the road to death. Not for a moment was there a doubt in their mind of that. It was not after the manner of Max Robinson to allow men he had plundered to live. It was not well for him to have too many men in the system hating him with that fierce hate which can only come through personal injury.

But they walked with their shoulders square, with their chins up and in their swinging stride there was no hint of condemned men on their way to the scaffold.

Reaching the door of Robinson's office they did not wait for the guard to announce them. Vince beat a tattoo upon the metal.

"Come in," said the pirate, and once more they stood before the beautifully carved desk behind which sat the most feared, most hated man of the solar system.

Robinson regarded them with narrowed eyes, but his throat gurgled with cruel laughter.

"This asteroid of yours," he said, "is very precious. It is rich beyond dreams. It is full of gold."

"It is full of lead and, at present, cluttered up with damned robbers," said Vince softly.

Robinson seemed not to hear him, but Vernon, watching closely, knew that his brother's words had flicked him on the raw.

"It is regrettable," purred the pirate, "that having discovered such a vast deposit of gold, it should be lost to you. Under the circumstances your fortitude has been truly amazing. You have earned something better than the fate which I generally mete out to my . . . my . . ."

"Victims," suggested Vince.

"That's it," beamed Robinson. "How did you think of the word?"

"I am way ahead of you all of the time," Vernon told him.

Robinson, however, was determined not to lose face by losing his temper. He had deliberately set out to taunt these men in an attempt to break them. He forced himself to maintain his light tone.

He wagged his head.

"I have taken all I want," he said. "More, perhaps, than I was rightly entitled to, for after all it was your mine. You discovered it. Still there is plenty more. I don't plan on returning, for there are many other such treasures in the system and the treasure itself means nothing to Max Robinson, rather the satisfaction of acquiring it."

"I hope," said Vince, "that you have derived considerable satisfaction from our explorations."

Robinson bowed, mocking them.

"Exactly," he said, "So I have decided not to kill you. I will leave you here with your mine. I have done enough wrong in my life. I am sorely in need of a few acts of mercy to counterbalance my sins."

Vernon stirred at Vince's side, but his brother reached out with a hand and gripped him. He steadied . . . waiting for the joker in Robinson's proposal.

"It is regrettable, however," stated the pirate, "that I am short on oxygen tanks. All I shall be able to give you will be three tanks. One for each of you and one to be divided between you as you see fit."

He stared solemnly at them.

"I am sorry to say, too, that I shall be obliged to take your ship out of your reach temporarily. If I left it where you could use it immediately, I fear that you might hasten to Mars and report my presence in this part of the solar system and it does not suit my plans to have my presence known for some time."

"Canny," declared Vince, "always the old fox."

Robinson grinned.

"I am going to take your ship and anchor it just a few miles away, on the Twin, where you can see it. One of my crew, a reputable instructor of mathematics in an Earth college before he committed a certain indiscretion and sought my protection, informs me that in the matter of a few thousand years the revolutions of the two asteroids will slow down and their orbits will close in, until they finally come together, joining one another. When that occurs you can reach your ship and return to Earth or Mars without harming me in the least."

"If the oxygen holds out," suggested Vince.

"I never thought of that," declared the pirate. "Maybe the oxygen wouldn't last that long."

"I'm afraid it wouldn't," said Vince.

"At least," pointed out the other, "you will have the satisfaction of always having your ship in sight when the Twin is in view."

A Desperate Chance

As he spoke Vince leaped. His body, striking against the desk, shoved it backward and toppled the pirate out of his chair. The chair thudded against the carpeted floor. A vase tottered and fell from a shallow wall bracket, smashing to a thousand bits as it struck against a piece of statuary standing beneath it.

Vince, his body bruised by the force of its impact against the heavy desk, scrambled to his feet.

Vernon was vaulting the desk, disappeared behind it. With a single effort, Vince followed. Vernon and Robinson were locked on the floor in a tangle of flying arms and legs.

Vince flung himself into the struggle. His hands found and closed with a vise-like grip upon a massive throat.

There was a hammering of feet in the corridor.

"Quick," screamed Vince, "The trick Kan taught us."

Like a flash Vernon was on his feet. With a thud he placed his left knee into the small of Robinson's back, bearing down with his entire weight. Up and back Vince forced the upper part of the body and then, with his fingers still wrapped like tentacles of steel about the pirate's throat, put his full strength into a final thrust. There was a sharp snap as the vertebrae slipped out of place.

Vince released his grip and the body slumped to the floor.

The door burst inward. The brothers vaulted the desk as one man and were in the center of the dozen members of the crew before a gun could be used. With fists working like driving pistons the two went to the attack. Back and forth the fight surged across the room, with the pirates afraid to use their guns at such close quarters.

Vince accounted for his first opponent with a clean smash to the temple, but fumbled the second blow when his fist slid off the granite chin of the second man. Someone hit him hard over the heart and he retaliated with a blow that lifted the man off his feet and sent him staggering. A monstrous fist lashed at his head and almost floored him. Groggy as he was, he failed to duck another fist that smashed him against the wall. A face appeared in front of him and he flailed at it. A red smear appeared on the face as it slumped out of his line of vision. Then there were other fists hitting him . . . hitting hard.

He caught sight of Vernon in the center of the melee in the middle of the room; saw a man wilt as his brother drove his fist into his threat; saw his brother toppled as someone struck him from behind. Then a fist he could not duck, hard as he tried . . . a moment of dull pain, of flashing lights within his head and then . . . nothing.

He awoke with the glare of electric bulbs in his eyes and a throbbing pain in his head. Weakly he gained a sitting position and glanced about him.

Members of the crew thronged the room, all of them clutching weapons. A short distance away Vernon was struggling to his feet.

Walking unsteadily, his brother advanced toward him. Vince forced his aching body to rise and faced Vernon.

"It was a good fight," said Vernon, "while it lasted."

He grinned, wryly. Vince noted that one of his front teeth was missing and that bloodstains were about his mouth.

"Our last good fight, kid," said Vince.

The pirates rimmed them in a tight circle, watching them warily.

"Why don't they polish us off, kid?" asked Vince.

"Orders from Robinson," Vernon explained, "he is still alive."

"What's that!"

"Robinson is still alive."

"The hell you say," exclaimed Vince. "He's the first man I ever knew who could outlive old Kan's trick."

"Too tough to kill. Born to hang," said Vernon.

There was a stir at the edge of the circle which hemmed them in. It parted to let two men pass through. The two cradled a broken man in their arms.

Robinson glared at the brothers out of haggard eyes. His legs dangled grotesquely, seeming to reach despairingly toward the floor. His face was a twisted mask of pain and anger.

"You thought to kill me," he boomed.

"I am sorry," said Vince.

"Sorry!"

"Sorry I didn't succeed."

Robinson was muttering to himself.

"Delirious," said Vernon and Vince nodded.

But they were mistaken.

"Hard men to break," mumbled the pirate, "but loneliness on an asteroid, with a space ship just out of reach, will break you. Too bad I won't be here to see you fight over the third oxygen tank. Too bad I can't hear you scream when you watch the ship, so near . . . yet just too far. Yes, it is too bad I can't wait to see you break."

Vince, his fists clenched hard at his side, took a step toward the man.

"Listen, Robinson, you won't be anywhere again. You are just a twisted cripple. You'll never walk again. There isn't a man in God's creation who can mend that back of yours. Your spinal column is shattered . . . and you are hanging on by a thread. You will live, knowing every minute that just one little twist, one wrong move may send you to eternity. I hope to God you live a hundred years and fear every moment you will die.

"You are a broken man . . . a useless worn-out shell. These hands broke you . . . broke you, do you hear . . . and I am damn glad we were able to do it . . . you sneering, low-lived swine!"

"Take him out," commanded Robinson.

Men sprang forward, and pinioned their arms behind them, forcing them to the door.

The Twin was rising over the rim of the tumbling world.

Two men, seated on a rocky ridge, arms thrown over one another's shoulders, stared up at it. Against its dull lustre could be seen a speck of silver, etched in familiar outline, the *Space Pup*.

"We'll see it just once more," said Vince, "Our oxygen won't last more than another revolution of the asteroids."

"What are we going to do with this?" Vernon touched the extra tank with the toe of his boot.

"You know what we are going to do with it."

Vernon nodded.

"We'll furnish a great newspaper story some day," he said, "if we are ever found. Two dead men in space suits with a tank full of oxygen at their feet. Mystery—why didn't one of them use the oxygen?"

"I have something I want to say," said Vince. "Hard to word it. Would think a fellow could say things to his brother . . . but you know how it is."

"Sure. Better not say it. I feel the same way."

"You've been regular," declared Vince.

"Not so bad yourself," replied Vernon.

"It's not hard to die with you, kid. I always pictured us going out differently. Maybe with guns flaming in some out of way station or with the old *Space Pup* busted wide open somewhere out in space . . . but not like this. Doesn't matter after all. . . ."

"Why should it?" demanded Vernon.

They sat silently, watching the Twin climb rapidly toward the zenith. Dust spurted in the mine pits as a few tiny meteors plunged down on the asteroid.

"If one of those hit us, it would be over in a minute," observed Vernon.

"Look!" screamed Vince. "The Twin is falling!"

Vernon jerked his head upward.

The Twin was falling! Falling with a rotary motion around the axis of its length. Even as he watched it seemed to draw closer!

"A meteor," exclaimed Vince, his voice tense, "a large meteor. Struck it and threw it out of its orbit! That's the only thing that can account for it."

"It is bringing the *Space Pup* back to us!" said his brother.

"It will crush the *Space Pup*," declared Vince. "Likely smash us, too. It will land smack on top of us."

"It won't hurt the *Space Pup*," argued Vernon. "See, it is rotating. The top will be turned toward us when it strikes. The ship will be on top. It will be safe!"

"By God, you're right," yelled Vince. "Here, kid, we're getting out of here! Grab a handful of rocks and jump as you've never jumped before! At an angle to carry you out over the edge."

He stooped and scooped up handfuls of rubble.

"Get going!" he screamed at his brother.

Vernon was running. Running with long leaps toward the nearer edge of the planetoid, gaining speed at every leap. Then he shot upward, as if he had been catapulted from a gigantic sling shot. Up and up he went, out and out, until he was a speck against the blackness.

Bouncing along over the surface, Vince put all of his strength into a tremendous leap as he struck the rock beneath with both feet planted firmly. He seemed to be rushing out, away from the asteroid, at an express train speed. Rapidly the bloated space suit encasing his brother seemed to leap to meet him. Then he was floating free in space, looking back at the Twin rushing downward upon the slab of rock he had so recently quitted. He could see that the rotary motion of the Twin, probably imparted to it when a meteor had struck with force enough, not only to knock it out of its orbit, but to also reverse its directional spin, had brought the *Space Pup* to the upper side. The two planetoids were so close now that the ship could not possibly be crushed between them. They were due to crash any moment now and the *Space Pup* was on top!

He clawed with his hands at empty space, swinging his body around until his back was toward the asteroid. Then with all his strength he heaved a rock straight away from him. With a rush his body moved backwards, slowed down, glided. Another thrown rock and another leap . . . another . . . another. Over his shoulder he could see out of the tail of his eye that he was proceeding in the right direction.

A short distance away he could see Vernon also heaving rocks.

Another rock . . . but this time his body did not slow to a glide. It kept on moving. He realized that he was falling, that he was influenced by gravity!

Sudden fear assailed him. Had he miscalculated? Had he been captured again by the first asteroid before the Twin had struck? Or had the Twin already struck?

Desperately he attempted to twist about. He succeeded and glimpsed jagged rock surface beneath him. The matter of landing without ripping his suit or cracking his helmet ports took all of his attention during the next few seconds.

He struck on his two feet, tumbled and rolled, his arms shielding his helmet. The ground seemed to be pitching and rocking. He could feel it quivering and moving beneath him. Like an earthquake. He gained his feet, but lost his balance again.

As he fell he caught sight of a familiar silvery shape looking large before him, swaying and rocking as the surface of the asteroid swayed and rocked. He was on the Twin, which must have already struck the first asteroid . . . and the *Space Pup* was only a few rods away!

He spread his body flat on the surface to keep from being tossed about as the two slabs of rock, suddenly thrown together with terrific force, danced a jog in space.

Where was Vernon? Had he landed? Or was he miles behind? As soon as the Twin struck, the first asteroid also must have been knocked out of its orbit. Both must now be rushing through space. If Vernon had not been close enough to be captured by the gravity of the two, he would now be somewhere out there in the darkness alone, and perhaps helpless.

A wave of illness swept over Vince at that thought. Would he be able to find him in time? Or would he only pick up a corpse, a man floating in space, dead from lack of air?

He raised his head to stare at the *Space Pup* and a cry of gladness welled up into his throat. A man was crawling toward him over the weaving surface. Vernon! His brother . . . safe!

Words beat in upon his.

"Vince, are you all right? Vince! Vince, you're all right, aren't you?"

"Sure, I'm all right, kid."

The two crawled together and locked arms.

"We took an awful chance, kid," said Vince.

"It was the only thing to do," replied Vernon. "We couldn't stay and be smashed in the collision."

Arm in arm, they crawled over the buckling, gyrating world toward the *Space Pup*.

GOOD NESTERS ARE DEAD NESTERS

This story was originally published in the July 1945 issue of .44 Western Magazine, *and I feel sure that it was not Clifford D. Simak who put the title "Good Nesters Are Dead Nesters!" on it—Cliff's journals are reasonably comprehensive for the period in which this story was written, and that title never appears in them.*

But in looking over those journals, I have noted that two of Cliff's Westerns seem to be good candidates for having gone through the metamorphosis of names I referred to: a story that Cliff called "Hate Ramrods a Lobo Range," for which he was paid $125 in 1945, and a story named "Sixguns Write the Law," for which he received $177 in 1944. The latter story seems the best candidate, since the hero of "Good Nesters" is a frontier lawyer. Moreover, while I do not know to whom "Hate Ramrods a Lobo Range" was sent, "Sixguns Write the Law" was sent to Popular Publications, *which was the company that published* .44 Western Magazine.

And this is going to sound strange, but . . . the thing that sticks with me most about this story is that the hero, Crane, just keeps on being wrong—he's not the kind of hero who gets it all right from the start.

—dww

Chapter One
Lawman—Keep Out!

She didn't move, just sat on the doorstep of the nester's shack and stared with hollow eyes across the emptiness of Coyote Flats.

Finally she spoke, "He just rode up and shot him," her voice was flat—flat with the grief and weariness of utter defeat.

Chester Crane swung off the big roan, stood for a moment looking from the woman to the sprawled figure on the dusty ground.

The woman spoke again and her voice was impersonal, a monotone, as if the crumpled man who lay there was someone she had never seen before. "He never done a thing. We was just trying to make ourselves a home. And then this man rode up . . ."

Her voice broke, but her face remained unchanged—a pinched and haggard face that seemed drained of life.

A child came timidly to the cabin door and stood beside the woman, staring at Crane with big, blue owl-like eyes.

"When did it happen?" Crane asked.

She seemed to see him for the first time, looking at him with eyes that were great hollows in her parchment face.

"You say your name is Crane?"

"That's right," Crane told her. "County attorney from over at Wildcat City. Just riding past . . ."

"You're a lawman?"

"Sort of," said Crane. "You see, I . . ."

For the first time her voice became human speech, lost the hollow emptiness: "They why don't you put a stop to things like this? Why do you let them kill us? We ain't done a thing. We got a right to be here. We ain't hurting no one. Ain't right that folks can ride up and kill us. Like we was dogs . . ."

Her voice broke again and for a moment Crane thought she was going to weep, almost wished she would, for this was unnatural. Unnatural that a woman should sit on a doorstep without a single tear and her man dead in the yard less than twenty feet away.

Crane strode across the yard, stooped to lift the dead man. The vest, he saw, was dyed with blood, and there was a jagged hole where the bullet had come out his back. Jack Robinson had been shot at close range by a heavy gun.

The body was heavy and Crane staggered with its weight. The woman stood aside to let him in the doorway.

Inside, the shack was wretched poverty. A stove, with one leg missing, was propped up on a stone. A rickety table stood in the center of the single room. Several boxes, which served in place of chairs, were pushed beneath it. In one corner of the room was a home-made bunk.

Carefully, Crane laid the body on the bunk, reached up and took a slicker from a peg, spread it across the body. The battered, worn boots of the dead man stuck out grotesquely from beneath the coat.

Mrs. Robinson had stepped inside, stood beside the table. The little girl was huddled against her, clutching at her skirt.

"What else can I do for you?" asked Crane. "I could hitch up your team and take you to a neighbor's."

She shook her head. "Just stop in somewhere and tell them what has happened. They will come and help me."

"One other thing," said Crane. "Did you see the man who did it?"

She nodded. "His name is Charley. He rides for the Angle O."

"Red-headed?"

She nodded and for the first time Crane saw the brightness of tears as she looked at him.

"That would be Charley Kirk," said Crane.

"I never knew his last name," she told him.

"But what are you going to do?" asked Crane. "You can't stay here."

"I don't know, mister," she said. "I ain't thought about it none. There just don't seem to be nothing I can do."

There was no brightness in her eyes now and the face was a mask again—a tight and terrible mask etched with loneliness and despair too deep for tears, too deep for anything but numbness.

"I'm sorry," said Crane. "I'll do everything I can."

But it was almost as if she didn't hear him.

On his horse, Crane looked back. The woman was sitting on the doorstep again and the little girl had climbed into her lap. Both of them were staring out across the flats.

The nearest cabin was a smudge on the horizon and Crane lifted the roan into a gallop, heading for it.

"Good Lord," Crane told himself, "it isn't human."

Unbelievable, almost. Unbelievable that a puncher, even Charley Kirk, should ride up and kill a man without provocation.

Made all the more unbelievable because Charley rode for Old John Fenton's Angle O. Fenton, Crane told himself, might be ornery and hard-fisted, but he wasn't the kind of man who would send out a hired hand to do his killing for him. If Fenton had wanted the nester killed he would have ridden out and done the job himself.

And, another thing Crane could not forget was that Old John Fenton was Betty Fenton's father.

Nick Gulick was perched on the top rail of a rickety corral when Crane pulled up his horse beside the shack. Smoke drooled upward into Gulick's left eye from the brown paper cigarette that dangled from his mouth.

"Howdy, Crane," he said, and there was a raspy purr to his voice that set Crane's nerves on edge.

"Something going on over at Robinson's?" he asked. "I heard a shot or two."

"Robinson's been killed," replied Crane. "Mrs. Robinson asked me to ride by and let you know."

Gulick sat silently on the fence, like a perching crow, black hat pulled down across his eyes.

"We'll have to figure out something for Mrs. Robinson," said Crane. "Looks like there isn't more than a meal or two ahead left in the house. And she's just sitting there . . ."

Gulick spat viciously in the dust. "We got to do something for all of us," he said. "Them damn cowmen act like they own the country. A good dose of lead is what they need."

"Wanted to talk to you about that," said Crane. "I'm trying to get some of the boys to come in to a meeting at the court house tonight. Talk this over. See if we can't figure out some way you fellows can get along together."

A sour grin twisted Gulick's face. "Forget about the meeting, friend." He patted the holstered gun hanging at his side.

"You're wrong there, Gulick," Crane told him, soberly. "More killings isn't the answer to what's wrong. Start a range war and all of you will be wiped out. That's what I'm trying to head off."

"We'll handle this ourselves—the feller who dry-gulched Robinson will be walking on air!"

Crane's words were cold and clipped: "I'm warning you, Gulick. You fellows do a rope job and I'll have you in and I'll do my level best to see that you're convicted."

"Mister," snarled Gulick, "you're spoiling the view. Get out of here. Now git pronto!"

"O.K.," Crane told him. "It's your land."

He wheeled the roan and headed westward.

What's the use, he thought. When even the nesters feel that way, what's the use of trying to iron the situation out. The cattlemen—they would be stiff-necked, of course, because they figured that the land was rightfully theirs and they had the guns to back up what they thought. But the nesters were a different proposition. Plowmen, farmers, sod busters—they weren't fighting men.

Crane shook his head, felt the weariness of the day upon him. He had ridden since morning, from ranch to ranch, from shack to shack, to tell about the meeting. And almost everywhere the answer had been the same. Polite evasion, open derision, downright skepticism.

There was something wrong, something deadly, a sinister thing that stalked the range.

The sun was low in the sky when Crane reached the short stretch of trail that ran though the badlands before climbing up to the higher plain and then Wildcat City.

Coming down the trail to meet him was a flapping figure on a mule.

Crane pulled to one side as the rider drew up to him.

"Hello, Sam," said Crane.

Sam Lee, Chinese cook at the Angle O, grinned at him.

"You miss him," he said. "Missy, she in town."

"Anything wrong?" asked Crane. "Anything happen at the ranch?"

"Boss say ranch no place for her," Sam told him. "Say all hell soon going to break loose."

He hammered the mule's ribs with his heels and the huge sleeves of his jacket flapped grotesquely.

"Get back quick," he explained. "Supper late again and they throw Sam in the horse tank."

The mule's ears bobbed, its feet stirred and Sam Lee moved down the trail.

Crane sat his horse staring after him and called. "At that rate of speed, they'll drown you, sure!"

Chapter Two
The Lid Is Off!

Sheriff Ed Lyon was crestfallen and disgusted. Ponderously, he edge his feet off the desk and dropped them to the floor.

"It does beat all hell," he said. "Just when I was settling down for some comfortable years."

"I'll get out a warrant," said Crane, "and you'll bring Charley in."

Sheriff Lyon stroked his mustache. "Cripes, you don't know what you're asking. Anything might happen. Somebody might be laying for me . . ."

"They won't be laying for you," Crane pointed out, "because they won't expect you."

"Look," argued the sheriff, "let us put it this way. Let's send out word to Charley that we'd like to see him. Maybe, after all, it wasn't him that done it. Can't believe a thing a woman says. No, sir, not a thing. Plumb flighty—all of them."

Crane pounded the desk with his fist. "You're going out and you're bringing Charley back! That country is a keg of dynamite and if Kirk gets away with one killing, there's apt to be a good deal more."

The sheriff shrugged himself to his feet. "Though you was going to settle it peaceable," he said accusingly. "Talking about a meeting, getting all the boys together . . ."

Crane shook his head. "I'm afraid it fizzled out. There won't be more than five or six. Bartley was the only one that seemed interested."

Sheriff Lyon belched good naturedly. "Fine fellow, that Bartley. Even if he is from the east. Gets along good with everyone. They all like him. Even loaned his neighbors money when the bank refused them."

"Where will I find you," asked Crane, "when I have the warrant made out?"

"Down at the Silver Slipper," the sheriff told him. "Got to fortify myself."

"Just be sure," Crane warned, "that you aren't petrified."

"Man can't go sheriffing without having himself a drink," Lyon declared.

Turning on his heel, Crane went out the door and down the steps.

Dusk had fallen and the stars were coming out. The business places along the street threw orange and yellow light across the sidewalk. The town seemed almost deserted.

Crane cursed under his breath, thinking about the sheriff. More than likely the old fool would go down to the Silver Slipper and get himself tanked up and then use that as an excuse for not going out.

Two strikes against you before you're even started, Crane told himself. A sheriff that isn't worth the powder to blow him plumb to hell and some strange undercurrent out there on the range—an undercurrent sweeping cattlemen and nesters toward a holocaust of hate.

Funny about that, he thought. Something there that one can't put his finger on. Some hidden factor . . .

He went up the stairs to his office above the bank two steps at a time, paused in astonishment when he saw light streaming from the open door.

A big bear of a man sat on a chair tilted in the corner and a girl was in the chair behind the desk.

John Fenton's chair bumped forward and he bellowed at Crane: "Come in, young fellow, come in."

Crane grinned. "Hello, John," he said.

He nodded to the girl. "I met Sam on the trail. He said that you were here."

She smiled at him. "You have a nice office, Chet. It's the first time I have seen it."

It wasn't nice, Crane knew, but it pleased him to hear her say it. Some day, maybe, it would be a nice place, with shelves of law books and leather chairs and a desk that wasn't all nicked and marred and burned from forgotten cigarets.

John Fenton sat straight in his chair, legs spread wide, hands planted on his knees. His gold watch chain was looped across his paunch and the handkerchief he wore around his neck had slid over to one side. The single gun he carried sagged beside the chair.

"Can't spend much time," he said. "Got to be getting back. Just dropped in to have a word with you."

"I was hoping you were staying for the meeting," Crane told him.

Fenton shook his head. "That's what I'm here about. Got to pondering over it after you had left. Better forget about the meeting, son."

"But why?" asked Crane. "Certainly you want to . . ."

"Sure, I do," Fenton told him. "Sure, I'd like to see it settled without gunsmoke. But it can't be done. It's coming, no matter what you do. And you're hurting yourself by mixing into it. The folks won't understand. The nesters will think you're siding the ranchers and the ranchers will swear you're throwing in with the nesters. You can't win either way—you got to keep out of it."

"John, I can't do that," Crane said slowly. "If I did I'd be laying down on my job. The people of this county elected me to help to keep the peace. And I'm going to do just that! When a man is killed, that's murder. You may look at it different, but to me it's murder."

Fenton's face flushed red and his jaw thrust out. "You're a damn fool," he shouted. "I come here and try to set you straight and you preach to me like this!"

"Thanks for your good intentions, anyhow," said Crane.

"They'll come in here and ride you out on a rail," yelled Fenton. "If you interfere . . ."

Crane snapped at him angrily. "Interfere! You mean that you aren't going to let anything interfere with this little range war you are cooking up? You figure that it's your right to go out and shoot up the nesters?"

"None of them have been shot yet," snarled Fenton. "Shot at, maybe, and threatened some."

"One of them was shot this afternoon," said Crane, "and I'm drawing up a warrant to arrest the man who did it."

Fenton stared at him, blind with rage.

"Kirk," said Crane, slowly. "Charley Kirk—one of your men."

Fenton stormed to his feet. "I don't believe it, Crane."

Crane shrugged his shoulders. "I have an eyewitness who will testify in court."

"You're crazy," shrieked Fenton. "You'll never arrest him."

"But I will," Crane told him. "See that he's there when Lyon comes to get him. I'm holding you responsible for producing him. And be sure that Lyon comes back. I don't want a thing to happen to him."

Fenton clenched his weather beaten, rope-tough fists. "If it weren't for my daughter, I'd give you . . ."

"Father!" said Betty softly. "Father, you calm down. Both of you should be ashamed."

Fenton turned brusquely on his heel and strode toward the door. Crane swung around to face the girl.

He shook his head. "It can't be helped, I guess. I'm sorry it had to be your dad."

"You must be terribly busy," Betty told him, "getting out that warrant."

She came around the desk and walked toward the door. Crane stood and watched her go, listened to her footsteps go down the hall and stairs.

Crane walked behind the desk, sat down slowly.

Good Lord, he thought, it can't be Fenton. It simply can't be Fenton who is behind all this. And yet it had been one of Fenton's men who had killed Robinson.

He opened a drawer, selected the proper form, laid it on his desk, reached for the pen.

Half an hour later Crane found Sheriff Lyon bending an elbow at the Silver Slipper, got him aboard a horse and headed in the right direction. Then he went to the town's one and only restaurant for some food.

Night had fallen when he came out of the restaurant and walked toward the courthouse. The town was quiet—quiet and strangely empty.

A dim figure rose from the courthouse steps and made room for him. Crane sat down, staring at the man.

"Bartley," he said. "Glad that you came. Don't look like any of the others did."

The tiny night breeze rustled the one lone tree that stood in the courthouse yard. From down in the badlands came the hooting of an owl.

Bartley took off his spectacles, polished them with a handkerchief.

"I wouldn't brood over it," he said. "You did your best. It's not your fault you failed. These men, every one of them, are obsessed with the conviction they are right. The cattlemen were here first and they took the land and held it, figured it was theirs.

"And now the government tells them it's not. They are told that it belongs to anyone who wants to file on it and carry out the requisites set down by the homestead law. So the cattlemen stand aside and see their water holes grabbed up, see the grass their cattle fed on turned over by the plow."

Crane nodded, listening to the smooth eastern speech of the man who sat beside him.

"If someone could just get them together and talk sense to them," he said. "There isn't one of them that's vicious. There's not a single killer among the lot of them."

Bartley put the spectacles back on again.

"I know it," he said. "It's just that each one thinks he's right. The nester knows he's right because he's backed by law and the cattleman knows he's right because he's convinced the law is wrong."

They sat silently, listening to the wind in the one lone tree, to the owl down in the badlands.

Finally Crane stirred uneasily. "Guess there's no one coming," he said. "I should have known they wouldn't."

Hoofs suddenly pounded from the far end of the street, came nearer.

Crane leaped to his feet.

A lathered horse came storming down the street in a cloud of dust, a swaying man clutching at the saddle. As he watched, Crane saw the man totter, almost fall, clutch at the saddlehorn and keep his seat.

With a single spring, Bartley was out in the street, leaping at the fleeing animal, hand reaching for the bridle. The hand closed and hauled savagely, swung the horse's head around. Bartley's heels plowed through the dust, leaving long gouges.

The man in the saddle swayed, bent in the middle, grasped at the horn and missed.

Crane ran to catch him, eased him to the ground.

Bending he peered into the sweat-streaked face, felt the stickiness of blood seeping through the dust-stained shirt.

The man croaked at him.

"All hell's broke loose," he said.

"Here," Crane yelled at Bartley. "Help me with him."

Bartley released the horse and the animal trotted down the street and stopped, reins dragging.

"It's Gamble," said Bartley softly. "Gamble from the Lazy M."

Men were running down the sidewalk, racing across the street.

"We'll have to get him to the doctor," said Crane.

"All gone," Gamble whispered at them. "All gone. Haystacks burning. Buildings gone . . ."

Crane gazed across the man at Bartley.

"It's started," Bartley said.

Crane straightened, spoke to the men who stood in a circle around them.

"Get him to the doctor, fellows. I have work to do."

Bartley already was racing down the street, long legs pumping like two busy pistons, guns flapping at his hips.

A hand gripped Crane's sleeve and he swung around.

Betty Fenton, shawl tied around her head, looked up at hm.

"What's happened, Chet?" she cried. "Who was that?"

"That was Gamble," Crane told her. "He was burned out."

He started to move away and she ran after him.

"Chet, where are you going?"

"To see your dad," he said. "Maybe I can talk some sense into him. Maybe he can stop this."

"I'm going with you." Her voice was almost sobbing.

He swung about and faced her.

"You're staying here," he said, grimly.

"But, Chet . . ."

He swung around, ran for the office. He had to get his gun, get to the livery stable as soon as the Lord would let him.

Chapter Three
Death to the Invader!

On top of the break where the plain surged down into the badlands spur, Crane hauled the roan to a halt. He sat and looked out across the black gulf that was Coyote Flats.

A darkness that was specked by tiny flecks of red.

The moon was just below the eastern horizon and spread a faint glow across the eastern sky. But the moon-glow was not the only light. Other glows were reflected in the sky—red, angry lights that marked the sites of ranch and homestead.

Burning haystacks, burning buildings, burning homes! The quick crack of the rifle in the night, the sudden coughing of a hidden gun—and then the roll of hoofs back into the blackness.

He had but one slim chance to make his play. Time to back his puny hand to the very limit. If that failed, there would be hell to pay tomorrow, for this was just a starter. Tonight there were buildings and a few stray shootings, but tomorrow would bring the payoff when grim-lipped men rode to exact bloody vengeance for the ashes that had been homes.

Carne started down the trail, plunging into the darkness of the fantastic badlands, going slowly, picking his way, sure-footed as a cat.

Crane heard what might have been a shot. The horse shied and stopped. Crane bent forward, staring into the blackness. Something moved out there, just beyond the horse's head, and Crane's hand dropped to grasp the holstered gun.

"Crane?"

"That's right," said Crane. "Who are you?"

"Just one of the boys," said the shadow, and the words had a raspy sound that set Crane's nerves on edge.

"What do you want?" demanded Crane.

"Just warning you," the voice rasped. "This is as far as you go. You better turn around."

Suddenly Crane knew the man. It was the same man that had ordered him off his land—Gulick, the nester.

"I got a gun," said Gulick, "and I ain't a-mind to fool. You better turn around and head back for Wildcat."

Crane's hand tightened on the gun, drew it free of leather.

"Gulick, I'm coming through. Don't try to stop me!"

The nester's voice rose to a high-pitched shriek. "I'm warning you . . ."

Crane raked the roan with his spurs, hauled back on the reins. The roan leaped, striking viciously at the shadow that barred the trail.

Gulick screamed and the roan was thundering down the trail, stumbling in the dark, catching himself, regaining his balance.

A rifle bawled from above and Crane, bending low, face almost against the horse's flying mane, heard the sullen whine of the bullet overhead. The rifle spoke again and again, churning with a deadly yammer as Gulick worked the lever.

The roan checked himself with stiff legged jumps, swung around a turn, cantered down an incline, crossed a brook and trotted up a rise.

Crane was puzzled. Why should Gulick be laying for him? If anyone should regard him as their friend it should be the nesters, for on other ranges the cattle outfits had risen and driven the nesters out without the law so much as raising its eyebrows. He had tried to help them.

Someone must have posted Gulick there. That was the only answer. Someone who wanted to see this range war started and carried out to its bitter end. Someone who would profit by it.

Crane's busy mind groped for answers, found none. Nothing but a blank wall of contradictions. Someone who wanted to see the range burst into flaming war had posted Gulick there—and had posted him because he knew Crane would be riding that way.

The roan shied suddenly, dancing off the path.

"Something scare you, boy?" asked Crane—and then he saw it, the huddled patch of blackness that lay beside the trail.

For a long moment, Crane sat the horse, staring at the thing. Then, slowly, he swung from the saddle, approached it and knelt down.

It was a man, he saw, but the darkness hid the face. Finding a match, he flicked the sulphur head across his thumbnail, held the cupped flame in his hand.

The light flickered, throwing tiny shadows. Slowly Crane lowered it toward the face of the man lying in the trail, gasped at what he saw.

The dead face of Sheriff Ed Lyon stared back at him and the dancing shadows of the flickering match made it appear the sheriff's lips were twisting, so that it seemed he tried to speak.

Crane's hand shook and the match went out. He fumbled for another one, took long seconds before he found it and snapped it across his thumb.

The sheriff was dead. There was no doubt of that. There was a tiny, bluish hole just above his left eye.

And as he stared at the ashy face, Crane remembered the last thing the sheriff had told him:

"*You don't know what you're asking. Anything might happen. They might be laying for me.*"

Something twitched at Crane's sleeve and a whiplash report burst the night wide open.

The match flame leaped and fluttered, then snuffed out and the rifle spoke again, its muzzle flash flaring from across the gully.

Crane hurled himself to one side, hauling at his gun.

The rifle chugged again with an angry cough and pebbles jumped and rattled where the bullet struck.

Hunkered on the slope below the trail, Crane jerked up his gun and squeezed the trigger, shooting at the spot of blackness where the muzzle flash had been.

But even as he fired, Crane knew that the man with the rifle would be no longer there—that somewhere out in the darkness he was crawling closer, running catfooted along the talus of the slope.

Crane leaped to his feet, staggered up the slope toward the trail. Hoofs stamped above him and he made for the sound, collided against a furry wall that nickered at him.

Clawing for the saddle, Crane found it, felt the horse lifting into a lope even as he swung to leather.

Crouching low, Crane waited for the whiplike crack of Gulick's rifle, but it did not come.

Half a mile farther on the trail left the badlands, swung out onto Coyote Flats. The eastern sky was a mighty lantern with the moon just behind the farthest hills and to the south a garish flame curled toward the sky—a haystack going up. Even as Crane watched, the flame died down and became an ember glowing in the dark.

The roan stretched out, glad to leave the badlands behind. Crane kept a close watch of the night. There were riding men out here on the flats who would shoot at anything that moved and there was no sense of taking chances.

From the north came a spatter of shots, thinned by the distance and the wind.

The country became broken again and Coyote Flats was left behind. Just ahead lay the Angle O.

Crane swung the big roan down a timbered gully, slowed to a walk. Wouldn't do, he told himself, to come in with a rush. Anyone who did that tonight was simply asking for it.

The timber ended and Crane hauled the roan to a sudden halt. The ranch buildings were gone and in their place tiny wisps of smoke curled upward in the moonlight.

Fenton had been burned out and that meant there wasn't a chance in the world to get any help from him. All hell wouldn't stop the old rancher now from wiping out every nester that came before his guns.

Crane sat in the saddle, staring at the piles of ashes, at the three sprawled bodies which lay between what had been the house and the big hay barn.

The smell of woodsmoke was strong in Crane's nostrils and the moonlight gave the place a ghostly look.

Slowly he got down from the roan, walked to the three bodies one by one, staring at them, apprehension and the strong sense of defeat growing with every step he took. If one of these men were John Fenton . . .

But none of them was. He recognized one of them as an Angle O puncher, the other two were strangers.

It was all over, he knew. All over as far as he was concerned. He might just as well ride back to town and stay there. There was nothing left that he could do.

A soft sound brought him swinging around, hand dropping to his gun. But there was nothing. The ashes lay beneath the moonlight and the three dead men stared startled at the sky.

Gun half drawn, he strode back to the roan, skin crawling on his back.

Shoulders hunched, he sat in the saddle and thought, his mind confused and twisted.

He jerked erect at a new sound, the distant sound of hoof beats coming through the timber of the gully. Hoof beats coming fast.

Crane swung the roan around, unlimbered his gun and waited. A running horse burst from the timber and headed toward him and the moonlight made the rider's head a shower of molten gold.

"Betty!" cried Crane.

She screamed—then stopped abruptly.

Crane spurred forward, grasped her horse's bridle. The girl seemed scarcely to see him. She sat frozen in the saddle, staring at the ruins.

"Betty," he said softly and she looked at him, eyes wide with terror.

"Those men," she cried. "Those men on the ground!"

He shook his head. "Nobody that we know."

He saw relief flood across her face.

"Dad?" she asked.

"He isn't here," Crane told her. "There's no one here."

Soft feet padded behind him and Crane swung around. Sam Lee trotted toward them, slippers slapping in the dust, wide sleeves flapping.

"Missy, missy," he chanted in a high pitched squeak. "What you here for?"

"I had to come," she told him. "I heard about the trouble and I had to come."

Crane, watching her, saw that she was close to tears.

"You shouldn't have," he told her, almost angrily. "That's what your dad took you into town for. So that you wouldn't be here when the shooting started. He wanted you out of the way—he was afraid . . ."

A sudden thought struck him. "You came through the badlands?"

She nodded.

"There was no one there? No one stopped you?"

"I didn't see a soul," she said.

Her hand reached out and clutched his sleeve. "Oh, Chet, just look at it."

Crane sat, staring at the ashes that had been a ranch house, the dull eyes of fire still shining at him. Beside him the girl was sobbing quietly.

"Everything gone," she said. "Poor Dad. Poor Dad."

"He'll rebuild again," Crane told her, trying to be comforting. "He's bucked worse things than this before."

"But we don't have any money, Chet," the girl protested. "Last fall Dad counted on ten carloads of cattle and there were only four."

"Rustlers," said Crane, remembering how the ranges had been cleaned.

"Nesters," she corrected and her voice was bitter with the savage bitterness of any cattleman.

Crane stirred in his saddle. "We can't stay here," he said, "and town's a long ways off. This range is filled with men and guns."

The girl was silent.

"Bartley would put us up," said Crane, "if he still has a place."

He swung his horse and the girl followed. Swiftly the horses trotted for the timber.

Once out of the timber, the country was flooded with the molten moonlight. The night was quiet, giving no hint of the savage forces that were abroad.

Crane and the girl rode silently, heading for the Bartley spread. Betty sobbed quietly at times, remembering the devastation that had struck the Angle O. Crane thought, chin sunk on his chest.

He had been wrong in suspecting Fenton as the man behind the range war, he admitted to himself. There could be no better proof of that than the burned out ranch.

The Bartley buildings still were standing, although two haystacks still glowed, the smouldering fire dimmed by the heavy pile of ash.

Crane and the girl rode slowly down the slope toward the ranch. A horseman rode out from the barns and sat in his saddle waiting them.

"Who is it?" he shouted.

"Crane and Betty Fenton. That you, Nordby?"

Frank Nordby, Bartley's foreman, spurred forward.

"What's happening out on the range?" he asked.

"Fenton's place is wiped out," Crane told him. "I don't know about the others. Saw some fires when I was riding in."

"They tried to get us," said Nordby, "but we were waiting for them. They fired a couple of stacks but we drove them off before they got the buildings."

He spoke to Betty. "Sorry, ma'm, to hear about your place."

Crane said: "We figured maybe Bartley would let us stay here until morning. It's a long ride back to town."

"Sure," said Nordby. "Glad to. He's down at the house. Ask my wife to fix you up some chow."

He pulled to a halt when they came opposite the barns. "I have to stay here," he said. "Some of the boys are helping me watch. You go on down."

In the shadow of the hay barn a match flared briefly as it lit a cigarette. A man's voice grumbled and then a short, vicious laugh.

Nordby wheeled away and Crane and the girl rode on toward the ranch house.

"Chet," Betty whispered.

"What is it?"

"That man who laughed. It sounded like Charley Kirk."

"Charley—You must be wrong. What would Kirk be doing here?"

Betty's voice wavered. "Maybe I was wrong. But for a minute it sounded like him."

Mrs. Nordby answered their knock at the door and let them in.

"Land sakes alive," she squealed. "Do come right in, Betty, I ain't seen you in a . . ."

A voice came from inside the house. "Who's that?"

Before she could answer Bartley was at the door of his office, across the hall from the living room, his huge frame blocking out the light that came from the open door.

"Oh, Crane," he said. "Glad to see you. And you, Miss Fenton. Won't you come on in. We'll talk while Mrs. Nordby rustles up some coffee."

He led the way into the office and closed the door.

"A bad night," he told them. "An extremely bad night."

"Fenton's burned out," Crane told him. "And there were a lot of other fires."

Bartley shook his head. "Too bad. This will set back the country a good five years or more. If they only would have listened to reason—That chair over there, Miss Fenton. You will find it comfortable. Cigar, Crane?"

Crane shook his head, sank into a chair. "Just want to rest," he said. "Rest and think. Try to figure it out. You know, Bartley, there is something wrong. Something more than just a clash between nesters and ranchers. I've been trying to figure it out."

Bartley stood spraddle-legged in the center of the room, hands behind his back, cigar clenched viciously in his mouth.

"You know, Crane, I like this country. And when I think of what tonight has done . . ."

He stopped suddenly.

Crane settled back in the chair, let his eyes run about the room. Shelves of books, the heavy desk littered with papers, a small iron safe crouched in one corner.

The door burst open and a man stood in it, a man with a black hat pulled low, almost to his eyes.

"Say, boss," he blurted. "I . . ."

His words cut off and he gulped, staring at Crane.

Bartley wheeled on him angrily. "You damn fool, don't you know better . . ."

He caught himself, turned back slowly to the two within the room.

"Please pardon me," he said softly. "I will be back directly."

Crane sat frozen, staring at Gulick, who was slowly backing from the doorway as Bartley strode toward it. And as he stared, the tumbling questions that swirled within his brain suddenly clicked together and he had the answer.

Chapter Four
Range War Maker

So Bartley was the man behind it all. . . . Bartley was the one who had set Gulick to watch the badlands trail and turn him back. And now it all was clear—clear that it had to be Bartley and no one else. For Bartley was the only one who could have known he would ride that trail.

I can't be mistaken, Crane told himself. Unbelievable as it may be, I simply can't. For it all fits together. Gulick out there watching the trail and then Gulick stepping into this room and calling Bartley boss.

Gulick—and the man who had laughed out there at the barn when they were coming in. The man that Betty had said sounded like Kirk. It was Kirk, of course. For Kirk would be Bartley's man, just as Gulick was. Men Bartley had hired to stir up trouble on the range, men to set the ranchers and the nesters at one another's throats.

"What is the matter, Chet?" Betty's voice came low and tense across the room.

Crane came out of the chair, stood staring at the iron safe in the corner.

"Betty," he said. "Betty, tell me. Did Bartley ever lend your dad some money?"

"Yes, he did. Two thousand dollars. After Dad found he was short of shipping stock."

"And how was it to be paid? A note. Just a promise . . ."

"A mortgage," Betty told him. "Dad insisted on that. Said it was the only way to do business. The bank had turned him down, you see."

The bank turned him down, Crane knew, because it knew his range was stripped. But Bartley loaned him the money, knowing when he loaned it that Fenton never could pay back, that he, Bartley, would see to it that he could never pay.

And now, with his buildings gone, Fenton would come to his good friend Bartley to tell him he couldn't pay—that he even needed a bigger loan than he already had. And Bartley, in his suave, eastern voice, would say that he was sorry, but conditions had changed and he needed the two thousand he had already loaned. . . .

"Look, Betty," said Crane swiftly. "Bartley has loaned money to just about everyone in this whole country. The mortgages, more than likely, are in that safe over in the corner. Now he's trying to ruin them with a range war so they can't pay him back . . ."

"But," the girl protested, "Bartley is our friend . . ."

She stopped short, staring at Crane with fear-widened eyes. Her fingers nervously spun an ink well standing on the desk.

"Chet, the man who laughed out there by the barn. He was the man who killed the nester. The man who started . . ."

Crane nodded. "Exactly. He set the whole thing off. Bartley told him to."

Crane spun on his heel, stalked to the door and jerked it open, then froze, staring at the small, black, wicked mouth of the sixgun that pointed at his stomach's pit.

Behind the gun Charley Kirk's face twisted in a grimace of ironic glee.

"All right, Crane," he said, "this is what I was laying for. Knew that sooner or later you'd come charging out like a red-flagged bull. Unbuckle that gun belt of yours and toss it out to me."

Slowly Crane lifted his hands to the buckle of the belt.

"Hurry up," snarled Kirk. "Get a hustle on."

Beyond Kirk, in the living room, stood Bartley, with his back to the huge stone fireplace, the cigar still in his mouth, a grin upon his face. Beside him stood Gulick, watching, but unsmiling.

Trapped, thought Crane. Trapped, neat without a chance.

Kirk took a quick step forward, hand reaching out, his face a twisted snarl.

"Do I have to tear it off . . ."

Crane heard the whistle of the thing that went past his head, heard the crunch as it struck Kirk full in the face and sent him reeling back into the hall, his face streaked with running black.

The ink well bounced upon the floor, spewing ink along the rug.

In the living room Bartley was diving for the floor and Gulick's arm was pistoning for the sixgun at his side. With a swift, sure motion, Crane's hand swept back, freed his own gun of leather, brought it spinning out.

A table crashed, hit by Bartley's shoulder, and the lamp which sat upon it went smashing out into the center of the room.

Gulick's gun spit fire and a bullet crunched into the door casing just above Crane's head. Crane snapped a quick shot at the crouching man, shooting in the flaring light of the flaming oil that ran swiftly along the rug from the shattered lamp.

Gulick's gun snarled wickedly and Crane felt the wind of the lead as it plunged past to smack into the wall.

"Betty!" yelled Crane.

"Here I am, Chet."

He flicked his gaze to one side for a single second, saw her crouched against the wall, handing reaching for the gun that Kirk had dropped.

"Down the hall!" he shouted at her. "Out the back way."

Crouched, he squinted into the flames that danced through the living room, saw Bartley leaping through an open window, Gulick still hunched against the fireplace, gun up, his face an ugly leer in the flickering light.

The sixgun snarled and Crane flinched at the spear of pain that ran along his ribs where the bullet scraped.

He jerked his own gun up, but the flames leaped up and hid the man who crouched beside the fireplace.

On the floor Kirk groaned and sat up, hand groping for his gun. Crane swung and struck, gun barrel whistling. Kirk fell back, sprawled in a grotesque heap.

"I guess," said a soft voice behind him, "I didn't hit him hard enough."

Crane grunted. "That ink well was a swell idea," he said.

He reached out his hand to the girl.

"Quick," he told her. "We got to vamoose . . . get out of here."

Outside Bartley's voice was bellowing orders . . . orders for men to put out the fire . . . orders for men to cover the back of the house . . .

"Run!" gasped Crane.

Something flicked past Crane's throat, scarcely brushing the skin, like the dull blade of a knife had been stroked across it swiftly. A sledge hammer hit him in the leg and the world was a spinning thing of snarling faces, of shouting mouths, of belching guns.

Slowly he fought his way back, dimly conscious of the dragging seconds that marched by—hearing from far away a single voice with a note of hysteria. . . .

Fighting, he forced his eyelids open, saw the moonlight that lay upon the boards. His hand moved, feeling of the boards, inching along with groping fingers reaching—fingers that touched something that was not board, something that was cold and smooth, metal-like.

Slowly his fingers crept around it, closed around it, tightened. A gun, his brain told him—a gun.

The voice came again:

"I'll shoot—one of you make a move toward me and I'll shoot!"

Crane twisted his head, saw the girl standing on the porch, not more than six feet away, her back against the house, gun in her hand.

Beyond her, at one end of the porch, stood a ring of men—waiting for the girl to waver.

His hand tightened on the gun, drew it closer, inch by inch.

At the other end of the porch a man moved, swiftly, like a striking snake, leaping toward the girl.

Crane's finger squeezed the trigger with a vicious pressure and the gun jumped in his hand. The leaping man jerked in midstride, was falling back, like a straight tree falling. His head cracked as he hit the porch. This must have been the gun someone else dropped—for his gun was empty.

The girl screamed: "Chet!" The knot of men suddenly swirled forward, then were staggering and stumbling while out in the moonlight a single gun coughed steadily—a husky cough.

With a yell, Crane surged to his feet, wabbled unsteadily, one leg stiff and sore. At the end of the porch men were going over the railing while the husky gun still kept up its throaty rattle.

Then the porch was empty and five bodies lay where three had been before.

"Missy!" yelled a high-pitched voice. "Missy, run!"

Crane wheeled around, saw the scarecrow figure of Sam Lee standing in the yard. Smoke trailed from the muzzle of the tiny gun almost hidden in his hand.

"Missy, run!" he shrilled again.

The girl was beside Crane, her voice anxious. "Chet, are you all right?"

He shoved at her. "Get going. I'm all right."

His leg was like a dead weight as he ran. The cook, he saw, was heading toward a lop-eared mule that waited with drooping head and canted hips.

A rifle bellowed from the ranch house and kicked up a shower of dust just ahead of Crane. Other guns rattled and snarled and ahead of Crane the girl stumbled and went down.

Breath sobbing in his throat, fear squeezing at his heart, Crane ran toward the huddled gingham figure. Kneeling beside her, he pulled at her shoulder, saw the dark streak that ran across her temple.

"Betty!" he cried. "Betty!" She did not answer. A tiny trickle of darkness ran across her cheek.

Feet padded and Crane looked up. Sam Lee was coming back.

Crane yelled fiercely at him: "Go back, Sam. Find Fenton. Tell him Bartley's the man he wants . . ."

For a moment the cook stood uncertainly, then swung around and galloped for the mule. Gently, Crane lifted the girl in his arms, staggered to his feet, stood unsteadily with a dull dread and terror washing over him.

Hoofs pounded briefly and then were gone. Sam Lee was on his way.

Stiffly, swinging his wounded leg to clear the ground, Crane walked back toward the ranch house. Men were running toward him, but he did not falter. He recognized the man who was in the lead of those running toward him and he stopped and waited, drawing the girl's body close against his chest.

Bartley halted six feet away, directly in front of him and Bartley's men circled to both sides, watching Crane out of the corners of their eyes.

"I'm sorry, Crane," said Bartley. "Sorry that Miss . . ."

"Bartley," said Crane, dully, "if she's dead, I'll kill you!"

"Shut up!" a voice rasped.

"You're mistaken, Crane," said Bartley, softly. "Your killing days are over."

One of the men stepped forward, took the girl from Crane's arms. He stared into her face a long time.

"She ain't dead, mister," he said.

"Take her to the house," snarled Bartley. "Have Mrs. Nordby take care of her."

The voice behind Crane asked. "Shall I let him have it, boss?"

"Not yet, Gulick," said Bartley. "I want to talk to him."

Chapter Five
Live and Die By the Gun

Crane stood before the desk in Bartley's office. In the chair behind it, Bartley lolled, cleaning his fingernails with a pocket knife.

"I suppose," said Bartley, "that you figure I'm plenty sore at you. You killed some of my men and you set fire to the house and you raised hell in general. And I suppose you sent the Chinaman to get word to Fenton. But that doesn't matter. None of it matters. My men by this time have probably shot the Chink and we put the fire out. So everything's all right. I hold all the aces. You must do as I say."

He stared at Crane and Crane saw that his eyes were opaque, devoid of any lustre or expression—the eyes of a poker player and a killer.

"Go on," snarled Crane. "Next thing you'll be telling me is that you and I are pals."

Bartley sighed. "Crane, you've got brains and I like a man with brains."

"You do all right yourself," Crane told him bitterly. "You had everybody fooled. All the nice, subtle touches. Even set fire to a couple of your haystacks so it looked as if someone had tried to get you, too."

Bartley closed the knife, put it in his pocket, sat straight in the chair.

"You know, Crane, we could go a long ways if we pulled together. Why don't you just go back to town. Take Miss Fenton with you. I'll see to it that you get along. County attorney now, judge a little later, after that a senator."

Crane shifted his weight off the wounded leg. "You can guarantee that, Bartley?"

"Hell, yes. There's nothing to it. I'm not stopping with this valley. Once I have it, there are other things to do. Honestly, Crane, you western folks are simple. Easy for a man like me. Why I ever spent all those years in the east trying to get along when there were pickings like this here is something I'll never understand."

"And you want me to go along?"

Bartley nodded.

"All I have to do is keep my mouth shut?"

"That's all," Bartley told him. "That and doing a few things for me when I need them done."

"How about Betty?"

"She keeps her mouth shut, too. That's part of the bargain. You marry her and she'd have to keep still then. Can't involve her husband in a thing like this."

He waved his hand. "Hell, I'll even do more than that. I'll tear up her old man's mortgage. Or I'll buy him out for more than the place is worth."

"Just supposing," suggested Crane, "that I don't go for it? Suppose I tell you that the deal is off?"

"You won't," Bartley told him, easily. "I'm offering you a chance you'll never get again. You forced my hand, of course, but it's one of those things that happen. Things a man must be ready for."

"But, suppose . . ."

"Crane," said Bartley, "if you refuse, neither you nor the girl will get back to town alive."

Hoofs thundered across the yard, came to a skidding halt. Bartley half rose from his chair, facing toward the door. Running feet drummed across the porch, burst into the hall.

"Boss," yelled the running man. "Boss, he got away!"

Bartley's face suddenly was white—parchment white with anger, and his voice was a whiplash that snarled across the room.

"Who got away?"

It was Kirk, Crane saw. Kirk, standing in the doorway, red hair sticking up inside a bloody bandage wound around his head.

"The Chink," gasped Kirk. "He got into the badlands and we lost him. The boys are still out hunting . . ."

"Damn you," roared Bartley, "didn't I tell you to shoot him. Cut him down on sight . . . didn't I . . ."

Crane spun on his heel to face the open window, took one swift step and hurled himself toward the opening in a long, smooth leap. His stiff leg, dragging, caught the sill and threw him off his balance so that he stumbled as he struck the ground beneath.

Behind him he heard Bartley's bellow of anger and the swift beat of running feet.

Before him a figure suddenly loomed, a running man with a drawn gun. Crane hurled himself in a fierce, slashing block, felt the impact of his body cut the man's legs from beneath him. On hands and knees Crane jumped to his feet, saw the shine of the gun where it had been dropped and pounced to scoop it up.

The man he had hit was scrambling to his knees, growling in his throat.

A gun crashed and a bullet plowed a dusty furrow across the yard. Kirk, red hair bristling in the moonlight, was coming down the porch steps, slowly and deliberately, and his smoking sixgun was leveled for a second shot.

Crane snapped up the gun he held, worked the trigger. Splinters leaped in a spray from the step beside Kirk's knee.

The gun in Kirk's hand blinked with a fiery eye and a twitching hand plucked at Crane's sleeve.

The gun jerked up in his hand and steadied and his finger closed against the trigger. Then the gun spat and jumped and Kirk was stumbling down the steps, as if he had missed his footing.

Feet scuffed behind him and Crane swung around, saw the man to whom the gun belonged charging, with his head lowered and his long arms reaching out.

Crane danced aside, one leg dragging, brought down the gun as one outstretched, groping hand brushed against his coat. The gun barrel spatted viciously against the hatted head and the charging man crumpled in the dust.

A gun blasted from the doorway of the ranch house and Crane heard the soft whisper of lead as the bullet whined past. Feet were coming through the night, thumping feet that ran. Over by the barn a bull-like voice roared out an oath.

Crane ran, twisting, across the yard. Before him loomed a canted stock tank and he plunged behind it, lay huddled against the steel, listening to the thump of feet and the shouting voices.

A bullet hit the edge of the tank and richocheted away with a banshee howl. Another punched through the bottom, left a jagged hole. Crane forced his body against the ground.

It was a fool play, he told himself. Something he should not have done. He should have stayed back there in the office and talked with Bartley, should have taken the proposition that he made.

For now he didn't have a chance. The tank would not stop bullets and with his game leg he wasn't worth a hoot for running. It would be just a matter of time, he knew, before they smoked him out—either that, or until some lucky shot, punching through the steel, caught him where it counted.

A goner, for sure, that was what he was. And not himself alone, but Betty as well. Betty upstairs in the ranch house with Mrs. Nordby.

If he'd said yes to Bartley, he and Betty could have ridden back to town, safe at last from this night of fire and smoke—with the promise of a judgeship and later on a senator—a senator with Bartley's crooked power behind him.

A sixgun bellowed and a bullet punched another hole through the bottom of the tank.

Pretty soon they'll flank me, Crane told himself. Come creeping up from both sides while those in front keep me pinned down by firing at the tank.

Bartley's voice lifted in the night:

"Crane, come out of there. You haven't got a chance. Come out and we'll forget all about it."

Crane huddled close against the tank, the words ringing in his ears.

A second chance—a chance to get himself out of this mess. A chance to get that judgeship and to be a senator. A chance to save Betty and to marry her.

"Go to hell," Crane roared.

Bartley's answer was smooth and soft. "All right, you asked for it."

Quietly, Crane drew his feet beneath him, crouching. Four shots. He had four shots left in the gun and he would come out smoking. He would come out in the open and he'd get Bartley and maybe Gulick before the bullets cut him down. He'd die like a man, on both his feet instead of hiding behind a tank.

A sixgun banged down toward the barn—and then another. A man shouted. Hoofs drummed and were drowned out by the crash of sixguns.

Crane leaped free of the tank.

Moonlight made the yard almost like daylight and men were running desperately for shelter while other men, mounted on horses, were sweeping in from the barn with sixguns flaming.

Running, twisting like a hunted rabbit, with a mounted man no more than six jumps behind him, a man was heading toward Crane . . . heading toward Crane without seeing him. A hunted man running from the breath of death.

The sixgun in the hand of the mounted man spat and the fleeing runner stumbled, hit the ground like an empty sack. The mounted man's gun came up again and Crane, frozen in his tracks, saw death in the deadly bore that came in line with him.

Then the horse reared, hoof slashing in the moonlight and the gun came up in a gesture of salute.

"John!" yelled Crane and John Fenton yelled back something that Crane could not make out.

Fenton was racing back toward the barn and Crane stood,

weak kneed, staring after him. One second more and that gun would have blazed and there'd been no chance of missing. John Fenton would have killed him without knowing who he was.

The gunfire down at the barn was slackening and voices were shouting to holed-up men to come out with their hands above their heads.

"So Sam got through," thought Crane. "Sam and his lop-eared mule. A wonderful lot, these Chinese."

The ranch house door creaked and a man came swiftly across the porch.

"Bartley!" yelled Crane.

Bartley, headed for the horse, swung in mid-stride and for a frozen second the two stood staring across the space of a dozen feet.

The man's hand was moving like a striking snake—flashing for his gun. Crane swung up his own gun even as moonlight struck fire on Bartley's leaping from the holster.

The two shots were almost like one, one single crash of hate that rolled across the night. Crane felt the tiny whisper of wind that was a bullet going past his cheek and pressed the trigger again, then eased up, letting the hammer back.

Out in the yard Bartley was folding up, fighting to keep his feet, swaying like a tree battling with the wind. The gun dropped from his nerveless hand and the man sagged, sagged slowly to the ground, crumpling into a huddled pile of clothes.

For a long moment, Crane stood there, looking at the man. Then, deliberately, he threw his gun away, sent it wheeling across the yard to hurtle into the dust. No more killing now.

He climbed the porch steps awkwardly, stumped into the hall.

"Betty!" he called.

And from somewhere upstairs a voice answered him and he heard the sound of quick, sure feet coming toward the stairs. He'd get to be a senator, but the honest way—with a wife that would be proud of him.

DESERTION

Those familiar with the works of Clifford D. Simak will recognize this story as the fourth episode in the book City*, but, strangely, it appears that it was the first of those episodes to be written (it was sent to editor John W. Campbell Jr. in July of 1943). Its appearance in* Astounding Science Fiction*, which bought it for fifty dollars (less than Cliff would be paid for the subsequent related stories), was postponed while the preceding three stories were written and published (see my introduction to Open Road Integrated Media's edition of* City *for more detail). "Desertion" would finally appear in the November 1944 issue of the magazine, and I believe that it would have won Best SF Story of the Year if any such awards had existed at the time—for this may be the greatest single piece of imagination in all of Cliff's work. It demonstrates an incredible ability to imagine, and then portray, an alien world, and alien life, in terms that make you wish you could be there/do that. . . . How did a former Wisconsin farm boy who became a big-city newsman manage to do that?*

This story takes place entirely on Jupiter, and the planet is recognizable as the Jupiter of Cliff's earlier story "Clerical Error." I sometimes wonder if Cliff, in the back of his mind, might have played with the idea of doing more stories with the Lopers. . . .

—dww

Four men, two by two, had gone into the howling maelstrom that was Jupiter and had not returned. They had walked into the keening gale—or rather, they had loped, bellies low against the ground, wet sides gleaming in the rain.

For they did not go in the shape of men.

Now the fifth man stood before the desk of Kent Fowler, head of Dome No. 3, Jovian Survey Commission.

Under Fowler's desk, old Towser scratched a flea, then settled down to sleep again.

Harold Allen, Fowler saw with a sudden pang, was young—too young. He had the easy confidence of youth, the straight back and straight eyes, the face of one who never had known fear. And that was strange. For men in the domes of Jupiter did know fear—fear and humility. It was hard for Man to reconcile his puny self with the mighty forces of the monstrous planet.

"You understand," said Fowler, "that you need not do this. You understand that you need not go."

It was formula, of course. The other four had been told the same thing, but they had gone. This fifth one, Fowler knew, would go too. But suddenly he felt a dull hope stir within him that Allen wouldn't go.

"When do I start?" asked Allen.

There was a time when Fowler might have taken quiet pride in that answer, but not now. He frowned briefly.

"Within the hour," he said.

Allen stood waiting, quietly.

"Four other men have gone out and have not returned," said Fowler. "You know that, of course. We want you to return. We don't want you going off on any heroic rescue expedition. The main thing, the only thing, is that you come back, that you prove man can live in a Jovian form. Go to the first survey stake, no farther, then come back. Don't take any chances. Don't investigate anything. Just come back."

Allen nodded. "I understand all that."

"Miss Stanley will operate the converter," Fowler went on. "You need have no fear on that particular point. The other men were converted without mishap. They left the converter in apparently perfect condition. You will be in thoroughly competent hands. Miss Stanley is the best qualified conversion operator in the Solar System. She has had experience on most of the other planets. That is why she's here."

Allen grinned at the woman and Fowler saw something flicker across Miss Stanley's face—something that might have been pity, or rage—or just plain fear. But it was gone again and she was smiling back at the youth who stood before the desk. Smiling in that prim, school-teacherish way she had of smiling, almost as if she hated herself for doing it.

"I shall be looking forward," said Allen, "to my conversion."

And the way he said it, he made it all a joke, a vast, ironic joke.

But it was no joke.

It was serious business, deadly serious. Upon these tests, Fowler knew, depended the fate of men on Jupiter. If the tests succeeded, the resources of the giant planet would be thrown open. Man would take over Jupiter as he already had taken over the other smaller planets. And if they failed—

If they failed, Man would continue to be chained and hampered by the terrific pressure, the greater force of gravity, the weird chemistry of the planet. He would continue to be shut within the domes, unable to set actual foot upon the planet, unable to see it with direct, unaided vision, forced to rely upon the awkward tractors and the televisor, forced to work with clumsy tools and mechanisms or through the medium of robots that themselves were clumsy.

For Man, unprotected and in his natural form, would be blotted out by Jupiter's terrific pressure of fifteen thousand pounds per square inch, pressure that made terrestrial sea bottoms seem a vacuum by comparison.

Even the strongest metal Earthmen could devise couldn't exist under pressure such as that, under the pressure and the alkaline rains that forever swept the planet. It grew brittle and flaky, crumbling like clay, or it ran away in little streams and puddles of ammonia salts. Only by stepping up the toughness and strength of that metal, by increasing its electronic tension, could it be made to withstand the weight of thousands of miles of swirling, choking gases that made up the atmosphere. And even when that was done, everything had to be coated with tough quartz to keep away the rain—the bitter rain that was liquid ammonia.

Fowler sat listening to the engines in the sub-floor of the dome—engines that ran on endlessly, the dome never quiet of them. They had to run and keep on running. For if they stopped the power flowing into the metal walls of the dome would stop, the electronic tension would ease up and that would be the end of everything.

Towser roused himself under Fowler's desk and scratched another flea, his leg thumping hard against the floor.

"Is there anything else?" asked Allen.

Fowler shook his head. "Perhaps there's something you want to do," he said. "Perhaps you—"

He had meant to say write a letter and he was glad he caught himself quick enough so he didn't say it.

Allen looked at his watch. "I'll be there on time," he said. He swung around and headed for the door.

Fowler knew Miss Stanley was watching him and he didn't want to turn and meet her eyes. He fumbled with a sheaf of papers on the desk before him.

"How long are you going to keep this up?" asked Miss Stanley and she bit off each word with a vicious snap.

He swung around in his chair and faced her then. Her lips were drawn into a straight, thin line, her hair seemed skinned back from her forehead tighter than ever, giving her face that queer, almost startling death-mask quality.

He tried to make his voice cool and level. "As long as there's any need of it," he said. "As long as there's any hope."

"You're going to keep on sentencing them to death," she said. "You're going to keep marching them out face to face with Jupiter. You're going to sit in here safe and comfortable and send them out to die."

"There is no room for sentimentality, Miss Stanley," Fowler said, trying to keep the note of anger from his voice. "You know as well as I do why we're doing this. You realize that Man in his own form simply cannot cope with Jupiter. The only answer is to turn men into the sort of things that can cope with it. We've done it on the other planets.

"If a few men die, but we finally succeed, the price is small. Through the ages men have thrown away their lives on foolish things, for foolish reasons. Why should we hesitate, then, at a little death in a thing as great as this?"

Miss Stanley sat stiff and straight, hands folded in her lap, the lights shining on her graying hair, and Fowler, watching her, tried to imagine what she might feel, what she might be thinking. He wasn't exactly afraid of her, but he didn't feel quite comfortable when she was around. Those sharp blue eyes saw too much, her hands looked far too competent.

She should be somebody's Aunt sitting in a rocking chair with her knitting needles. But she wasn't. She was the top-notch conversion unit operator in the Solar System and she didn't like the way he was doing things.

"There is something wrong, Mr. Fowler," she declared.

"Precisely," agreed Fowler. "That's why I'm sending young Allen out alone. He may find out what it is."

"And if he doesn't?"

"I'll send someone else."

She rose slowly from her chair, started toward the door, then stopped before his desk.

"Some day," she said, "you will be a great man. You never let a chance go by. This is your chance. You knew it was when this dome was picked for the tests. If you put it through, you'll go up a notch or two. No matter how many men may die, you'll go up a notch or two."

"Miss Stanley," he said and his voice was curt, "young Allen is going out soon. Please be sure that your machine—"

"My machine," she told him, icily, "is not to blame. It operates along the co-ordinates the biologists set up."

He sat hunched at his desk, listening to her footsteps go down the corridor.

What she said was true, of course. The biologists had set up the co-ordinates. But the biologists could be wrong. Just a hairbreadth of difference, one iota of digression and the converter would be sending out something that wasn't the thing they meant to send. A mutant that might crack up, go haywire, come unstuck under some condition or stress of circumstance wholly unsuspected.

For Man didn't know much about what was going on outside. Only what his instruments told him was going on. And the samplings of those happenings furnished by those instruments and mechanisms had been no more than samplings, for Jupiter was unbelievably large and the domes were very few.

Even the work of the biologists in getting the data on the Lopers, apparently the highest form of Jovian life, had involved more than three years of intensive study and after that two years of checking to make sure. Work that could have been done on Earth in a week or two. But work that, in this case, couldn't be done on Earth at all, for one couldn't take a Jovian life form to Earth. The pressure here on Jupiter couldn't be duplicated outside of Jupiter and at Earth pressure and temperature the Lopers would simply have disappeared in a puff of gas.

Yet it was work that had to be done if Man ever hoped to go about Jupiter in the life form of the Lopers. For before the converter could change a man to another life form, every detailed physical characteristic of that life form must be known—surely and positively, with no chance of mistake.

* * *

Allen did not come back.

The tractors, combing the nearby terrain, found no trace of him, unless the skulking thing reported by one of the drivers had been the missing Earthman in Loper form.

The biologists sneered their most accomplished academic sneers when Fowler suggested the co-ordinates might be wrong. Carefully they pointed out, the co-ordinates worked. When a man was put into the converter and the switch was thrown, the man became a Loper. He left the machine and moved away, out of sight, into the soupy atmosphere.

Some quirk, Fowler had suggested; some tiny deviation from the thing a Loper should be, some minor defect. If there were, the biologists said, it would take years to find it.

And Fowler knew that they were right.

So there were five men now instead of four and Harold Allen had walked out into Jupiter for nothing at all. It was as if he'd never gone so far as knowledge was concerned.

Fowler reached across his desk and picked up the personnel file, a thin sheaf of paper neatly clipped together. It was a thing he dreaded but a thing he had to do. Somehow the reason for these strange disappearances must be found. And there was no other way than to send out more men.

He sat for a moment listening to the howling of the wind above the dome, the everlasting thundering gale that swept across the planet in boiling, twisting wrath.

Was there some threat out there, he asked himself? Some danger they did not know about? Something that lay in wait and gobbled up the Lopers, making no distinction between Lopers that were *bona fide* and Lopers that were men? To the gobblers, of course, it would make no difference.

Or had there been a basic fault in selecting the Lopers as the type of life best fitted for existence on the surface of the planet?

The evident intelligence of the Lopers, he knew, had been one factor in that determination. For if the thing Man became did not have capacity for intelligence, Man could not for long retain his own intelligence in such a guise.

Had the biologists let that one factor weigh too heavily, using it to offset some other factor that might be unsatisfactory, even disastrous? It didn't seem likely. Stiffnecked as they might be, the biologists knew their business.

Or was the whole thing impossible, doomed from the very start? Conversion to other life forms had worked on other planets, but that did not necessarily mean it would work on Jupiter. Perhaps Man's intelligence could not function correctly through the sensory apparatus provided Jovian life. Perhaps the Lopers were so alien there was no common ground for human knowledge and the Jovian conception of existence to meet and work together.

Or the fault might lie with Man, be inherent with the race. Some mental aberration which, coupled with what they found outside, wouldn't let them come back. Although it might not be an aberration, not in the human sense. Perhaps just one ordinary human mental trait, accepted as commonplace on Earth, would be so violently at odds with Jovian existence that it would blast all human intelligence and sanity.

Claws rattled and clicked down the corridor. Listening to them, Fowler smiled wanly. It was Towser coming back from the kitchen, where he had gone to see his friend, the cook.

Towser came into the room, carrying a bone. He wagged his tail at Fowler and flopped down beside the desk, bone between his paws. For a long moment his rheumy old eyes regarded his master and Fowler reached down a hand to ruffle a ragged ear.

"You still like me, Towser?" Fowler asked and Towser thumped his tail.

"You're the only one," said Fowler. "All through the dome they're cussing me. Calling me a murderer, more than likely."

He straightened and swung back to the desk. His hand reached out and picked up the file.

Bennett? Bennett had a girl waiting for him back on Earth.

Andrews? Andrews was planning on going back to Mars Tech just as soon as he earned enough to see him through a year.

Olson? Olson was nearing pension age. All the time telling the boys how he was going to settle down and grow roses.

Carefully, Fowler laid the file back on the desk.

Sentencing men to death. Miss Stanley had said that, her pale lips scarcely moving in her parchment face. Marching men out to die while he, Fowler, sat here safe and comfortable.

They were saying it all through the dome, no doubt, especially since Allen had failed to return. They wouldn't say it to his face, of course. Even the man or men he called before his desk and told they were the next to go, wouldn't say it to him.

They would only say: "When do we start?" For that was formula.

But he would see it in their eyes.

He picked up the file again. Bennett, Andrews, Olson. There were others, but there was no use in going on.

Kent Fowler knew that he couldn't do it, couldn't face them, couldn't send more men out to die.

He leaned forward and flipped up the toggle on the intercommunicator.

"Yes, Mr. Fowler."

"Miss Stanley, please."

He waited for Miss Stanley, listening to Towser chewing half-heartedly on the bone. Towser's teeth were getting bad.

"Miss Stanley," said Miss Stanley's voice.

"Just wanted to tell you, Miss Stanley, to get ready for two more."

"Aren't you afraid," asked Miss Stanley, "that you'll run out of them? Sending out one at a time, they'd last longer, give you twice the satisfaction."

"One of them," said Fowler, "will be a dog."

"A dog!"

"Yes, Towser."

He heard the quick, cold rage that iced her voice. "Your own dog! He's been with you all these years—"

"That's the point," said Fowler. "Towser would be unhappy if I left him behind."

It was not the Jupiter he had known through the televisor. He had expected it to be different, but not like this. He had expected a hell of ammonia rain and stinking fumes and the deafening, thundering tumult of the storm. He had expected swirling clouds and fog and the snarling flicker of monstrous thunderbolts.

He had not expected the lashing downpour would be reduced to drifting purple mist that moved like fleeing shadows over a red and purple sward. He had not even guessed the snaking bolts of lightning would be flares of pure ecstasy across a painted sky.

Waiting for Towser, Fowler flexed the muscles of his body, amazed at the smooth, sleek strength he found. Not a bad body, he decided, and grimaced at remembering how he had pitied the Lopers when he glimpsed them through the television screen.

For it had been hard to imagine a living organism based upon ammonia and hydrogen rather than upon water and oxygen, hard to believe that such a form of life could know the same quick thrill of life that humankind could know. Hard to conceive of life out in the soupy maelstrom that was Jupiter, not knowing, of course, that through Jovian eyes it was no soupy maelstrom at all.

The wind brushed against him with what seemed gentle fingers and he remembered with a start that by Earth standards the wind was a roaring gale, a two-hundred-mile an hour howler laden with deadly gases.

Pleasant scents seeped into his body. And yet scarcely scents, for it was not the sense of smell as he remembered it. It was as if his whole being was soaking up the sensation of lavender—and yet not lavender. It was something, he knew, for which he had no word, undoubtedly the first of many enigmas in terminology. For the words he knew, the thought symbols that served him as an Earthman would not serve him as a Jovian.

The lock in the side of the dome opened and Towser came tumbling out—at least he thought it must be Towser.

He started to call to the dog, his mind shaping the words he meant to say. But he couldn't say them. There was no way to say them. He had nothing to say them with.

For a moment his mind swirled in muddy terror, a blind fear that eddied in little puffs of panic through his brain.

How did Jovians talk? How—

Suddenly he was aware of Towser, intensely aware of the bumbling, eager friendliness of the shaggy animal that had followed him from Earth to many planets. As if the thing that was Towser had reached out and for a moment sat within his brain.

And out of the bubbling welcome that he sensed, came words.

"Hiya, pal."

Not words really, better than words. Thought symbols in his brain, communicated thought symbols that had shades of meaning words could never have.

"Hiya, Towser," he said.

"I feel good," said Towser. "Like I was a pup. Lately I've been feeling pretty punk. Legs stiffening up on me and teeth wearing down to almost nothing. Hard to mumble a bone with teeth like that. Besides, the fleas give me hell. Use to be I never paid much attention to them. A couple of fleas more or less never meant much in my early days."

"But . . . but—" Fowler's thoughts tumbled awkwardly. "You're talking to me!"

"Sure thing," said Towser. "I always talked to you, but you couldn't hear me. I tried to say things to you, but I couldn't make the grade."

"I understood you sometimes," Fowler said.

"Not very well," said Towser. "You knew when I wanted food and when I wanted a drink and when I wanted out, but that's about all you ever managed."

"I'm sorry," Fowler said.

"Forget it," Towser told him. "I'll race you to the cliff."

For the first time, Fowler saw the cliff, apparently many miles away, but with a strange crystalline beauty that sparkled in the shadow of the many-colored clouds.

Fowler hesitated. "It's a long way—"

"Ah, come on," said Towser and even as he said it he started for the cliff.

Fowler followed, testing his legs, testing the strength in that new body of his, a bit doubtful at first, amazed a moment later, then running with a sheer joyousness that was one with the red and purple sward, with the drifting smoke of the rain across the land.

As he ran the consciousness of music came to him, a music that beat into his body, that surged throughout his being, that lifted him on wings of silver speed. Music like bells might make from some steeple on a sunny, springtime hill.

As the cliff drew nearer the music deepened and filled the universe with a spray of magic sound. And he knew the music came from the tumbling waterfall that feathered down the face of the shining cliff.

Only, he knew, it was no waterfall, but an ammonia-fall and the cliff was white because it was oxygen, solidified.

He skidded to a stop beside Towser where the waterfall broke into a glittering rainbow of many hundred colors. Literally many hundred, for here, he saw, was no shading of one primary to another as human beings saw, but a clearcut selectivity that broke the prism down to its last ultimate classification.

"The music," said Towser.

"Yes, what about it?"

"The music," said Towser, "is vibrations. Vibrations of water falling."

"But, Towser, you don't know about vibrations."

"Yes, I do," contended Towser. "It just popped into my head."

Fowler gulped mentally. "Just popped!"

And suddenly, within his own head, he held a formula—the formula for a process that would make metal to withstand the pressure of Jupiter.

He stared, astounded, at the waterfall and swiftly his mind took the many colors and placed them in their exact sequence in the spectrum. Just like that. Just out of blue sky. Out of nothing, for he knew nothing either of metals or of colors.

"Towser," he cried. "Towser, something's happening to us!"

"Yeah, I know," said Towser.

"It's our brains," said Fowler. "We're using them, all of them, down to the last hidden corner. Using them to figure out things we should have known all the time. Maybe the brains of Earth things naturally are slow and foggy. Maybe we are the morons of the universe. Maybe we are fixed so we have to do things the hard way."

And, in the new sharp clarity of thought that seemed to grip him, he knew that it would not only be the matter of colors in a waterfall or metals that would resist the pressure of Jupiter, he sensed other things, things not yet quite clear. A vague whispering that hinted of greater things, of mysteries beyond the pale of human thought, beyond even the pale of human imagination. Mysteries, fact, logic built on reasoning. Things that any brain should know if it used all its reasoning power.

"We're still mostly Earth," he said. "We're just beginning to learn a few of the things we are to know—a few of the things that were kept from us as human beings, perhaps because we were human beings. Because our human bodies were poor bodies. Poorly equipped for thinking, poorly equipped in certain senses that one has to have to know. Perhaps even lacking in certain senses that are necessary to true knowledge."

He stared back at the dome, a tiny black thing dwarfed by the distance.

Back there were men who couldn't see the beauty that was Jupiter. Men who thought that swirling clouds and lashing rain obscured the face of the planet. Unseeing human eyes. Poor eyes. Eyes that could not see the beauty in the clouds, that could not see through the storm. Bodies that could not feel the thrill of trilling music stemming from the rush of broken water.

Men who walked alone, in terrible loneliness, talking with their tongue like Boy Scouts wigwagging out their messages, unable to reach out and touch one another's mind as he could reach out and touch Towser's mind. Shut off forever from that personal, intimate contact with other living things.

He, Fowler, had expected terror inspired by alien things out here on the surface, had expected to cower before the threat of unknown things, had steeled himself against disgust of a situation that was not of Earth.

But instead he had found something greater than Man had ever known. A swifter, surer body. A sense of exhilaration, a deeper sense of life. A sharper mind. A world of beauty that even the dreamers of the Earth had not yet imagined.

"Let's get going," Towser urged.

"Where do you want to go?"

"Anywhere," said Towser. "Just start going and see where we end up. I have a feeling . . . well, a feeling—"

"Yes, I know," said Fowler.

For he had the feeling, too. The feeling of high destiny. A certain sense of greatness. A knowledge that somewhere off beyond the horizons lay adventure and things greater than adventure.

Those other five had felt it, too. Had felt the urge to go and see, the compelling sense that here lay a life of fullness and of knowledge.

That, he knew, was why they had not returned.

"I won't go back," said Towser.

"We can't let them down," said Fowler.

Fowler took a step or two, back toward the dome, then stopped.

Back to the dome. Back to that aching, poison-laden body he had left. It hadn't seemed aching before, but now he knew it was.

Back to the fuzzy brain. Back to muddled thinking. Back to the flapping mouths that formed signals others understood. Back to eyes that now would be worse than no sight at all. Back to squalor, back to crawling, back to ignorance.

"Perhaps some day," he said, muttering to himself.

"We got a lot to do and a lot to see," said Towser. "We got a lot to learn. We'll find things—"

Yes, they could find things. Civilizations, perhaps. Civilizations that would make the civilization of Man seem puny by comparison. Beauty and, more important—an understanding of that beauty. And a comradeship no one had ever known before—that no man, no dog had ever known before.

And life. The quickness of life after what seemed a drugged existence.

"I can't go back," said Towser.

"Nor I," said Fowler.

"They would turn me back into a dog," said Towser.

"And me," said Fowler, "back into a man."

THE GOLDEN BUGS

On June 11, 1958, Clifford D. Simak wrote in his journal that plotting was "going well" for the "bacteria" story, and by the June 14, he was referring to the story as "Bug-Killer." However, on the June 24, he wrote that he had eleven pages written but was not satisfied, and that he might lay it aside and start over. He spent some time working on several other stories, and in July, he and Kay decided that their new house was not working for them; they decided to sell it. Thereafter, he made no mention of the story in his journal until, on September 24. He wrote that he had finished "The Golden Bugs." He then sent the story to H. F. Gold and John W. Campbell Jr., but both of them rejected it; so he sent it to Robert Park Mills in the middle of November. Mills, after first saying that he wanted to hold it for a few months before accepting it, finally bought it in April of 1959. It was published in the June 1960 issue of the Magazine of Fantasy & Science Fiction.

Readers may find it interesting to know that in a journal entry dated September 29, 1957, Cliff recorded that while he had been out rock-hunting, he met a man who taught him about agates and that he found his first one. After that, rocks and stones played a part in a number of Cliff's stories.

—dww

It started as a lousy day.

Arthur Belsen, across the alley, turned on his orchestra at six o'clock and brought me sitting up in bed.

I'm telling you, Belsen makes his living as an engineer, but music is his passion. And since he is an engineer, he's not content to leave well enough alone. He had to mess around.

A year or two before he'd gotten the idea of a robotic symphony, and the man has talent, you have to give him that. He went to work on this idea and designed machines that could read—not only play, but read—music from a tape, and he built a machine to transcribe the tapes. Then he built a lot of these music machines in his basement workshop.

And he tried them out!

It was experimental work, quite understandably, and there was redesigning and adjusting to be done and Belsen was finicky about the performance that each machine turned out. So he tried them out a lot—and loudly—not being satisfied until he had the instrumentation just the way he thought it should be.

There had been some idle talk in the neighborhood about a lynching party, but nothing came of it. That's the trouble, one of the troubles, with this neighborhood of ours—they'll talk an arm off you, but never do a thing.

As yet no one could see an end to all the Belsen racket. It had taken him better than a year to work up the percussion section and that was bad enough. But now he'd started on the strings and that was even worse.

Helen sat up in bed beside me and put her hands up to her ears, but she couldn't keep from hearing. Belsen had it turned up loud, to get, as he would tell you, the feel of it.

By this time, I figured, he probably had the entire neighborhood awake.

"Well, that's it," I said, starting to get up.

"You want me to get breakfast?"

"You might as well," I said. "No one's going to get any sleep with that thing turned on."

While she started breakfast, I headed for the garden back of the garage to see how the dahlias might be faring. I don't mind telling you I was delighted with those dahlias. It was nearly fair time and there were some of them that would be at bloom perfection just in time for showing.

I started for the garden, but I never got there. That's the way it is in this neighborhood. A man will start to do something and never get it done because someone always catches him and wants to talk awhile.

This time it was Dobby. Dobby is Dr. Darby Wells, a venerable old codger with white chin whiskers, and he lives next door. We all call him Dobby and he doesn't mind a bit, for in a way it's a badge of tribute to the man. At one time Dobby had been an entomologist of some repute at the university and it had been his students who had hung the name on him. It was no corruption of his regular name, but stemmed rather from his one-time interest in mud-dauber wasps.

But now Dobby was retired, with nothing in the world to do except hold long and aimless conversations with anyone he could manage to nail down.

As soon as I caught sight of him, I knew that I was sunk.

"I think it's admirable," said Dobby, leaning on his fence and launching into full-length discussion as soon as I was in voice distance, "for a man to have a hobby. But I submit it's inconsiderate of him to practice it so noisily at the crack of dawn."

"You mean that," I said, making a thumb at the Belsen house, from which the screeching and the caterwauling still issued in full force.

"Exactly," said Dobby, combing his white chin whiskers with an air of grave deliberation. "Now, mind me, not for a moment would I refuse the man the utmost admiration . . ."

"Admiration?" I demanded. There are occasions when I have a hard time understanding Dobby. Not so much because of the pontifical way in which he talks as because of the way he thinks.

"Precisely," Dobby told me. "Not for his machines, although they are electronic marvels, but for the way in which he engineers his tapes. The machine that he rigged up to turn out those tapes is a most versatile contraption. Sometimes it seems to be almost human."

"When I was a boy," I said, "we had player pianos and the pianos ran on tapes."

"Yes, Randall, you are right," admitted Dobby, "the principle was there, but the execution—think of the execution! All those old pianos had to do was tinkle merrily along, but Belsen has worked into his tapes the most delicate nuances . . ."

"I must have missed them nuances," I told him, without any charity at all. "All I've heard is racket."

We talked about Belsen and his orchestra until Helen called me in for breakfast.

I had no sooner sat down than she dragged out her grievance list.

"Randall," she said, with determination, "the kitchen is positively crawling with grease ants again. They're so small you can hardly see them and all at once they're into everything."

"I thought you got rid of them," I said.

"I did. I tracked them to their nest and poured boiling water into it. But this time it's up to you."

"Sure thing," I promised. "I'll do it right away."

"That's what you said last time."

"I was ready to," I told her, "but you beat me to it."

"And that isn't all," she said. "There are those wasps up in the attic louvres. They stung the little Montgomery girl the other day."

She was getting ready to say more, but just then Billy, our eleven-year-old, came stumbling down the stairs.

"Look, Dad," he cried excitedly, holding out a small-size plastic box. "I have one here I've never seen before."

I didn't have to ask one what. I knew it was another insect. Last year it had been stamp collecting and this year it was insects—and that's another thing about having an idle entomologist for a next door neighbor.

I took the box without enthusiasm.

"A lady bug," I said.

"No, it's not," said Billy. "It's too big to be a lady bug. And the spots are different and the color is all wrong. This one is gold and a ladybug is orange."

"Well, look it up," I said, impatiently. The kid will do anything to keep away from reading.

"I did," said Billy. "I looked all through the book and I couldn't find it."

"Oh, for goodness sakes," snapped Helen, "sit down and eat your breakfast. It's bad enough to be overrun with ants and wasps without you spending all your time catching other bugs."

"But, Mom, it's educational," protested Billy. "That is what Dr. Wells says. He says there are 700,000 known families of insects . . ."

"Where did you find it, son?" I asked, a bit ashamed of how we both were hopping onto him.

"Right in my room," said Billy.

"In the house!" screamed Helen. "Ants aren't bad enough . . ."

"Soon as I get through eating, I'll show it to Dr. Wells."

"Now, don't you pester Dobby."

"I hope he pesters him a lot," Helen said, tight-lipped. "It was Dobby who got him started on this foolishness."

I handed back the box and Billy put it down beside his plate and started in on breakfast.

"Randall," Helen said, taking up her third point of complaint. "I don't know what I'm going to do with Nora."

Nora was the cleaning woman. She came in twice a week.

"What did she do this time?"

"It's what she doesn't do. She simply will not dust. She just waves a cloth around and that is all there's to it. She won't move a lamp or vase."

"Well, get someone else," I said.

"Randall, you don't know what you're talking about. Cleaning women are hard to find and you can't depend on them. I was talking to Amy . . ."

I listened and made the appropriate replies. I've heard it all before.

As soon as I finished breakfast, I took off for the office. It was too early to see any prospects, but I had some policies to write up and some other work to do and I could use the extra hour or two.

Helen phoned me shortly after noon and she was exasperated.

"Randall," she said, without preamble, "someone has dumped a boulder in the middle of the garden."

"Come again," I said.

"You know. A big rock. It squashed down all the dahlias."

"Dahlias!" I yipped.

"And the funny thing about it is there aren't any tracks. It would take a truck to move a rock that big and . . ."

"Now, let's take this easy. How big, exactly, is this boulder?"

"It's almost as tall as I am."

"It's impossible!" I stormed. Then I tried to calm myself. "It's a joke," I said. "Someone played a joke."

I searched my mind for someone who might have done it and I couldn't think of anyone who'd go to all the trouble involved in that sort of joke. There was George Montgomery, but George was a sobersides. And Belsen, but Belsen was too wrapped up in music to be playing any jokes. And Dobby—it was inconceivable he'd ever play a joke.

"Some joke!" said Helen.

Nobody in the neighborhood, I told myself, would have done a trick like that. Everyone knew I was counting on those dahlias to win me some more ribbons.

"I'll knock off early," I told her, "and see what can be done about it."

Although I knew there was precious little that could be done about it—just haul the thing away.

"I'll be over at Amy's," Helen said. "I'll try to get home early."

I went out and saw another prospect, but I didn't do too well. All the time I was thinking of the dahlias.

I knocked off work in the middle of the afternoon and bought a spray-can of insecticide at a drugstore. The label claimed it was effective against ants, roaches, wasps, aphids and a host of other pests.

At home, Billy was sitting on the steps.

"Hello, son. Nothing much to do?"

"Me and Tommy Henderson played soldier for a while, but we got tired of it."

I put the insecticide on the kitchen table, then headed for the garden. Billy trailed listlessly behind me.

The boulder was there, squarely in the middle of the dahlia patch, and every bit as big as Helen said it was. It was a funny looking thing, not just a big slab-sided piece of rock, but a freckled looking job. It was a washed-out red and almost a perfect globe.

I walked around it, assessing the damage. There were a few of the dahlias left, but the better ones were gone. There were no tracks, no indication of how the rock might have gotten where it was. It lay a good thirty feet from the alleyway and someone might have used a crane to hoist it off a truck bed, but that seemed most unlikely, for a heavy nest of utility wires ran along the alley.

I went up to the boulder and had a good, close look at it. The whole face of it was pitted with small, irregular holes, none of them much deeper than a half an inch, and there were occasional smooth patches, with a darker lustre showing, as if some part of the original surface had been knocked off. The darker, smoother patches had the shine of highly polished wax, and I remembered something from very long ago—when a one-time pal of mine had been a momentary rock collector.

I bent a little closer to one of the smooth, waxy surfaces and it seemed to me that I could see the hint of wavy lines running in the stone.

"Billy," I asked, "would you know an agate if you saw one?"

"Gosh, Dad, I don't know. But Tommy would. He is a sort of rockhound. He is hunting all the time for different kinds of rocks."

He came up close and looked at one of the polished surfaces. He wet his thumb against his tongue and rubbed it across the waxy surface to bring out the satin of the stone.

"I don't know," he said, "but I think it is."

He backed off a ways and stared at the boulder with a new respect.

"Say, Dad, if it really is an agate—if it was one big agate, I mean, it would be worth a lot of money, wouldn't it?"

"I don't know. I suppose it might be."

"A million dollars, maybe."

I shook my head. "Not a million dollars."

"I'll go get Tommy, right away," he said.

He went around the garage like a flash and I could hear him running down the driveway, hitting out for Tommy's place.

I walked around the boulder several times and tried to estimate its weight, but I had no knowledge I could go on.

I went back to the house and read the directions on the can of insecticide. I uncapped and tested it and the sprayer worked.

So I got down on my knees in front of the threshold of the kitchen door and tried to find the path the ants were using to come in. I couldn't see any of them right away, but I knew from past experience that they are little more than specks and almost transparent in the bargain and mighty hard to see.

A glittery motion in one corner of the kitchen caught my eye and I wheeled around. A glob of golden shimmer was running on the floor, keeping close to the baseboard and heading for the cabinet underneath the kitchen sink.

It was another of the outsize lady bugs.

I aimed the squirt can at it and let it have a burst, but it kept right on and vanished underneath the cabinet.

With the bug gone, I resumed looking for the ants and found no sign of them. There were none coming in the door. Or going out, for that matter. There were none on the sink or the work table space.

So I went around the corner of the house to size up Operation Wasp. It would be a sticky one, I knew. The nest was located in the attic louvre and would be hard to get at. Standing off and looking at it, I decided the only thing to do was wait until night, when I could be sure all the wasps were in the nest. Then I'd put up a ladder and climb up and let them have it, then get out as fast as I could manage without breaking my fool neck.

It was a piece of work that I frankly had no stomach for, but I knew from the tone of Helen's voice at the breakfast table there was no ducking it.

There were a few wasps flying around the nest, and as I watched a couple of them dropped out of the nest and tumbled to the ground.

Wondering what was going on, I stepped a little closer and then I saw the ground was littered with dead or dying wasps. Even as I watched, another wasp fell down and lay there, twisting and squirming.

I circled around a bit to try to get a better look at whatever might be happening. But I could make out nothing except that every now and then another wasp fell down.

I told myself it was all right with me. If something was killing off the wasps it would save me the job of getting rid of them.

I was turning around to take the insecticide back to the kitchen when Billy and Tommy Henderson came panting in excitement from the backyard.

"Mr. Marsden," Tommy said, "that rock out there is an agate. It's a banded agate."

"Well, now, that's fine," I said.

"But you don't understand," cried Tommy. "No agate gets that big. Especially not a banded agate. They call them Lake Superior agates and they don't ever get much bigger than your fist."

That did it. I jerked swiftly to attention and went pelting around the house to have another look at the boulder in the garden. The boys came pounding on behind me.

That boulder was a lovely thing. I put out my hand and stroked it. I thought how lucky I was that someone had plopped it in my garden. I had forgotten all about the dahlias.

"I bet you," Tommy told me, his eyes half as big as saucers, "that you could get a lot of money for it."

I won't deny that approximately the same thought had been going through my mind.

I put out my hand and pushed against it, just to get the solid and substantial feel of it.

And as I pushed, it rocked slightly underneath the pressure!

Astonished, I pushed a little harder, and it rocked again.

Tommy stood bug-eyed. "That is funny, Mr. Marsden. By rights, it hadn't ought to move. It must weigh several tons. You must be awful strong."

"I'm not so strong," I told him. "Not as strong as that."

I tottered back to the house and put away the insecticide, then went out and sat down on the steps to do some worrying.

There was no sign of the boys. They probably had run swiftly off to spread the news throughout the neighborhood.

If that thing were an agate, as Tommy said it was—if it really was one tremendous agate, then it would be a fantastic museum piece and might command some money. But if it were an agate, why was it so light? No ten men, pushing on it, should have made it budge.

I wondered, too, just what my rights would be if it should

turn out to be actually an agate. It was on my property and it should be mine. But what if someone came along and claimed it?

And there was this other thing: How had it gotten there to start with?

I was all tied up in knots with my worrying when Dobby came trundling around the corner of the house and sat down on the steps beside me.

"Lots of extraordinary things going on," he said. "I hear you have an agate boulder in the garden."

"That's what Tommy Henderson tells me. I suppose that he should know. Billy tells me he's a rockhound."

Dobby scratched at his whiskers. "Great things, hobbies," he said. "Especially for kids. They learn a lot from them,"

"Yeah," I said, without enthusiasm.

"Your son brought me an insect for identification after breakfast time this morning."

"I told him not to bother you."

"I am glad he brought it," Dobby said. "It was one I'd never seen before."

"It looked like a lady bug."

"Yes," Dobby agreed, "there is some resemblance. But I'm not entirely certain—well, fact of the matter is, I'm not even sure that it is an insect. To tell the truth, it resembles a turtle in many ways more than it does an insect. There is an utter lack of bodily segmentation, such as you'd find in any insect. The exoskeleton is extremely hard and the head and legs are retractible and it has no antennae."

He shook his head in some perplexity. "I can't be sure, of course. Much more extensive examination would be necessary before an attempt could be made at classifying it. You didn't happen to have found any more of them, have you?"

"I saw one running on the floor not so long ago."

"Would you mind, next time you see one, grabbing it for me?"

"Not at all," I said. "I'll try to get you one."

I kept my word. After he had left I went down into the basement to look up a bug for him. I saw several of them, but couldn't catch a one. I gave up in disgust.

After supper, Arthur Belsen came popping from across the alley. He was in a dither, but that was not unusual. He is a birdlike, nervous man and it doesn't take too much to get him all upset.

"I hear that boulder in your garden is an agate," he said to me. "What do you intend to do with it?"

"Why, I don't know. Sell it, I suppose, if anyone wants to buy it."

"It might be valuable," said Belsen. "You can't just leave it out there. Someone might come along and pinch it."

"Guess there's nothing else to do," I told him. "I certainly can't move it and I'm not going to sit up all night to guard it."

"You don't need to sit up all night," said Belsen. "I can fix it for you. We can rig up a nest of trip wires and hook up an alarm."

I wasn't too impressed and tried to discourage him, but he was like a beagle on a rabbit trail. He went back to his basement and came out with a batch of wire and a kit of tools and we fell to work.

We worked until almost bedtime getting the wires rigged up and an alarm bell installed just inside the kitchen door. Helen took a sour view of it. She didn't like the idea of messing up her kitchen, agate or no agate.

In the middle of the night the clamor of the bell jerked me out of bed, wondering what all the racket was. Then I remembered and went rushing for the stairs. On the third step from the bottom I stepped on something that rolled beneath my foot and sent me pitching down the stairs into the living room. I lit sprawling and skidded into a lamp, which fell on top of me and hit me on the head. I brought up against a chair, tangled with the lamp.

A marble, I thought. That damn kid has been strewing marbles all over the house again! He's too big for that. He knows better than to leave marbles on the stairs.

In the bright moonlight pouring through the picture window I saw the marble and it was moving rapidly—*not rolling, moving!* And there were a lot of other marbles, racing across the floor. Sparkling golden marbles running in the moonlight.

And that wasn't all—in the center of the living room stood the refrigerator!

The alarm bell was still clanging loudly and I picked myself up and got loose from the lamp and rushed for the kitchen door. Behind me I heard Helen yelling at me from the landing.

I got the door open and went racing in bare feet through the dew-soaked grass around the corner of the house.

A puzzled dog was standing by the boulder. He had managed to get one foot caught in one of Belsen's silly wires and he was standing there, three-legged, trying to get loose.

I yelled at him and bent over, scrabbling in the grass, trying to find something I could throw at him. He made a sudden lurch and freed himself. He took off up the alley, ears flapping in the breeze.

Behind me the clanging bell fell silent.

I turned around and trailed back to the house, feeling like a fool.

I suddenly remembered that I had seen the refrigerator standing in the living room. But, I told myself, that must be wrong. The refrigerator was in the kitchen and no one would have moved it. There was, first of all, no reason for a refrigerator to be in the living room; its place was in the kitchen. No one would have wanted to move it and even if they did, they'd have made noise enough to wake the house if they'd tried to do it.

I was imagining things, I told myself. The boulder and the bugs had got me all upset and I was seeing things.

But I wasn't.

The refrigerator still stood in the center of the living room. The plug had been pulled out of the outlet and the cord trailed across the floor. A puddle of water from the slowly-thawing box had soaked into the carpet.

"It's ruining the carpet!" Helen shrieked at me, standing in a corner and staring at the errant refrigerator. "And the food will all be spoiled and . . ."

Billy came stumbling down the stairs, still half asleep.

"What's going on?" he asked.

"I don't know," I said.

I almost told him about the bugs I'd seen running in the house, but caught myself in time. There was no use upsetting Helen any more than she was right then.

"Let's get that box back where it belongs," I suggested, as matter-of-factly as I could. "The three of us can do it."

We tugged and shoved and hauled and lifted and got it back in its proper place and plugged it in again. Helen found some rags and started to mop up the sopping carpet.

"Was there something at the boulder, Dad?" asked Billy.

"A dog," I told him. "Nothing but a dog."

"I was against it from the start," declared Helen, on her knees, angrily mopping carpet. "It was a lot of foolishness. No one would have stolen the boulder. It isn't something you can just pick up and carry off. That Arthur Belsen's crazy."

"I agree with you," I told her, ruefully. "But he is a conscientious sort of fellow and a determined cuss and he thinks in terms of gadgets . . ."

"We won't get a wink of sleep," she said. "We'll be up a dozen times a night, chasing off stray dogs and cats. And I don't believe the boulder is an agate. All we have to go on is Tommy Henderson."

"Tommy is a rockhound," Billy told her, staunchly defending his pal. "He knows an agate when he sees one. He's got a big shoe box full of ones he's found."

And here we were, I thought, arguing about the boulder, when the thing that should most concern us—the happening with the most brain-twisting implications—was the refrigerator.

And a thought came to me—a floating, random thought that came bumbling out of nowhere and glanced against my mind.

I shivered at the thought and it came back again and burrowed into me and I was stuck with it:

What if there were some connection between the refrigerator and the bugs?

Helen got up from the floor. "There," she said, accusingly, "that is the best that I can do. I hope the carpet isn't ruined."

But a bug, I told myself—no bug could move a refrigerator. No bug, nor a thousand bugs. And what was more and final, no bug would want to move one. No bug would care whether a refrigerator was in the living room or kitchen.

Helen was very businesslike. She spread the wet cloth out on the sink to dry. She went into the living room and turned out the lights.

"We might as well get back to bed," she said. "If we are lucky, we can get some sleep."

I went over to the alarm beside the kitchen door and jerked the connections loose.

"Now," I told her, "we can get some sleep."

I didn't really expect to get any. I expected to stay awake the rest of the night, worrying about the refrigerator. But I did drop off, although not for very long.

At six thirty Belsen turned on his orchestra and brought me out of bed.

Helen sat up, with her hands against her ears.

"Oh, not again!" she said.

I went around and closed the windows. It cut down the noise a little.

"Put the pillow over your head," I told her.

I dressed and went downstairs. The refrigerator was in the kitchen and everything seemed to be all right. There were a few of the bugs running around, but they weren't bothering anything.

I made myself some breakfast, then I went to work. And that was the second day hand-running I'd gone early to the office. If this kept up, I told myself, the neighborhood would have to get together and do something about Belsen and his symphony.

Everything went all right. I sold a couple of policies during the morning and lined up a third.

When I came back to the office early in the afternoon a wild-eyed individual was awaiting me.

"You Marsden?" he demanded. "You the guy that's got an agate boulder?"

"That's what I'm told it is," I said.

The man was a little runt. He wore sloppy khaki pants and engineer boots. Stuck in his belt was a rock hammer, one of those things with a hammer on one end of the head and a pick on the other.

"I heard about it," said the man, excitedly and a bit belligerently, "and I can't believe it. There isn't any agate that ever ran that big."

I didn't like his attitude. "If you came here to argue . . ."

"It isn't that," said the man. "My name is Christian Barr. I'm a rockhound, you understand. Been at it all my life. Have a big collection. President of our rock club. Win prizes at almost every show. And I thought if you had a rock like this . . ."

"Yes?"

"Well, if you had a rock like this, I might make an offer for it. I'd have to see it first."

I jammed my hat back on my head.

"Let us go," I said.

In the garden, Barr walked entranced around the boulder. He wet his thumb and rubbed the smooth places on its hide. He leaned close and inspected it. He ran a speculative hand across its surface. He muttered to himself.

"Well?" I asked.

"It's an agate," Barr told me, breathlessly. "Apparently a single, complete agate. Look here, this sort of pebbled, freckled surface—well, that's the inverse imprint of the volcanic bubble inside of which it formed. There's the characteristic mottling on the surface one would expect to find. And the fractures where the surface has been nicked show subconchoidal cleavage. And, of course, there is the indication of some banding."

He pulled the rock hammer from his belt and idly banged the boulder. It rang like a monstrous bell.

Barr froze and his mouth dropped open.

"It hadn't ought to do that," he explained as soon as he regained some of his composure. "It sounds as if it's hollow."

He rapped it once again and the boulder pealed.

"Agate is strange stuff," he said. "It's tougher than the best of steel. I suppose you could make a bell out of it if you could only fabricate it."

He stuck the hammer back into his belt and prowled around the boulder.

"It could be a thunderegg," he said, talking to himself. "But no, it can't be that. A thunderegg has agate in its center and not on the surface. And this is banded agate and you don't find banded agate associated with a thunderegg."

"What is a thunderegg?" I asked, but he didn't answer. He had hunkered down and was examining the bottom portion.

"Marsden," he asked, "how much will you take for this?"

"You'd have to name a figure," I told him. "I have no idea what it's worth."

"I'll give you a thousand as it stands."

"I don't think so," I said. Not that I didn't think it was enough, but on the principle that it's never wise to take a man's first figure.

"If it weren't hollow," Barr told me, "It would be worth a whole lot more."

"You can't be sure it's hollow."

"You heard it when I rapped it."

"Maybe that's just the way it sounds."

Barr shook his head. "It's all wrong," he complained. "No banded agate ever ran this big. No agate's ever hollow. And you don't know where this one came from."

I didn't answer him. There was no reason for me to.

"Look here," he said, after a while. "There's a hole in it. Down here near the bottom."

I squatted down to look where his finger pointed. There was a neat, round hole, no more than half an inch in diameter; no haphazard hole, but round and sharply cut, as if someone might have drilled it.

Barr hunted around and found a heavy weed stalk and stripped off the leaves. The stalk, some two feet of it, slid into the hole.

Barr squatted back and stared, frowning, at the boulder.

"She's hollow, sure as hell," he said.

I didn't pay too much attention to him. I was beginning to sweat a little. For another crazy thought had come bumbling along and fastened onto me:

That hole would be just big enough for one of those bugs to get through!

"Tell you what," said Barr. "I'll raise that offer to two thousand and take it off your hands."

I shook my head. I was going off my rocker linking up the bugs and boulder—even if there were a bug-size hole drilled into the boulder. I remembered that I likewise had linked the bugs with the refrigerator—and it must be perfectly obvious to anyone that the bugs could not have anything to do with either the refrigerator or the boulder.

They were just ordinary bugs—well, maybe not just ordinary bugs, but, anyhow, just bugs. Dobby had been puzzled by them, but Dobby would be the first, I knew, to tell you that there were many insects unclassified as yet. This might be a species which suddenly had flared into prominence, favored by some strange quirk of ecology, after years of keeping strictly undercover.

"You mean to say," asked Barr, astonished, "that you won't take two thousand?"

"Huh?" I asked, coming back to earth.

"I just offered you two thousand for the boulder."

I took a good hard look at him. He didn't look like the kind of man who'd spend two thousand for a hobby. More than likely, I told myself, he knew a good thing when he saw it and was out to make a killing. He wanted to snap this boulder up before I knew what it was worth.

"I'd like to think it over," I told him, warily. "If I decide to take the offer, where can I get in touch with you?"

He told me curtly and gruffly said good-bye. He was sore about me not taking his two thousand. He went stumping around the garage and a moment later I heard him start his car and drive away.

I squatted there and wondered if maybe I shouldn't have taken that two thousand. Two thousand was a lot of money and I could have used it. But the man had been too anxious and he'd had a greedy look.

Now, however, there was one thing certain. I couldn't leave the boulder out here in the garden. It was much too valuable to be left unguarded. Somehow or other I'd have to get it into the garage where I could lock it up. George Montgomery had a block and tackle and maybe I could borrow it and use it to move the boulder.

I started for the house to tell Helen the good news, although I was pretty sure she'd read me a lecture for not selling for two thousand.

She met me at the kitchen door and threw her arms around my neck and kissed me.

"Randall," she caroled, happily, "it's just too wonderful."

"I think so, too," I said, wondering how in the world she could have known about it.

"Just come and look at them," she cried. "The bugs are cleaning up the house!"

"They're what!" I yelled.

"Come and look," she urged, tugging at my arm. "Did you ever see the like of it? Everything's just shining!"

I stumbled after her into the living room and stared in disbelief that bordered close on horror.

They were working in battalions and they were purposeful about it. One gang of them was going over a chair back, four rows of them in line creeping up the chair back, and it was like one of those before-and-after pictures. The lower half of the chair back was so clean it looked like new, while the upper half was dingy.

Another gang was dusting an end table and a squad of others was working on the baseboard in the corner and a small army of them was polishing up the television set.

"They've got the carpeting all done!" squealed Helen. "And this end of the room is dusted and there are some of them starting on the fireplace. I never could get Nora to even touch the fireplace. And now I won't need Nora. Randall, do you realize that these bugs will save us the twenty dollars a week that we've been paying Nora? I wonder if you'll let me have that twenty dollars for my very own. There are so many things I need. I haven't had a new dress for ages and I should have another hat and I saw the cutest pair of shoes the other day . . ."

"But bugs!" I yelled. "You are afraid of bugs. You detest the things. And bugs don't clean carpeting. All they do is eat it."

"These bugs are cute," protested Helen, happily, "and I'm not afraid of them. They're not like ants and spiders. They don't give you a crawly feeling. They are so clean themselves and they are so friendly and so cheerful. They are even pretty. And I just love to watch them work. Isn't it cunning, the way they get together in a bunch to work. They're just like a vacuum cleaner. They just move over something and the dust and dirt are gone."

I stood there, looking at them hard at work, and I felt an icy finger moving up my spine, for no matter how it might violate common sense, now I knew that the things I had been thinking, about the refrigerator and the boulder, had not been half as crazy as they might have seemed.

"I'm going to phone Amy," said Helen, starting for the kitchen. "This is just too wonderful to keep. Maybe we could give her some of the bugs. What do you think, Randall? Just enough of them to give her house a start."

"Hey, wait a minute," I hollered at her. "These things aren't bugs."

"I don't care what they are," said Helen, airily, already dialing Amy's number, "just so they clean the house."

"But, Helen, if you'd only listen to me . . ."

"Shush," she said, playfully. "How can I talk to Amy if you keep—Oh, hello, Amy, is that you . . ."

I saw that it was hopeless. I retreated in complete defeat.

I went around the house to the garage, intending to move some stuff to make room for the boulder at the back.

The door was open. Inside was Billy, busy at the work bench.

"Hello, son," I said, as cheerfully as I could manage. "What's going on?"

"I'm making some bug traps, Dad. To catch some of the bugs that are cleaning up the house. Tommy's partners with me. He went home to get some bait."

"Bait?"

"Sure. We found out that they like agates."

I reached out and grabbed a studding to hold myself erect. Things were going just a bit too fast to take.

"We tried out the traps down in the basement," Billy told me. "There are a lot of the bugs down there. We tried everything for bait. We tried cheese and apples and dead flies and a lot of other things, but the bugs weren't having any. Tommy had an agate in his pocket, just a little gravel agate that he had picked up. So we tried that . . ."

"But why an agate, son? I can't think of anything less likely . . ."

"Well, you see, it was this way, Dad. We tried everything . . ."

"Yes," I said, "I can see the logic of it."

"Trouble is," Billy went on, "we have to use plastic for the traps. It's the only thing that will hold the bugs. They burst right out of a trap made of anything but plastic . . ."

"Now, just a minute there," I warned him. "Once you catch these bugs, what do you intend to do with them?"

"Sell them, naturally," said Billy. "Tommy and me figured everyone would want them. Once the people around here find out how they'll clean a house, everyone will want them. We'll charge five dollars for half a dozen of them. That's a whole lot cheaper than a vacuum cleaner."

"But just six bugs . . ."

"They multiply," said Billy. "They must multiply real fast. A day or two ago we had just a few of them and now the house is swarming."

Billy went on working on the trap.

Finally he said: "Maybe, Dad, you'd like to come in with us on the deal. We need some capital. We have to buy some plastic to make more and better traps. We might be able to make a big thing out of it."

"Look, son. Have you sold any of the bugs?"

"Well, we tried to, but no one would believe us. So we thought we'd wait until Mom noised it around a bit."

"What did you do with the bugs you caught?"

"We took them over to Dr. Wells. I remembered that he wanted some. We gave them to him free."

"Billy, I wish you'd do something for me."

"Sure, Dad. What is it?"

"Don't sell any of the bugs. Not right away at least. Not until I say that it's O.K."

"But, gee, Dad . . ."

"Son, I have a hunch. I think the bugs are alien."

"Me and Tommy figured that they might be."

"You what!"

"It was this way, Dad. At first we figured we'd sell them just as curiosities. That was before we knew how they would clean a house. We thought some folks might want them because they looked so different, and we tried to figure out a sales pitch. And

Tommy said why don't we call them alien bugs, like the bugs from Mars or something. And that started us to thinking and the more we thought about it the more we thought they might be really bugs from Mars. They aren't insects, nor nothing else so far as we could find. They're not like anything on Earth . . ."

"All right," I said. "All right!"

That's the way kids are these days. You can't keep up with them. You think you have something all nailed down and neat and here they've beat you to it. It happens all the time.

I tell you, honestly, it does nothing for a man.

"I suppose," I said, "that while you were figuring all this out, you also got it doped how they might have got here."

"We can't be really sure," said Billy, "but we have a theory. That boulder out in back—we found a hole in it just the right size for these bugs. So we sort of thought they used that."

"You won't believe me, son," I told him, "but I was thinking the same thing. But the part that's got me stumped is what they used for power. What made the boulder move through space?"

"Well, gee, Dad, we don't know that. But there is something else. They could have used the boulder for their food all the time they traveled. There'd be just a few of them, most likely, and they'd get inside the boulder and there'd be all that food, maybe enough of it to last them years and years. So they'd eat the agate, hollowing out the boulder and making it lighter so it could travel faster—well, if not faster, at least a little easier. But they'd be very careful not to chew any holes in it until they'd landed and it was time to leave."

"But agate is just rock . . ."

"You weren't listening, Dad," said Billy, patiently. "I told you that agate was the only bait they'd go for."

"Randall," said Helen, coming down the driveway, "if you don't mind, I'd like to use the car to go over and see Amy. She wants me to tell her all about the bugs."

"Go ahead," I said. "Any way you look at it, my day is shot. I may as well stay home."

She went tripping back down the driveway and I said to Billy: "You just lay off everything until I get back."

"Where you going, Dad?"

"Over to see Dobby."

I found Dobby roosting on a bench beneath an apple tree, his face all screwed up with worry. But it didn't stop him talking.

"Randall," he said, beginning to talk as soon as I hove in sight, "this is a sad day for me. All my life I've been vastly proud of my professional exactitude in my chosen calling. But this day I violated, willingly and knowingly and in a fit of temper, every precept of experimental observation and laboratory technique."

"That's too bad," I said, wondering what he was talking about. Which was not unusual. One often had to wonder what he was getting at.

"It's those damn bugs of yours," Dobby accused me explosively.

"But you said you wanted some more bugs. Billy remembered that and he brought some over."

"And so I did. I wanted to carry forward my examination of them. I wanted to dissect one and see what made him go. Perhaps you recall my telling you about the hardness of the exoskeletons."

"Yes, of course I do."

"Randall," said Dobby, sadly, "would you believe me if I told you that exoskeleton was so hard I could do nothing with it. I couldn't cut it and I couldn't peel it off. So you know what I did?"

"I have no idea," I declared, somewhat exasperated. I hoped that he'd soon get to the point, but there was no use in hurrying him. He always took his time.

"Well, I'll tell you, then," said Dobby, seething. "I took one of those little so-and-sos and I put him on an anvil. Then I picked up a hammer and I let him have it. And I tell you frankly that I am not proud of it. It constituted, in every respect, a most improper laboratory technique."

"I wouldn't let that worry me at all," I told him. "You'll have to simply put this down as an unusual circumstance. The important thing, it seems to me, is what you learned about the bug . . ."

And then I had a terrible thought. "Don't tell me the hammer failed!"

"Not at all," said Dobby, with some satisfaction. "It did a job on him. He was smashed to smithereens."

I sat down on the bench beside him and settled down to wait. I knew that in due time he'd tell me.

"An amazing thing," said Dobby. "Yes, a most amazing thing. That bug was made of crystals—of something that looked like the finest quartz. There was no protoplasm in him. Or, at least," he qualified, judiciously, "none I could detect."

"But a crystal bug! That's impossible!"

"Impossible," said Dobby. "Yes, of course, by any earthly standard. It runs counter to everything we've ever known or thought. But the question rises: Can our earthly standards, even remotely, be universal?"

I sat there, without saying anything, but somehow I felt a great relief that someone else was thinking the same thing I had thought. It went to prove, just slightly, that I wasn't crazy.

"Of course," said Dobby, "it had to happen sometime. Soon or late, it should be almost inevitable that some alien intelligence would finally seek us out. And knowing this, we speculated on monsters and monstrosities, but we fell far short of the actual mark of horr . . ."

"There's no reason at the moment," I told him, hastily, "that we should fear the bugs. They might, in fact, become a useful ally. Even now they are co-operating. They've seemed to strike up some sort of deal. We furnish them a place to live and they, in turn . . ."

"You're mistaken, Randall," Dobby warned me solemnly. "These things are alien beings. Don't imagine for a moment that they and the human race might have a common purpose or a single common concept. Their life process, whatever it may be, is entirely alien to us. So must be their viewpoints. A spider is blood-brother to you as compared with these."

"But we had ants and wasps and they cleaned out the ants and wasps."

"They may have cleaned out the ants and wasps, but it was no part, I am sure, of a co-operative effort. It was no attempt on their part to butter up the human in whose dwelling place they happened to take refuge, or set up their camp, or carve out their beachhead, however you may put it. I have grave doubt that they are aware of you at all except as some mysterious and rather shadowy monstrosity they can't bother with as yet. Sure they killed your insects, but in this they did no more than operate on a level common with their own existence. The insects might have been in their way or they may have recognized in them some potential threat or hindrance."

"But even so, we can use them," I told him impatiently, "to control our insect pests, or carriers of disease."

"Can we?" Dobby asked. "What makes you think we can? And it would not be insect pests alone, but rather all insects. Would you, then, deprive our plant life of its pollination agents—to mention just one example of thousands?"

"You may be right," I said, "but you can't tell me that we must be afraid of bugs, of even crystal bugs. Even if they should turn out to be a menace, we could find a way in which to cope with them."

"I have been sitting here and thinking, trying to get it straight within my mind," said Dobby, "and one thing that has occurred to me is that here we may be dealing with a social concept we've never met with on this planet. I'm convinced that these aliens must necessarily operate on the hive-mind principle. We face not one of them alone nor the total number of them, but we face the sum total of them as a single unit, as a single mind and a single expression of purpose and performance."

"If you really think they're dangerous, what would you have us do?"

"I still have my anvil and my hammer."

"Cut out the kidding, Dobby."

"You are right," said Dobby. "This is no joking matter, nor is it one for an anvil and a hammer. My best suggestion is that the area be evacuated and an atom bomb be dropped."

Billy came tearing down the path.

"Dad!" he was yelling. "Dad!"

"Hold up there," I said, catching at his arm. "What is going on?"

"Someone is ripping up our furniture," yelled Billy, "and then throwing it outdoors."

"Now, wait a minute—are you sure?"

"I saw them doing it," yelled Billy. "Gosh, will Mom be sore!"

I didn't wait to hear any more. I started for the house as fast as I could go. Billy followed close behind me and Dobby brought up the rear, white whiskers bristling like an excited billy goat.

The screen door off the kitchen was standing open as if someone had propped it, and outside, beyond the stoop, lay a pile of twisted fabric and the odds and ends of dismembered chairs.

I went up the steps in one bound and headed for the door. And just as I reached the doorway I saw this great mass of stuff bulleting straight toward me and I ducked aside. A limp and gutted love seat came hurtling out the door and landed on the pile of debris. It sagged into a grotesque resemblance of its former self.

By this time I was good and sore. I dived for the pile and grabbed up a chair leg. I got a good grip on it and rushed through the door and across the kitchen into the living room. I had the club at ready and if there'd been anybody there I would have let him have it.

But there was no one there—no one I could see.

But there was plenty else to see.

The refrigerator was back in the center of the room and heaped all about it were piles of pots and pans. The tangled coil springs from the love seat were leaning crazily against it and scattered all about the carpeting there were nuts and bolts, washers, brads and nails and varying lengths of wire.

There was a strange creaking noise from somewhere and I glanced hurriedly around to find out what it was. I found out, all right.

Over in one corner, my favorite chair was slowly and deliberately and weirdly coming apart. The upholstery nails were rising smoothly from the edging of the fabric—rising from the wood as if by their own accord—and dropping to the floor with tiny patterings. As I watched, a bolt fell to the floor and one leg bent underneath the chair and the chair tipped over. The upholstery nails kept right on coming out.

And as I stood there watching this, I felt the anger draining out of me and a fear come dribbling in to take its place. I started to get cold all over and I could feel the gooseflesh rising.

I started sneaking out. I didn't dare to turn my back, so I backed carefully away and I kept my club at ready.

I bumped into something and let out a whoop and spun around and raised my club to strike.

It was Dobby. I just stopped the club in time.

"Randall," said Dobby calmly, "it's those bugs of yours again."

He gestured toward the ceiling and I looked. The ceiling was a solid mass of golden-gleaming bugs.

I lost some of my fear at seeing them and started to get sore again. I pulled back my arm and aimed the club up at the ceiling. I was ready to let the little stinkers have it, when Dobby grabbed my arm.

"Don't go getting them stirred up," he yelled. "No telling what they'd do."

I tried to jerk my arm away from him, but he hung onto it.

"It is my considered opinion," he declared, even as he wrestled with me, "that the situation has evolved beyond the point where it can be handled by the private citizen."

I gave up. It was undignified trying to get my arm loose from Dobby's clutching paws and I likewise began to see that a club was no proper weapon to use against the bugs.

"You may be right," I said.

He let go my arm. "Maybe you better call the cops," he told me.

I saw that Billy was peering through the door.

"Get out of there," I yelled at him. "You're in the line of fire. They'll be throwing that chair out of here in another minute. They're almost through with it."

Billy ducked back out of sight.

I walked out to the kitchen and hunted through a cupboard drawer until I found the phone book. I looked up the number and dialed the police.

"This is Sergeant Andrews talking," said a voice.

"Now, listen closely, Sergeant," I said. "I have some bugs out here . . ."

"Ain't we all?" the sergeant asked in a happy tone of voice.

"Sergeant," I told him, trying to sound as reasonable as I could, "I know that this sounds funny. But these are a different kind of bug. They're breaking up my furniture and throwing it outdoors."

"I tell you what," the sergeant said, still happy. "You better go on back to bed and try to sleep it off. If you don't, I'll have to run you in."

"Sergeant," I told him, "I am completely sober . . ."

A hollow click came from the other end and the phone went dead.

I dialed the number back.

"Sergeant Andrews," said the voice.

"You just hung up on me," I yelled. "What do you mean by that? I'm a sober, law-abiding, taxpaying citizen and I'm entitled to protection, and even if you don't think so, to some courtesy as well. And when I tell you I have bugs . . ."

"All right," said the sergeant, wearily. "Since you are asking for it. What's your name and address?"

I gave them to him.

"And Mr. Marsden," said the sergeant.

"What is it now?"

"You better have those bugs. If you know what is good for you, there better be some bugs."

I slammed down the phone and turned around.

Dobby came tearing out of the living room.

"Look out! Here it comes!" he yelled.

My favorite chair, what was left of it, came swishing through the air. It hit the door and stuck. It jiggled violently and broke loose to drop on the pile outside.

"Amazing," Dobby panted. "Truly amazing. But it explains a lot."

"Tell me," I snapped at him, "what explains a lot?"

I was getting tired of Dobby's ramblings.

"Telekinesis," said Dobby.

"Tele-what?"

"Well, maybe only teleportation," Dobby admitted sheepishly. "That's the ability to move things by the power of mind alone."

"And you think this teleportation business bears out your hive-mind theory?"

Dobby looked at me with some astonishment. "That's exactly what I meant," he said.

"What I can't figure out," I told him, "is why they're doing this."

"Of course you can't," said Dobby. "No one expects you to. No one can presume to understand an alien motive. On the surface of it, it would appear they are collecting metal, and that well may be exactly what they're doing. But the mere fact of their metal grabbing does not go nearly far enough. To truly understand their motive . . ."

A siren came screaming down the street.

"There they are," I said, racing for the door.

The police car pulled up to the curb and two officers vaulted out.

"You Marsden?" asked the first one.

I told him that I was.

"That's funny," said the second one. "Sarge said he was stinko."

"Say," said the first one, staring at the pile of wreckage outside the kitchen door, "what is going on here?"

Two chair legs came whistling out the door and thudded to the ground.

"Who is in there throwing out that stuff?" the second cop demanded.

"Just the bugs," I told them. "Just the bugs and Dobby. I guess Dobby's still in there."

"Let's go in and grab this Dobby character," said the first one, "before he wrecks the joint."

I stayed behind. There was no use of going in. All they'd do would be ask a lot of silly questions and there were enough of them I could ask myself without listening to the ones thought up by someone else.

A small crowd was beginning to gather. Billy had rounded up some of his pals and neighbor women were rushing from house to house, cackling like excited chickens. Several cars had stopped and their occupants sat gawping.

I walked out to the street and sat down on the curbing.

And now, I thought, it all had become just a little clearer. If Dobby were right about this teleportation business, and the evidence said he was, then the boulder could have been the ship the bugs had used to make their way to Earth. If they could use their power to tear up furniture and throw it out the house, they could use that selfsame power to move anything through space. It needn't have been the boulder; it could have been anything at all.

Billy, in his uninhibited, boyish thinking, probably had struck close to the truth—they had used the boulder because it was their food.

The policemen came pounding back out of the house and stopped beside me.

"Say, mister," said one of them, "do you have the least idea what is going on?"

I shook my head. "You better talk to Dobby. He's the one with answers."

"He says these things are from Mars."

"Not Mars," said the second officer. "It was you who said it might be Mars. He said from the stars."

"He's a funny-talking old coot," complained the first policeman. "A lot of the stuff he says is more than a man can swallow."

"Jake," said the other one, "we better start doing something about this crowd. We can't let them get too close."

"I'll radio for help," said Jake.

He went to the police car and climbed into it.

"You stick around," the other said to me.

"I'm not going anywhere," I said.

The crowd was good-sized by now. More cars had stopped and some of the people in them had gotten out, but most of them just sat and stared. There were an awful lot of kids by this time and the women were still coming, perhaps from blocks away. Word spreads fast in an area like ours.

Dobby came ambling down the yard. He sat down beside me and started pawing at his whiskers.

"It makes no sense," he said, "but, then, of course, it wouldn't."

"What I can't figure out," I told him, "is why they cleaned the house. Why did it have to be spic and span before they started piling up the metal? There must be a reason for it."

A car screeched down the street and slammed up to the curb just short of where we sat. Helen came bustling out of it.

"I can't turn my back a minute," she declared, "but something up and happens."

"It's your bugs," I said. "Your nice house-cleaning bugs. They're ripping up the place."

"Why don't you stop them, then?"

"Because I don't know how."

"They're aliens," Dobby told her calmly. "They came from somewhere out in space."

"Dobby Wells, you keep out of this! You've caused me all the trouble I can stand. The idea of getting Billy interested in insects! He's had the place cluttered up all summer."

A man came rushing up. He squatted down beside me and started pawing at my arm. I turned around and saw that it was Barr, the rockhound.

"Marsden," he said, excitedly, "I have changed my mind. I'll give you five thousand for that boulder. I'll write you out a check right now."

"What boulder?" Helen asked. "You mean our boulder out in the back?"

"That's the one," said Barr. "I got to have that boulder."

"Sell it to him," Helen said.

"I will not," I told her.

"Randall Marsden," she screamed, "you can't turn down five thousand! Think of what five thousand . . ."

"I can turn it down," I told her, firmly. "It's worth a whole lot more than that. It's not just an agate boulder any longer. It's the first spaceship that ever came to Earth. I can get anything I ask."

Helen gasped.

"Dobby," she asked weakly, "is he telling me the truth?"

"I think," said Dobby, "that for once he is." The wail of sirens sounded down the street.

One of the policemen came back from the car.

"You folks will have to get across the street," he said. "As soon as the others get here, we'll cordon off the place."

We got up to start across the street.

"Lady," said the officer, "you'll have to move your car."

"If you two want to stay together," Dobby offered, "I'll drive it down the street."

Helen gave him the key and the two of us walked across the street. Dobby got into the car and drove off.

The officers were hustling the other cars away.

A dozen police cars arrived. Men piled out of them. They started pushing back the crowd. Others fanned out to start forming a circle around the house.

Broken furniture, bedding, clothing, draperies from time to time came flying out the kitchen door. The pile of debris grew bigger by the moment.

We stood across the street and watched our house be wrecked.

"They must be almost through by now," I said, with a strange detachment. "I wonder what comes next."

"Randall," said Helen, tearfully, clinging to my arm, "what do we do now? They're wrecking all my things. How about it—is it covered by insurance?"

"Why, I don't know," I said. "I never thought of it."

And that was the truth of it—it hadn't crossed my mind. And me an insurance man!

I had written that policy myself and now I tried desperately to remember what the fine print might have said and I had a sinking feeling. How, I asked myself, could anything like this be covered? It certainly was no hazard that could be anticipated.

"Anyhow," I said, "we still have the boulder. We can sell the boulder."

"I still think we should have taken the five thousand," Helen told me. "What if the government should move in and just grab the boulder off?"

And she was right, I told myself. This would be just the sort of thing in which the government could become intensely interested.

I began to think myself that maybe we should have taken that five thousand.

Three policemen walked across the yard and went into the house. Almost at once they came tearing out again. Pouring out behind them came a swarm of glittering dots that hummed and buzzed and swooped so fast they seemed to leave streaks of their golden glitter in the air behind them. The policemen ran in weaving fashion, ducking and dodging. They waved their hands in the air above their heads.

The crowd surged back and began to run. The police cordon broke and retreated with what dignity it could.

I found myself behind the house across the street, my hand still gripping Helen's arm. She was madder than a hornet.

"You needn't have pulled me along so fast," she told me. "I could have made it by myself. You made me lose my shoes."

"Forget your shoes," I told her sharply. "This thing is getting serious. You go and round up Billy and the two of you get out of here. Go up to Amy's place."

"Do you know where Billy is?"

"He's around somewhere. He is with his pals. Just look for a bunch of boys."

"And you?"

"I'll be along," I said.

"You'll be careful, Randall."

I patted her shoulder and stooped down to kiss her. "I'll be careful. I'm not very brave, you know. Now go and get the boy."

She started away and then turned back. "Will we ever go back home?" she asked.

"I think we will," I said, "and soon. Someone will find a way to get them out of there."

I watched her walk away and felt the chilly coldness of the kindness of my lie.

Would we, in solemn truth, ever go back home again? Would the entire world, all of humanity, ever be at home again? Would the golden bugs take away the smug comfort and the warm security that Man had known for ages in his sole possession of a planet of his own?

I went up the backyard slope and found Helen's shoes. I put them in my pocket. I came to the back of the house and peeked around the corner.

The bugs had given up the chase, but now a squadron of them flew in a lazy, shining circle around and just above the house. It was plain to see that they were on patrol.

I ducked back around the house and sat down in the grass, with my back against the house. It was a warm and blue-sky summer day; the kind of day a man should mow his lawn.

A slobbering horror, I thought, no matter how obscene or fearful, might be understood, might be fought against. But the cold assuredness with which the golden bugs went directly to their purpose, the self-centered, vicious efficiency with which they operated, was something else again.

And their impersonal detachment, their very disregard of us, was like a chilly blast upon human dignity.

I heard footsteps and looked up, startled.

It was Arthur Belsen and he was upset.

But that was not unusual. Belsen could get upset at something that was downright trivial.

"I was looking for you everywhere," he chattered. "I met Dobby just a while ago and he tells me these bugs of yours . . ."

"They're no bugs of mine," I told him sharply. I was getting tired of everyone talking as if I owned the bugs, as if I might be somehow responsible for their having come to Earth.

"Well, anyway, he was telling me they are after metal."

I nodded. "That's what they're after. Maybe it is precious stuff to them. Maybe they haven't got too much of it wherever they are from."

And I thought about the agate boulder. If they had had metal, certainly they'd not have used the agate boulder.

"I had an awful time getting home," said Belsen. "I thought there was a fire. There are cars parked in the street for blocks and an awful crowd. I was lucky to get through."

"Come on and sit down," I told him. "Stop your fidgeting."

But he paid no attention to me.

"I have an awful lot of metal," he said. "All those machines of mine down in the basement. I've put a lot of time and work and money into those machines and I can't let nothing happen to them. You don't think the bugs will start branching out, do you?"

"Branching out?"

"Well, yes, you know—after they get through with everything in your house, they might start getting into other houses."

"I hadn't thought of it," I said. "I suppose that it could happen."

I sat there and thought about it and I had visions of them advancing house by house, cleaning out and salvaging all the metal, putting it into one big pile until it covered the entire block and eventually the city.

"Dobby says that they are crystal. Isn't that a funny thing for bugs to be?"

I said nothing. After all, he was talking to himself.

"But crystal can't be alive," protested Belsen. "Crystal is stuff that things are made of. Vacuum tubes and such. There is no life in it."

"Don't try to fight with me," I told him. "I can't help it if they are crystal."

There seemed to be a lot of ruckus going on out in the street and I got to my feet to peer around the corner of the house.

For a moment there was not a thing to see. Everything looked peaceful. One or two policemen were running around excitedly, but I couldn't see that anything was happening. It looked just as it had before.

Then a door slowly, almost majestically, detached itself from one of the police cars parked along the curb and started floating toward the open kitchen door. It reached the door and made a neat left turn and disappeared inside.

A rear vision mirror sailed flashing through the air. It was followed by a siren. Both disappeared within the house.

Good Lord, I told myself, the bugs are going after cars!

Now I saw that a couple of the cars were already minus hoods and fenders and that some other doors were missing.

The bugs, I thought, had finally really hit the jackpot. They wouldn't stop until they'd stripped the cars clean down to the tires.

And I was thinking, too, with a strange perverse reaction, that there wasn't nearly room enough inside the house to pack all those dismantled cars. What, I wondered, would the bugs do when the house was full?

A half dozen policemen dashed across the street and started for the house. They reached the lawn before the bug patrol above the house became aware of them and swooped down in a screaming, golden arc.

The policemen ran back pell-mell. The bug patrol, its duty done, returned to circling the house. Fenders, doors, tail lights, head lights, radio antennae, and other parts of cars continued to pour into the house.

A dog came trotting out of nowhere and went across the lawn, tail wagging in friendly curiosity.

A flight of bugs left the patrol and headed down toward him.

The dog, startled by the whistle of the diving bugs, wheeled about to run.

He was too late.

There was the sickening thud of missiles hitting flesh. The dog leaped high into the air and fell over on his back.

The bugs swooped up into the air again. There were no gaps in their ranks.

The dog lay twitching in the yard and blood ran in the grass.

I ducked back around the corner, sick. I doubled up, retching, trying hard to keep from throwing up.

I fought it off and my stomach quieted down. I peeked around the corner of the house.

All was peaceful once again. The dead dog lay sprawling in the yard. The bugs were busy with their stripping of the cars. No policemen were in sight. There was no one in sight at all. Even Belsen had disappeared somewhere.

It was different now, I told myself. The dog had made it different.

The bugs no longer were a mystery only; now they were a deadly danger. Each of them was a rifle bullet with intelligence.

I remembered something that Dobby had said just an hour or so ago.

Evacuate the area, he had said, then drop an atom bomb.

And would it come to that? I wondered. Was that the measure of the danger?

No one, of course, was thinking that way yet, but in time they might. This was just the start of it. Today the city was alerted and the police were on the scene; tomorrow it might be the governor sending in some troops. And in time it would be the federal government. And after that, Dobby's solution might be the only answer.

The bugs hadn't spread too far as yet. But Belsen's fear was valid; in time they would expand, pushing out their beachhead block by block as there were more and more of them. For Billy had been right when he had said they must multiply real fast.

I tried to imagine how the bugs could multiply, but I had no idea.

First of all, of course, the government probably would try to make contact with them, would attempt to achieve some communication with them—not with the creatures themselves, perhaps, but rather with that mass mind which Dobby had figured them to have.

But was it possible to communicate with creatures such as these? On what intellectual level might one approach them? And what good could possibly come of such communication if it was established? Where was the basis for understanding between these creatures and the human race?

And I realized, even as I thought all this, that I was thinking with pure panic. To approach a problem such as the bugs presented, there was need of pure objectivity—there could be no question of either fear or anger. The time had come for Man to discard the pettiness of one-planet thinking.

It was no problem of mine, of course, but thinking of it, I saw a deadly danger—that the eventual authority, whoever that might be, might delay too long in its objectivity.

There had to be a way to stop the bugs, there must be some measure to control them. Before we tried to establish contact, there must be a way in which we could contain them.

And I thought of something—of Billy telling me that to hold them once you caught them you had to have a plastic trap.

I wondered briefly how the kid had known that. Perhaps it had been no more than simple trial and error. After all, he and Tommy Henderson must have tried several different kinds of traps.

Plastic might be the answer to the problem I had posed. It could be the answer if we acted before they spread too far.

And why plastic, I wondered. What element within plastic would stop them cold and hold them once they were entrapped within it? Some factor, perhaps, that we would learn only after long and careful study. But it was something that did not matter now; it was enough we knew that plastic did the trick.

I stood there for a time, turning the matter in my mind, wondering who to go to.

I could go to the police, of course, but I had a feeling I would get little hearing there. The same would be true of the officials of the city. For while it was possible they might listen, they'd have to talk it over, they'd have to call a conference, they'd feel compelled to consult some expert before they did anything about it. And the government in Washington, at the moment, was unthinkable.

The trouble was that no one was scared enough as yet. To act as quickly as they should they'd have to be scared silly—and I had had a longer time to get scared silly than any of the rest.

Then I thought of another man who was as scared as I was.

Belsen.

Belsen was the man to help me. Belsen was scared stiff.

He was an engineer and possibly he could tell me if what I had been thinking was any good or not. He could sit down and figure how it might be done. He'd know where to get the plastic that we needed and the best type of it to use and more than likely he'd know how to go about arranging for its fabrication. And he might, as well, know someone it would do some good to talk to.

I went back to the corner of the house and had a look around.

There were a few policemen in sight, but not too many of them. They weren't doing anything, just standing there and watching while the bugs kept on working at the cars. They had the bodies pretty well stripped down by now and were working on the engines. As I watched I saw one motor rise and sail toward the house. It was dripping oil and chunks of caked grease and dust were falling off of it. I shivered at the thought of what a mess like that would do to Helen's carpeting and the decorating.

There were a few knots of spectators here and there, but all of them were standing at quite a distance off.

It looked to me as if I'd have no trouble reaching Belsen's house if I circled round the block, so I started out.

I wondered if Belsen would be at home and was afraid he might not be. Most of the houses in the neighborhood seemed to be deserted. But it was a chance, I knew, that I had to take. If he wasn't at his house, I'd have to hunt him down.

I reached his place and went up the steps and rang the bell. There wasn't any answer, so I walked straight in.

The house seemed to be deserted.

"Belsen," I called.

He didn't answer me and I called again.

Then I heard footsteps clattering up a stairs.

The basement door came open and Belsen stuck his head out.

"Oh, it's you," he said. "I'm glad you came. I will need some help. I sent the family off."

"Belsen," I said, "I know what we can do. We can get a monstrous sheet of plastic and drop it on the house. That way they can't get out. Maybe we can get some helicopters, maybe four of them, one for each corner of the sheet . . ."

"Come downstairs," said Belsen. "There's work for both of us."

I followed him downstairs into his workroom.

The place was orderly, as one might expect from a fussbudget such as Belsen.

The music machines stood in straight and shining lines, the work bench was immaculate and the tools were all in place. The tape machine stood in one corner and it was all lit up like a Christmas tree.

A table stood in front of the tape machine, but it was far from tidy. It was strewn with books, some of them lying flat and open and others piled haphazardly. There were scribbled sheets of paper scattered everywhere and balled-up bunches of it lay about the floor.

"I cannot be mistaken," Belsen told me, jittery as ever. "I must be sure the first time. There'll be no second chance. I had a devil of a time getting it all figured out, but I think I have it now."

"Look, Belsen," I said, with some irritation, "I don't know what hare-brained scheme you may be working on, but whatever it may be, this deal of mine is immediate and important."

"Later," Belsen told me, almost hopping up and down in his anxiety. "Later you can tell me. I have a tape I have to finish. I have the mathematics all worked out . . ."

"But this is about the bugs!"

Belsen shouted at me: "And so is this, you fool! What else did you expect to find me working on? You know I can't take a chance of their getting in here. I won't let them take all this stuff I've built."

"But, Belsen . . ."

"See that machine," he said, pointing to one of the smaller ones. "That's the one we'll have to use. It is battery powered. See if you can get it moved over to the door."

He swung around and scurried over to the tape machine and sat down in front of it. He began punching slowly and carefully on the keyboard and the machine began to mutter and to chuckle at him and its lights winked on and off.

I saw there was no sense in trying to talk to him until he had this business done. And there was a chance, of course, that he knew what he was doing—that he had figured out some way either to protect these machines of his or to stop the bugs.

I walked over to the machine and it was heavier than it looked. I started tugging at it and I could move it only a few inches at a time, but I kept on tugging it.

And suddenly, as I tugged away, I knew without a question what Belsen must be planning.

And I wondered why I hadn't thought of it myself; why Dobby, with all his talk of A-bombs, hadn't thought of it. But, of course, it would take a man like Belsen, with his particular hobby, to have thought of it.

The idea was so old, so ancient, so much a part of the magic past that it was almost laughable—and yet it ought to work.

Belsen got up from the machine and lifted a reel of tape from a cylinder in its side. He hurried over to me and knelt down beside the machine I'd tugged almost to the door.

"I can't be sure of exactly what they are," he told me. "Crystal. Sure, I know they're crystalline in form, but what kind of crystals—just what type of crystals? So I had to work out a sort of sliding shotgun pattern of supersonic frequencies. Somewhere in there, I hope, is the one that will synchronize with whatever structure they may have."

He opened a section of the small machine and started threading in the tape.

"Like the violin that broke the goblet," I said.

He grinned at me nervously. "The classical example. I see you've heard of it."

"Everyone has," I said.

"Now listen to me carefully," said Belsen. "All we have to do is flip this switch and the tape starts moving. The dial controls the volume and it's set at maximum. We'll open up the door and we'll grab the machine, one on each side of it, and we'll carry it as far as we can before we set it down. I want to get it close."

"Not too close," I cautioned. "The bugs just killed a dog. Couple of them hit him and went through him without stopping. They're animated bullets."

Belsen licked his lips. "I figured something like that."

He reached out for the door.

"Just a minute, Belsen. Have we got a right to?"

"A right to what?" he asked.

"A right to kill these things. They're the first aliens to come to visit us. There's a lot we might learn from them if we could only talk to them . . ."

"Talk to them?"

'Well, communicate. Get to understand them."

And I wondered what was wrong with me, that I should be talking that way.

"After what they did to the dog? After what they did to you?"

"Yes, I think," I said, "even after what they did to me."

"You're crazy," Belsen screamed.

He pulled the door wide open.

"Now!" he shouted at me.

I hesitated for a second, then grabbed hold.

The machine was heavy, but we lifted it and rushed out into the yard. We went staggering with it almost to the alley and there the momentum of our rush played out and we set it down.

I looked up toward my house and the bug patrol was there, circling at rooftop height, a flashing golden circle in the light of the setting sun.

"Maybe," Belsen panted, "maybe we can get it closer."

I bent to pick it up again and even as I did I saw the patrolling circle break.

"Look out!" I screamed.

The bugs were diving at us.

"The switch!" I yelled. "The switch!"

But Belsen stood there, staring at them, frozen, speechless, stiff.

I flung myself at the machine and found the switch and flipped it and then I was groveling in the dirt, rooting into it, trying to make myself extremely thin and small.

There was no sound and, of course, I had known there would be none, but that didn't stop me from wondering why I didn't hear it. Maybe, I thought, the tape had broken; maybe the machine had failed to work.

Out of the tail of my eye I saw the patrol arrowing down on us and they seemed to hang there in the air, as if something might have stopped them, but I knew that was wrong, that it was simply fright playing tricks with time.

And I was scared, all right, but not as scared as Belsen. He still stood there, upright, unable to move a muscle, staring at oncoming death in an attitude of stricken disbelief.

They were almost on top of us. They were so close that I could see each one of them as a dancing golden mote and then suddenly each little mote became a puff of shining dust and the swarm was gone.

I climbed slowly to my feet and brushed off my front.

"Snap out of it," I said to Belsen. I shook him.

He slowly turned toward me and I could see the tension going from his face.

"It worked," he said, in a flat sort of voice. "I was pretty sure it would."

"I noticed that," I said. "You're the hero of the hour."

And I said it bitterly, without even knowing why.

I left him standing there and walked slowly across the alley.

We had done it, I told myself. Right or wrong, we'd done it. The first things from space had come and we had smashed them flat.

And was this, I wondered, what would happen to us, too, when we ventured to the stars? Would we find as little patience and as little understanding? Would we act as arrogantly as these golden bugs had acted?

Would there always be the Belsens to outshout the Marsdens? Would the Marsdens always be unable or unwilling to stand up before the panic-shouting—always fearful that their attitude, slowly forming, might be antisocial? Would the driving sense of fear and the unwillingness to understand bar all things from the stars?

And that, I told myself, was a funny thing for me, of all people, to be thinking. For mine was the house the bugs had ruined.

Although, come to think of it, they might have cost me not a dime. They might have made me money. I still had the agate boulder and that was worth a fortune.

I looked quickly towards the garden and the boulder wasn't there!

I broke into a run, breath sobbing in my throat.

I stopped at the garden's edge and stared in consternation at the neat pile of shining sand.

There was one thing I'd forgotten: that an agate, as well as bugs and goblet, was also crystalline!

I turned around and stared back across the yard and I was sore clean through.

That Belsen, I thought—him and his sliding shotgun pattern!

I would take one of those machines of his and cram it down his throat!

Then I stopped dead still. There was, I realized, nothing I could do or say.

Belsen was the hero, exactly as I had said he was.

He was the man, alone, who'd quashed the menace from the stars.

That was what the headlines would be saying, that was what the entire world would think. Except, perhaps, a few scientists and others of their kind who didn't really count.

Belsen was the hero and if I laid a finger to him I'd probably be lynched.

And I was right.

Belsen *is* the hero.

He turns on his orchestra at six o'clock each morning and there's no one in the neighborhood who'll say a word to him.

Is there anyone who knows how much it costs to soundproof an entire house?

FULL CYCLE

On December 20, 1954, Clifford D. Simak sent a story entitled "Gypsy Trailers" to H. F. Gold of Galaxy Science Fiction, *but Gold rejected it, as did* Astounding Science Fiction *and the* Magazine of Fantasy & Science Fiction *during the course of the next few months. But as the end of March neared, Cliff sent the story to Robert A. W. Lowndes, who offered to buy it in mid-April, but would pay for it only upon publication. The story was published in the November 1955 issue of* Science Fiction Stories *(which was referred to by most people as the* Original Science Fiction Stories*).*

You might look at this story as a completely different take on the concept of "ghost cities" that turns up, in various forms, in a number of Cliff's stories. Or perhaps as a precursor of the later Simak stories that showed universities trying to survive societal collapse.

—dww

I

The letter sent the life of Amby Wilson crashing decorously down about his ears. It was a form affair, with the address typed in with a newer, blacker ribbon; it said:

Dr. Ambrose Wilson

Department of History

It is with regret that I must inform you the board of regents at their meeting this morning decided the university will cease to function at the end of the present term.

Contributing to the decision were the lack of funds and the progressive dwindling of the student body. You, of course, have been aware of the situation for some time, but nevertheless . . .

There was more of it, but Amby didn't read it. What still was left unread, he knew, would be no more than the grossest of platitudes.

It had been bound to happen.

The regents had hung on in the face of monstrous difficulties; the university was virtually deserted. The place that once had rung with life and pulsed with learning was now no better than a ghost school.

As the city was a ghost city.

And I a ghost, thought Amby.

He made an admission to himself, an admission he would not have made a day or hour ago: For thirty years or more he had lived in an unreal and unsubstantial world, clinging to the old, vague way of life as he first had known it. And to make that vague life the more substantial, he had banished to an intellectual outer limbo any valid consideration of the world beyond the city.

And good reason that he should, he thought; good and valid reason. What was outside the city had no link with this world of his. A nomad population—an almost alien people, who had built a neo-culture rich in decadence, concocted half of provincialism, half of old folk-tales.

There was nothing there, he thought, of any value to a man like him, nothing worth the consideration of a man like him. Here in this university he had kept alight a feeble glow of the old learning and the old tradition; now the light had flickered out and the learning and tradition would go down into the darkness.

And that, he knew, was no attitude for a historian to take; history was the truth and the seeking after truth. To gloss over, to ignore, to push away an eventful fact—no matter how distasteful—was not the way of history.

Now history had caught up with him and there were two alternatives. He could go out and face the world or he could hide from it. There was no compromise.

Amby picked up the letter between his fingertips, as if it might be something dead and left out in the sun too long. Carefully he dropped it in the wastebasket; then he got his old felt hat and clapped it on his head.

He marched out of the classroom without looking back.

II

When he got home, a scarecrow was perched on the front steps. When it saw him coming, it pulled itself together and got up. "Evening, Doc," it said.

"Good evening, Jake," said Amby.

"I was just fixing to go fishing," Jake told him.

Amby sat down carefully on the steps and shook his head. "Not tonight; don't feel up to it. They're closing down the university."

Jake sat down beside him and stared across the street at the city wilderness. "I suppose that ain't no big surprise to you."

"I've been expecting it," said Amby. "Nobody attends any more except some *stuffy* kids. All the *nomies* go to their own universities, if that is what they call them. Although to tell you the honest truth, Jake, I can't see how schools like those could give them very much."

"Well, you're fixed all right, I guess," said Jake, consolingly. "You been working all these years; you probably been able to put away a little. Now with me it's different. We been living hand-to-mouth and we always will."

"I'm not too well fixed," said Amby, "but I'll get along somehow. I probably haven't too long left; I'm almost seventy."

"There was a day," said Jake, "when they had a law that paid a man to quit at sixty-five. But the *nomies* threw that out, just like they did everything."

He picked up a short length of dead branch and dug absent-mindedly at the grass. "I always figured, someday I'd get me enough together so I could buy a trailer. You can't do a thing unless you got a trailer. It does beat all how times can change. I remember when I was a kid it was the man who owned a house that was all set for life. But now a house don't count for nothing. You got to have a trailer."

He got up in sections, stood with his rags fluttering in the wind, looking down at Amby. "You ain't changed your mind about that fishing, Doc?"

"I'm all beat out," said Amby.

"With you not working any more," Jake said, "us two can get in a powerful lot of hunting. The place is full of squirrels and the young rabbits will soon be big enough to eat. This fall there'll be a sight of coons. Now that you ain't working, I'll split the skins with you."

"You still can keep the skins," said Amby.

Jake stuck his thumbs into his waistband and spat upon the ground. "Might just as well spend your time out in the woods as anywhere. Used to be a man could make some money if he was lucky at his prowling, but prowling now is just a waste of time. The places all have been worked over and it's getting so it's downright dangerous to go inside of them. You never know when something might give way and come down and hit you or when the floor will drop out from underneath you."

He hitched up his britches. "Remember that time we found the box with all the jewelry in it?"

Amby nodded. "I remember that; you almost got enough to buy the trailer that time."

"Ain't it a fact? It does beat all how a man can fritter cash away. I bought a new gun and a batch of cartridges and some clothes for the family—and God knows, we needed them—and a good supply of grub; and before I knew it there wasn't near enough left over to even think about a trailer. In the old days a man could have bought one on time. All he'd needed would be ten per cent to pay down on it. But you can't do that no more. There ain't even any banks. And no loan companies. Remember, Doc, when the place crawled with loan companies?"

"It all has changed," said Amby. "When I think back it can't seem possible."

But it was, of course.

The city was gone as an institution; the farms had become corporations and people no longer lived in houses—only the *stuffies* and the squatters.

And folks like me, thought Amby.

III

It was a crazy idea—a sign of old age and feeble-mindedness, perhaps. A man of sixty-eight, a man of competence and settled habits, did not go charging off on a wild adventure even if his world had crashed about his ears.

He tried to quit thinking of it, but he couldn't quit. He thought about it all the time that he cooked supper, and while he ate supper, and later when he washed the dishes.

With the dishes done, he went into the living room, carrying the kitchen lamp. He set the lamp on a table beside another lamp and lit the second lamp. *Must be a sign a man's eyes are wearing out*, he thought, *when he needs two lamps to read by*. But kerosene lamps, at best, were poor things; not like electricity.

He picked a book out of the shelves and settled down to read, but he couldn't read; he couldn't keep his mind on what he tried to read. He finally gave it up.

He took one of the lamps, walked to the fireplace and held it high so that the lamplight fell upon the painting there. And he wondered as he raised the lamp if she would smile at him tonight; he was fairly sure she would, for she was always ready with a tiny smile when he needed it the most.

He wasn't sure at first if she were smiling; then he saw she was, and he stood there looking at her and her smile.

There had been many times of late when he talked with her, for he remembered how ready she had always been to listen to him, how he had talked out his troubles and his triumphs—although, come to think of it, his triumphs had been few.

But he could not talk to her tonight; she would not understand. This world in which he lived without her would seem to her so topsy-turvy as to be past all understanding. And if he tried to talk to her about it, she would be disturbed and troubled and he must not let that happen.

You'd think, he told himself, upbraiding himself, that I'd be content to leave well enough alone. I have a place to hide. I could live out my life in comfort and in safety. And that, he knew, was the way he wanted it to be.

But there was that nagging voice which talked inside his brain: *You have failed your task and failed it willingly. You have shut your eyes and failed. You have failed by looking backwards. The true historian does not live in the past alone. He must use the past to understand the present; and he must know them both if he is to see the trend toward the future.*

But I do not want to know the future, said the stubborn Dr. Ambrose Wilson.

And the nagging voice said: *The future is the only thing that is worth the knowing.*

He stood silently, holding a lamp above his head, staring at the painting almost as if he expected it to speak, as if it might give a sign.

There wasn't any sign. There couldn't be a sign, he knew. It was no more than a painting of a woman, dead these thirty years. The sensed nearness, the old sharp memory, the smile upon the lips were in the heart and mind—not in the square of canvas with clever brush strokes that preserved across the years the bright illusion of a loved face.

He lowered the lamp and went back to his chair.

There was so much to say, he thought, and no one to say it to—although the house might listen if he talked to it as an ancient friend. It had been a friend, he thought. It had been lonely often with her no longer here—but not as lonely in the house as away from it, for the house was a part of her.

He was safe here, safe in this anachronistic house, safe in the abandoned city with its empty buildings; comfortable in this city gone back to wilderness, filled with squirrels and rabbits, colorful and fragrant now with the bloom of gone-wild lilacs and escaped daffodils, prowled by squatters who hunted the thickets of its lawns for game and prowled its crumbling structures to find some salvage they might sell.

Queer, he thought, the concepts upon which a culture might be founded, the fantastic acceptance standards which evolved in each society.

Some forty years ago, the cleavage of the culture had first started; it had not come all at once, but quickly enough so that historically it must be regarded as an abrupt rather than a gradual cleavage.

It had been the Year of Crisis, he remembered, when the drums of fear had thudded through the land and a man had lain in bed, tensed and listening for the coming of the bomb, knowing even as he listened that he'd not hear it if it came.

Fear was the start of it, he thought; and what and where would be the end?

He sat huddled in his chair, cringing from the dark barbarism that lay beyond the city—an old man caught between the future and the past.

IV

Jake said, "She's a beauty, Doc." He got up to walk around it once again.

"Yes, sir," he said, patting it, "She surely is a beauty. I don't think I can rightly say I ever saw a finer trailer. And I've seen lots of them."

"We may be doing a lot of traveling in it," Amby told him. "We want one that will stand up. The roads, I understand, aren't what they used to be. The *nomies* chisel on the road tax, and the government hasn't got much money to keep the roads in shape."

"It won't take long," Jake said confidently. "All we got to do is just kind of look around. In no time at all we'll find a camp that will take us in. Stands to reason there'll be one of them that could find a use for us."

He went over to the trailer and carefully wiped a spot of dust off its shiny surface with his ragged shirt sleeve.

"We ain't none of us scarcely slept a wink since you told us, Doc. Myrt, she can't understand it; she keeps saying to me, 'Why is Doc taking us along? We ain't got no claim on him; all we been is neighbors.'"

"I'm a bit too old," said Amby, "to do it by myself. I have to have someone along to help out with the driving and the other chores. And you've been looking forward all these years to going trailering."

"That's a fact," admitted Jake. "Doc, you never spoke a truer word. I wanted it so bad I could almost taste it; and by the looks of it, so have all the rest of us. You ought to see the throwing away and packing that's going on over at the house. Myrt is plain beside herself. I tell you, Doc, it ain't no safe place to go until Myrt calms down a bit."

"Maybe I ought to do some packing myself," said Amby. "Not that there's much to do; I'll just leave the most of it behind."

But he didn't stir. He didn't want to face it.

It would be hard to leave his home—although that was old-fogey thinking, for there were no longer any homes. "Home" was a word out of an era left behind. "Home" was another nostalgic word for old men like him to mumble in their dim remembering. "Home" was the symbol of a static culture that had failed in the scales of Man's survival. To put down roots, to stay and become encumbered by possessions—not only physical, but mental and traditional as well—was to die. To be mobile and forever poised on the edge of flight, to travel lean and gaunt, to shun encumbrances, was the price of freedom and life.

Full cycle, Amby thought—*we have come full cycle. From tribe to city, now back to tribe again.*

Jake came back from the trailer and sat down again. "Tell me, Doc; tell me honest now—why are you doing it? Not that I ain't glad you are, for otherwise I'd never in all my born days get out of this here rat trap. But I can't somehow get it through my head why you are pulling stakes. You ain't a young man, Doc, and . . ."

"I know," said Amby; "maybe that's the reason. Not too much time left, and I have to make the best use of it I can."

"You're sitting pretty, Doc, and not a worry in the world. Now that you've retired, you could take it easy and have a lot of fun."

"I've got to find out," said Amby.

"Find out what?"

"I don't know; just what is happening, I guess."

They sat quietly, looking at the trailer in all its shining glory. From some distance down the street came the faint clatter of pots and pans and a suddenly raised voice.

Myrt still was busy packing.

V

The first evening they stopped at a deserted campsite across the road from an idle factory.

It was an extensive camp and it had the look of being occupied only recently, as if the trailers might have pulled out just a day or two before. There were fresh tire tracks in the dust; scraps of paper still blew about the area, and the ground beneath some of the water faucets still was damp.

Jake and Amby sat in the trailer's shade and looked at the silent buildings just across the road.

"Funny thing," said Jake, "about this place not running. Sign up there says it's a food processing plant. Breakfast food, looks like. Figure maybe it shut down because there wasn't any market for the stuff it makes?"

"That might be it," said Amby. "But seems there should be a market for breakfast cereal, at least some sort of market for it. Enough to keep it running, although maybe not at full capacity."

"Figure there was some kind of trouble?"

"No sign of it," said Amby. "Looks as if they just up and left."

"There's that big house up on the hill. Look, up thataway . . ."

"I see it now," said Amby.

"Might be where the *stuffy* lives."

"Could be."

"Wonder what it would be like to be a *stuffy*? Just sit and watch the cash come rolling in. Let other people work for you. Have everything you want. Never want for nothing."

"I imagine," Amby told him, "that the *stuffies* have their troubles, too."

"I'd like to have them kind of troubles. I'd just plumb love to have them kind of troubles for a year or two."

He spat on the ground and hauled himself erect. "Might go out and see if I could get me a rabbit or a squirrel," he said. "You feel like coming with me?"

Amby shook his head. "I'm a little tuckered out."

"Probably won't find nothing anyhow. Close to a camp like this, the game must be all cleaned out."

"After a while," said Amby, "when I'm rested up a bit, I might take a walk."

VI

The house was a *stuffy* house, all right. One could almost smell the money of it. It was large and sprawling, very neatly kept, and surrounded by extensive grounds full of flowers and shrubs.

Amby sat down on a stone wall just outside the grounds and looked back the way he'd come. There below him lay the factory and the deserted camping grounds, with his trailer standing alone in the great level, trampled area. The road wound away to a far horizon, white in the summer sun, and there was nothing on it—not a single car or truck or trailer. And that, he thought, was not the way it had been. Once the roads had been crawling with machines.

But this was a different world than the one he'd known. It was a world that he'd ignored for more than thirty years, and it had grown alien in those thirty years. He had shut himself away from it and lost it; now that he sought it once again, he found it puzzling and at times a little terrifying.

A voice spoke behind him. "Good evening, sir."

Amby turned and saw the man—middle-aged or more, and the tweeds and pipe. Almost, he thought, like the age-old tradition of the English country squire.

"Good evening," Amby said. "I hope I'm not intruding."

"Not at all. I saw you camped down there; very glad to have you."

"My partner went out hunting, so I took a walk."

"You folks changing?"

"Changing?"

"Changing camps, I mean. There used to be a lot of it. Not much any more."

"You mean changing from one camp to another?"

"That's it. A process of settling down, I take it. Get dissatisfied with one setup, so go out and hunt another."

"By now," said Amby, "the shakedown period must be almost over. By now each man must have found his place."

The *stuffy* nodded. "Maybe that's the way it is. I don't know too much about it."

"Nor I," Amby told him. "We're just starting out. My university closed down, so I bought a trailer. My next door neighbors came along with me. This is our first day."

"I've often thought," said the man, "that it might be fun to do a little touring. When I was a boy we used to go on long motoring trips and visit different places; but there doesn't seem to be much of that any more. Used to be places where you could stop the night—motels, they called them. And every mile or so there were eating places and service stations where you could buy gasoline. Now the only place where you can get anything to eat, or buy some gas, is at one of the camps; lots of times, I understand, they don't care to sell."

"But we aren't touring. We hope to join a camp."

The *stuffy* stared at him for a moment, then he said: "I wouldn't have thought so, looking at you."

"You don't approve of it?"

"Don't mind me," the *stuffy* said. "Right at this moment, I'm a little sour on them. Just the other morning they all drove out on me. Closed down the plant. Left me sitting here."

He climbed up on the wall and sat down alongside Amby. "They wanted to take me over completely, you understand," he said, settling down to a minute recounting of it. "Under the existing contract they already ran the plant. They bought the raw materials and set up their own work schedules and kept up maintenance. They decided plant operation policy and set production schedules. I'd have had to ask their permission just to go down there and visit. But it wasn't enough for them. Do you know what they wanted?"

Amby shook his head.

"They wanted to take over marketing. That was all that I had left and they wanted to take that away from me. They were all set to shove me out completely. Pay me a percentage of the profit and cut me out entirely."

"Somehow," Amby said, "that doesn't sound quite fair."

"And when I refused to sign, they just packed up and left."

"A strike?"

"I suppose you could call it that. A most effective one."

"What do you do now?"

"Wait until another camp comes down the road. There'll be one along sometime. They'll see the plant standing idle, and if they're industrial and think they can handle it, they'll come up and see me. Maybe we can make a deal. Even if we can't, there'll be another camp along. There's always floating camps. Either that or swarms."

"Swarms?"

"Like bees, you know. A camp gets overcrowded. Too many to handle the contract that they have. So it up and swarms. Usually a bunch of young folks just starting out in life. A swarm is usually easier to deal with than the floaters. The floaters, often as not, are a bunch of radicals and malcontents who can't get along with anyone, while the youngsters in a swarm are anxious to get started at something of their own."

"That all sounds well enough," said Amby, "but how about the ones who left you? Could they afford just to pull stakes and go?"

"They're loaded," said the *stuffy*. "They worked here almost twenty years. They got a sinking fund that would choke a cow."

"I didn't know," said Amby.

There was so much, he thought, that he didn't know. Not only the thinking and the customs, but even a lot of the terminology was strange.

It had been different in the old days when there'd been a daily press; when a new phrase or a new thought became public property almost overnight; when the forces that shaped one's life were daily spread before one in the black and white of print. But now there were no papers and no television. There was still radio, of course; but radio, he thought, was a poor medium to keep a man in touch; even so, it was not the kind of radio he'd known and he never listened to it.

There were no papers and no television, and that wasn't all by any means. There was no furniture, for there was no need of furniture in a trailer with everything built in. There were no rugs, no carpeting, no drapes. There were few luxury items, for there was no room for luxury items in the confines of a trailer. There were no formal and no party clothes, for no one in a trailer camp would dress—there was no room for an extensive wardrobe and the close communal life would discourage all formality. Such dress as there might be in a trailer camp undoubtedly would run heavily to sportswear.

There were no banks or insurance firms or loan companies. Social security had gone down the drain. There was no use for banks or loan companies; the credit union setup, dating from the old trade unionism, would have replaced them on a tight communal basis. And an extension of the old union health and welfare fund, once again on a tight communal basis, had replaced any need of social security, governmental welfare aid, or health insurance. And the war chest idea—once again grafted from unionism—had made each trailer camp an independent, self-sufficient governmental unit.

It worked all right, for there was little that a resident of a trailer camp could spend his money on. The old flytraps of entertainment; the need of expensive dress; the overhead of house furnishings—all had been wiped out. Thrift had become an enforced virtue—enforced by circumstance.

A man didn't even pay taxes any more—not to speak of, anyhow. State and local governments long ago had fallen by the wayside. There remained nothing but the federal government, and even the federal government had lost much of its control—as it must have known it would on that day of forty years ago. All that need now be paid was a trifling defense tax, and a slightly heavier road tax, and the *nomies* screamed loud and lustily against the paying of the road tax.

"It's not like it used to be," said the *stuffy*. "This trade unionism got entirely out of hand."

"It was about all the people had to tie to," Amby told him. "It was the one surviving piece of logic, the one remaining solid thing that was left to them. Naturally, they embraced it; it took the place of government."

"The government should have done it differently," said the *stuffy*.

"They might have if we hadn't got so frightened. It was the fear that did it; it would have been all right if we hadn't got afraid."

Said the *stuffy*: "We'd been blown plumb to hell if we hadn't got afraid."

"Maybe so," said Amby. "I can remember how it happened. The order went out to decentralize, and I guess industry must have known a good deal more about what the situation was than the most of us; it got out and scattered, without any argument. Maybe they knew the government wasn't fooling and maybe they had some facts that weren't public knowledge. Although the public facts, as I remember them, ran rather to the grim side."

"I was just in my teens then," said the *stuffy*, "but I remember something of it. Real estate worth nothing. Couldn't sell city property at a fraction of its worth. And the workers couldn't stay there, for their jobs had moved away—away out in the country. Decentralization took in a lot of country. The big plants split up, some of them into a lot of smaller units and there had to be a lot of miles between each unit."

Amby nodded. "So there'd be no target big enough for anyone to waste a bomb on. Make it cost too much to wipe out an industry. Where one bomb would have done the job before, now it would take a hundred."

"I don't know," said the *stuffy*, still unwilling to concede. "Seems to me the government could have handled it a little differently instead of letting the thing run on the way it did."

"I suspect the government had a lot on its mind right then."

"Sure it had, but it had been in the housing business up to its ears before. Building all sorts of low-cost housing projects."

"It had the job of helping industry get those new plants set up. And the trailers solved the housing problem for the moment."

"I suppose," the *stuffy* said, "that was the way it was."

And that, of course, was the way it had been.

The workers had been forced to follow their jobs—either follow them or starve. Unable to sell their houses in the cities when the bottom dropped out of the real estate market almost overnight, they compromised on trailers; and around each fractionated industry grew up a trailer camp.

They grew to like the trailer life, perhaps, or they were afraid to build another house for fear the same thing might happen yet again—even if some could afford to build another house, and there were a lot of them who couldn't. Or they may have become disillusioned and disgusted—it did not matter what. But the trailer life had caught on and stayed, and people who were not directly affected by decentralization had gradually drifted into the trailer camps, until even most of the villages stood empty.

The cult of possessions had been foresworn. The tribe sprang up again.

Fear had played its part, and freedom—the freedom from possessions, and the freedom to pick up and go without ever looking back—and unionism, too.

For the trailer movement had killed the huge trade union setup. Union bosses and business agents, who had found it easy to control one huge union setup, found it a sheer impossibility to control the hundred scattered units into which each big local had been broken. But within each trailer camp a local brand of unionism had caught on with renewed force and significance. It had served to weld each camp into a solid and cohesive unit. It had made the union a thing close to each family's heart and interest. Unionism, interpreted in the terms of the people and their needs, had provided the tribal pattern needed to make the trailer system work.

"I'll say this much for them," the *stuffy* said. "They were an efficient bunch. They ran the plant better than I could have run it; they watched the costs and they were forever dinging up short-cuts and improvements. During the twenty years they worked here they practically redesigned that plant. That's one of the things they pointed out to me in negotiations. But I told them they'd done it to protect their jobs, and that may have been the thing that made them sore enough to leave."

He tapped his pipe out on the wall. "You know," he said, "I'm not too sure but what I'm right. It'll more than likely take any new gang that moves in a month or so to figure out all the jack-leg contraptions that this bunch of mine rigged up. All I hope is that they don't start it up too quick and wreck the whole shebang."

He polished the bowl of his pipe abstractedly. "I don't know. I wish I could figure that tribe out—just for my peace of mind, if nothing else. They were good people and mostly sensible. They were hard workers and up to a month ago easy to get along with. They lived normal lives for the most part, but there were things about them I couldn't understand. Like the superstitions that grew up. They'd worked up a sizable list of taboos, and they were hell on signs of exorcism and placation. Oh, sure, I know we used to do it—cross your fingers and spit over your left shoulder and all that sort of stuff—but with us it was all in fun. It was just horseplay with us. A sort of loving link with a past we were reluctant to give up. But these people, I swear, believed and lived by it."

"That," said Amby, "bears out my own belief that the culture has actually degenerated into the equivalent of tribalism, perhaps further than I thought. Your small, compact, enclosed social groups give rise to that sort of thing. In a more integrated culture, such notions are laughed out of existence; but in protected soil they take root and grow."

"The farm camps are the worst," the *stuffy* told him. "They have rainmaking mumbo-jumbo and crop magic and all the rest of it."

Amby nodded. "That makes sense. There's something about the enigma of the soil and seed that encourages mysticism. Remember the wealth of mythology that grew up around agriculture in prehistoric times—the fertility rites, and the lunar planting tables, and all the other fetishes."

He sat on the stone wall, staring off across the land; out of the dark unknown of the beginning of the race, he seemed to hear the stamp of calloused feet, the ritual chant, the scream of the sacrifice.

VII

The next day, from the top of a high hill, they sighted the farm camp. It was located at the edge of a grove of trees a little distance from a row of elevators, and across the plains that stretched in all directions lay the gold-green fields.

"Now that's the kind of place I'd like to settle into," said Jake. "Good place to raise the kids and it stands to reason you wouldn't have to kill yourself with work. They do farming mostly with machinery and you'd just ride around, steering a tractor or a combine or a baler or something of the sort. Good healthful living, too, out in the sun and open air and you'd get to see some country, more than likely. When the harvest is done the whole kit and caboodle would just pull stakes and go somewhere else. Out to the southwest maybe for the lettuce or the other garden stuff, or out to the coast for fruit or maybe even south. I don't know if there's any winter farming in the south. Maybe you know, Doc."

"No, I don't," said Amby.

He sat beside Jake and watched Jake drive; Jake, he admitted to himself, was a fine man at the wheel; a man felt safe and confident with Jake driving. He never went too fast; he took no chances, and he knew how to treat a car.

In the back seat the kids were raising a ruckus, and now Jake turned his attention to them. "If you young'uns don't quiet down, I'm going to stop this here outfit and give you all a hiding. You kids know right well you wouldn't be raising all this rumpus if your Ma was with you instead of back there in the trailer. She'd smack your ears for fair and she'd get you quietened down."

The kids paid no attention, went on with their scuffling.

"I been thinking," Jake said to Amby, his duty as a father now discharged, "that maybe this is the smartest thing you ever done. Maybe you should have done it sooner. Stands to reason an educated man like you won't have no trouble finding a good place in one of these here camps. Ain't likely they got many educated men and there's nothing, I've always said, like an education. Never got one myself and maybe that's why I set such a store by it. One of the things I hated back there in the city was watching them kids run wild without a lick of learning. Myrt and me did the best we could, but neither of us know much more than our ABC's and we weren't proper teachers."

"They probably have schools in all the camps," said Amby. "I've never heard they had, but they have some sort of universities—and before anyone could go to college he'd have to have some sort of elementary education. I rather imagine we'll find the camps equipped with a fair communal program. A camp is a sort of mobile village and more than likely it would be run like one, with schools and hospitals and churches and all the other things you'd expect to find in towns—although all of them, I imagine, will have certain overtones of trade unionism. Culture is a strange thing, Jake, but it usually spells out to pretty much the same in the end result. Differing cultures are no more than different approaches to a common problem."

"I declare," said Jake, "it's a pleasure just to sit here and listen to all that lingo that you throw around. And the beauty of it is you sound just like you know what all them big words mean."

He swung the car off the highway onto the rutted road that ran up to the camp. He slowed to a crawl and they bumped along.

"Look at it," he said. "Ain't it a pretty sight. See all that washing hung out on the lines and those posies growing in the window boxes on the trailers and that little picket fence some of the folks have set up around the trailers, just like the yards back home. I wouldn't be none surprised, Doc, if we find these folks people just like us."

They reached the camp and swung out of the road, off to one side of the trailers. A crowd of children had gathered and stood watching them. A woman came to the door of one of the trailers and stood, leaning against the doorway, staring at them. Some dogs joined the children and sat down to scratch fleas.

Jake got out of the car. "Hello, kids," he said.

They giggled shyly at him.

Jake's kids piled out of the back seat and stood in a knot beside their father.

Myrt climbed down out of the trailer. She fanned herself with a piece of cardboard. "Well, I never," she declared.

They waited.

Finally an old man came around the end of one of the trailers and walked toward them. The kids parted their ranks to let him through. He walked slowly, with a cane to help him. "Something I can do for you, stranger?"

"We was just looking around," said Jake.

"Look all you want," the oldster told him.

He glanced at Amby, still sitting in the car. "Howdy, oldtimer."

"Howdy," said Amby.

"Looking for anything special, oldtimer?"

"I guess you could say we are looking for a job; we hope to find a camp that will take us on."

The old man shook his head. "We're pretty well full up. But you better talk to the business agent; he's the one to see."

He turned and yelled to the group of staring kids. "You kids go and hunt up Fred."

They scattered like frightened partridges.

"We don't get many folks like you any more," the old man said. "Years ago there were lots of them, just drifting along, looking for whatever they could find. A lot of folks from the smaller towns and a lot of them DF's."

He saw the look of question on Amby's face.

"Displaced farmers," he said. "Ones who couldn't make a go of it and once they took off parity there were a lot of them. Maddest bunch you ever saw. Fighting mad, they were. Had come to count on parity; thought they had it coming to them. Figured the government had done them dirt and I suppose it had. But it did dirt to a lot of the rest of us as well. You couldn't bust things up the way they were busted up without someone getting hurt. And the way things were, you couldn't expect the government to keep on with all their programs. Had to simplify."

Amby nodded in agreement. "You couldn't maintain a top-heavy bureaucracy in a system that had become a technological tribal system."

"I guess you're right," the old man agreed in turn. "So far as the farmers were concerned, it didn't make much difference anyhow. The small land holdings were bound to disappear. The little farmer just couldn't make the grade. Agriculture was on its way toward corporate holdings even before D.C. Machinery was the thing that did it. You couldn't farm without machinery and it didn't pay to buy machinery to handle the few acres on the smaller farms."

He walked closer to the car and stroked one fender with a gnarled hand. "Good car you got here."

"Had it for a long time," Amby told him. "Took good care of it."

The old man brightened. "That's a rule we got around here, too. Everyone has to take good care of everything. Ain't like it was one time when, if you busted something, or it wore out, or you lost it, you could run down the corner and get another one. Pretty good camp that way. Young fellers spend a lot of their spare time dinging up the cars. You should see what they've done to some of them. Yes, sir, there's some of them cars they've made almost human."

He walked up to the open car window and leaned on the door. "Darn good camp," he said. "Any way you look at it. We got the neatest crops around; and we take good good care of the soil; and that's worth a lot to the *stuffy* who owns the place. We been coming back to this same place every spring for almost twenty years. If someone beats us here, the *stuffy* won't even talk to them. He always waits for us. There ain't many camps, I can tell you, that can say as much. Of course, in the winter we wander around considerable but that's because we want to. There ain't a winter place we been we couldn't go back to anytime we wanted."

He eyed Amby speculatively. "You wouldn't know nothing about rain-making, now would you?"

"Some years ago I did some reading on what had been done about it," Amby told him. "Cloud seeding, they called it. But I forget what they used. Silver—something. Some kind of chemical."

"I don't know anything about this seeding," the old man said; "and I don't know if they use chemicals or not."

"Of course," he said, anxious not to be misunderstood, "we got a bunch of the finest rain-makers that you ever saw, but in this farming business you can't have too many of them. Better to have one or two too many than one or two too few."

He looked up at the sky. "We don't need no rain right now and it ain't right to use the power, of course, unless you have some need of it. I wish you'd come when we needed rain, for then you could stay over and see the boys in action. They put on quite a show. When they put on a dance everyone turns out to watch."

"I read somewhere once," said Amby, "about the Navahos. Or maybe it was the Hopis . . ."

But the old man wasn't interested in Navahos or Hopis. "We got a fine crew of green-thumbers, too," he said. "I don't want to sound like bragging, but we got the finest crew . . ."

The children came charging around the parked trailers, yelling. The old man swung around. "Here comes Fred."

Fred ambled toward them. He was a big man, bareheaded, with an unruly thatch of black hair, bushy eyebrows, a mouthful of white teeth. "Hello, folks," he said. "What can I do for you?"

Jake explained.

Fred scratched his head, embarrassed and perplexed. "We're full up right now; fact is, we're just on the edge of swarming.

I don't see how we can take on another family. Not unless you could offer something special."

"I'm handy at machinery," Jake told him; "I can drive anything."

"We got a lot of drivers. How about repair? Know anything about welding? Can you operate a lathe?"

"Well, no . . ."

"We have to repair our own machines and keep them in top running shape. Sometimes we have to make parts to replace ones that have been broken. Just can't wait to get replacements from the factory, we're kind of jacks-of-all-trades around here. There's a lot more to it than driving. Anyone can drive. Even the women and the kids."

"Doc here," said Jake, "is an educated man. Was a professor at the university until the university shut down. Maybe you could find some use . . ."

Fred cheered up. "You don't say. Not agronomy . . ."

"History," Amby told him. "I don't know anything but history."

"Now that's too bad," said Fred. "We could use an agronomist. We're trying to run some experimental plots, but we don't know too much about it. We don't seem to get nowhere."

The old man said to Amby: "The idea is to develop better strains. It's our stock in trade. One of our bargaining points. Each camp furnishes its own seed and you can get a better deal out of the *stuffy* if you have top-notch strains. We got a good durham, but we're working on corn now. If we could get some that matured ten days sooner, say . . ."

"It sounds interesting," said Amby, "but I couldn't help you. I don't know a thing about it."

"I'd sure work hard," said Jake, "if you just gave me a chance. You wouldn't find a more willing worker in your entire camp."

"Sorry," the business agent told him. "We all are willing workers. If you're looking for a place your best bet would be a swarm. They might take you in. An old camp like us don't take newcomers as a rule; not unless they got something special."

"Well," said Jake, "I guess that's it."

He opened the door and got into the car. The kids swarmed into the back seat. Myrt climbed back into the trailer.

"Thanks," Jake said to the business agent. "Sorry we took up your time."

He swung the car around and bumped back to the road. He was silent for a long time. Finally he spoke up. "What the hell," he asked, "is an agronomist?"

VIII

That was the way it was everywhere they went:

--Are you one of those cybernetic fellows? No? Too bad. We could sure use one of those cybernetic jerks.

--Too bad. We could use a chemist. Messing around with fuels. Don't know a thing except what we dig out. One of these days the boys will blow the whole camp plumb to hell.

--Now if you were a lifter. We could use a lifter.

--You know electronics, maybe. No? Too bad.

--History. Afraid we got no use for history.

--You know any medicine? Our Doc is getting old.

--Rocket engineer? We got some ideas. We need a guy like that.

--History? Nope. What would we do with history?

But there was a use for history, Amby told himself. "I know there is a use for it," he said. "It has always been a tool before. Now, suddenly, even in a raw, new society such as this, it could not have lost its purpose."

He lay in his sleeping bag and stared up at the sky.

Back home, he thought, it was already autumn; the leaves were turning and the city, in the blaze of autumn, he recalled, was a place of breathless beauty.

But here, deep in the south, it still was summer and there was a queer, lethargic feel to the deep green of the foliage and the flint-hard blueness of the sky—as if the green and blue were stamped upon the land and would remain forever, a land where change had been outlawed and the matrix of existence had been hard cast beyond any chance of alteration.

The trailer loomed black against the sky; now that Jake and Myrt had quit their mumbling talk inside of it, he could hear the purling of the stream that lay just beyond the campsite. The campfire had died down until it was no more than a hint of rose in the whiteness of the ash, and from the edge of the woods a bird struck up a song—a mockingbird, he thought, although not so sweet a song as he had imagined a mockingbird would sing.

That was the way it was with everything, he thought. Nothing was the way you imagined it. Most often a thing would be less glamorous and more prosaic than one had imagined it; and then, suddenly, in some unexpected place one would encounter something that would root him in his tracks.

The camps, once he'd seen two or three of them, had fallen into patterns—good solid American, sound business-practice patterns; the peculiarities had ceased to be peculiarities once he had come to understand the reason for them.

Like the weekly military drills, for instance, and the regular war games, with every man-Jack of the camp going through maneuvers or working out in all seriousness, grimly, without any horseplay, a military problem—with the women and the children scattering like coveys of quail to seek out hiding places from imaginary foes.

And that was why, he knew, the federal government could get along on its trifling defense tax. For here, at hand, subject to instantaneous call, was a citizen soldiery that would fight a total, terrible war such as would rip to pieces and hunt down with frontier efficiency and Indian savagery any enemy that might land upon the continent. The federal government maintained the air force, supplied the weapons, conducted the military research and provided the overall command and planning. The people, down to the last and least of them, were the standing army, ready for instant mobilization, trained to hair-trigger readiness, and operative without a dime of federal cost.

It was a setup, he realized now, having seen the war games and the drill, that would give pause to any potential enemy. It was something new in the science of warfare. Here stood a nation that presented no target worth the bomb that might be dropped upon it, fostering no cities to be seized and held, no industries which might be ravaged in their entirety, and with every male inhabitant between the ages of 16 and 70 a ready, willing fighter.

He lay there, pondering the many things he'd seen, the strangely familiar and the unfamiliar.

Like the folkways that had grown up within each camp, compounded of legend, superstition, magic, remembered teachings, minor hero-worship and all the other inevitable odds and ends of close communal living. And the folkways, he realized, were a part of the fierce, partisan loyalty of each man and woman for their own home camp. Out of this had arisen the fantastic rivalry, hard at times to understand, which existed among the camps, manifesting itself all the way from the bragging of the small fry to the stiff-necked refusal of camp leaders to share their knowledge or their secrets with any other camp. Hard to understand, all of it, until one saw in it the translation of the old tradition that had been the soul and body of American business practice.

A queer layout, thought Dr. Ambrose Wilson, lying in his sleeping bag in the depth of southern night—a queer layout, but a most effective one, and understandable within its terms of reference.

Understandable except for one thing—something on which he could not lay a finger. A feeling, perhaps, rather than a fact—a feeling that somewhere, somehow, underneath this whole new fabric of the neo-gypsy life, lay some new factor, vital and important, that one could sense but could never lay a name to.

He lay there, thinking of that new and vital factor, trying to sift out and winnow the impressions and the clues. But there was nothing tangible; nothing to reach out and grasp; nothing that one could identify. It was like chaff without a single grain, like smoke without a fire—it was something new and, like all the other things, perhaps, entirely understandable within its frame of reference. But where was the reference, he wondered.

They had come down across the land, following the great river, running north to south, and they'd found many camps—crop camps with great acreages of grain and miles of growing corn; industrial camps with smoking chimneys and the clanking of machines; transportation camps with the pools of trucks and the fantastic operation of a vast freightage web; dairy camps with herds of cattle and the creameries and cheese factories where the milk was processed and the droves of hogs that were a sideline to the dairying; chicken camps; truck farming camps; mining camps; road maintenance camps; lumbering camps and all the others. And now and then the floaters and the swarms, wanderers like themselves, looking for a place.

Everywhere they'd gone it had been the same. A chorus of "too bad" resounding down the land, the swarms of staring children and the scratching dogs and the business agent saying there was nothing.

Some camps had been friendlier than others; in some of these they'd stayed for a day or week to rest up from their travels, to overhaul the motor, to get the kinks out of their legs, to do some visiting.

In those camps he had walked about and talked, sitting in the sun or shade, as the time of day demanded; it had seemed at times he had got to know the people. But always, when it seemed that he had got to know them, he'd sense the subtle strangeness, the nebulous otherness, as if there were someone he could not see sitting in the circle, someone staring at him from some hidden spying spot; and he'd know then that there lay between him and these people a finely-spun fabric of forty years forgotten.

He listened to their radios, communal versions of the 1960 ham outfits, and heard the ghostly voices come in from other camps, some nearby, some a continent away, a network of weird communication on the village level. Gossip, mostly, but not entirely gossip, for some of it was official messages—the placing of an order for a ton of cheese or a truckload of hay, or the replacement for some broken machine part—or possibly the confirmation of a debt that one camp owed another for some merchandise or product, and oftentimes a strange shuffling of those debts from one camp to another, promise paying promise. And what of it was gossip had a special sense, imprinted with the almost unbelievable pattern of this fantastic culture which overnight had walked out of its suburbia to embrace nomadism.

And always there was magic, a strangely gentle magic used for the good of people rather than their hurt. It was, he thought, as if the brownies and the fairies had come back again after their brief banishment from a materialistic world. There were quaint new ceremonies drawing from the quaintness of the old; there were good-luck charms and certain words to say; there was a resurgence of old and simple faith forgotten in the most recent of our yesterdays, an old and simple faith in certain childish things. *And perhaps*, he thought, *it is well that it is so.*

But the most puzzling of all was the blending of the ancient magic and the old beliefs with an interest just as vital in modern technology—cybernetics going hand in hand with the good luck charm, the rain dance and agronomy crouching side by side.

All of it bothered him in more ways than one as he sought an understanding of it, tried to break down the pattern and graph it mentally on a historic chart sheet; for as often as the graph seemed to work out to some sensible system it would be knocked out of kilter by the realization he was working with no more than surface evidence.

There was always something missing—that sensed and vital factor.

They had traveled down the continent to a chorus of "too bad"; Jake, he knew, was a worried man, as he had every right to be. Lying in his sleeping bag night after night, he'd listened to them talking—Jake and Myrt—when the kids had been asleep and he should have been. And while he'd taken care, out of decency, not to be close enough or listen hard enough to catch their actual words, he had gathered from the tones of their mumbling voices what they had talked about.

It was a shame, he thought; Jake's hopes had been so high and his confidence so great. It was a terrible thing, he told himself, to see a man lose his confidence, a little day by day—to see it drain away from him like blood-drip from a wound.

He stirred, settling his body into the sleeping bag, and shut his eyes against the stars. He felt sleep advance upon him like an ancient comforter; and in that hazy moment he had drifted from the world and yet not entirely lost it, he saw once again, idealized and beautiful, the painting that hung above the fireplace, with the lamplight falling on it.

IX

The trailer was gone when he awoke.

He did not realize it at first, for he lay warm and comfortable, with the fresh wind of morning at his face, listening to the gladness of the birds from each tree and thicket, and the talking of the brook as it flowed among its pebbles.

He lay thinking how fine it was to be alive and vaguely wondering what the day would bring and thankful that he did not fear to meet it.

It was not until then that he saw the trailer was no longer there; he lay quietly for a moment, uncomprehending, before the force of what had happened slapped him in the face.

The first wave of panic washed over him and swiftly ebbed away—the cold fear of loneness, the panic of desertion—retreating before the dull red glow of anger. He found his clothes inside the sleeping bag and swiftly scrambled out. Sitting on the bag to dress, he took in the scene and tried to reconstruct how it might have happened.

The camp lay just beyond a long dip in the road and he remembered how they had blocked the trailer's wheels against the slope of ground. More than likely Jake had simply taken away the blocks, released the brakes, and rolled down the hill, not starting the motor until well out of hearing.

He got up from the sleeping bag and walked numbly forward. Here were the stones they'd used to block the trailer and there the tracks of the tires straight across the dew.

And something else: Leaning against a tree was the .22 rifle that had been Jake's most prized possession and beside it an old and bulging haversack.

He knelt beside the tree and unstrapped the haversack. There were two cartons of matches, ten boxes of ammunition, his extra clothing, food, cooking and eating utensils, and an old raincoat.

He knelt there, looking at it all spread upon the ground and he felt the burning of the tears just behind his eyelids. Treachery, sure—but not entirely treacherous, for they'd not forgotten him. Thievery and desertion and the worst of bad intentions, yet Jake had left him the rifle that had been his good right arm.

Those mumbled conversations that he had listened to—could they have been plotting together rather than just worried talk? And what if he had listened to the words rather than the mumble, what if he had crept and listened and learned what they were planning—what could he have done about it?

He repacked the haversack and carried it and the rifle to his sleeping bag. It would be a lot to carry, but he would take it slow and easy and he would get along. As a matter of fact, he consoled himself, he was not too badly off; he still had his billfold and the money that remained. He wondered, without caring much, how Jake, without a cent, would get gasoline and food when he needed it.

And he could hear Jake saying, in those mumbled nightly talks: "*It's Doc. That's why they won't take us in. They take one look at him and know the day is not far off when he'll be a welfare charge. They aren't taking on someone who'll be a burden to them in a year or two.*"

Or: "*It's Doc, I tell you, Myrt. He flings them big words around and they are scared of him. Figure he won't fit. Figure he is snooty. Now take us. We're common, ordinary folks. They'd take us like a shot if we weren't packing Doc.*"

Or: "*Now us, we can do any kind of work, but Doc is specialized. We won't get nothing unless we cut loose from Doc.*"

Amby shook his head. It was funny, he thought, to what lengths a man would go once he got desperate enough. Gratitude and honor, even friendship, were frail barriers to the actions of despair.

And I, he asked himself. What do I do now?

Certainly not the first thing that had popped into his head—turning around and heading back for home. That would be impossible; in another month or so, snow would have fallen in the north and he would be unable to get through. If he decided to go home, he'd have to wait till spring.

There was one thing to do—continue southward, traveling as he had been traveling, but at a slower pace. There might even be some merit in it. He would be by himself and would have more time to think. And here was a situation that called for a lot of thinking, a lot of puzzling out. Somewhere, he knew, there had to be an answer and a key to that factor he had sensed within the camps. Once he had that factor, the history graph could be worked out, and he would have done the task he had set out to do.

He left the haversack and rifle on the sleeping bag and walked out to the road. He stood in the middle of it, looking first one way and then the other. It was a long and lonely road and he must travel it as lonely as the road. He'd never had a child, and of recent years he'd scarcely had a friend. Jake, he admitted now, had been his closest friend; but Jake was gone, cut off from him not only by the distance and the winding road, but by this act which now lay between them.

He squared his shoulders, with an outward show of competence and bravery which he did not feel, and walked back to pick up the sleeping bag, the haversack and rifle.

X

It was a month later that he stumbled on the truckers' camp, quite by accident.

It was coming on toward evening; he was on the lookout for a place to spend the night when he approached the intersection and saw the semi-trailer parked there.

A man was squatted beside a newly-lighted campfire, carefully feeding small sticks to the flame. A second man was unpacking what appeared to be a grub-box. A third was coming out of the woods with a bucket, probably carrying water from a nearby stream.

The man tending the fire saw Amby, and stood up. "Howdy, stranger," he called. "Looking for a place to camp?"

Amby nodded and approached the campfire. He took the haversack and sleeping bag off his shoulder and dropped them to the ground. "I'd be much obliged."

"Glad to have you," said the man. He hunkered down beside the fire again and went on nursing it. "Ordinarily we don't camp out for the night. We just stop long enough to cook a bite to eat, then hit the road again. We got a bunk in the job so one of us can sleep while another drives. Even Tom has got so he's pretty good at driving."

He nodded at the man who had brought in the water. "Tom ain't a trucker. He's perfesser at a university, on a leave of absence."

Tom grinned across the fire at Amby. "Sabbatical."

"So am I," said Amby. "Mine is permanent."

"But tonight we'll make a night of it," went on the trucker. "I don't like the sound of the motor. She's heating up some, too. We'll have to tear it down."

"Tear it down right here?"

"Why not? Good a place as any."

"But . . ."

The trucker chuckled. "We'll get along all right. Jim, my helper over there—he's a lifter. He'll just h'ist her out and bring her over to the fire and we'll tear her down."

Amby sat down by the fire. "I'm Amby Wilson," he said. "Just wandering around."

"Rambling far?"

"From up in Minnesota."

"Far piece of walking for a man your age."

"I came part of the way by car."

"Car break down on you?"

"My partner ran off with it."

"Now," the trucker said, judiciously, "that's what I'd call a lousy, lowdown trick."

"Jake didn't mean any harm; he just got panicky."

"You try to track him down?"

"What's the use of trying? There's no way that I can."

"You could get a tracer."

"What's a tracer?"

"Pop," the trucker asked, "where the hell you been?"

And it was a fair question, Amby admitted to himself.

"A tracer," said Tom, "is a telepath. A special kind of telepath. He can track down a mind and find it almost every time. A kind of human bloodhound. It's hard work and there aren't many of them; but as the years go by we hope there will be more—and better."

A tracer is a telepath!

Just like that, without any warning.

A special kind of telepath—as if there might be many other kinds of them.

Amby sat hunched before the fire and looked cautiously around to catch the sheltered grin. But they were not grinning; they acted, he thought, as if this matter of a telepath was very commonplace.

Could it be that here, he wondered, within minutes after meeting them, these people had been the first to say the word that made some sense out of the welter of folklore and magic he'd encountered in the camps?

A tracer was a telepath; and a lifter might be a teleporter; and a green-thumber very well might be someone who had an inherent, exaggerated sympathy and understanding for the world of living things.

Was this, then, the missing factor he had sought; the differentness sensed in the camps; the logic behind the rain-makers and all the other mumbo-jumbo that he had thought of as merely incidental to an enclosed social group?

He brought his hands together between his knees, locking his fingers together tightly, to keep from trembling. *Good Lord,* he thought, *if this is it, so many things explained! If this is the answer that I sought, then here is a culture that is unbeatable!*

Tom broke in upon his thinking. "You said you were on a sabbatical as well as I. A permanent one, you said. Are you a school man, too?"

"I was," said Amby, "but the university closed down. It was one of the old universities, and there was no money and not many students."

"You're looking for another school post?"

"I'd take anything; it seems that no one wants me."

"The schools are short on men. They would snap you up."

"You mean these trailer universities."

Tom nodded. "That is what I mean."

"You don't think much of them?" the trucker asked, his hackles rising.

"I don't know anything about them."

"They're good as any schools there ever were," the trucker said. "Don't let no one tell you different."

Amby hunched forward toward the fire, the many questions, the hope and fear bubbling in his mind. "This tracer business," he said. "You said a tracer was a special kind of telepath. Are there others—I mean, are there other possibilities?"

"Some," said Tom. "There seems to be a lot of special talent showing up these days. We catch a lot of them in the universities and we try to train them, but there isn't much that we can do. After all, how could you or I train a telepath? How would you go about it? About the best that we can do is to encourage each one of them to use such talent as he has to the best advantage."

Amby shook his head, confused. "But I don't understand. Why do you have them now when we never used to have them?"

"Perhaps there may have been some of them before D. C. There must have been, for the abilities must have been there, latent, waiting for their chance. But maybe, before this, they never had a chance. Maybe they were—well, killed in the rush. Or the abilities that there were may have been smothered under the leveling influence of the educational system. There may have been some who had the talents, and were afraid to use them for fear of being different in a culture where differentness was something to point a finger at. And being afraid, they suppressed them, until they weren't bothered by them.

And there may have been others who used their talents secretly to their own advantage. Can you imagine what a lawyer or a politician or a salesman could have done with telepathy?"

"You believe this?"

"Well, not all of it. But the possibilities exist."

"What do you believe, then?"

"Folks are smarter now," the trucker said.

"No, Ray, that isn't it at all. The people are the same. Perhaps there were special talents back before D. C., but I don't think they showed up as often as they show up now. We got rid of a lot of the old restrictions and conventionalities. We threw away a lot of the competition and the pressure when we left the houses, and all the other things we had thought we couldn't get along without. We cut out the complexities. Now no one is breathing down our necks. We don't have to worry so much about keeping up with the man next door—because the man next door has become a friend and is no longer a yardstick of our social and economic station. We aren't trying to pack forty-eight hours of living into every twenty-four. Maybe we're giving ourselves the chance to develop what we missed before."

Jim, the helper, had hung a pot of coffee on a forked stick over the fire and now was cutting meat.

"Pork chops tonight," said Ray, the trucker. "We were passing by a farm camp this morning and there was this pig out in the road and there wasn't nothing I could do . . ."

"You almost wrecked the truck to get him."

"Now, that's a downright libel," Ray protested. "I did my level best to miss him."

Jim went on cutting chops, throwing them into a big frying pan as he sliced them off.

"If you're looking for a teaching job," said Tom, "all you got to do is go to one of the universities. There are a lot of them. Most of them not large."

"But where do I find them?"

"You'd have to ask around. They move around a lot. Get tired of one place and go off to another. But you're lucky now. The south is full of them. Go north in the spring, come south in the fall."

The trucker had settled back on his haunches and was building himself a cigaret. He lifted the paper to his mouth and licked it, twirling it in shape. He stuck it in his mouth and it drooped there limply while he hunted for a small twig from the fire to give himself a light.

"Tell you what," he said, "why don't you just come along with us? There's room for everyone. Bound to find a bunch of universities along the way. You can have your pick of them. Or you might take it in your mind to stick with us right out to the coast. Tom is going out there to see some shirt-tail relatives of his."

Tom nodded. "Sure. Why don't you come along."

"Ain't like it was in the old days," said the trucker. "My old man was a trucker then. You went hell-for-leather. You didn't stop for nothing—not even to be human. You just kept rolling."

"That was the way with all of us," said Amby.

"Now we take it easy," said the trucker. "We don't get there as fast, but we have a lot more fun and there ain't no one suffering if we're late a day or two."

Jim put the pan of chops on the bed of coals.

"It's a lot easier trucking, too," said Ray, "if you can get a lifter for a helper. Nothing to loading or unloading if you have a lifter. And if you get stuck in the mud, he can push you out. Jim here is the best lifter that I ever saw. He can lift that big job if he has to without any trouble. But you got to keep after him; he's the laziest mortal I ever saw."

Jim went on frying chops.

The trucker flipped the cigaret toward the fire and it landed in the pan of chops. Almost immediately it rose out of them; described a tiny arc and fell into the coals.

Jim said: "Ray, you got to cut out things like that. Watch what you are doing. You wear me out just picking up behind you."

The trucker said to Amby, "How about joining up with us? You'd see a lot of country."

Amby shook his head. "I'll have to think about it."

But he was dissembling. He didn't have to think about it.

He knew he wasn't going.

XI

He stood by the dead campfire at the intersection and waved goodbye to them, watching the semi-trailer disappear down the road in the early morning mist.

Then he bent down and picked up the haversack and the sleeping bag and slung them on his shoulder.

He felt within himself a strange urgency—a happy urgency. And it was fine to feel it once again after all these months. Fine again to know he had a job to do.

He stood for a moment, staring around at the camping grounds—the dead ash of the fire, the pile of unused wood, and the great spot on the ground where the grease from the motor of the truck soaked slowly in the soil.

He would not have believed it, he knew, if he had not seen it done—seen Jim lift the motor from the truck once the bed bolts had been loosened, lift it and guide it to rest beside the fire without once lying hands upon it. Again he had watched the stubborn nuts that defied the wrench turn slowly and reluctantly without a tool upon them, then spin freely to rise free of the thread and deposit themselves neatly in a row.

Once, long ago it seemed, he'd talked with a *stuffy* who had told him how efficiently a camp had run his plant, complaining all the while of how they'd rejiggered it until it would take any other camp a month at least to figure out the sheer mechanics of it.

Efficient! Good Lord, of course they were efficient! What new methods, what half-guessed new principles, he wondered, may have gone into that rejiggered plant?

All over the country, he wondered, how many new principles and methods might there be at work? But not regarded as new principles by the camps that had worked them out; regarded rather as trade secrets, as powerful points in bargaining, as tribal stock-in-trade. And in the whole country, he wondered, how many new talents might there be, how many applicable variations of those specific talents?

A new culture, he thought—an unbeatable culture if it only knew its strength, if it could be jarred out of its provincialism, if it could strip from its new abilities the veil of superstition. And that last, he knew, might be the toughest job of all; the magic had been used to cloak annoying ignorance and as an explanation for misunderstanding. It offered a simple and an easy explanation, and it might be hard to substitute in its stead the realization that at the moment there could be little actual knowledge and no complete understanding—only an acceptance and a patience against the day when it might be understood.

He walked over to the tree where he had leaned his rifle and picked it up. He swung it almost gayly in his hand and was astonished at the familiarity of it, almost as if it were a part of him, an extension of his hand.

And that was the way it was with these people and the possibilities. They'd gotten so accustomed to the magic, that it had become a part of everyday; they did not see the greatness of it.

The possibilities, once one thought of them, were fantastic. Develop the abilities and within another hundred years the sputtering radios would be gone, replaced by telepaths who would blanket the nation with a flexible network of communications that never would break down, that would be immune to atmospheric conditions—an intelligent, human system of communication without the inherent limitations of an electronic setup.

The trucks would be gone, too, with relays of teleporters whisking shipments from coast to coast (and all points in between), fast and smooth and without a hitch and, once again, without regard to weather or to road conditions.

And that was only two facets of the picture. What of all the others—the known, the suspected, the now-impossible?

He walked from the campsite out to the road and stood for a moment, wondering. Where was that camp where they had asked if he was a rocket engineer? And where had been the camp that had been in the market for a chemist because the boys were fooling around with fuels? And where, he wondered, would he be able to pick up a lifter? And perhaps a good, all-purpose telepath.

It wasn't much, this thing he had in mind, he admitted to himself. But it was a start. "Give me ten years," he said. "Just ten years is all I ask."

But even if he had no more than two, he had to make a start. For if he made the start, then perhaps there'd be someone who would carry on. Someone had to make a start. Someone like himself, perhaps, who could look upon this neo-tribal world objectively and in the light of the historic past. *And there may not be many of us left*, he thought.

He might have a hard job selling them, he knew, but he thought he knew the pitch.

He set off up the road and he whistled as he went.

It wasn't much, but it would be spectacular if he could accomplish it. Once it had been done, it would be a thing that every camp would spy and scheme and cheat and steal to do.

And it would take something such as that, he knew, to knock some sense into their heads; to make them see the possibilities; to set them to wondering how they might turn to use the other strange abilities which had blossomed here in the soil of a new society.

Now where was that camp where they'd been in need of a rocket engineer?

Up the road somewhere. Up the winding, lonely road that was no longer lonely.

Just up the road a piece. A hundred miles or two. Or was it more than that?

He jogged along, trying to remember. But it was hard to remember. There had been so many days and so many camps. A landmark, he thought—I was always good at landmarks.

But there had been too many landmarks, too.

XII

He wandered up the road, stopping at the camps and the answer that he got became monotonous.

"Rockets? Hell, no! Who'd fool around with rockets?"

And he wondered: Had there ever been a camp where they'd said they could use a rocket engineer? Who would fool around with rockets? What would be the use of it?

The word went ahead of him, by telepath perhaps, by radio, by fast-running word of mouth, and he found himself a legend. He found them waiting for him, as if they had been expecting him, and they had a standard greeting that soon became a joke.

"You the gent who's looking for the rockets?"

But with their joking and the legend of him, he became one of them; and yet, even in becoming one of them, he still stood apart from them and saw the greatness that they missed, a greatness that they had to—*had to*—be awakened to. And a greatness that mere words and preaching would never make come alive for them.

He sat at the nightly communal gabfests, slept in those trailers that had room for an extra person, and helped at little tasks and listened to the yarning. And in turn did some yarning of his own. Time after time he felt again the strangeness and the otherness; but now that he recognized it, it did not disturb him—and sometimes, looking around the circle, he could spot the one who had it.

Lying in a bunk at night, before he went to sleep, he thought a lot about it and finally it all made sense to him.

These abilities had been with Man always, perhaps even from the caves, and then, as now, Man had not understood the power and so had not followed it. Rather he had followed along another path—ignoring mind for hand—and had built himself a wonderful and impressive and complex culture of machines. He'd built with his hands and with mighty labor the vast, complex machines which did what he might have done with the power of mind alone had he but chosen to do so. Rather he had hidden the mental power behind semantics of his own devising, and in seeking after intellectual status had laughed into disrepute the very thing he sought.

This thing which had happened, Amby told himself, was no quirk in the development of the race, but as sure and certain as the sun. It was no more than a returning to the path it had been intended all along that Man should follow. After centuries of stumbling, the human race once more was headed right again. And even if there had been no decentralization, no breakup of the culture, it would eventually have happened, for somewhere along the line of technology there must be a breakdown point. Machines could only get so big. There had to be an end somewhere to complexity, be it in machines or living.

Decentralization may have helped a little, might have hurried the process along by a thousand years or so, but that was all it amounted to.

And here once again Man had devised clever words—commonplace words—to dim the brightness of this frightening thing he could not understand. A teleporter was called a lifter; a telepath a tracer or a talker, the ability to follow worldlines a bit into the future was called second sight, while one who practiced it was usually called a peeker. And there were many other abilities, too—unrecognized or little better than half-guessed—all lumped under the general term of magic. But this did not matter greatly. A common and a homey word served just as well as correct terminology, and might even in the end lead to a readier acceptance. The thing that did matter greatly was that this time the abilities not be lost and not be pushed aside. Something would happen, something had to happen, to shock these people into a realization of what they really had.

So he went from camp to camp and now there was no need to ask the question, for the question went before him.

He went along the roads, a legend, and now he heard of another legend, a man who went from camp to camp dispensing medicines and cures.

It was only a rumor at first, heard oftener and oftener; finally he found a camp where the healer had stopped no more than a week before. Sitting around a campfire that evening, he listened to the wonder of the healer.

"Mrs. Cooper complained for years," an old crone told him. "Was sickly all the time. Kept to her bed for days. Couldn't keep nothing on her stomach. Then she took one bottle of this stuff and you should see her now. Sprightly as a jay."

Across the fire an old man nodded gravely. "I had rheumatiz," he said. "Just couldn't seem to shake it. Misery in my bones all the blessed time. The camp doc, he couldn't do a thing. Got a bottle of this stuff . . ."

He got up and danced a limber jig to put across his point.

In not one camp, but twenty, the story was the same—of those who left their beds and walked; of miseries disappeared; of complaints gone overnight.

Another one of them, Amby told himself. Another piece of magic. A man with the art of healing at his fingertips. Where would it end, he wondered.

Then he met the healer.

He came on the deserted camp after dusk had fallen. It was just at the hour when the suppers should be over, and the dishes done, and people would be gathering to sit around and talk. But there was not a soul around the trailers—except a dog or two at the garbage cans—and the streets that ran between the trailers echoed in their emptiness.

He stood in the center of the camp, wondering if he should shout to attract attention, but he was afraid to shout. Slowly he wheeled about, watching narrowly for the slightest motion, for the first pinprick of wrongness. It was then he saw the flare of light at the south edge of the camp.

Advancing cautiously toward it, he caught the murmur of the crowd when he was still a good ways off. He hesitated for a moment, doubtful if he should intrude, then went slowly forward.

The crowd, he saw, was gathered at the edge of a grove just beyond the camp. They were squeezed into a close-packed knot before a solitary trailer. The scene was lighted by a half dozen flares thrust into the ground.

A man stood on the steps that led up to the trailer's door, and his voice floated faintly to where Amby stood; but faint as the words might be, there was a familiar pattern to them. Amby stood there, thinking back to boyhood, and a small town he had not thought of for years, and the sound of banjo music and the running in the streets. It had been exciting, he remembered, and they'd talked of it for days. Old Lady Adams, he remembered, had sworn by the medicine she'd bought, and waited patiently for years for the medicine show to come back to town again so she could get some more. But it never came again.

He walked forward to the edge of the crowd and a woman turned her head to tell him, whispering fiercely, "It's him!", as if it might be the Lord Almighty. Then she went back to listening.

The man on the steps was in full spiel by this time. He didn't talk so loud, but his voice carried and it had a quietness and a pompous, yet human, authority.

"My friends," he was saying. "I'm just an ordinary man. I wouldn't have you think different. I wouldn't want to fool you by saying I was somebody, because in fact I ain't. I don't even talk so good. I ain't much good at grammar. But maybe there are a lot of the rest of you who don't know much grammar, either, and I guess the most of you can understand me; so it'll be all right. I'd like to come right down there in the crowd and talk to each one of you, face to face, but you can hear me better if I stand up here. I'm not trying to put on any airs by standing up here on these steps. I ain't trying to put myself above you.

"Now I've told you that I wouldn't fool you, not even for a minute. I'd rather cut my tongue out and throw it to the hogs than tell you a thing that wasn't true. So I ain't going to make no high-flown claims for this medicine of mine. I'm going to start right out by being honest with you. I'm going to tell you that I ain't even a doctor. I never studied medicine. I don't know a thing about it. I just like to think of myself as a messenger—someone who is carrying good news.

"There's quite a story connected with this medicine and if you'll just hold still for a while I'd like to tell it to you. It goes a long ways back and some of it sounds almost unbelievable, but I wish you would believe me, for every word is true. First, I'll have to tell you about my old grandma. She's been dead these many years, God rest her. There never was a finer or a kinder woman and I remember when I was just a lad . . ."

Amby walked back from the crowd a ways and sat down limply on the ground.

The gall of the guy, he thought, the sheer impertinence!

When it was all over, when the last bottle had been sold, when the people had gone back to the camp and the medicine man was gathering up the flares, Amby rose and walked forward.

"Hello, Jake," he said.

XIII

Jake said, "Well, I tell you, Doc, I was kind of backed against the wall. We was down to nothing. No money for gasoline or grub and begging hadn't been so good. So I got to thinking, sort of desperate like. And I thought that just because a man's been honest all his life doesn't mean he has to keep on being honest. But for the life of me, I couldn't see how I could profit much even from dishonesty, except maybe stealing and that's too dangerous. Although I was ready to do most anything."

"I can believe that," Amby said.

"Aw, Doc," pleaded Jake, "What you keep pouring it on for? There ain't no sense of you staying sore. We was sorry right away we left you; we would have turned around right away and come back again, except that I was scared to. And, anyhow, it worked out all right."

He flipped the wheel a little to miss a rock lying in the road.

"Well, sir," he said, continuing with his story, "it does beat all how things will happen. Just when you figure you are sunk, something will turn up. We stopped along this river, you see, to try to catch some fish and the kids found an old dump there and got rooting around in it, the way kids will, you know. And they found a lot of bottles—four or five dozen of them—all of them alike. I imagine someone had hauled them out long ago and dumped them. I sat looking at those bottles, not having much of anything else to do, and I got to wondering if I had any use for them or if it would be just a waste of space hauling them along. Then all of a sudden it hit me just like that. They were all full of dirt and some of them were chipped, but we got them washed and polished up and . . ."

"Tell me, what did you put in the bottles?"

"Well, Doc, I tell you honest, I just don't remember what I used for that first batch."

"Nothing medicinal, I take it."

"Doc, I wouldn't have the slightest notion of what goes into medicine. The only thing to be careful of is not to put in anything that will kill them or make them very sick. But you got to make it unpleasant or they won't think it's any good. Myrt, she fussed some about it to start with, but she's all right now. Especially since people claim the stuff is doing them some good, although how in the world it could I can't rightly figure out. Doc, how in the world could stuff like that be any good at all?"

"It isn't."

"But folks claim it helps. There was this one old geezer . . ."

"It's conditioned faith," said Amby. "They're living in a world of magic and they're ready to accept almost anything. They practically beg for miracles."

"You mean it's all in their heads?"

"Every bit of it. These people have lost their sophistication, or you'd never got away with it; they'll accept a thing like that on faith. They drink the stuff and expect so confidently it will help them that it really does. They haven't been battered since they were old enough to notice with high-power advertising claims. They haven't been fooled time after time by product claims. They haven't been gypped and lied to and cajoled and threatened. So they're ready to believe."

"So that's the way it is," said Jake. "I'm glad to know; I worried some about it."

The kids were scuffling in the back seat and Jake chewed them out, but the kids went on scuffling. It was like old times again.

Amby settled back comfortably in the seat, watching the scenery go by. "You're sure you know where this camp is?"

"I can see it, Doc, just like it was yesterday. I remember thinking it was funny those guys would need a rocket engineer."

He looked slantwise at Amby. "How come you're in such a lather to find this camp of theirs?"

"I got an idea," Amby told him.

"You know, Doc, I was thinking now that you're back we might team up together. You with your white hair and that big lingo that you use . . ."

"Forget it," Amby said.

"There ain't no harm in it," protested Jake. "We'd give them a show. That's what brought them out at first. It ain't like it used to be back before D.C., when there was television and the movies and baseball games and such. There ain't much entertainment now and they'd come out just to hear us talk."

Amby didn't answer.

It was good to be back again, he thought. He should be sore at Jake, but somehow he couldn't be. They'd all been so glad to see him—even the kids and Myrt—and they were trying so hard to make up for their deserting him.

And they'd do it all over again if the occasion ever arose where they thought it would be to their advantage; but in the meantime they were good people to be with, and they were heading where he'd wanted to go. He was satisfied. He wondered how long he would have had to hunt before he found the rocket camp if Jake had not turned up again. He wondered, vaguely, if he'd ever found it.

"You know," Jake said, "I been thinking it over and I might just run for congress. This medicine business has given me a lot of practice at public speaking and I know just the plank to run on—abolish this here road tax. I never heard anyone in all my life as burned up at anything as these folks are at the road tax."

"You couldn't run for congress," Amby told him. "You aren't a resident of any place. You don't belong to any camp."

"I never thought of that. Maybe I could join up with some camp long enough to . . ."

"And you can't abolish the road tax if you want to keep the roads."

"Maybe you're right at that, Doc. But it does seem a shame these folks are pestered by the road tax. It sure has them upset."

He squinted at the dials on the instrument panel. "If we don't have any trouble," he said, "We'll be at that camp of yours by tomorrow evening."

XIV

They said, "It won't work." But that was one of the things he had known they'd say.

"It won't work if you don't co-operate," said Amby. "To do it you need fuel."

"We got fuel."

"Not good enough," said Amby; "not nearly good enough. This camp just down the road is working on some fuels."

"You want us to go down there with our hats in hand and . . ."

"Not with your hats in hand. You have something; they have something. Why don't you make a trade?"

They digested that, sitting in a circle under the big oak tree that grew in the center of the camp. He watched them digesting it—the hard and puzzled faces, the shrewd, nineteenth-century Yankee faces, the grease-grimed hands folded in their laps.

All around were the trailers with their windowboxes and their lines of washing, with the women-faces and the children-faces peering out of doors and windows, all being very silent; this was an important council, and they knew their place.

And beyond the trailers the great stacks of the farm machinery plant.

"I tell you, mister," said the business agent. "This rocket business is just a hobby with us. Some of the boys found some books about it and read up a little and got interested. And in a little while the whole camp got interested. We do it like some other camps play baseball or hold shooting matches. We aren't hell-for-leather set on doing something with it. We're just having fun."

"But if you could use the rockets?"

"We ain't prejudiced against using them, but we got to think it through."

"You would need some lifters."

"We've got lifters, mister; we got a lot of them. We pick up all we can. They cut down the operation costs, so we can afford to pay them what they ask. We use a lot of them in the assembly plant."

One of the younger men spoke up. "There's just one thing about it. Can a lifter lift himself?"

"Why couldn't he?"

"Well, you take a piece of pipe. You can pick it up without any trouble, say. But if you stand on it, you can tug your muscles out and you can't even budge it."

"A lifter can lift himself, all right," said the business agent. "We got one fellow in assembly who rides around at work—on the pieces he is lifting. Claims it's faster that way."

"Well, all right, then," said Amby. "Put your lifter in a trailer; he could lift it, couldn't he?"

The business agent nodded. "Easily."

"And handle it? Bring it down again without busting it all up?"

"Sure he could."

"But he couldn't move it far. How far would you say?"

"Five miles, maybe. Maybe even ten. It looks easy, sure, but there's a lot of work to it."

"But if you put rockets on the trailer, then all the lifter would have to do would be to keep it headed right. How hard would that be?"

"Well, I don't rightly know," the business agent said. "But I think it would be easy. He could keep it up all day."

"And if something happened? If a rocket burned out, say. He could bring it down to earth without smashing anything."

"I would say he could."

"What are we sitting here for, then?"

"Mister," asked the business agent, "what are you getting at?"

"Flying camps," said Amby. "Can't you see it, man! Want to move somewhere else, or just go on vacation—why, the whole camp would take to the air and be there in no time."

The business agent rubbed his chin. "I don't say it wouldn't work," he admitted. "My guess is that it would. But why should we bother? If we want to go somewhere else we got all the time there is. We ain't in any hurry."

"Yes," said another man, "just tell us one good reason."

"Why, the road tax," Amby said. "If you didn't use the roads, you wouldn't have to pay the tax."

In the utter silence he looked around the circle, and he knew he had them hooked.

CLIFFORD D. SIMAK, during his fifty-five-year career, produced some of the most iconic science fiction stories ever written. Born in 1904 on a farm in southwestern Wisconsin, Simak got a job at a small-town newspaper in 1929 and eventually became news editor of the *Minneapolis Star-Tribune*, writing fiction in his spare time.

Simak was best known for the book *City*, a reaction to the horrors of World War II, and for his novel *Way Station*. In 1953 *City* was awarded the International Fantasy Award, and in following years, Simak won three Hugo Awards and a Nebula Award. In 1977 he became the third Grand Master of the Science Fiction and Fantasy Writers of America, and before his death in 1988, he was named one of three inaugural winners of the Horror Writers Association's Bram Stoker Award for Lifetime Achievement.

DAVID W. WIXON was a close friend of Clifford D. Simak's. As Simak's health declined, Wixon, already familiar with science fiction publishing, began more and more to handle such things as his friend's business correspondence and contract matters. Named literary executor of the estate after Simak's death, Wixon began a long-term project to secure the rights to all of Simak's stories and find a way to make them available to readers who, given the fifty-five-year span of Simak's writing career, might never have gotten the chance to enjoy all of his short fiction. Along the way, Wixon also read the author's surviving journals and rejected manuscripts, which made him uniquely able to provide Simak's readers with interesting and thought-provoking commentary that sheds new light on the work and thought of a great writer.

CPSIA information can be obtained
at www.ICGtesting.com
Printed in the USA
JSHW020521090922
30281JS00001B/11

9 781504 073929